Critical Acclaim for A.R. Homer's

The Mirror of Diana

For all who love pulsating fiction....breathtaking plot twists.
--Midwest Book Review

A magnificent tale told with stunning passion...masterful touches of literary suspense.
--Bonnie Toews, author of *Treason and Triumph*

A hold-your-breath page turner...a tale you won't forget!
--Lou Stanek, Ph.D., author and critic

Set in an historically-accurate wartime Italy...faithfully captures the details of wartime life and the images of a beautiful place. Bravissimo!
--Rosario d'Agata, President of *Association Dianae Lacus*

A compelling and poignant story of love and war ... offers many history lessons; excellent characters.
--*Writer's Digest* reviewer

THE SOBS
of
AUTUMN'S
VIOLINS

◆　◆　◆　◆　◆

A Novel of War and Love

A. R. HOMER

Llumina Press

2780015

This book is a work of fiction. Any resemblance to actual events, locales or persons, living or dead, is entirely coincidental.

ISBN: 1-59526-482-5

Printed in the United States of America by Llumina Press

Library of Congress Control Number: 2005906637

The long sobs of autumn's violins
Wound my heart with a monotonous languor

Message broadcast by the BBC in June 1944 to alert the French
Resistance to the coming Normandy invasion

Les sanglots longs des violins de l'automne
Blessent mon coeur d'une langeur monotone

Verlaine. *Chanson d'automne*

❖ ❖ ❖ ❖ ❖

To all those whose courage, ingenuity, and love of country
kept the D-Day secret safe, that precious lives might be spared
in the invasion of France, 1944

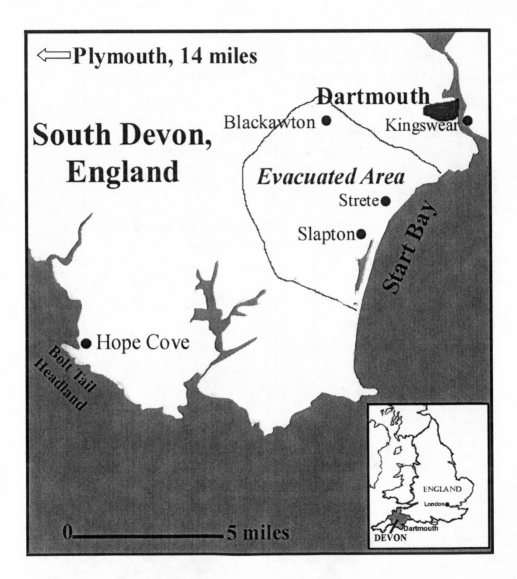

Plymouth, 14 miles

South Devon, England

Dartmouth

Blackawton

Kingswear

Evacuated Area

Strete

Slapton

Start Bay

Hope Cove

Bolt Tail Headland

0 ———————— 5 miles

ENGLAND

London

Dartmouth

DEVON

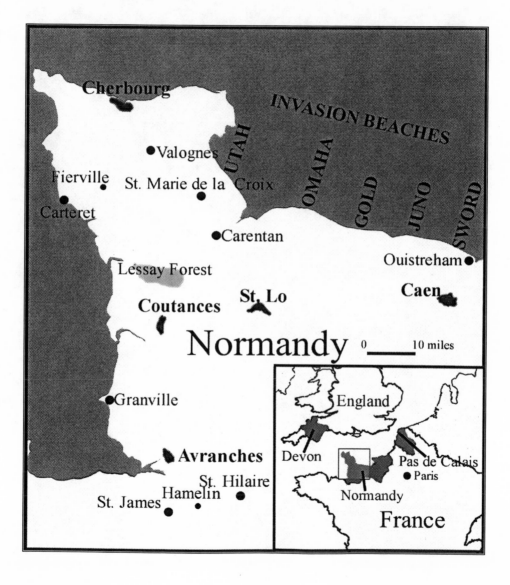

Prologue

It is spring, 1944. For four years, Europe has been occupied by the Germans. In England, Supreme Commander Eisenhower prepares almost two million servicemen to invade the continent and defeat Hitler's Nazi legions.

The invasion – code-named Operation Overlord – is shrouded in secrecy and deception. Above all, Hitler must be deceived about the place and time of the coming offensive. And Hitler knows that his armies must defeat it, or he will lose the war.

In England, a spy for the Germans seeks to betray his own country and deliver the invasion's secrets to his Nazi paymasters. If Hitler knows where and when the landings will come, the invasion will be doomed and the course of history changed forever.

A Diary. May 22ⁿᵈ 1944. Somewhere in England

Last night, I lay awake and turned it over in my mind until dawn. It's a long shot, I know, and I'm still not sure I can pull it off. I'm so near, but I still need one good throw of the dice.

There were the usual faces in the pub tonight with the usual mindless chatter about the war. "We're all in this together," some idiot said. Maybe not all of us, I thought. Certainly not me.

If only they knew. Over the years, I have grown to loathe my own government more and more. What they have done to me and my family can never be forgiven. Dad, I wish you could be here to watch Churchill and those revolting Americans get a bloody nose.

With one smile from Lady Luck I'll have within my grasp a secret so colossal it will decide who wins the war. And it won't be Churchill and his American friends.

May 23ʳᵈ

1944

*P*hilippe Josse. Why? She had seen the evidence, yet still asked the question. She pictured his face. Was Philippe a traitor?

"Stop all engines." The captain's order drove the image away. She watched the officer as he peered over his charts. So young. He was probably little older than her own twenty-four years.

"Stop all engines, sir."

The echo came from the man squatting tightly at the controls, barely discernible in the red, subdued artificial light.

"Up periscope."

Not even thirty, she thought, as she saw the captain peer into the lens, his half-closed eyes revealing few lines. She wondered what tale of the war had brought him here, in command of one of His Majesty's submarines. He'd probably be behind some desk in a bank if it hadn't been for the war. Her eyes scanned the other men, watching dials, pulling levers. All with tales to tell, no doubt. She could not ask them for their tales, just as they would not ask for hers.

The captain moved brusquely from the periscope to the map table and marched his calipers swiftly across the chart, his odor lingering in the air as he passed her. She felt out of place in the tight band of men. The smell of stale men hung everywhere, perhaps with a hint of fear; the smell of men at war.

But she was not out of place. It was her war, too. Beneath her overalls was the simple peasant dress of a French country girl, every stitch made in France. Hidden in the folds were the messages she was to deliver, and, strapped to her right thigh, disguised by the full folds of her skirt, was a Walther 9mm pistol. In the blouse pocket were her papers, with the forged stamp of the German authorities. Name: Jeanne Busson. Occupation: Dairy worker. As soon as the submarine put her ashore on the French coast, that was who she would be. A British agent, codenamed Monkey. She would no longer be....but that was another story. Her tale.

"We'll be ready in about five minutes, er, miss." The captain looked up at her from the chart. She could see he didn't know how to address her. Her clothes carried no insignia of rank. It was clear he wanted the operation to be over, to drop her off at the appointed spot, and to retreat into the manly cocoon. Some mariners believed only ill-luck came from having a woman aboard.

The ice-cold snake of fear slithered through her stomach once again. It was her fifth visit – sometimes she was parachuted in, sometimes, like today, she was landed by submarine – but it never got any easier. She knew her chances of surviving this line of work – roughly fifty-fifty. She knew the probability that if death did come, it would not come as a relatively quick release by an impartial bullet, but as a slow, agonizing, and solitary snuffing out at the hands of sadists. And she knew the worst fate of all – that under duress she might betray those who depended upon her, just as she depended upon them. She willed these thoughts from her mind, but the ice-cold snake did not go away.

She undid the buttons of the overalls, pushed them to her ankles and stepped out. For some reason, the captain averted his eyes, as if witnessing some intimacy that he should not see. She curbed a smile and picked up the overalls, folding them neatly, as if she were folding the tablecloth at home. It made her think of her father, waiting for his 'nice cup of tea,' and the homey familiarity of that brief image brought a bit of comfort.

Her lips tightened as she snapped into the essential routine of an agent-courier about to be landed on French soil. She checked her dress and made sure that the papers and pistol were secure. Then she reached into her blouse pocket for her false ID.

Jeanne Busson. It was her mother's maiden name. She, herself, had been born in France. But her father was English – she was a consequence of the last war. Soon after the armistice, her mother had walked into the marketplace at Amiens and bumped into her father. He was a sergeant at the army camp, awaiting demobilization.

"Blow main ballast."

Her thoughts were interrupted as the captain gave the order. She felt the vessel shudder as it began to lift to the surface.

She recalled her mother's face, smiling, but always gaunt, lined and old before her time. It was the tuberculosis. Her father had tried to explain after her death, when Jeanne was a frightened fourteen years old, but she had needed time to understand. After her mother's death, her father had returned to England and she had had to face a new life. New schools, new friends, new country.

"Open conning tower hatch."

Now she was going back again, and on this mission she was even more on edge. Her earlier visits had been dangerous, but she had a special task this time. She grabbed the old suitcase containing her wireless and followed the captain up the conning tower steps, leaving the musty staleness, and drawing the welcome cool sea air into her lungs. A half moon bounced off the rippling sea that slapped against the hull. In the barest light, she could make out the land. The men below on the deck pulled out the raft from its storage and pushed it towards the side of the hull.

Suddenly, there was a brief, barely discernible flash of light from the land.

"There it is." The captain lowered his binoculars. "My men will row you ashore and then return to the ship. I am to pick you up in two days' time. Thursday 0230 hours. Same location. There'll be the usual signal. *Bonne chance!* " He smiled.

She began to climb down the ladder to the deck.

3

The craft with the two men bobbed in the water. She measured the distance and leapt into the raft, and the men pulled vigorously on the oars. As the flimsy craft drew away from the submarine, she began to think again of the purpose of her mission. The image of Philippe Josse again came to her. Philippe Josse, French Resistance leader. The man she had orders to kill.

Dartmouth, Devon, England. 10:15p.m.

Tom Ford ran the last few yards to escape the sudden shower and pushed on the latch to the saloon bar of The Cherub Inn.

"Doesn't it ever stop raining here?" His slight southern accent caused a few heads to turn, but only briefly; the novelty of seeing an American had worn thin months ago. He shook the rain from his cap and hung it on the back of the door.

"Sometimes." The bartender reached for a glass from the shelf. "It baint rain one day last August, oi think."

The Devon burr of the bartender, still barely comprehensible to Tom even after six months in England, caused a titter to come up from the wooden tables. A few faces turned to him and nodded, but most continued to stare sullenly into their glasses. A foursome of old faces did not shift from the dominoes they held in their hands.

"It's only a shower. Soon be gone. How be 'e today, Cap'n?"

"Apart from being wet, I'm fine." He'd told the bartender many times he was a major, but if the man hadn't learned by now, he never would.

"What be your pleasure?" The bartender held the glass ready and poised his hand above the row of pumps.

He resisted the temptation to tell him that his pleasure, right at that moment, was to be sitting on the front porch of his folks' home in Chapel Hill, North Carolina, basking in the warmth of the late spring sun. He could picture it: the temperature in the seventies, the neighbors in the garden enjoying a weenie roast, his father puttering with his car in the driveway.

"Beer, Cap'n?"

The American nodded. That would be another pleasure: an ice cold beer, instead of the unappetizing glass of tepid liquid that the bartender pushed across the bar. He wondered why the Brits hadn't rationed their beer; virtually everything was rationed – meat, eggs, even candy – but there seemed to be a never-ending supply of tepid colored water. Maybe Churchill had ordered the brewing of beer as a top priority of the war, up there with aircraft production.

Stop whining, he told himself as he thrust his lip into the inch of froth at the top of the glass. He recalled the leaflet the Army had given him when he, one of the first to be posted to England, had arrived the previous November. 'Do not complain. Remember the Brits have been involved in a punishing war since 1939.'

He took a window seat and looked across the river, peering through the darkness at the mass of military craft clogging Dartmouth harbor so tightly that it was almost possible to walk to Kingswear on the other side without getting your feet wet. The big day when they were headed for the Far Shore was not far away.

He knew, first hand, that the Brits had endured a punishing war. He had seen Plymouth, scarred by the bombing raids of the early years. Rows of houses laid low, pushed into piles of rubble so that buses could ply the streets again. Yes, they had suffered; but he didn't share that suffering. He just wanted to do his job, get the war over, and hightail it back home. The glass came to his lips again. His job wasn't heroic, he knew. Intelligence.

Not for him the storming of Hitler's Europe. Just listening to radio traffic, monitoring messages, decoding and enciphering, probing to find German weaknesses. He felt uneasy when he realized men would be risking their lives on the information he garnered.

He thought of the men readying themselves for the night's exercise. A half-dozen ships, with thousands of men, heading out into the English Channel, preparing to launch a practice landing on innocuous Slapton Sands. Innocuous, except for the fact that live shells would come from warships offshore. Real fire, for a practice. He wondered if the big brass knew what they were doing. Why didn't they save the real fire for the enemy on the Far Shore?

He took another sip of beer, his mind wandering to his own North Carolina shore, where he had taken his wife Wilma before his posting to England.

"You look as if you're a thousand miles away, Yank!" The old man was waiting for the dominoes to be shuffled, the long ash about to fall from his cigarette.

"Yep." Tom replied curtly, a false smile hiding his true feelings.

Not a thousand miles. More like four thousand. Wilma would be walking their dog, Bruiser. Or perhaps she was over at her mother's for lunch. He'd always liked her mother. Apple pie and motherhood, a true American woman. Wilma didn't want to go in for motherhood. It wasn't that she didn't want to have children, she said, but it was the war; who knew what could happen? In truth, he hadn't wanted to marry, and he had used the same argument. But, all across America, young men of draft age and their sweethearts had rushed into churches, synagogues, and Justice of the Peace offices.

Paradoxically, the same reasons were used to justify marriage as to argue against it: the uncertainty of the world in general and their lives in particular. 'Don't get married,' said one school of thought; 'it's too risky – you don't know what the future will bring.' 'Get married,' said the opposing point of view; 'love and life are always a gamble, and you don't know what the future will bring.'

Confused and scared, and with his overseas posting imminent, Tom and Wilma had harkened to the latter voice and a hastily-organized wedding had taken place just a few weeks before his departure for England. Two months later and an ocean away, he had welcomed New Year 1944 in Devon, England.

5

A shout from the domino table broke across his thoughts. "Right, we've got 'em in the dead hole!" Tom could never understand the game, which involved complex math that the old men performed correctly in the blink of an eye. He called for another pint and noticed that the shower had passed, but the wind lingered as the night swept in across the river. He thanked his lucky stars that he wasn't on one of those ships out in Start Bay.

The envelope brushed against his hand as it went into his pocket in search of his cigarettes. He pulled it out and let it lie on the table before him. The date stamp was early April, over a month ago. In the early days, she had written every week, sometimes twice a week, but, since February, the frequency of her letters had dropped off. Perhaps there was something wrong with the mail service, he thought, and then bit his lip. There was nothing wrong with the mail, but there was probably something wrong between Wilma and him, and he couldn't just run around the block to put it right.

He did not pull the letter from the envelope; he had read it so many times he almost knew it by heart.

April 12, 1944

Dearest Tom,

I have just baked a "Victory Cake" from a Betty Crocker recipe – no eggs, no milk, no butter. And guess what else – no taste! Even so, how I wish you were here to share it with me.

Tom, I know that I should be doing all that I can to buck up your spirits – after all, you're the one who's serving our country. But I sit in our tiny apartment listening only to the clock, feeling my life ebbing away with every tick. I've had a lot of time to think things over. Do you think we may have made a mistake? The early part of a marriage is when two people especially need to be together – so they can share experiences, both good and bad. Instead, you're living in a whole new world, and here I am fending for myself alone.

Tom, I'm worried. Yesterday, I saw a man and a woman walking by the river holding hands, looking into each other's eyes, laughing, and I suddenly broke out into tears. I don't know why, but I'm young, and I feel I'm missing out on something.

I'm sorry, Tom, for getting all serious on you – but it seems to me that everyone thinks of the hardships of the boys abroad, and there is little compassion for those of us left behind.

Anyway, Mom and Dad are coming over for dinner (which is why I baked the cake) and I've got to go squeeze the yellow food coloring into the Nucoa. You'd surely think they'd find a better way to make white margarine look like butter!

Hope all is going well for you; please write soon.

Love,
Wilma

He slammed the beer glass down, causing the eyes of the bar to look at him, briefly, before returning to their dominoes. Wilma had never been ardent

6

in her letters, but, early on, there had been some warmth. However, it wasn't what Wilma felt that tore him apart – it was that reading her words made him realize that he felt exactly the same as she did. They seemed separated by a gulf much wider than the Atlantic Ocean.

His thoughts drifted off to Gwen…

He had met her a month before at a little get-together at All Saints' Church. The good ladies of the parish had sought to foster good relations between the newly-arrived Yanks and the Brits. He hadn't really wanted to go to the shindig, but there had been pressure put on by the brass, who wanted to build bridges, as they put it.

He had walked into the musty church hall decorated with the curious hand-made poster showing John Bull shaking the hand of Uncle Sam, and had seen her in a corner of the hall. She was serving punch, and he had been suddenly seized with an overwhelming desire for punch. He had watched her eyes moving quickly from face to face as people sought a drink. Eventually, her eyes had found his and paused for a moment before she ladled the punch into his glass.

He had tried to think of something clever to say, but he had not been blessed with a gift for gab and knew he wouldn't have the guts to go beyond the usual pleasantries. But he'd eventually found courage to ask her out for a drink. Instead, she'd taken him to a concert, where she'd seemed rapt listening to Bach. They hadn't talked much, and when he'd asked for another date, she'd said she was busy. But there had been a smile, and she'd given him her phone number. He'd waited a few days before calling her, but her father had answered the phone, telling him that she'd gone to visit her aunt in Gravesend and wouldn't be back for some time.

Tom sighed. He'd probably never see her again.

Normandy, Occupied France. 10:30 p.m.

The first task was to get Jeanne to a safe house. Henri and Bertrand had handled her before on several visits. All three walked away from the coastal path to where the bicycles were hidden.

"We have a long way to go, this time. About thirty kilometers." Henri ground out his cigarette and swung his leg over the saddle. *"Allons-y!"*

Jeanne strapped the case containing her radio to the pannier, tucked the hem of her skirt into her underwear and pedaled after the Frenchmen. She had no problems with the fast pace they set. The tough physical exercises in the secret training camp had honed her body; the pedals spun rapidly beneath her feet, and the tall hedgerows of the *bocage* flew by. She relied on Henri for the route: he would know how to avoid the towns and known German outposts. To meet with any German patrol at night was an almost-certain death sentence.

Henri braked quickly, his right hand flapping. *"Arrête! Arrête!"* She stopped and lifted her ear to an unwelcome sound.

"A car. At this time of night, it can only be Germans." Henri ran, pushing his bicycle towards a gate leading to a field behind the hedgerow. Bertrand followed him. The noise of the car engine came closer. Jeanne hurried to the gate, but slipped on the mud and fell, her bicycle clattering to the ground. She looked up and could hear the car clearly, less than two hundred meters away, just around the bend; there was no time to reach the gate. She tossed her bicycle into the deep ditch at the side of the road and threw herself after it, pressing her body down into the watery mud.

She waited for the car to pass, but her heart sank as she heard it stop. They had seen her. She began to feel for the pistol strapped to her thigh, but stopped. No movement. Lie still. She heard the door of the car open, followed by raucous laughter. She felt the fear, but did not move. Lie still. She heard the boots scrape across the road towards her position in the ditch. She heard the click of an automatic weapon.

"Schnell, schnell, Heinrich!" The shout came from the car.

The warm liquid splashing on her ankles surprised her. Her mind leapt, but she forced herself to lie still. The German was urinating on her. He had stopped for a piss. She heard a grunt, and the boots scraped their way back to the car. There was more laughter as the car sped off, the noise of the engine dying away.

"I was about to shoot them." Bertrand waved his weapon in the air. That was the click she had heard.

"He pissed on me." She pulled out a handkerchief and started wiping her legs. "He pissed on me."

"It's better than a bullet in the head." Henri smiled.

"Only just!" She smiled, and they all burst into laughter, releasing the tension that had consumed them.

The Cherub Inn, Dartmouth. 10:50 p.m.

"Last orders, gentleman, please!"

As the bartender called out, the door of the bar flew open, and the wind almost hurled a tiny uniformed figure into the room.

"Put the wood in t'hole, missus!" The gruff voice came from the domino table. Tom could see she was flustered as her petite frame struggled to close the door.

"I'm sorry, but I've got a puncture and I can't get the wheel off – one of the nuts is stuck. Can anyone help?"

Tom could tell she was not local – her voice was refined, upper-class. From her uniform, he could see she was a Wren – the name the Brits gave to the women in the Women's Royal Naval Service. She removed her white naval cap, revealing a mass of blond hair swept up in the latest fashion.

"Perhaps I can call the garage, miss?" The bartender's suggestion made her more frustrated.

"And wait hours? It's only a rusted nut!" So pale, thought Tom. No sun in England.

The domino players shuffled their feet and looked away. Dominoes clearly came before gallantry.

"Perhaps I can help, miss?"

Tom got up and walked towards her, surprised to find he towered at least a foot over her.

"Thank you." She glanced at his epaulette, replaced her cap and saluted. "Major."

He grabbed his cap and followed her to the door.

"So much for the bulldog spirit!" She tossed the remark over her shoulder as she left. There were mutterings as Tom closed the door behind them.

"Thank Heavens the rain has stopped." She looked up at the night sky and then bent down over the offending wheel. "I'm sorry to trouble you, but the last nut just will not budge." She kicked at the tire angrily.

"That's okay. No problem."

He reached down and grabbed the wrench. Thirty seconds later, the veins in his temples bulging, he managed to get the nut to move. He flipped off the nut and pulled the wheel free. He turned and was astonished to find her diminutive figure holding the spare wheel. She crouched down, slammed the wheel over the bolts, spun the nuts finger-tight and secured them with the wrench before he had time to offer his help.

"Thank you." She smiled up at him as she put the wheel and the wrench into the trunk. "You're very kind."

He shrugged his shoulders. What sort of women were the Brits breeding now? What had the war done to them?

"Perhaps I can return the favor?" She moved to the front of the car. "You're based at HMS Britannia, I presume?"

He looked perplexed. He wasn't aware he was based on a Royal Navy ship.

"I'm sorry," she smiled, "it's what we used to call the Royal Naval College before you Americans took it over."

"Oh, the college," he stammered. "Yes, I'm based there."

"Then allow me to offer you a lift." Her hand waved towards the car. "I've got to go there. Picking up some red stripe," she glanced at her watch, "in half an hour."

"Red stripe?" His eyebrows lifted.

"I'm sorry. Two nations divided by a common language." She laughed. "Staff Officer. VIP." She opened the door. "Welcome aboard." Her laugh rang out again. "Get in."

"How long have you been driving for the navy?"

"My goodness, it must be four years now. It's not as bad as it was then – some of us were dispatch riders, out all hours dodging bombs in the blitz. One of our girls in Plymouth was blown off her motorbike, yet still ran through the bombs to deliver her message. She got a gong for that."

"Gong?"

"Sorry – a medal. They stopped recruiting soon after that. Too dangerous, they said." He watched as she ran through the gears, still unaccustomed at seeing a woman in naval uniform. He knew some women who could drive a car, but his father would as soon let his mother behind the wheel as ask her to change a tire.

She stopped at a crossroad and turned to him.

"Have you been here long?"

"Since last November."

"That long ago. Most Americans arrived only recently. You must be getting used to us by now."

She slammed the car into second gear and he grabbed at the dashboard as she threw the car into a tight turn through the narrow streets.

"I'm still not used to driving on the wrong side of the road in the dark with hooded headlights!"

"But have you tried our hospitality? Most Americans seem to stick together. I see you go to the pub. Would you like to go to a real pub?"

"A real pub? You mean one that sells cold beer?"

"Well, not really." She smiled. "But at least a pub with real people, young people. The inmates of The Cherub Inn have been fighting the war from their barstools for the last four years. I suppose they did their bit in the last show, but there's more atmosphere in a funeral home."

She paused at a crossroads and swung left. "Better go the back way. There's so much of your military on the road. How about coming out to a real pub?"

She giggled as he hesitated. "Don't get the wrong end of the stick – I wasn't proposing a date. There's quite a few of us – we go over to The Hope and Anchor in Hope Cove on Fridays, when we can get off duty. You can meet the gang and get away from the war for a couple of hours. Maybe even learn a few words of English!"

She smiled, disarmingly, and he felt more at ease. "And it won't be a hen party – my friend Danny will be there."

"Is Danny your boyfriend?"

"Not really. He's a very good friend. He gave a basic training session on signaling for some of us Wrens, and we've been friends ever since. I'm sure you'll like him. Do come and meet him at The Hope and Anchor."

"I might just give it a try." He needed a break, he thought, as he began to convince himself. "If I can get time."

"Good." She turned the car into the college driveway. "What job do you do?"

"Intelligence."

"Well, that's one way to stop a conversation." She smiled again. "You would have a great time with Daddy. He's also into some hush-hush work. Spends most of his time in London. You'd both find lots of things *not* to talk about!"

She pulled the car over. "Here we are." He stepped out. She wound down her window. "I know this seems awfully silly, but what's your name?"

"Tom. Tom Ford. Look, if I can, I'll take you up on that offer. Can you give me a call on Friday? I'll be here at the college."

She nodded and he turned to go up the steps, but her voice called after him.

"Haven't you forgotten something?"

His brow furrowed.

"You don't know my name." She smiled and his face reddened again. "It's Sally, Sally Fortescue. I'm based at HMS Cicala."

"Where's your ship moored?"

His question brought forth another gale of laughter.

"It's not moored anywhere. It's the top two floors of the Royal Dart Hotel in Kingswear, across the river." She waved. "Now I must find my bigwig. I'll give you a ring on Friday."

May 24th

1944

Royal Navy Radar Operations, Plymouth, England. 1:30 a.m.

Acting Lieutenant Danny Sullivan walked down the corridor toward his office. *Acting Lieutenant.* It still stuck in his throat. They'd given him his pips only because he knew everything about radar; otherwise he wouldn't have stood a chance against the Royal Navy old boys' network. The others in the officers' mess sometimes looked at him disdainfully, but he was past caring about it. He did his job and got on with it. Doing his bit, as he father would say.

Doing his bit. His father had 'done his bit' in the Great War – wounded and gassed. The government had promised him 'a land fit for heroes.' Instead they had taken his land away from him. Danny was bitter; he knew life was not fair, and fairness in war was a lunatic concept. But it was one thing when the enemy hurt you, and another thing when your own country did.

Late in the previous year, his mother and father had been told by the government to get out of their farm near Blackawton and leave that part of Devon. There had been rumors about a mass evacuation from the whole of South Hams since September, but nobody believed them. Then, in November, the government told them that everyone in sixteen towns and the surrounding countryside had six weeks to get out – their farms and villages were to be handed over to the Yanks. Three thousand people were forced to move so that the Yanks could practice assault landings for the big invasion of the Far Shore.

Like everyone else in the area, his mother and father had packed up all their belongings. Like everyone else, they had somehow found rooms miles away in someone else's house to live. Like other farmers, his father had made arrangements for some of his animals to be moved and kept; others had to be sold for a pittance. Of course, the government had told them they'd get their land back after the war – whenever that would be.

But unlike everyone else, his father wouldn't be going back. The move from his lifelong roots had sickened him; a heart attack had ended his life. He would never again see his beloved farm – the farm he was born and grew up in, the farm in which he was married and raised a family. That's what he got for 'doing his bit.'

Danny forced himself to push his bitterness aside as he sat down at his desk and sifted through the reports. His eyes grew large and he looked up at the clock. Half past one. And a heap of shit brewing up.

"When did this report come in, Hadley?" He waved the paper towards the sallow-faced petty officer at the desk in the corner.

"About ten minutes ago, sir." The 'sir' came after a pause, as if begrudging the younger man's seniority.

"I think there's something up." Danny's eyes scanned the report again. "I'm going to look for myself."

14

He bounded across the office and headed for the stairs. If what he thought was correct, the American landing exercise in Start Bay was in trouble. Big trouble. His feet skipped rapidly down the stairs to the basement, where he flashed his security pass to the guard. The bomb-proof door slammed behind him and it took a few moments to adjust to the darkened room, lit only by the cathode ray tubes lined up across a long desk in front of the far wall.

"Where's Vector S-4?" He looked up and down the row of operators huddled over the screens.

"Here, sir." The operator on the left raised a hand, without lifting his eyes from his equipment.

Danny went across and peered over the shoulder of the operator, watching the sweep back and forth across the screen.

"There's the American exercise, sir."

The operator's voice was matter-of-fact as his finger circled a series of blips about six miles offshore. Danny knew that it was a big practice landing on Slapton Sands, a rehearsal for the invasion to come. It was the third practice of the month: dawn landings, live ammunition, shelling of the beach, the works. He'd heard that eight Americans had been killed by friendly fire during the first practice. He wondered if the bigwigs knew what they were doing, killing their own men.

Danny identified the larger blips on the screen. LSTs. Landing Ship Tanks. Five of them, all loaded to the gunwales with men, tanks, trucks. And fuel. Thousands of gallons of petrol.

He flipped the controls, intensifying the screen definition, and picked out a smaller image, ahead of the others. His brow furrowed.

"Who is the escort duty?"

"HMS Lily, sir."

Danny took off his naval cap and ran his fingers through his red hair.

"There they are again, sir." The operator's voice rose with concern.

"Where?" Danny peered at the screen.

"Vector three, sir." The operator's finger pointed to several hazy dots, about fifteen miles south-east of the American flotilla. "It's not a good signal, sir, the images come and go. Do you think the weather's affecting the scan?"

Danny looked hard and counted the indistinct blips. "No, they're vessels. Very low in the water. Any news from the Cherbourg station?" He picked up the duty log. Navy Headquarters in Plymouth permanently kept two submarines fifty miles across the Channel outside Cherbourg harbor to watch for German vessels coming out.

"Nothing, sir." The operator continued the sweep. Danny watched the dots as they began to swing, slowly, to the north-west, towards the convoy. Where had they come from? Had they slipped out of Cherbourg unnoticed?

"Not submarines, sir. Too many of them."

"You're absolutely correct, seaman. They're E-boats!"

His mind raced. E-boats. German motor torpedo boats. Small, but with 300 horse-power engines, a top speed of almost forty knots, each armed with cannon and four torpedoes. He looked back at the screen. If that lot got in the midst of the American exercise, there would be hell to pay. He glanced at the clock. Coming up to two o'clock.

"They're closing, sir!"

Danny looked again as the arc swept across the screen. Less than twelve miles. He reached for the telephone.

"Get me signals, please."

He waited for the connection. Despite the urgency, he spoke slowly and clearly.

"Officer of the watch here. Please send message to Commander-in-Chief Plymouth: Nine E-boats twelve miles east-south-east of Convoy T Tango 4. Speed 25 knots. Bearing north-north-west."

Danny waited patiently as the Wren radio operator read the message back.

"Time that at," he looked up at the clock, "0205 hours."

He waited for the confirmation, put down the telephone and looked again at the screen. The arc swept the screen again. The dots were closing fast.

Normandy. Five kilometers from St. Marie de la Croix. 2:15 a.m.

Jeanne followed the two men as they swung their bicycles onto a rutted path leading away from the road. The darkness of the night enveloped the squat stone cottage at the end of the path. It was a different safe house from last time. Every visit produced a new safe house. Take no chances. Don't give the Germans a clue. Philippe had always insisted…she felt anguished as she thought of him. She bit her lip. The man she had orders to kill.

"You're to see Philippe in St. Marie de la Croix in the morning." Henri's voice cut across her thoughts. "Eleven o'clock. The church. Try to get some sleep. *A bientôt*." He tipped his cap as the two men turned their bicycles and disappeared back down the path.

Jeanne unstrapped the case containing her wireless set from the pannier on the rear wheel of her bicycle, offering a brief prayer that it had not been damaged when it had been thrown in the ditch. She opened the cottage door, bridling at the musty smell coming from the dark interior. She swung her rucksack from her back and delved in it for her flashlight.

The door creaked in protest as she closed it behind her and switched on the flashlight. A large sepia photograph of a nineteenth century French matriarch looked down from the wall onto a table that offered an oil lamp and a box of matches, as well as a baguette, some slices of ham, and a bottle of wine. She lit the lamp and, as its light flickered into life, she saw the fire had already been laid in the hearth; another match soon brought forth flames and the sound of crackling wood. In the corner of the room was a cot with blankets and a pillow.

It was nearly half past two. She knew she should grab a few hours of sleep, but, despite the weariness that weighed on her eyes, there was something she needed to do. She searched around the cottage and unearthed an old bucket from a cupboard. Opening the door, she looked cautiously around the yard before going to the pump and drawing water.

She dropped the latch behind her, rummaged in a chest of drawers for a towel, and then took off her clothes. The smell of the German's urine had to be washed from her legs. The water was cold, but she sat in front of the fire, the flames flickering patterns over her as she scrubbed at her body. She would deal with her mud-stained clothes later.

She got into the cot and pulled the blankets over her. She was tired, but sleep would not come. She kept seeing the image of Philippe Josse's face. How could he be a traitor?

At sea. Lyme Bay.
Twelve miles from the Devon coast. 2:15 a.m.

PFC Jake Rudd looked at the half moon that flickered over the sea and sighed heavily. He was bored and frustrated. No smoking on the ship. So the ship was crammed with tanks, trucks and gas, but would one cigarette matter? He looked around for any officers, tapped his pocket, and pulled out a pack. The monotonous throbbing of the ship's engines added to his boredom. Another exercise. He could just make out the shape of the LST ahead of his vessel, plowing its way towards the destination: all five LSTs would hit the beach just after dawn. He peered at his watch in the thin moonlight. Just after two. In four hours, he'd drive his jeep up over Slapton Sands onto the coast road. He'd done it twice already.

He sat in his jeep, one of many lined up across the deck four abreast, ready to be driven off when the ship reached the shore. He ducked down beneath the dashboard, struck a match, and drew deeply on the cigarette.

The scrape of a boot on the deck made him jump. He looked furtively as he crushed the cigarette out on the floor of the jeep. "Smoking again, Rudd?" The voice was low and authoritative. He steeled himself for the worst as he glanced in the wing mirror. The figure, silhouetted by the moon, came alongside the jeep. He jumped as the dark shape bounded the last few paces and thrust its face through the window.

"Boo!"

"Aw, it's you, Grainger." Rudd heaved a sigh of relief. "Don't do that, you bastard. You scared the living shit out of me!"

Grainger guffawed and held his nose. "Yep, sure can smell it!"

"You're just a bastard, Grainger. A mother-fucking bastard!"

"You be sure my papa and mama were married proper." Grainger's southern drawl irked Rudd. "In church. Decent folk. Not like you Yankee white trash."

Rudd grabbed the door handle and leapt out. He went to grapple with Grainger, but the big Southerner held up his hand.

"D'ya hear that?" Rudd stopped and they both craned their heads to the wind. "Hear what? If this is another of your stupid tricks, Grainger, I'll—"

"No. Honest. Listen." They stood still for a few moments.

"There's nothing, Grainger, you're hearing things."

"Yep, and the things ah'm hearin' are motors. High pitch, squealin' motors."

Rudd cupped his hands to his ears. "Probably one of the other ships."

"Can't be. It's too—"

A great noise, followed by a huge burst of flame, shattered the still darkness of the night. The vessel in front of them had exploded into flame.

"Holy shit!" Moments later, there was another roar. The deck plates beneath them erupted, hurling them into the air. They were dead before they hit the water.

US Navy Headquarters. Dartmouth, Devon. 4:30 a.m.

Tom Ford rubbed the sleep from his eyes as he approached the door to Colonel Kessler's office. Four-thirty in the morning was not a pleasant time to be dragged from bed. Particularly to be told there had been an attack on the exercise off Slapton Sands. He paused at the doorway, checking his uniform and adjusting his tie. It might have been the middle of the night, but Kessler was a stickler for details and protocol. He knocked and entered. Kessler looked at him, awaiting Tom's salute, which he returned as he stood up.

"This situation is intolerable, Ford."

"You mean the attack, sir?"

"What else would I be talking about?" Kessler's face reddened with contempt as he shouted.

"Let me convey to you, Major Ford, the consequences of this attack. Two hours ago, German E-boats beat up our convoy during a landing exercise on Slapton Sands. I had a phone report an hour ago. At least two ships sunk. Hundreds dead. Without any warning." Tom watched the colonel pace up and down behind his desk.

"Why didn't you intelligence people have any warning of the attack? Can't you see how stupid I will look at Headquarters? Not to mention the top brass. The phones have been ringing off the hooks. Ike is screaming mad."

"We had nothing, sir. No information, no warning."

"No warning?" The colonel stopped his pacing and stared menacingly.

"Nothing, sir. We monitored all the German radio traffic for the past week, as usual. Even the Brits had nothing to give us, and they've been at this job far longer—"

"The Brits?" Kessler's voice rose sharply, his eyes bulging with rage. "Don't talk to me about the Brits! They gave one ship as an escort – one old stinking tin can…." He got up and slammed his fist on the desk. "I don't want excuses. I want action, Ford, action!"

"I'll get an investigation underway at once, sir."

"An investigation? That would be useful, Ford." Kessler's voice dripped with sarcasm. "It might very well be useful to Ike to know why he's lost two ships and hundreds of men." The colonel pushed his face inches from Tom's. "That is the least of your worries, Ford."

"Sir?"

"Your first priority is to hush up the whole affair."

"Hush it up? But, sir—"

"No one is to know about it. It never happened." He shouted out the words as he stared into Tom's incredulous eyes. "Ike's direct order." He stabbed a finger on the desk to emphasize the authority.

"But there'll be injured men, sir. They'll talk. And the medical staff—"

"Threaten everyone with court-martial if they talk." He saw the surprise on Tom's face. "It's approved." His finger pointed upwards. "From the top. The Brits are doing the same. Everyone realizes the dangers if word gets out – the impact on the men waiting to go to the Far Shore, the damage to civilian morale, that sort of thing."

Tom began to grapple with the size of the task. "Very well, sir." He saluted and turned to leave.

"I've not finished yet, Major." Kessler spoke sharply.

Tom stopped. "And then the investigation, sir?"

Kessler looked at him coldly. "You disappoint me, Ford. I told you that was the least of your problems. Have you not thought of the security aspects?"

Kessler stood up and walked away from his desk. "What if the German E-boats have captured somebody? Picked someone up from the sea. What if that man was a BIGOT?"

Tom stiffened at the word. A BIGOT. As an intelligence officer, he was a BIGOT, the code name for someone who knew the time and place of the coming cross-Channel invasion. Originally, it had been used for the North African landings as 'TOGIB', meaning 'To Gibraltar.' The story was that, with so many rubber stamps left over, the letters had been inverted for the landing on the Far Shore.

The whole counter-intelligence game had been – was – to delude the Germans, to keep them guessing about the coming invasion. Only about a hundred officers knew the time and place of the landings: the BIGOTS. The rest of the army knew as much as the Germans.

"I see you are suitably impressed with the importance of this issue, Ford." He reached into a folder and pulled out a sheet of paper. "Here is a list of the BIGOTS known to be on the exercise. I want every single one to be accounted for. If there's one missing, the whole invasion could be in danger."

Tom picked up the paper. "Will there be anything else, sir?"

"There will be no investigation. Dismissed."

The safe house in Normandy. 5 a.m.

Jeanne could not sleep. The problem of Josse gnawed at her. She found it difficult to believe he was a traitor, despite all the evidence.

She had first met him a year earlier, as he was beginning to build up a Resistance unit supplied with British arms. She had admired his tact and diplomacy as he had welded disparate men into a team. Some were local patriots, some young hotheads; others were just frightened men trying to escape the compulsory labor draft that the Germans imposed to send Frenchmen off to Germany as slave labor for their war machine. Philippe had made them into a fighting unit, readying itself for the invasion they knew would surely come. But she also knew him to be hard, even ruthless, with anyone who challenged his authority.

He had masked his Resistance activity behind his position as mayor of St. Marie de la Croix, a position in which he pretended to accommodate the German occupier. It was a dangerous game, but she admired the way he played it. Until Major Priestley called her into his office two weeks ago.

"Please sit down, Jeanne." He had used her service alias, as always. Major Alistair Priestley always went by the book.

His eyes looked at her from a tired face that had seen better days. He sleeked down his thinning red hair as he opened a folder. About forty, Jeanne guessed. From what she knew, he had spent the late thirties as an attaché in the Berlin embassy, but his diplomatic career had led nowhere. He was a little eccentric, but he was hard-working. And he was thorough and methodical, with a painstaking eye for detail. She presumed these qualities – and his fluency in three languages – had got him his command position in Special Operations Executive.

"I trust you are well?" He raised a bushy eyebrow as he looked at her from behind his desk. She nodded, but was immediately on her guard; Priestley rarely engaged in small talk. He looked at her steadily for a few moments.

"We have a tricky assignment for you." He took out a pipe and pouch. "A rather nasty one, in fact."

She waited patiently as he tamped his pipe and lit it. He looked at her through the billowing cloud of smoke.

"You remember the fiasco with the Dutch resistance?"

She nodded. She knew it all too well. The Germans had captured the Dutch agents, complete with codes, and had taken over the whole network, forcing the Dutch to act as if they were still genuine. Drop sites had been designated; hundreds of rifles and tons of equipment had been parachuted straight into the welcoming arms of the Germans. Worse still, British agents had been dropped – one of them her friend, Yvette – and never seen again. Special Operations Executive took a long time to realize that something was wrong until the Germans, knowing they couldn't play their cunning game anymore, arrogantly sent SOE a final message thanking them for their contribution to the German war effort. She remembered talking to Yvette the night before her drop....

"We believe one of our sections in Normandy has been turned, too." Priestley's voice was matter-of-fact.

"Are you saying that French *resistants* are being forced to work for the Germans?"

"It's worse than that, Jeanne. We believe the betrayal comes from within the group."

Her eyes widened. "Which group is it, Major?"

He drew deeply on his pipe. "St. Marie de la Croix." He exhaled the smoke slowly, awaiting her reaction.

"But that's impossible! That's the group of—"

"Philippe Josse." He ended the sentence for her. "Precisely."

"But I know Philippe. I've worked with him. He wouldn't do that."

"He looks gilt-edged, I know." He pulled his spectacles from his pocket and put them on as he opened a dossier on his desk. His hand plucked out a sheet of paper and he began to read.

"Philippe Josse. Born 1895. Began training for the priesthood, but rallied to the colors when the First War broke out. Fought at Verdun. Wounded. Decorated war hero."

He paused and looked at her. "Wonderful testimonial."

"It's been verified?" She felt defensive.

"Oh, yes, of course. There's more." His eyes returned to the paper. "Became a successful farmer after the war. Never married. Entered politics. Conservative – opposed Blum and the Popular Front. Elected mayor of St. Marie de la Croix in 1937."

His brow furrowed as he flicked through the dossier. "Strangely, there's no indication that he supported Pétain."

She grimaced at the name. Pétain had done a deal with Hitler after the defeat of France in 1940 in order to become head of a puppet French state. Supporters of Pétain almost always collaborated with the Germans.

"Pity." He returned to the original sheet. "Arrested by the Germans in August 1940, supposedly for protesting too much about maltreatment of the citizens of St. Marie de la Croix. That's probably when they turned him."

"How can you say that in view of all the other evidence?" She tried to keep anger from her voice.

"Jeanne," he gave her a look asking for patience, "I haven't finished with all the evidence." He leaned back in his chair, making a church steeple with his fingers. "Of our last five drops, two have been met by reception committees. German reception committees." He looked up at her. "Shades of Holland, eh? Josse professes that it was a mixture of bad luck and an increase in German security."

"What if it were? Perhaps it could be bad luck." She knew she shouldn't press the case, but she did. When she saw a rare smile on Priestley's face, she knew she had made a mistake.

"Ah, but you haven't seen these." He reached into the dossier and brought out two photographs. "One of our agents who was on an entirely different mission took them." His fingers pushed the images across the desk to her. "Recognize anyone?"

She picked up the photos and instantly recognized Philippe. The thinning hair, the broad walrus moustache on the heavy-set face. He was talking to a man, a small man with pointed features, a sharp face beneath a German military cap.

"The other man," he spoke diffidently, anticipating her question, "is Hermann Richter. The man our agent had been watching." He got up and walked around the desk to peer at the photos over her shoulder. "The photos were taken in the *Parc Paysager* in St. Lô. Hermann Richter is the head of the Gestapo in Normandy."

The memory of the meeting kept her awake. She got up from the bed, cut the bread and nibbled on the ham that her unseen hosts had left. The wine beckoned; she pulled the cork free and drank from the bottle. She shivered as she recalled the memory of the meeting, even though she basked in the heat of the open fire. The thought of falling into Richter's hands filled her with terror.

She put another log on the fire and sat down in front of it, cradling her knees with her arms. She wasn't afraid to kill – on one raid she had shot a German – but this time it was personal: she could see the face of the man she was to kill; she knew him.

She looked into the fire, raised the bottle to her lips again and drank freely. It wasn't for King and Country she'd accepted the assignment. She returned to the cot, feeling the effect of the wine explode in her stomach. She remembered Yvette, who had dropped into Holland and disappeared forever; Yvette, her crooked smile and nervous laugh, never to be seen again. That's why she was doing it. She pushed her pistol under the pillow, doused the light and pulled the blanket over her. It would soon be daylight. Her eyes closed; she hoped there would be no dreams.

Slapton Sands, Devon. 7 a.m.

Tom pulled the jeep over to the side of the road. Already four feet high and ten yards long, the horrific stack of bodies made him sick. He stepped out of the jeep and fought his stomach's need to retch. A platoon of black soldiers was adding bodies to the pile, tossing them as if they were bales of hay.

He looked out across Start Bay, as the gulls cawed and swooped over more lifeless forms bobbing in the water. Small boats spluttered amongst them, as if fishing, plucking the bodies from the sun-speckled water. It wasn't real, his mind shrieked at him; it hadn't happened. The screech of tires on the coastal road pulled him back to reality. A young lieutenant came running towards him.

"It's a mess, a complete fucking mess!" The young face looked at him for a moment, outraged, until he recognized Tom's rank. "Sir!" He sprang to attention and saluted.

"I agree, Lieutenant." He returned the salute. "But you never saw it. Neither did I." He looked into the man's disbelieving face. "No mention must ever be made of these events. You must tell all your men. No mention. Under threat of court martial." There was a menace in his voice that the young officer could not fail to understand. "Do I make myself clear?"

"Yes, sir!" The lieutenant looked at him incredulously.

Tom avoided the young man's eyes and looked out to the sea lapping on the beach. For some reason, he thought of Thornton Wilder's *Our Town*, which he'd seen while on leave in London a few weeks before. The dead buried up on the hill in Grover's Corner were allowed to relive one day, one ordinary day – a paradise forever denied the guys lying in the hideous stack of bodies. None would ever again hear the thwack of ball hitting bat, would ever enjoy a beer with the guys in the bar, or would ever feel his girl's soft hand. And there were many more yet to join them.

He thrust the thought aside. "It's a matter of security." He paused to allow the noise of two passing Sherman tanks to die away. "Where are the wounded?"

"Some are at the other end of the beach, sir." He pointed toward the village of Strete at the far end of the coast road. "But most of the wounded have been shipped out to a hospital at Sherborne." Tom knew that Sherborne was a fair distance away, nearly a hundred miles; the brass were taking no chances that workers in local hospitals might link a sudden influx of casualties with the rumors that were certain to be circulating.

Tom saluted the lieutenant and leapt back into his jeep. "Don't forget – complete secrecy," he shouted as the tires bit into the sand-strewn road.

He pulled over at the far end of the beach. The on-shore breeze flapped at his pants as he stepped down from the jeep. A huddle of men gathered on the sand. One was lying on a stretcher, his head swathed in bandages reddened with blood. The others made no attempt to get to their feet as he approached. Saluting officers was beyond them. Their haggard faces looked down at their boots, but their thoughts were still locked in the nightmare of the previous night.

"What happened?" He tossed the question in their direction, but there was no response. Although he understood their feelings of hopelessness, he reached out to touch one man on the shoulder.

"What's your name, soldier?"

The face turned to him sullenly. "Lutz, sir." The man's voice was low, quavering.

"What happened out there, soldier?" Tom nodded toward the sea. The soldier looked at him steadily for a few moments.

"Sir, we were hoping *you* were going to tell *us*."

"It was hell, sir." Another voice cut in before Tom could react to the insubordination. "They threw everything at us – cannon fire, torpedoes, the lot. We never had a chance."

There was a honk as a truck bearing a Red Cross came down the hill at the northern end of the beach. Several men jumped down, including a lieutenant, who approached Tom and saluted.

"Lieutenant Henderson, sir. I'm responsible for getting these wounded men to Sherborne."

"Very well." Tom drew the officer to one side. "I know they're in bad shape, but you've got to tell them they are ordered – and I mean ordered – not to say anything of last night. Under penalty of court martial." His eyes fixed on the lieutenant's look of surprise.

"The same goes for you, too, Lieutenant Henderson." He saluted and turned on his heel towards his jeep without waiting for the return salute.

Something was not right, he knew. Hush it up. Cover the whole stinking mess up. Ship the bodies out to London and tell the survivors to shut the fuck up. Those were his orders.

He knew that, later in the day, he would have to make the ninety mile drive to Sherborne to ensure that every survivor knew that to talk of the disaster was a military crime.

But another problem pressed him. The ten 'BIGOTS.' The men who were missing after the operation – the men who knew the designated landing beaches in France. If the Germans had captured any one of them....

St. Marie de la Croix, Manche, Normandy. 11 a.m.

She looked up at the church of St. Marie de la Croix. The huge Gothic stone façade surrounded a rose window above heavy oak doors, and the spire above pointed toward a clear blue morning sky. She reached for the latch, but her instincts told her to look behind her. There were two German soldiers walking together down the Rue de l'Eglise. She saw one yawn in the boredom of his routine patrol, as she covered her head with a scarf and pushed on the door.

Her eyes adjusted to the darkness of the interior of the church. The stained glass windows set high above the nave allowed little of the morning light into a darkened House of God. A few filtered sunbeams danced fitfully around the altar. She looked past the font, nestled in the west end of the church, and saw that all the pews were empty, save two. In one, an old woman knelt, her lips pressed to her clasped hands in supplication; on the northern side, away from the aisle, she saw the broad shoulders of the man she knew was waiting for her.

Even from the back of the church, she could sense the power that emanated from him. Relaxed but alert, ready to spring into action in the briefest of moments, he gazed steadily at the altar before him. He turned slightly at the sound of her echoing footfall, and she recognized the swarthy features and walrus moustache of Philippe Josse. The man she had orders to kill.

She hesitated as the latch on the sacristy door rattled and a priest, his long robe swaying, made his way to the altar. He bowed in obeisance and lit a candle. Her hand clutched the pistol in her pocket and then released it. Not now. The old woman would pose no problem, but with the priest and the German patrol outside, it was too risky. And, for some reason, she felt it was not the place. She had lost all faith in God when Brian had died early in the war, but she still felt unable to defile the church. She went to the pew and sat at the aisle, a few feet from him. Crossing herself, she knelt and began to mutter, as if praying.

She looked at him from the corner of her eye and saw that he nodded, almost imperceptibly, before returning his eyes to the altar. She continued muttering until the priest had walked back and closed the sacristy door behind him.

"*Eh bien, ma petite singe*, it's good to see you again." There was a genuine warmth in his voice that made her feel uneasy. She recalled the nickname he had given her in her first visit, after he had learned her codename. *Singe.* Monkey. Again, she felt uncomfortable, balancing their previous friendship against the task she had to do. She thought again of Yvette's death to strengthen her resolve.

The old woman in the pew opposite got up, crossed herself and left the church. Perhaps she should do it now, put an end to him and any last vestige of doubt within her. The rattle of the latch echoed throughout the church. She stiffened. Perhaps it was a trap; perhaps he had already planned her betrayal. For a long second she waited, expecting the rasp of military boots on the stone floor and the guttural tones of a German voice. There was nothing, only the slither of soft shoes as another peasant woman shuffled her way to the altar.

"What's up, Jeanne? You look so nervous." Josse spoke quietly. "It is unlike you."

She fought quickly to regain her composure. The sweet incense caught in her throat and she coughed. "It's nothing – I have a slight cold."

He gave a low chuckle. "England is the land of colds. Why have you come?"

The quiet of the church hung over them. She dug into her coat pocket and brought out an envelope, which she slipped along the pew until it touched his broad fingers. "I've brought something that cannot be trusted to the wireless." She knelt again and spoke behind the disguise of praying. "It's the operations plan for your group for the period leading up to…" Her voice trailed away; he nodded his understanding. She saw him slip the envelope under his coat.

The document, she knew, had been fabricated by Priestley. In it was nothing more than the routine actions that any resistance group would be expected to do. It mentioned nothing of the coming invasion, of which she herself knew little more than that it was coming.

"There's some money, too – French francs printed in London. The notes have been handled deliberately so they appear worn."

"It will be very useful." He stood up, genuflected and crossed himself, preparing to go. "When do you leave, Jeanne?"

"Not yet. There's something else." Now was the time to float out the bait, she thought, as she got up and turned to him. "Supplies are to be brought in tonight."

His fingers tugged on his moustache. "There's to be a drop?"

"No, not a drop. There have been faulty drops in the past that the Germans captured." She watched his face for any emotion, but there was none. "We need accuracy, a guarantee that you'll get the supplies." Priestley had made sure the supplies would be no more than a few cases of rifles; if the consignment were to be betrayed, the Germans would profit little. She pulled on the knot of her scarf, tightening it around her head. "We'll need the big field at Labouchère's farm for the landing. The arrival is scheduled for midnight. Can you fix it? It's very short notice, I know."

A broad smile came to his face. "Of course. It is rather short notice, but it can be done. Do you remember the Bar Coq d'Or by the Town Hall?" She nodded. "Be there at eight-thirty this evening. From there we'll go to Labouchère's farm. Bertrand and Henri will come, too. No need for more. They'll arrange for the landing lights to be ready. *A ce soir.*"

He took her hand as he turned to go. She watched his huge frame walk back along the aisle. She knew when she would complete her mission. At Labouchère's farm. She would do it there.

Labouchère's Farm. Near St. Marie de la Croix. 11 p.m.

Jeanne was tense. She felt for the pistol in her coat pocket, but the solid touch of the steel did little to reassure her. She glanced at her watch. Just another hour to the landing, another hour until....

The huge field behind Labouchère's farmhouse lay before her, enveloped in the darkness of night. The wind had brushed the clouds from the sky but the heat of the day still hung in the air. Jeanne felt perspiration on her brow, but she knew it was not caused by the weather. From the barn came the voices of the Frenchmen as they prepared for the landing.

"This plane – is it a Hudson?" She jumped sharply at the voice behind her, and turned to see Philippe's huge figure as a large shadow. "Jeanne, you seem nervous. I thought you were supposed to keep watch. What if I had been a German?"

Her doubts about Philippe resurfaced, like an unwelcome denizen from the depths of her mind. He was acting so normally, preparing for the landing. There was no trace of anything unusual in his behavior. Still, the metal of the pistol pressed insistently against her thigh through the cloth of her pocket.

"Well, is it a Hudson?" He repeated the question. She nodded.

26

"*Bien*, the field is big enough. When we hear the plane, Henri and Bertrand will run down the landing area to light the flares. They'll then help me with the unloading. After the plane has left, we'll hide the supplies in Labouchère's barn. Then we'll all leave on our bicycles and disappear. You'll take watch while we unload."

She noted the meticulous planning which had always been his strong point. If there were to be a betrayal, it was not evident.

"Here, I hope you won't need this." He handed her one of the two rifles he was carrying. "I'm sorry we haven't got any machine pistols. Let's hope there are some in the supplies."

As they closed the barn door behind them, the feeble light of an oil lamp revealed Henri and Bertrand preparing the landing flares, small saucepans of gasoline into which they would throw lit rags when the time came. Philippe leapt across the straw-strewn floor of the barn. "Are you a fool, Bertrand?" He snatched the cigarette from the startled man's mouth and ground it out. "What do you think Labouchère would say if we burnt down his barn?" An ironic smile played on his lips. "Not to mention burning us all to a crisp."

"*Venez*." Josse trundled a cart from the corner of the barn. "Let's put the flares in place." The men began loading the pans onto the cart. "*Douçement, douçement*, Henri! Try not to spill any." When the loading had finished, they pushed the cart towards the door. "Jeanne," he turned to her after checking outside, "keep watch. If you hear anything suspicious, shine your flashlight out into the field briefly. If it's serious, shoot."

The muffled noise of the cart and the men died away as Jeanne took her place by an open window. She listened intently, but only the chirrup of crickets and other sounds of the rural night came back to her. She sat on a wooden crate and shook her head, angry with herself. Her mission was going badly. She should have shot him in the church, or outside, a few minutes ago. From now until the landing, Henri and Bertrand would always be with him, and it would be difficult. Besides, if there were a German attack, she would be caught in no-man's land, without an avenue of escape.

She cursed her own poor judgment. But what of Priestley's? His words rang in her ears. "You must complete your mission. At all costs." Did that mean shooting Henri and Bertrand as well? Perhaps Priestley had been wrong, after all. Philippe had not in any way acted like a traitor. Then she remembered the photo of him with the chief of the Gestapo. Her indecisiveness troubled her. Perhaps she was not cut out for the job.

The quandary tormented her until a noise snapped her back to the night. She released the safety catch from the rifle and looked through the window, but the sound of hushed French voices told her it was only the men returning. The dim shadow of Philippe's large frame led the way, pulling the now-empty cart. She swung the rifle in front of her, aligning the sights on the indistinct shape. *At all costs*. She could tell the others that

27

it had been a big mistake, that she had thought they were Germans. Her finger gently caressed the trigger. But she lowered the weapon. She could not be sure of the kill in the dark.

After they had pushed the cart into the barn, Jeanne resumed her place at the window, still listening for any sound intruding upon the night. The smell of crushed straw mingled with the fumes of the oil lamp, whose flickering, pale light played with the shadows in the barn. Bertrand and Henri lay on the bales of hay, their heavy-lidded eyes battling sleep. At her feet, his back to the wall, Philippe sat gazing at the lamp. She looked at her watch. Half past eleven.

"What will you do after the war, *ma petite singe*?" His voice surprised her. "Get married?"

"No." He had never asked personal questions before. She tried to keep a coolness in her voice, but the question had touched a raw nerve.

"I was married. My husband was killed in 1940." There was a catch in her voice as she recalled Brian. They had been so much in love. He had been a navigator with the R.A.F. They had been married only two months when he was sent on a bombing raid. He never came back. She had learned afterwards that the raid had dropped only propaganda leaflets, and she still cursed the authorities who had ordered such senseless operations. "I shall never marry again." There had been too much pain. She turned back to the window, hoping Philippe would say nothing more. Talking over personal things with a man she had to kill made her uneasy.

"I am sorry, I did not know. I try to understand, but it is difficult. I have never been married." He got up and stretched. "After the war, I shall go back to the Church, to go into orders. It will be late, I know, but it is what I have always truly wanted. After all this war, I shall seek peace with God. And maybe myself."

"And what if the Germans win the war?" She could not resist asking the question, probing him. He looked at her and she thought she detected a touch of guilt in his brown eyes. He shrugged his shoulders. "I had not thought—"

"*Écoutez!*" Henri's hushed call made them start.

They gathered at the window, ears straining. "*Oui, tu as raison.*" Philippe crossed himself before picking up his rifle. The noise of the aircraft grew louder. "*Vite, vite!*" He urged Henri and Bertrand through the door. "Light the lamps now!" The two men ran into the field. "Jeanne, you must come with us this time. We must all stick together throughout the landing."

Her brow furrowed. Surely she should remain in the barn to guard any approach from the road. She looked at him suspiciously, and was alarmed to find that he avoided her eyes. He beckoned her in the doorway and she followed, despite the ice-cold snake returning to her stomach.

The throb of the aircraft engine drew nearer. Bertrand and Henri ran hurriedly, lighting the two rows of flares that would outline the intended runway. The flames burst forth, casting a gentle orange hue about the field. The light caught the underside of the plane, now directly above them; the pilot dipped his wings to acknowledge them, before sweeping away to make his approach.

Jeanne looked carefully around the hedges surrounding the field, checking for any movement. If the landing had been betrayed, the Germans would make their move soon. She looked at Philippe, but found he was watching the plane's approach. She, too, watched as the wings wavered, then steadied as the pilot guided the plane on the approach to the lines of flares. The noise of the engines eased as the pilot throttled back, the plane quickly losing height as it neared touchdown.

Jeanne tensed as the wheels skidded on the wet grass. The plane slid off course, towards her. There was no time for her to get out of the way; at the last moment, the pilot opened the throttle slightly and straightened out, letting the aircraft run to the end of the field. Recovering from her shock, she looked at Philippe, but found his eyes, along with Henri's and Bertrand's, were fixed on the plane. The pilot taxied to the other end of the field and turned the aircraft. All four ran after the plane.

The pilot slid the cockpit window open. "Sorry about the landing." There was a nervous grin on his young face. "There are two men in the back to help unload. Six cases. Please hurry – I want to get out quickly."

Jeanne rapidly translated, and Henri complained as he ran toward the door opening on the plane. "Six cases? All this fuss for six cases?"

"Shut up, you fool, and get on with the job!" Philippe's harsh voice barked brutally. Jeanne had always found the contrast between his gentleness and his cruelty disturbing. Unseen hands passed out the first case, which the three men lifted away from the plane and placed on the ground. Jeanne's eyes scoured the hedges keenly, searching again for any movement. The second and third cases followed. Jeanne jumped as Henri shouted, but it was a cry of pain as the fourth case grated against his shin.

Jeanne was beginning to relax as the fifth case emerged. Surely Priestley was wrong; the evidence didn't tie up.

Suddenly, the whole field was bathed in the brilliant, blinding light of a searchlight.

She had been betrayed. Worse, she had let herself be betrayed. Josse was a traitor. She had fooled herself. These thoughts tumbled through Jeanne's mind in the instant she took to turn and raise her rifle. She struggled to see, still blinded by the searchlight. German voices shouted as her eyes began to pick out Philippe's form. She heard his voice, shouting, "Do not move!" She regained her vision and saw that his rifle was pointed straight at her head.

Jeanne ignored his order, pulling on the trigger of her rifle. It was jammed. Had he fixed that too? She tossed the weapon aside and reached for her pistol. Before she could pull it from her pocket, she heard the crack of his rifle; she gasped, but was astonished to hear the crash of glass as the searchlight went out, plunging the whole field back into the meager light afforded by the runway flares. As her eyes struggled to readjust, he was upon her, grabbing her in a bear hug. Her combat training produced an instant reaction: she brought her knee up into his groin. He grunted in pain, releasing her. She raised her right hand behind her head and picked out the spot on the nape of his neck for the killing blow. She was too slow. There was a dull thud on the back of her skull. She slumped to the ground, unconscious.

Her mind reached desperately for the real world. There was the sound of angry voices; her body was bouncing on the floor. Through her pain, she heard the scream – the scream of an aircraft engine with the throttle wide open. Perhaps it was a dream, a nightmare. She had a blurred vision of two R.A.F. men, cursing as they struggled to close the aircraft door against the slipstream. The plane began to climb into the sky and she saw Philippe below, surrounded by German soldiers. Small arms fire chased the plane as it reached for the safety of the black sky. As the struggling men closed the door, her eyelids became heavy. She began to slip back into unconsciousness. Why? She thought she heard the question repeated in French. *Pourquoi?* She tried to identify the voice, but darkness claimed her.

May 25th

1944

Jeanne made her way between the Nissen huts set up in the gardens of the old mansion that served as headquarters. She still wasn't sure what she was going to say to Priestley. There had been two – maybe three – chances to kill Philippe Josse and she'd missed out on all of them.

Yet she had escaped – and she was sure the Frenchman had helped her. Bertrand, who had also escaped on the plane, had confirmed it; after the searchlight had been put out of action, Josse had passed her unconscious form to him and told him to board the plane.

The bright, early morning sunshine reflected from the windows at the rear of the house, but did little to penetrate the fog of doubt in her mind. She remembered the blow on the back of the head. After that, it was hazy. Had Philippe betrayed her? She had taken a few hours' sleep to recover, and she was still a little dazed, but she knew that Priestley would insist on a debriefing. She didn't look forward to the meeting.

She opened the French doors leading from the patio and walked down the corridor to the drawing room that served as Priestley's office. The door was open and Priestley was sitting at his desk, a shroud of smoke from his pipe rising above his red hair. She was surprised there was no anger on his face. He pointed with the stem of his pipe to a vacant chair and she sat down.

"I'm sorry—" She began to stammer, but he ignored her.

"It's good to see you back safe and sound, Jeanne." He half smiled, but his amiable manner changed abruptly. "However, you failed in your mission and we now have a serious situation on our hands."

His hand reached for the brief report she had written on her return. He glanced at the piece of paper and then fixed her with angry eyes. He tossed the report onto his desk. "It would appear from this that you had several opportunities to fulfill your mission, yet you spurned every single one. Why?"

"I…," she hesitated, "…I don't know."

Priestley placed his pipe in an ashtray and stood up. "You don't know?" He turned from her and looked disinterestedly at the portrait of Churchill hanging above the mantelpiece. "Or is it that you were too squeamish – that you lacked the guts to do the job?"

She felt a hot flush rush to her face. "No!" There was anger in her voice now. "My record shows—"

"Your record shows that you killed one unimportant German some time ago." He turned sharply on his heel to face her. "But your record now shows that you fouled up on a most important mission." He walked slowly behind her chair. "Killing Josse was too much for you. You couldn't handle it, could you?"

"Yes…no." She fought the urge to cry; she would not let him see her cry. She breathed slowly, deliberately. "I felt something was wrong."

"You *felt* something was wrong? You are supposed to be a trained agent. You saw the evidence, even though I had no need to show you. In case you hadn't noticed, we are fighting a war. Since when do your feelings matter?"

"Perhaps my feelings were right." She turned to look up at him. "How can you explain why he helped me to escape?"

He sat down and sighed, like a schoolmaster dealing with a petulant schoolgirl. "In the same way I can explain why Josse is in German hands in St. Lô prison."

"But doesn't that fact support my argument?" she spoke loudly, as if trying to convince herself. Priestley propped up his face with his hands, looked down at his desk and shook his head.

"You are a naïve fool, Jeanne." He picked up the report again and tapped on the paper. "You say here yourself that you think Josse betrayed you. He's playing the role of double agent." He looked at her condescendingly. "He let you escape – even helped you escape – so that we would still trust him. Then, when the stakes are higher, he tells the Germans."

"But he's in prison—"

Priestley's sardonic laugh interrupted her. "Quite soon, we shall no doubt hear of an amazing escape. It's been done before." He shook his head again and started to clean up the papers on his desk. "But that will be someone else's problem."

"Someone else?" She looked at him, puzzled.

"Yes, I've had my fill of running agents, particularly those with *feelings*."

He dwelt on the last word. "I applied for a damned good position some time ago and I've been offered the post. Real work – top secret."

"But who am I to report to? When do I go back to France?"

"I can't tell you that, because I'm not allowed to know." He looked at her angrily; she should have known the protocol. "My successor will contact you via the usual channels." He stood up, indicating the conclusion of the meeting. "But I have to say that when he reads my report of this mission, it's unlikely that you'll ever be going back to France." He dismissed her from the room with a wave and picked up his pipe. "You're on permanent leave."

She managed to close the door behind her before the tears started.

Special Agents Headquarters. 9 p.m.

Alistair Priestley drummed his fingers on his desk. It had been essential for Jeanne to kill Josse, and she had failed. Now the whole plan was threatened. He viewed it as a personal failure as he always did when someone in his charge did not carry out his orders.

He sighed. Throughout his life, he'd always been driven by his work. He had a single-mindedness of purpose, a view that nothing in the world mattered as much as his work. His devotion to it pushed out any possibility of a life outside it – he had never married and had few friends and no hobbies – but what did a personal life matter when work was all-consuming? And now

Jeanne had snatched from him the satisfaction he always felt when some piece of work within his purview was done well; worse, she had jeopardized the plan. There was little he could do.

But from other quarters there was one big consolation. He lit his pipe and picked up the letter from his desk. It was the notification of his transfer, his promotion.

He made sure his office door was shut and opened the bottom drawer, pulling out a bottle of scotch and a glass. Promotion. He deserved some self-congratulation. The bottle clinked against the glass as he poured a generous measure. He'd worked hard for the promotion, and he'd earned it. The scotch rolled around his mouth. At last his talents had been recognized.

It had been a long battle, mainly against his fellow officers. He remembered how they'd looked down on him with an air of disdain. They knew him as a grammar school upstart who'd put himself through a provincial university. He was not one of them – not public school and Oxford. No matter; he didn't care to socialize with them anyway – it was his work that mattered.

He picked up his promotion letter and read it again. Now he was being moved nearer the center of power. He felt a thrill: the center of power – it opened up all sorts of opportunities.

He scribbled a few notes on Jeanne Busson's file. Perhaps the mess she had made could be sorted out later.

A Diary. Somewhere in England.

I read in the paper this morning that Gandhi, the pathetic man in knotted diapers, will be released from prison soon. What a misguided little man he is — his naïve assumption that conflict can be resolved non-violently betrays a lack of understanding of the human psyche that is worse than infantile.

People don't need to be taught how to become sheep — they already are sheep. Most of the British people are sheep. They allow a stupid system that rewards the useless aristocracy because their equally useless ancestors were rewarded. Yet people of merit, like me, get nothing. And this robbery is accepted by the people — even the poor — as a revered tradition, divinely ordained.

And, at the top of this pile of aristocratic manure, sits the Royal Family, their backsides regularly kissed by Churchill. What was it that fat toady said? 'We will fight on the beaches.' What hypocrisy! Everyone else would fight on the beaches, but not him. He'd be off to Canada, along with the Royal Family — and the nation's gold reserves.

Well, Mr. Winston Spencer Churchill, you may yet have the pleasure of enjoying Ottawa. When I get the secret of the invasion to my contact in Germany. And it will be soon.

May 26th

1944

US Naval Headquarters. Dartmouth, Devon. 9 a.m.

Tom lit a Lucky Strike and looked out of the window. He saw the huge flotilla gathered in the harbor below him, the ships stretching, cheek by jowl, all along the River Dart, which twinkled in the sunlight. The English weather continued to bemuse him. No rain for two days, not since the day before the …. Despite the warm sun shafting down onto his desk, he shuddered as he recalled the events.

His visit to Sherborne and other hospitals that had cared for the wounded had gone as well as could have been expected. All the survivors had been seen and they had been told of the need for absolute secrecy: they had to 'forget' about the calamitous night, and it was made clear to them what would happen if there was any loose talk.

The Brits had done the same with the medical staff and the whole 'hush-up' operation had been implemented rigorously. It could be called a job well done, but Tom did not feel satisfied. Shit happened in war, but why the cover-up?

At first, Tom had thought the top brass had been caught with their pants down in some gross negligence they didn't want the world to see. But now he realized that Operation Overlord, the upcoming invasion of Normandy, had to be protected at all costs. Everything, absolutely *everything,* about it had to be kept secret. And everything certainly included the ill-fated rehearsal for the invasion that had been taking place in Start Bay yesterday morning when the German E-boats had attacked.

The exercise area in Devon around Slapton Sands, with its tall hedgerows, was a dead ringer for the terrain of Normandy, with its *bocages,* where the real invasion would be launched. If the Germans realized what the exercise was – a rehearsal for the big invasion – and where it was taking place, they might just deduce the location in France where the real landings would occur. The success of Operation Overlord depended on surprise; lose the surprise and the invasion could be doomed, with the loss of thousands of Allied soldiers, and maybe even the war.

He stubbed out his cigarette and watched the final plume of smoke weave its way through the rays of the sun. After the 'hush-up,' the tracing of the missing BIGOTS was of paramount importance. If one of them had been captured by the Germans, it put the whole invasion plan into even greater jeopardy. Tom wondered how he, a BIGOT, would react if he were captured and tortured. He felt a cold drop of sweat form on his brow. Maybe he would talk.

He opened a folder and took out a list of the missing men. He read the names, then sighed heavily and let the list fall from his fingers. How he longed for the earlier days when he had first arrived in England. His main task had been breaking codes, a job he enjoyed. Ever since he was a kid, he'd been interested in puzzles, sending and receiving secret messages, then cracking the code. County chess champion when he was fourteen. He'd always liked intellectual problems. He'd majored in math at Duke, and was rarely happier than when faced with some apparently insoluble problem. His talent had led, when drafted, to a commission in the Intelligence Corps.

On his arrival in England, they had sent him to Bletchley, where the Brits had set up their code-breaking headquarters. He had thought he was good, but, when he met the strange collection of English oddballs and geniuses, he had soon realized he had a lot to learn. They had shown him how they had broken Germany's Enigma code, a code that changed its coordinates with every key-stroke. The Germans still thought the code was unbreakable, and the Brits' achievement was the most tightly-kept secret of the war. Except, of course, for the time and place of the coming invasion.

Then the Office of Strategic Services had decided that they, too, needed a code- breaking arm. Tom had been pulled in to help set up the unit. At first it had been exciting, but Tom had moved farther and farther from the hands-on end. Now he rarely saw a code, apart from the occasional garbled transmission that no one else could break. It was all executive work, like the hush-up operation and the missing BIGOTS.

The telephone jolted him from his thoughts.

"Hello, it's me." He was surprised that the voice was feminine and English. He tried to identify it, but was still searching his mind when the voice supplied it. "Sally. Sally Fortescue. You remember? The spare wheel?"

Tom smiled at the memory. "Why, yes. How are you?"

"I'm fine. Look, I hope you can make it today."

Tom realized that the disaster had made him completely forget about the visit to the pub. "I'm not sure. I'm very busy." He wondered if she knew about the attack. It was difficult to conceal everything. Perhaps she had been sworn to secrecy, too.

"Oh, please do try. There might be something special."

"Something special?"

"It's a surprise. One of our friends has invited us all to a birthday party."

"I'll do my darnedest, but I don't know. It depends how things work out this morning. If I can get away, I'll be there."

"Right. Do try to come. Must go now. Toodlepip."

Tom returned his attention to the list of missing BIGOTS. Ten names. Six had been found safe and sound. One had been identified among the wounded, and for one other, there would be no more war; his body had been found in the harvest of death that had been reaped from the sea.

Tom lingered over the three remaining names and looked up at the clock. In ten minutes, Captain Rosselli of the Seabees would arrive, with information, Tom hoped, of the other three. He didn't envy Rosselli's job. The Seabees' normal tasks were tough enough. Organized into Navy Combat Demolition Units, their job was to reconnoiter beaches and remove mines and obstacles before invading troops went ashore. The job Tom had given Rosselli and his unit perhaps wasn't as dangerous, but Tom knew he himself wouldn't have had the stomach for it. Ike and the top brass had given the utmost priority to tracking down the BIGOTS. Rosselli and his men had spent the whole of the day before combing the seabed, recovering the bodies and removing the dog tags. The Seabees were all volunteers, but it was a grisly task.

The phone rang to announce Rosselli's arrival. The door was opened by a small, unimposing man who looked young enough to have just come out of high school. His salute was casual, and with his other hand he grasped a small canvas bag. He held it reverentially, as if holding an urn of someone's ashes. Tom noticed that, despite his youth, the Captain's eyes had a look of weariness as he gently placed the bag on the desk.

"That's all we could find, Major. Eighty-seven." There was no emotion in the voice, but Tom wondered if he were churning inside. How many tags had the captain himself cut from the bodies?

"We searched a wide area, but I can't give an absolute guarantee that we found them all. Some were still in their trucks." A brief picture of the men at the bottom of the sea crossed Tom's mind, but he forced himself to brush it away.

"I'm sorry, Captain, it couldn't have been a very nice job." He realized he was choosing the wrong words and squirmed uncomfortably in his chair.

"It's all right, sir. Someone had to do it. And now, if you'll forgive me, I must go." Tom stood up from his desk and returned the salute.

"Sure. And good luck with your future operations." Tom had a vision of the young man swimming ashore in France and disarming mines.

The Captain turned in the doorway. "Thanks. But I tend to think we make our own luck." He saluted again and was gone.

Tom reckoned the young man had probably aged ten years in one day. He did not relish his own task as he took a knife from the drawer and cut the string at the top of the canvas bag. The dog tags clattered as they fell, randomly, onto the desktop. Like coins, Tom thought. The price of war. He picked one up, turning it in his fingers. Just two days earlier, it had been pressed against a warm body, full of hope. Tom closed his eyes and took a deep breath; he realized that, if his thinking continued along this line, he would never complete the task. He picked up a pencil and began to note the name and number on each tag, checking it against his BIGOT list.

Half an hour later, he had crossed out two more from his list. He assiduously went through the others again, double-checking. One was not there. He stared at the name left on the list and started. Major Glenn Dalton. It couldn't be. Not that Glenn Dalton. He checked the records again and let out a low sigh. He and Glenn had been at college together way back.

He picked up the phone and relayed the information on to Supreme Headquarters. As he put the receiver down, he wondered how Eisenhower would react when he learned one of the BIGOTS was missing.

There was nothing more he could do. He was sick of the war; he needed a break. He would go to the party. He let the list fall from his fingers, and wondered where his old college friend was at that moment.

Gestapo Headquarters, St. Lô. 10 a.m.

"My dear Major Dalton, may I welcome you to St. Lô by offering you some scotch?" *Sturmbannführer* Richter lifted the decanter from the silver salver resting on the sideboard of the Gestapo chief's office. Above the sideboard was the obligatory portrait of Hitler, his unfathomable brown eyes looking down on the luxuriously-furnished office. A young guard stood by the side of Dalton's chair.

"I can assure you, Major, that it is the finest twelve-year-old single malt." Richter looked across his desk to the tense figure of the American. Richter smiled, but his eyes lacked warmth. He was angry with the delay in getting the American to him, but he was indebted to the work of the *Kriegsmarine Schnellboote*. Three men had been captured during the attack. Two were NCOs, run-of-the-mill conscripts, but a ranking major was a real prize.

"Why not? I could do with a drink." Dalton looked at Richter's Gestapo shoulder flash and tried to keep his hand steady. He had been unconscious when the E-boat had plucked him from the water. He'd been somewhat surprised by the attention the Germans had given him. Doctors had checked him over and dressed his head wound; even his uniform had been cleaned and pressed. But he understood what they were seeking and felt afraid.

"Excellent." Richter poured two generous drafts and sat down, setting a glass before the American. He had decided upon the soft approach; although he knew there was little chance of success, he hoped it just might work. And, if the soft approach didn't work....

"Major, I will be honest with you." Richter sipped his whiskey. "You are, as you Americans say, up shit creek without a paddle." He smiled at his use of the American idiom, looking for any response from his prisoner, but was disappointed when no trace of a smile came to the American's lips. Richter became direct. "Perhaps you can tell me what you and your men were doing in Start Bay. Was it an exercise? An exercise for what?"

Richter watched carefully as Dalton downed the whiskey in one swallow. The American's hand shook as he placed the glass on the desk.

"I will tell you what I have to tell you." The American's voice was hesitant. "My name is Dalton. Glenn Dalton. Major in the United States Army. I am a prisoner of war and claim my rights under the Geneva Convention."

A hint of disappointment crossed Richter's face, but he persisted. "I am pleased you like the scotch, Major." He emptied his glass. "But there is no need to be so formal. You have been treated satisfactorily so far, have you not?" Dalton nodded, and Richter stood up, his look pensive as he walked behind Dalton's chair. "Do you know why we are at war, major?"

"That's obvious." Dalton flicked a finger towards the portrait of Hitler. "Because he declared war on the USA."

Richter quelled his rising anger. "It's not as simple as that. We are at war because of the British. The British hate us," Richter turned swiftly on his heel to face Dalton, "but they also hate you and the other Americans who have come across the ocean." He leaned over, spreading his hands on the table. "Have you heard the saying 'Perfidious Albion,' Major Dalton?"

Dalton nodded; in his studies of history, he had read such a description of the English.

"The British are merely using you, major." Richter spoke slowly, emphasizing every word. "They are willing to defend the British Empire to the last drop of American blood!"

Richter's humor could not penetrate Dalton's fear; he returned to the interrogation. "I am asking you to tell me about the landing practice. What is the plan?"

Dalton was breathing heavily, fear in his eyes as he looked at the Gestapo man. "You know the rules. I can only give you my name and rank. It's the Geneva Convention—"

Richter's patience snapped. "Do not remind me of the Geneva Convention again."

"Then I shall be treated as a prisoner of war – according to the rules?"

Richter nodded to the guard, who brought his fist down onto the American's face. Dalton raised his hands, cowering, but could not prevent another blow smashing into his eye.

"We have different rules here – you will be treated as I see fit!" Richter spat out the words and turned to the guard.

"Take this pathetic creature to his cell. Ensure there are no light and no food. Let's see how he likes twenty-four hours in solitary."

The guard dragged Dalton to his feet and Richter smiled when he saw the terror in the American's eyes.

Supreme Headquarters Allied Expeditionary Force. Southwick, England. 11 a.m.

"I don't like it." The voice had a gentle drawl and came from a wide mouth set in a round, care-lined face. The slender figure wore a newly-pressed U.S. Army uniform that carried epaulettes of four stars. His left hand held the report he was reading while the other brushed through his thinning hair. "If the Germans torture this major...," he paused as he sought the name in the report.

"Dalton, sir," the uniformed aide at his side offered.

"Whatever." A hand waved dismissively. "If he squeals, Operation Overlord is in jeopardy. We might have to postpone the invasion."

There was a hush around the conference table as Eisenhower's words sank in.

"Major Dalton has a very good record, sir." The aide consulted a dossier lying open on the table. "Served in North Africa."

The general's eyes fixed the aide. "I served in North Africa, too. But if some Nazi attached an electrode to my balls and pulled the switch, I'd probably sing like a canary." The aide blushed and averted his eyes.

"Precisely," Eisenhower continued. "I don't give a damn if he's the best soldier in Uncle Sam's Army. Not only do we have a major fuck-up with the training disaster," his hand tugged nervously at his right ear, "but now I've got this catastrophe on my hands." A sigh of frustration was followed by a few moments of reflection. "Let's see," he glanced at his watch, "they've had him for forty-eight hours now. Any news of him from over there?"

The aide shuffled his papers. "No news."

"Perhaps we can help, Ike." The thin, reedy voice came from a lean, wiry man in British uniform. The American turned to look at the lantern-jawed face on which sat a small moustache. The clipped tones continued. "Damn bad show all round, but we may have something."

There was a sigh from the aide, and Eisenhower stabbed him with a disapproving look. Since he had been made supreme chief of the combined operations, one of his major tasks had been to smooth out the wrinkles between his own people and the Brits. Sometimes, he himself felt the Brits were the most cussed people he had met.

"What news do you have, Monty?"

"Of course, it's not my particular field, but our security chappies have come up with something." Field Marshal Montgomery looked to his left, at a man dressed immaculately in a three-piece pin-striped suit, a gold chain straddling the vest pockets. Beneath a thick mane of silver hair, he wore a black eye patch, the legacy of a grenade wound in 1916. "Perhaps you should learn it from the horse's mouth." Monty looked at the man with the eye patch, whose eyebrows lifted at the introduction. "Sorry, old man." Monty's chuckle was forced. "Horse's mouth indeed."

The silver-haired man waited for the polite laughter to die. For four years, he had been the Head of the Special Operations Executive, the organization formed by Churchill, as the Prime Minister had put it, 'to set Europe ablaze': to direct sabotage and espionage in Nazi-occupied Europe. He was responsible for all the British agents sent to harass the Germans, to establish resistance groups and to prepare for the coming invasion. Few people knew his real identity; although he carried the rank of a brigadier-general, he preferred civilian dress.

"Gentleman, we do have information." He tucked his thumbs into his vest pockets and spoke with total assurance. "We have two agents on the ground in the immediate area. Of course, General, the American Office of Strategic Service has been informed."

The general nodded. "Go on."

The Englishman placed his hands on the table, revealing the gold studs at his cuffs. "The agents have just informed us that Major Dalton has been transferred to St. Lô prison this morning, where he is, unfortunately, in the hands of *Sturmbannführer* Hermann Richter." He paused for a moment. "As you probably know, Herr Richter is the head of the Gestapo in Normandy."

The group around the table shuffled in their seats as he continued. "Our information is that he was unharmed and unmarked when he was taken into the prison." He spread his hands wide. "Of course, we cannot be sure nothing has happened to him." He sat back in his chair and looked around the table. "But I believe we can get him out quickly."

Eisenhower leaned forward across the table towards the SOE man. "Did I hear you right? You've got two agents in the area and you think you can get him out?" There was an edge of sarcasm to his voice. "He's locked up in a prison, held by the Gestapo, surrounded by a sizeable chunk of the German army – and you can get him out with two agents?"

"With luck, yes." The voice remained calm, assured. "We'll need to send in an aircraft when we've released him from the jail. I've thought it through. My staff has been working on plans throughout the night."

Eisenhower was circumspect. "Well, you guys are the experts. How much time do you need?" His fingers drummed on the table.

"About two days."

"Too long. If the major is tortured and talks…" The fingers drummed more quickly and then stopped. "Colonel," he turned to the aide, "take this message to Lieutenant General Spaatz." The colonel flipped open his pad, ready to write the message to the chief of the US Strategic Air Force in Europe. "Unless countermanded by me personally, you are to execute a saturation bombing of high explosives tomorrow night. The target is to be the prison at St. Lô and its environs."

Eisenhower lit a cigarette and eased back in his chair. "That's all, gentlemen. I'll call another meeting when the situation is clearer."

There was a silence in the room as everyone realized Eisenhower's intention; if the agents could not rescue Dalton by the following night, he would be silenced by brute force.

The SOE head broke the silence. "Gentlemen, if I might have just a few more minutes of your time. The capture of a BIGOT points up the distressing vulnerability of our invasion plans and suggests a pressing need to strengthen Operation Fortitude. We must, in short, take every measure to ensure that Operation Fortitude is invincible."

All eyes in the room turned to him. Operation Fortitude was the huge plan to deceive Hitler and the Germans about the time and place of the coming invasion.

"I would like to propose an initiative aimed at doing just that." For the next ten minutes, the head of Special Operations Executive explained his plan. Finally, he sat back in his chair. "That's it. It may look like a long shot, but I believe it will work."

"I say go!" Montgomery tapped on the table.

"It might work." Eisenhower paused for a few minutes, his brow furrowed in concentration. "Yes, I'll approve. Please launch your plan."

The head of the SOE looked at his watch and stood up. "If you will excuse me, general." His hand reached for the scrambler telephone on the table. "I had made provisional arrangements pending your decision." The general's eyebrows lifted, but he nodded his assent.

"Connect me with the Kensington number, please." The intelligence chief waited briefly for the connection. "Harrison? Good. Please initiate the rescue of Major Dalton. Immediately. And prepare Operation First Violin. To await my orders."

St. Lô, Manche, Normandy. 11 a.m.

The towering twin spires of the Cathedral de Notre Dame in St. Lô cast their shadows across the square. Hermann Richter had admired the twelfth century architecture since he had first set eyes on it back in early 1941. He liked St. Lô, and was pleased that the western headquarters of the Gestapo in Normandy had been located there. The main headquarters were in Rouen, but he disliked the sprawling provincial town, whatever Monet thought of it.

He was happy in St Lô, so close to the Atlantic Ocean. He remembered what his father had told him: if you want to get on in a government position, get as far from Berlin as you can. Well, St Lô was far enough, and he was now Head of the Gestapo in Normandy. To progress further, he'd have to go back to Berlin, with all the political in-fighting crap; not to mention Bertha, a shrew of a wife who had spent the previous twenty years driving him up the greasy pole of ambition.

Hermann Richter was content enough as he walked around the Place Poissonerie. He was an *Alte Kämpfer* – one of the old battlers who had joined the Nazi Party in the early twenties, when Hitler was little more than a rabble-rousing tub thumper in Munich. The politics had drawn him in – who didn't want to avenge the socialist betrayal of November 1918 and deal with the Jewish Bolshevik conspiracy? But the action had pulled him, too. As a member of the Brownshirts – the *Sturmabteilung* – he had reveled in beating up communists and Jews.

He'd quickly risen through the ranks, but had been lucky enough to avoid the inner circle of Roehm, the leader of the Brownshirts, with its sordid clique of queers that Hitler had dealt with in 1934, butchering them all in what had become known as The Night of the Long Knives.

He was pleased with himself as he strode down the Rue des Halles towards the prison. He'd spent the last two years breaking French Resistance groups and targeting British agents; there had been some success, including the smashing of a major network. Perhaps he had been too good – there had been talk of using his services on the eastern front.

45

He chuckled as he neared the prison, thanking God that he was enjoying the spring sunshine in St. Lô and not wading through the mud in some hell-hole in Poland, waiting for the Reds to attack.

But he could not rest on his laurels. If the eastern front was waiting for the Russians, then he was waiting for the Americans and the British. They, too, were coming. He'd seen reports of over a million Americans in Britain. Rommel himself had described the enemy as a coiled spring waiting to be unleashed. But when would they strike? And where?

He stopped, sat down on the low wall in front of the prison and lit a cigarette. Soon. They would come soon, of that there was no doubt. It was already late May. There were only six opportunities – when the tide and the moon were right, the conditions favorable for an invasion landing. If they didn't come by July, they would be too late for that year. And if they waited until 1945, who knew what would happen? He himself had heard the strong rumors about wonder weapons – rocket planes and bombs – being developed by Hitler's scientists, weapons that could deal the enemy a fatal blow.

So, it had to be soon. You didn't have to be on the General Staff to know that. The real question was: where? He picked over the map of Europe in his mind.

Theoretically, the Allies could land anywhere from Norway to Bordeaux – anywhere provided the landing could be covered by planes based in England. But he knew that the choice boiled down to two main areas: the Pas de Calais or Normandy. The Pas de Calais would give the Allies a direct short thrust through Belgium to the heartland of Germany; Normandy would give them a hard slog, needing to defeat the *Wehrmacht* in France before taking the long route to the fatherland. Maybe they would try both.

He shook his head as he tossed his cigarette away, watching the sparks as it bounced on the pavement. Maybe Agent Blau, the spy in England, would penetrate allied security, but Richter knew he could not depend upon such luck. He walked towards the prison door. Perhaps the captured American major could give him the answer. But, for the moment, he'd let him stew in solitary. First, there was the problem of Philippe Josse.

Hope Cove, Devon. 12 noon.

The road widened as it dropped sharply to the harbor, the headland and the sea filling Tom's windshield. He pulled the jeep into the side of the road some way from the pub. Apart from a mass of bicycles, there weren't many vehicles and he didn't want to drive right up close, lest the Brits think he was just another flashy Yank. He walked down the road, which still fell steeply, to the little square around which stood two thatched houses. Beyond them lay the solid lines of the pub, its white-painted walls embracing the noonday sun.

He thought over some conversation pieces he might use, when his eyes were drawn to the cove, some fifty feet below the wall. The breaking waves spread their white fingers across the sand, pointing to a solitary small fishing boat beached at the last high tide. A strong breeze battled with the sheltering headland, fluffing up a few white horses to canter with the sunlight. He closed his eyes and listened to the gentle beat of the lapping waves, as the smell of brine and lobster pots teased his nostrils. He shook his head and walked toward the pub. It was difficult to believe that there was a war beyond this cove, a universal savagery of kill or be killed.

A cacophony of bar talk washed over him as he opened the door. Then the din died away as scores of eyes swung toward him. He felt self-conscious, as if he was in the wrong place. Perhaps he should not have worn his uniform; but, although most were civilians, he saw some in British naval whites, and a few in Royal Air Force blue.

"Tom, there you are – we thought you'd got lost!" Sally's cheery voice cut through the silence. "Come over here and join us." The bar resumed its animation, released from its curiosity as it realized the stranger was known.

"This is Danny." She introduced the young Royal Navy lieutenant at her side. "Danny, this is Tom – you know, the American I told you I met in the Cherub Inn." His handshake was firm, but Tom sensed that the red-haired man felt ill at ease.

"Hello. What's your poison? I'm afraid there's only the old sludge. No delivery till next week."

"Sludge?" There was a vacant look on Tom's face.

"It's what they call the beer." Again Sally's laugh. "There's no Scotch – unless you're a very good friend of the gaffer. Guess where all the whiskey goes?" Her face was playful as she answered her own question. "America."

Tom smiled, feeling embarrassed at the thought of the bottle of scotch he had brought for the party sitting in the back of his jeep. "I guess the sludge is fine."

"You may get to like it." Danny began to fight his way to the bar.

"Why don't we sit down?" Sally waved her hand at the chairs sprawled around a battered wooden table. As she sat down, she placed on the table a small, neatly-wrapped box with a 'Happy Birthday' tag. Tom hoped the bottle of scotch would be okay as a present.

Danny returned with the drinks. Tom took a pull on the frothy liquid in the large glass and, despite the lack of chill, was pleasantly surprised as the mellow taste washed over his tongue.

"It's good!" Tom reached for the pack of Lucky Strikes in his pocket. He struggled for something to open a conversation.

"Why the quiet when I came in?" He knew from their embarrassed looks that he'd made a mistake.

"In this place, they don't actually see many Americans. As you've found out, Tom, it's way off the beaten path." He found Sally's explanation somewhat lame.

"It's more than that." Danny looked at him nervously. "Can I explain?" He took a swig of his beer and continued.

"Well, everyone here knows that three thousand people had to leave their homes in the area behind Slapton Sands to make way for your exercises. Many people – including myself – had family and friends who were forced out. I'm sure it was probably very necessary, but it left a sour taste." There was a scarcely-hidden anger in the voice.

Tom grimaced. "I know the story. I'm sorry, but—"

"Look, there's Gwen out there!" Tom jumped at the mention of the name; the image of the dazzling smile that had accompanied the proffered cup of punch at the church came to his mind. He followed Sally's finger as it pointed through the window. But it was unmistakably her, sitting at a table in the pub's garden, her chin resting in her hands as she looked down at a book.

Before he could say anything, Sally headed for the door with her glass and package.

"Trying to hide from us, Gwen?" Sally's disarming laugh caused Gwen to look up from her book, her arm shielding her eyes from the sun.

"No, of course not; I've just walked down from the cottage. Don't you know it's nearly June? Why waste time in a smelly bar?"

"Well, anyway, how is the birthday girl? Happy Birthday!" Sally embraced Gwen. As they parted, Sally handed over her gift. "It's just a little something from Danny and me."

Gwen opened the box and drew out a set of earrings. "Sally, you shouldn't have. Must have cost the earth."

"Oh, I forgot." Sally looked embarrassed. "How rude of me. This is Tom, our new American friend."

Her eyes met his and there was warmth in the look of recognition. "I know – we've met before." Gwen recovered from her surprise and smiled at Tom. "Good to see you again. It's been a long time."

Too long, thought Tom. He shook her hand and returned the smile, his feet shuffling nervously. His earlier recollections were reinforced as he looked at her. She was a striking woman, almost as tall as he, with a long, slender neck, a proud jaw and full lips. Her smile was wide, as was the set of the eyes beneath the high forehead and swept-back auburn hair.

"You've already met?" Sally sounded a little like a disappointed schoolgirl. "Well, that's a turn up for the books. You are a dark one, Gwen."

"Oh, Sally, it was one of those ghastly do's at the church hall – you know, the sort of thing when we do our civic duty and make the Americans feel welcome." She realized she might be misunderstood and turned to him. "Which, of course, you are, Tom."

"I know the sort of affair of which you speak." Sally addressed Gwen, and then turned to beam a sly smile at Tom. "But sometimes I think it's the Americans who feel obliged to come and pretend that they're having fun."

Danny was not to be outdone. "Nonsense. In my experience, American GIs are always ready for any kind of party. After all, they're always on the lookout for some 'classy dames,' as they call our proper English girls."

"Okay, okay." Tom held his palms up toward Danny and laughed good-naturedly at the fun they seemed to be having at his expense. "I know what you Brits say about us: that we're 'overpaid, oversexed, and over here.' "

Danny laughed heartily and Gwen giggled while Sally shook her head in embarrassment.

"I think we'd better stop there," Sally sighed, "before war between the United States and Britain is declared. Let's go for a walk, shall we, Danny? You don't mind, do you, Gwen?"

Danny and Sally disappeared down the path to the headland. A foraging gull swooped down, screaming a loud, plaintive squawk. Tom glanced across at Gwen, found himself gazing into her warm eyes and looked down at the table.

St. Lô Prison. 12:30 p.m.

"Your game is not amusing!" Richter's voice echoed back from the walls. The room was bare, windowless. A table and two chairs stood drably in the dull light of a single bare bulb that cast its pallid illumination on the concrete walls. He walked behind Josse's chair. The Frenchman's face still bore scars and abrasions inflicted on his arrest. He looked up unconcernedly at the Gestapo man.

"Game? Your men beat me black and blue and you call it a game?"

"Don't try to be clever with me, Josse, I know what you're up to." Richter was angry. He breathed deeply. He had to be in control; anger was a sign of weakness.

"I'm up to nothing." Josse's voice was calm. "I'm just trying to help you. You got the consignment, didn't you?"

"Six cases of rifles? You call that a prize? What about the agent who escaped?" Richter found his voice rising and wondered why he allowed Josse to get to him. He decided to change tack and try to flush out the Frenchman. He affected a sigh and lowered his voice. "You said you wanted to help us, Josse. Why?" He watched his captive closely.

"I am the mayor of St. Marie de la Croix. I need to protect my people. And, although I am no great admirer of the Nazi Third Reich, it is necessary to halt the spread of communism, which I detest."

"Of course." Richter pulled out a pack of *Halbe-Fünf* cigarettes and saw Josse's eyes widen. He lit one slowly then made as if to put the red-and-gold pack on the table, but instead tossed it into his other hand and put it back into his pocket. "But surely there's more than that?"

"Maybe." There was a shrug of the shoulders.

"Maybe?" Richter blew smoke deliberately into Josse's face. "You tell me of arms drops, you betray men who are fighting for their country and you say 'Maybe?' "

He was surprised as Josse leapt to his feet, his face becoming crimson.

"I do not betray my country!" He slammed his huge fist down on the table. "My country has already been betrayed! Blum, the Popular Front, the socialists, the communists...," he hissed the last word, "...*they* betrayed my country. They are the anti-Christ."

"Is that why you're working for us?" Richter knew that the Catholic Church had done little to oppose the Nazis; indeed, in some areas, it had welcomed them with open arms.

"You eliminated the godless communists. That's good enough for me. You put Marshal Pétain in charge of France. And Laval. No more communists."

Richter suppressed his amusement. The 87-year-old Marshal – a French hero of the last war – was little more than a puppet for the Führer; the pathetic old man had been forced to watch the *Wehrmacht* take over his puppet Vichy state when the Allies had landed in North Africa in 1942. And Laval, even for Richter, was a little shit: true, he had his *Milice* round up Jews sometimes better than his own men; but if the Führer asked him to jump, he'd jump.

"Quite so." Richter pulled out his pack of cigarettes, and this time offered one to Josse. The Frenchman's hand shook a little as he accepted a light. Richter's eyebrows lifted a fraction. Nervous? Josse was usually imperturbable.

The Frenchman settled his thick-set frame back into the chair. "I'm sorry – I don't usually get emotional." He drew heavily on his cigarette. "But whenever I think about those anti-Christ communist bastards...." He clenched his fists for a moment, and then sat down.

Richter had known of Josse's religious inclinations but he had not been aware of their depth. Nevertheless, he decided to push on with his attack. "Yet, despite your avowed support for the Third Reich," he changed tack adroitly, "you allow a British agent to escape."

"The searchlight blinded me. Your men were too slow." Josse shrugged. "But it doesn't matter. It's of little importance."

Richter could scarcely contain his anger. "Of little importance?" He placed his face close to the Frenchman's. "The escape of a British agent is of little importance?" He walked around the table and confronted the Frenchman. "Josse, you have told me of five drops in the last three months. In two of the drops, we recovered the supply of weapons, although, strangely, there were no *resistants* for us to arrest."

His eyes narrowed as he watched the Frenchman for any reaction. Josse looked down at the table. "In the other three, my men were led in a wild goose chase around empty fields of Normandy."

"So, sometimes my information is incorrect." The voice was dismissive. "I've told you before: drops sometimes get cancelled at the last moment. Changes in the weather. Things happen."

A thin smile returned to Richter's face. The German walked back to his chair and sat down, fixing his prisoner with cold eyes. "Do not play games with me, Josse." He blew a long trail of smoke from his mouth. "I am very good at games, and I know yours." The German's control and self-confidence were now almost tangible, but the Frenchman did not break from the stare.

"Josse, it is my job to know how people think," he tapped the side of his nose, "and what they think." He leaned back leisurely in his chair, with the air of a schoolmaster lecturing a pupil.

"And what do I think?" The question was provocative, but Richter ignored the implication.

"You are thinking that you are worried about destroying your credibility with the English." Josse broke from the stare and looked down at his hands. Richter laughed and slapped his thigh. "You see, I am right! But do not worry, my friend – I understand! You are thinking that if everything they plan goes wrong, they will soon be aware of your game, and then," he drew his fingers across his throat, "*kaputt*. And you know the English can be ruthless killers."

Josse did not look up; he nodded, waiting for the German to continue.

"So, that is why you allowed the agent to escape." He threw down his cigarette and stood up as he ground it out. "But you must realize that you may lose credibility with us." There was menace in his voice.

Josse looked directly into Richter's eyes. "She'll be back. But it doesn't matter anyway. She's small fry." He took a final draw from his cigarette and ground it into the ashtray, the final wisps of smoke rising into the fetid air of the cell. "You're after the big secret, Herr Richter, aren't you?" He saw the German's eyes widen slightly. "And I'm the only man who can deliver it to you."

Hope Cove. 12.30p.m.

Tom's forefinger traced the rim of his glass. "What do you do in this goddamned war – apart from serving punch?"

Gwen laughed. "Nothing, I'm afraid." She raised her hands to the sides of her face, as if admitting some crime. "I look after my father – he was injured in the last show." Her lips pursed as she sipped from her glass. "Sometimes I do a little Land Army work when I visit my Aunt in Gravesend."

"Land Army?"

"Oh, of course, you wouldn't know." She smiled. "You see, with all the men being conscripted, there's a shortage of labor on the farms, so women fill the gaps. Actually," her eyes twinkled, "it's an excuse for us nice, middle-class gals to feel that we're doing our bit. But it's pretty ghastly. All muck and mud, sleeping in cold rooms and getting up at the crack of dawn. The farmers generally think we're a waste of time. But it's cheap labor for them." She looked at him and smiled. "I'm boring you, I'm sure."

"No, no…" He tried hard not to protest too much. "I'm fascinated by what you Brits have done to keep the ship afloat. You in the Land Army, Sally in the Wrens."

"Stiff upper lip and all that?" She leant back on her seat and laughed. "I suppose you've seen *Mrs. Miniver?*"

"Yes, I saw the movie when it came out two years ago. I thought it showed how heroic the Brits were."

"It's utter poppycock!" She laughed. "Sweet, of course, but total twaddle. Greer Garson buys a twee hat in the film, but hardly anyone buys a new hat nowadays. And as for Walter Pigeon's driving a sports car…" She saw the unbelieving look on his face. "I'm sorry, I didn't want to spoil your misconceptions."

"But look around this village," he protested, "it's idyllic – you wouldn't know there's a war on!"

"Yes, the countryside's not been badly hit – but the cities have taken a pasting."

She finished off her drink. "Let's not talk about it anymore. You've never told me what you do in this awful war."

"Intelligence."

"Oh, that must be exciting." Her face showed a keen interest. "Spies, secret codes and mysteries?"

"A little like that." He couldn't tell her that his latest assignment was to cover up the worst military disaster in the history of Uncle Sam's army. There was an awkward pause.

"I suppose you can't talk about it much. Pity. I love mysteries." She pointed to the book resting on the table. "I'm reading Conan Doyle again. You know, Sherlock Holmes. Have you read him? Is he popular in America?"

"Sure. Every American loves Sherlock Holmes. And most of them even know that in real life he goes by the name of Basil Rathbone." He laughed heartily and realized he hadn't laughed in a long time. It made him happy that she, too, laughed. "Seriously, I read him many years ago. I have to say I don't read much nowadays."

Her captivating smile reappeared. "But you should. Broadens the mind. You can learn a lot from reading. May I read to you what I just learned from Sherlock Holmes?" She picked up the book. "I'm sorry, I'll bore you."

"No, no, not at all." Somehow, he knew he wouldn't mind if she read the phone book to him. There was something about her that attracted him: her looks, of course, but there was something else, something he couldn't quite identify.

"Well, it's his methodology. Here, it's in *The Sign of the Four.*" She found her place and began reading. " 'My dear Watson, when you have eliminated the impossible, whatever remains, *however improbable,* must be the truth.' Isn't that a fantastic way to solve a mystery?"

"Perhaps. It doesn't appeal to the mathematician in me. Needs more precision, I think."

She raised an eyebrow. "You're sure I'm not boring you?"

"Nope – I mean yes." Why was he struggling with words?

She chuckled. "I understand. The mathematician inside you. Precision. Always important."

He laughed, and was pleased that his laughter brought a smile to her lips.

"But Sherlock Holmes triumphs over Moriarty. Checkmate." She smiled.

Tom fought the temptation to become lost in her smile. "Checkmate? That's a bit final, isn't it? I thought Moriarty led Holmes down the primrose path right to the very end. In fact, didn't Moriarty push Holmes over a waterfall? 'Checkmate' means 'the king is dead.' That's very final."

"Your precision again." She laughed and looked at him curiously. "You mentioned 'checkmate.' Do you play chess?"

"County champion when I was in high school." He realized it was almost a boast, but he was beginning to feel confident in her presence. Her eyebrows lifted, her eyes widening. "It was a small county." His voice was almost apologetic.

Her question surprised him. "What's your preferred opening as white – king's pawn or queen's pawn?"

"King's pawn." He answered automatically, a surprised look on his face.

"And against the Petroff Defense?"

"Trade the king's pawns. Aim to centralize my rooks on the open king's file—say, what is this?"

The curious exchange was interrupted by the return of Danny and Sally. "You two seem to be getting on like a house on fire." Sally looked coyly at Gwen, who returned a stern look that gave way to a mischievous smile.

"Are you all ready for my birthday lunch?" Gwen emptied her glass. "I've got a surprise." Her head turned from side to side, as if checking for eavesdroppers. "How does roast beef appeal to you?"

"Roast beef?" Danny's jaw dropped. "I thought it would be bangers and mash. You must be in the black market, Gwen. What's a good girl like you doing messing with spivs?"

"Ask me no questions and I'll tell you no lies." She feigned innocence. "And with the beef, there'll be roast potatoes and Yorkshire pudding, too."

"Yorkshire pudding?" Tom was confused. Pudding with roast beef?

"We'll explain later, Tom." Sally laughed and then looked at Gwen. "You're on!"

"And after this magnificent repast," Gwen paused, toying with them, "you can watch Tom and me play chess."

Danny broke the ensuing silence. "For roast beef, I'd face a Panzer division single-handed. But watching a game of chess...."

Gwen, her eyes smiling, looked at Tom as they all broke into laughter. He felt happy, and a little uneasy that he felt so.

St. Lô Prison. 1 p.m.

"Of course I'm after the big secret." Richter looked disdainfully at the Frenchman, whose usual florid face looked pale in the harsh glow of the solitary unshaded light bulb of the cell. The Gestapo man picked up a chair, spun it around and sat down, his hands gripping the back of the chair facing him. "I'm always after the big secret. Pray tell me, Josse," he slapped his thigh in amusement, "exactly what big secret I am after. How big is it?"

Josse stared at the cell floor, saying nothing. Richter stood up and shrugged. "So you don't want to play?" He made toward the door.

"When." Josse's voice was little more than a whisper. "And where."

Richter toyed with his cap for a few moments and then smiled. "I presume you are talking about a possible invasion?" He looked at the Frenchman, watching for the slightest reaction.

"It is not merely possible. It is certain." Josse looked at Richter impassively.

The German tossed his cap from one hand to the other. "I regret that I have to disappoint you, Josse, but I already know more-or-less when," he paused for a moment, "and roughly where."

"And what if I could tell you the exact date," Josse sniffed and wiped his hand across his moustache, "and precisely where."

"You?" Richter looked down contemptuously. "A small-town mayor? Someone who plays little spy games with the British?" He gave a sardonic snort. "Forgive me, Josse, but you are wasting my time." He pushed his cap onto his head. "You cannot tell me the time and place of the invasion." He called for the guard to open the cell.

"And the American will not tell you, either." Josse spoke softly, but it was enough to make Richter turn sharply. He waved the guard away and walked back to the table. "What American?"

"Please do not insult my intelligence, Herr Richter." He looked up and held the German's eyes with his own. "You may think me simple, but I am not a fool. Or do you think news doesn't travel in a prison?" A smile crossed his lips for an instant. "He was brought here this morning. He's in solitary." He shuffled on the bare wooden chair. "You are right, Herr Richter. I cannot tell you the secret. But give me some time with the American and he will tell me."

The German's eyes opened wide with incredulity and he laughed. "What makes you think that *I* cannot get the secret from the American myself, by interrogation?"

"You mean you're going to torture him?" Josse scoffed. "It will get you nowhere."

Richter shook his head. "Perhaps you now insult my intelligence, Josse. The so-called bravest men crumble when approached with a red hot poker."

"But you have no real threat against the American, Herr Richter."

"No threat?"

"You haven't got somebody to guarantee that he will tell the truth – his wife, or his girlfriend, or his sister—"

"Don't try to teach me my job, Josse. When I've finished with him, he'll talk."

"Without a doubt, but what will he tell you? His body screams in pain, he aches for release from the agony. So, he will tell you anything. That the Allied armies have so many divisions; that they will land in Norway, Denmark, the Pas de Calais, wherever. But how do you know, despite your torture, that it is true? You cannot verify it." There was a tobacco rasp to his dry chuckle. "You cannot be sure of whatever he tells you."

"You are beginning to bore me, Josse." He affected a yawn. "He will talk when I have finished with him. Or perhaps you can tell me another way to make the American give up his secrets?"

"The answer is simple, Herr Richter. You must get the American major to give up his secret willingly."

Richter let out a sardonic laugh. "So, I take the American out to dine and ask him nicely, 'Please, Major Dalton, I would be so obliged if you could tell me where the landings will be'."

"No, he will not tell *you.*" Josse toyed with the box of matches that lay on the table. "But he will tell me." He looked up at the German. "The plan is simple. You fix a way for me and the American to escape. When I prove to him my credentials as a Resistance leader, he will tell me. And then you will have the most valuable secret of the war, Herr Richter."

"Preposterous!" Richter laughed, dismissively. "I cannot possibly consider such an idea." He put on his cap and pulled the brim down hard. He called for the guard, waited for the door to be unlocked and stood in the doorway, looking back at the Frenchman. *"Undenkbar."* He shook his head. "Unthinkable."

Richter moved into the hall. The guard slammed the door and turned the key. "You wish to see the American now, *mein Herr?"*

Richter hesitated, stroking his chin. "Later."

He left the prison and walked back towards the square. Despite all his instincts, he was beginning to think along the lines of the unthinkable.

An hour later, a French warder entered Philippe Josse's cell. The mayor put down the book he was reading. Their eyes met, but no word was spoken as the tray with Josse's lunch was placed on the table. The warder left, locking the door behind him. Josse's fork played idly with the food before he lifted the plate to reveal a scrap of paper.

He read quickly, screwed up the paper, put it in his mouth, moistened it and swallowed. He returned to his book, selected a page and tore it out. With the stub of his pencil, he marked several letters on the page, folded it tightly and placed it under the plate. After half an hour, the warder returned and took away the tray.

May 26ᵗʰ 1944

The Atkinsons' cottage. Hope Cove, Devon. 2:15 p.m.

"You're late!" Gwen's father was looking out over the fence in front of the small cottage. Gwen whispered to Tom. "Don't forget what I told you. He can be awkward. Take everything he says with a pinch of salt." She turned back to her father as she pushed on the gate. "Stop fussing, Dad – the beef will be done to a tee."

Tom followed with Danny and Sally, his eyes taking in the attractive frontage of the cottage. The white-painted walls basked in the afternoon sun; roses on the lattice work by the side of the door were in full bloom.

"It's not good being late for dinner." Gwen's father retreated into the small hallway. "Two o'clock. It's always at two o'clock." He pulled his watch from his vest pocket. "It's nearly half past two!"

"Dad, it is my birthday, after all. Stop worrying, I'll soon fix things." Gwen hung her sweater on the hat stand. "Wouldn't you like to greet our guests?" She chided him. "You know Sally and Danny, and this is Tom, an American intelligence officer." She watched him nervously.

"American, eh?" He offered his hand as he looked Tom up and down. "Smart, I have to say that. Good crease in the trousers. Well-polished shoes."

Tom felt embarrassed and looked hopefully to Gwen for help. "For heaven's sake, Dad, this isn't the parade ground." She ushered her father into the living room and disappeared into the kitchen. Sally and Danny followed Tom into the small but neat room with a low, beamed ceiling. Danny whispered in Tom's ear. "Say little or nothing." He winked. "We've been here before. A bit old fashioned. I've known him since I was a lad."

"No wonder you're late." The grumble came from Gwen's father's chair. "Always late, Americans."

Tom looked across at Sally, who raised a finger to her lips.

"Three years late in the last war, two years late in this one." He lit a cigarette and coughed heavily.

"But they are helping us to win, Mr. Atkinson." Danny felt he had to come to Tom's aid.

"Granted – but they took their time about it." Another raucous cough followed.

"Anyway, to make up for the delay," Tom risked a half smile, "I've brought you this gift from the good old USA." His hand reached into his pocket and emerged with the bottle of single malt Scotch whiskey he had bought in the PX in Dartmouth. Mr. Atkinson threw his cigarette end into the fireplace and got up from his chair, his eyes agog. He took the bottle, cradling it in his hands like a mother with a baby.

For a few moments, nobody said a word, but the tableau was broken as Gwen emerged from the kitchen holding a dish on which sat the roast beef. "Dad, I've rarely seen you at a loss for words. Shouldn't you say something? Like 'thank you' for instance?"

56

"Yes...er, yes." He looked up at the American. "Thank you, young man."

"My name is Tom, sir."

"Then thank you, Tom." He looked down at the bottle and suddenly glanced back at Tom. "It's not illegal, is it?"

"Dad, for heaven's sake, stop being a curmudgeon!" Gwen put the dish on the table. "You didn't ask that question about the beef."

The old man looked shame-faced for a moment; he knew the beef had come from the black market. He composed himself, set the bottle on the table and began to carve the joint. "That's different – it's English beef." Gwen's eyes rolled upwards, and then glanced at Tom with a look beseeching his patience.

Danny's eyes moved between the bottle and the carved meat that was releasing its tempting aroma. "Roast beef and Scotch whiskey." He took his place at the table. "I must have died and gone to Heaven."

"Come on, Gwen, I'll help carry in the vegetables." Sally joined her friend as they moved around the table.

"And the Yorkshire pudding." Gwen winked at Tom as she handed around the plates.

After the last morsel of strawberry tart and clotted cream had disappeared, they all raised their glasses to Gwen. "Happy birthday! Many happy returns!" She acknowledged them with a modest smile.

"That was some meal!" Tom patted his stomach. "And the strawberry tart was absolutely delicious."

Gwen smiled her thanks. "They're our own strawberries – from the garden."

They were all replete from the meal and mellow from the whiskey. Gwen's father had retreated to his armchair behind a newspaper, while Sally vanished into the kitchen with Gwen to wash the dishes. Generous measures of the whiskey were poured into the men's glasses.

"Say, Danny," Tom sipped at his glass, "how come it's called Yorkshire pudding when it's served with roast beef? I thought pudding was a dessert."

Danny chuckled and heaved a great sigh. "We haven't used exact science to give names to our English culinary delights. It's a good job Gwen didn't serve you Toad in the Hole or Spotted Dick!"

"Spotted what?" Tom's face reddened as an unpleasant Army training film on hygiene came to mind.

There were sounds of laughter from the kitchen and Gwen's face appeared briefly in the doorway. "It's, well, like...," she smiled at Tom before bursting into laughter again. "Never mind." She disappeared back into the kitchen.

"Why, Spotted Dick is delicious." Mr. Atkinson was upset that his favorite dessert seemed to be under attack.

Gwen emerged, drying her hands on her apron and still giggling. "You're suddenly very quiet, Tom. Everything all right?"

"Yes, I'm fine." He grinned and winked at her. "I'm 'preparing my impromptu remarks,' as I believe your Winston Churchill once—"

"Don't mention that name in this house!" Mr. Atkinson's fists were clenched in anger and his face was beginning to redden.

"Dad, please—" Gwen bit her lip and sighed: Tom had accidentally stumbled into her father's long-standing grudge, the perceived evils of the prime minister.

But Mr. Atkinson was not to be deterred. "Churchill killed my cousin, George, in the Great War. George moved to Australia to seek his fortune, and when the war broke out he joined the army. A good boy was George, clever with his hands, wanted to be a mechanic, but he died young – slaughtered by the Turks at Gallipoli. Gallipoli – the hare-brained scheme of Churchill." The old man emptied his glass. "Churchill was Lord of the Admiralty then and was completely responsible. Thousands of Aussies and Kiwis died needlessly in the bloodbath. Churchill resigned in disgrace, and I thought we were rid of him."

Tom looked pensively down at his shoes as Gwen rolled her eyes.

"Gwen, I think your young American friend should know more about the political leader of his country's ally. Did you know, Tom, that in '26 Churchill tried to crush the unions? The miners had been out on strike for years – they had good reason: their wages had been chopped – and a countrywide sympathy strike was called. But Churchill stood solidly with the interests of big business; he forced the miners to crawl back to work on their knees. I'm a union man, and I can tell you—"

"Dad, stop being an old moaner. Why don't you show Danny your pigeons?" It was more an order than a question, Tom thought.

Danny took up the offer eagerly. "Have you still got that grizzle cock that won the Cherbourg race before the war? A fine bird, but it only just beat my uncle's! Are you breeding from him? Just think, after the war, we'll all be able to race again." The old man's temper subsided.

As Gwen opened a cabinet and pulled out a chessboard, Sally touched Gwen's arm. "Would you mind if I joined them in the garden, Gwen? It's such a nice afternoon. Besides, we're meeting my father for lunch in the Royal Castle Hotel tomorrow, and I want to keep an eye on Danny."

"Ah…" Gwen raised an eyebrow.

"It's nothing like that, Gwen." Sally flushed as she went out into the garden.

"You don't want to see the triumph of John Bull over Uncle Sam?" Gwen shouted after her as she put the chessboard on the table and flashed a challenging glance at Tom.

She smiled at him disarmingly as she began to set out the pieces. She shuffled two pawns behind her back and brought forward her clenched fists, each palm holding a pawn. Tom lightly touched her right hand, perhaps lingering longer than he should; she opened her palm to reveal its contents. "White. Lucky bugger." She made a final arrangement of her pieces. "It's always a big advantage to make the first move."

He looked at her, wondering if something was implied. He picked up his king's pawn and placed it firmly on the fourth rank.

Tom looked up at the clock on the mantelpiece. They'd been playing nearly an hour, and he felt pleased with his position. He'd played the risky Evans gambit, which she had accepted, her eyes challenging him from under her lashes. She had surprised him by withdrawing the attacked bishop to the king's file, but he had seized the initiative, won back the sacrificed pawn, then another. It was, he felt, only a matter of time.

"I must say you play well, Tom." Her eyes looked up from the board. "The position is a clear draw."

His eyebrows rose, briefly. His first reaction was to tell her that he had a winning position, that it needed only a dozen or so moves and he would sweep her opposition aside. But he quickly thought that would be ungallant; and then, just as quickly, he believed she was using her charm to prevent her fate.

Before he could decide between these two emotions, she spoke again. "Of course, we could fiddle around for a few more moves, but I don't think it would make any difference." She smiled at him across the board. "Or we could take a walk across the headland before you have to rush back to Dartmouth."

Tom felt very happy, knowing he would have resigned the position in exchange for a walk with her. "Okay, it's a draw." She responded with a smile that had a hint of triumph about it. But he also felt uneasy. He needed to tell her that he was a married man. His mind began to form the words, but she interrupted his thoughts.

"Wait until I tell Sally and Danny that an American county champion couldn't beat me." So it was the feminine guile, Tom thought. He began searching again for the words he knew he must say, but looked into her eyes and stopped. He picked up his officer's jacket from the back of the chair and put it on. "Come on, let's go see this headland." He opened the door for her. He would tell her later.

Major Ford's Quarters, Dartmouth. 11.30 p.m.

Tom looked at the cover of the book Gwen had given him: Sir Arthur Conan Doyle's *The Sign of the Four*. He put it on his bed and took off his jacket. Nearly midnight, but he was not yet ready for sleep; his mind was tormented with guilt. He should have told her he was married. There was no excuse for his behavior; he had treated her badly.

They hadn't said much during their walk, mainly talking about chess and Sherlock Holmes, but he knew that he was attracted to her. Several times he'd tried to tell her about his wife, and every time he'd spurned the opportunity, as if unable, or unwilling, to spoil the selfish pleasure of being with her.

He lit a cigarette and picked up the book. He would tell her. The next time he saw her, he would tell her everything. The well-thumbed book fell open naturally to the frontispiece, in which nestled a folded piece of paper. He opened it and was puzzled to see a series of five letters strung across the page. A whimsical smile came to his lips. It was a message written in code; she was challenging his decoding abilities.

Tom saw immediately that the message was too short to be deciphered by frequency analysis. More letters would have enabled him to use the frequency of the characters to find the real letters the characters represented. 'E', the most frequent vowel; 't', the most frequent consonant. He scanned the letter quickly; perhaps 'p' was 'e', the queen of vowels. Then his eyes caught the number written in the top right-hand corner: '37.'

He smiled, picked up the Sherlock Holmes book and turned to page 37. The first line would give him the key. Within five minutes he had unscrambled the message and was pleased to see that it was an invitation to have tea and play chess with her the next day.

May 27th

1944

Sturmbannführer Richter's Office. St. Lô. 10 a.m.

"Suppose I consider your mad scheme, Josse." Richter looked across his desk at the Frenchman who had been brought to his office. "How do I know that the American will tell you the truth? Or, for that matter, how do I know that you will tell me the truth?"

Josse looked at his captor, mindful of his cunning. "You don't. That's a fact."

"Then surely, if you were in my place, you would not take such a risk?" Richter stood up, turned to the window and looked out across the square.

"It depends." Josse looked pointedly at the pack of cigarettes on the desk. Richter nodded, and the Frenchman pulled one out and lit it. "I can be of no use to you at all in this place. I can't even make contact with the English agents." He drew deeply on the cigarette. "But outside, with the American major, who knows what I can find out?"

"Ah, the American major." Richter turned from the window, spinning on his heel. "I must soon turn my attention to him." He grinned. "A most pathetic character."

Josse shuddered involuntarily at the thought of what could happen in the cellar of the prison, where Richter conducted what he called his 'special interrogations.' "I told you it would be better for me to get the information from him." He flicked his ash into the ashtray and looked directly into Richter's eyes. "Painlessly."

Richter did not flinch from the stare. "I will be honest with you, Josse. I don't trust you." He waited for a reaction, but there was none. He heaved a sigh. "But then, you're probably thinking that I've made it my principle to trust no one. And, of course, you would be right."

Josse sat impassively, saying nothing. The German opened a desk drawer and pulled out a piece of paper. "However, I would suggest," he smiled at his choice of word, "an alternative plan. There is a large cell at the other end of the prison block. I intend to put you and the American in it together."

Josse raised an eyebrow and then shook his head. "It won't work." He ground out the cigarette. "It's an old trick. He'll take me for a stool pigeon."

"Maybe the trick is so old it will work. We shall see." Richter wrote on the paper, signed it and tapped on the desk with his pen. "The American will appreciate the change in his accommodation," he smiled thinly, "and circumstances. I'm sure you'll try, Josse." He called the guard, who escorted the Frenchman to the door. "Shall we say two days?"

Josse said nothing as the guard led him away.

Richter listened until the footsteps had died away, picked up the telephone and waited for the connection. "Put the American and Josse together in cell 79. And make the special arrangement. Yes, listening devices." He replaced the receiver and smiled.

The Atkinson's cottage, Hope Cove, Devon. 4 p.m.

Tom patted his lips with his napkin and sat back from the table.

"The English tea ceremony must be exported to the USA. Such delicious scones – that is the right word, isn't it? In the US, we call them 'biscuits,' and what you know as 'biscuits,' we call 'cookies.' See – I'm beginning to learn your lingo." He was pleased when she laughed. "Anyway, I'm sure glad I was able to decipher your code. If I hadn't, I'd have missed such a treat."

"If you hadn't solved it, I would have sent you the solution." Gwen realized the implication of what she had said and blushed a little. "Couldn't afford to waste such lovely scones and jam."

The message had said to come for a game of chess, but he felt there was something more. The blush on her cheeks matched the roses on the pattern of her cotton dress, which was tucked at the waist, showing her figure to good advantage. Tom saw that the dress had a slightly faded appearance, as if it had been laundered many times, and he recalled an English wartime motto he had learned since his arrival: 'make do and mend.' Clothing was rationed.

His eyes strayed down to a scattering of freckles above her scooped neckline before returning to her still-blushing face. She smiled and pushed back a few wisps of stray hair. He knew there was something between them, and he felt she knew it, too. When she'd asked him to come back, he had jumped at the chance, despite having to change rosters, and knowing that he would now have to work through the coming night.

"Well, Tom," Gwen's father pushed his chair away from the table and stood up. "I'd like to show you something." He walked towards the door. Tom looked across at Gwen, who smiled and nodded. "It's fine – I'll clear up the dishes. Don't keep him too long, Dad. There's chess, you know. I'm going to beat him this time." Her eyes twinkled at Tom.

Tom got up and followed the tall, erect figure that still walked with a military bearing, despite having left the army long ago. Tom wondered if Gwen got her height from him. The garden behind the house surprised him. The cobalt-blue irises in the border contrasted with the lush green of the lawn. The roses were flourishing, too, but most of the garden had vegetable plants in abundance – carrots, cauliflowers, clumps of potatoes, and runner beans climbing an improvised string frame.

"It looks like we're going to have a good year." The older man plucked a pod and examined it closely. "At least they can't say I didn't dig for victory."

Tom recalled the posters he'd seen at Plymouth railway station. 'Dig for Victory' they exhorted. Everyone was urged to grow their own vegetables, to reduce the demands on the convoys that were braving the U-boats in the Atlantic. Tom wondered how much difference it made; perhaps it could be measured in saved sailors' lives.

"Anyway, I didn't bring you out here to talk about vegetables." He cleared his throat and paused as if searching for the right words.

"It's about Gwen. I know you two have met a couple of times now. I know you've taken a shine to her."

Tom gulped. Was it so obvious that the old man could see it?

The old man fished in his pockets for his cigarettes. He lit one and tossed the match onto the compost heap. "It's just that she's everything to me, she's all I've got." He turned away, and Tom knew the old man was again looking into the past.

"Maybe…" Tom grasped for words. "Look, sir, if you'd rather I didn't see Gwen—"

"Good heavens, no." He turned his gaze back to Tom. "I haven't seen her so happy since—"

"Come on, Dad, you've had him long enough!" Gwen stood in the doorway, her hands on her hips in mock displeasure. "What can be more important than a game of chess?" She smiled the smile that bewitched Tom.

"You go in, Tom. I've got some things to do in the garden." The two men looked at each other and nodded in appreciation of the other's feelings. Tom felt strong pangs of guilt. What would the old man say if he knew he was married? He pushed the thought aside as he went into the cottage and saw Gwen setting up the chessboard. His turn with the black pieces. She would play a king's pawn opening, he knew. The Sicilian Defense.

One hour later, he was a pawn down and on the back foot. She kept smiling at him between moves, her eyes playing with his own. He wasn't sure if it was a genuine expression or whether she was using her wiles to gain an advantage. If it were the latter, she had succeeded: he could not concentrate.

"You're looking worried." That smile again.

He smiled back and decided to play her at her own game. "I must say you play well, Gwen." He glanced down at the board. "But the position is a clear draw."

Her eyes opened in disbelief, but he anticipated her protest. "Of course, we could fiddle around for a few more moves, but I don't think it will make any difference." He remembered her words from the day before and repeated them exactly. "Or we could take a walk across the headland before I have to rush back to Dartmouth."

She laughed and angled her head, looking at him from beneath her lashes. "Where on earth did you learn such a wicked trick?" She stood up and made for the door. "Okay, it's a draw. I'll let Dad know we're going for a walk."

The breeze stiffened, whipping off the sea and plucking at their hair, as the sun began to dip in the evening sky. They both knew their day together was coming to a close, but both were reluctant to let it go. He sneaked a look at his watch; he had to be back on duty in just over an hour.

"Come on, I know you've got to go." She surprised him by taking his hand and pulling him after her. He stumbled, but she grabbed him by the arms, staying his fall. He was impressed by her strength. He clutched at her to steady himself and she held him tightly. For several moments he looked into her eyes, feeling himself being tugged apart by the feelings within him.

"There's something you should know, Gwen." He eased himself away from her body.

"Please don't. Please don't say anything." She looked at him, and then lowered her eyes. "Not yet. I'm not ready for it. Not yet, please." She was fighting to control her own conflicting emotions. Tom realized she had misunderstood him, and cowardice drove his intentions to a remote part of his mind. He didn't want to hurt her. But he knew he couldn't lie to her forever. Or could he?

They walked back to the cottage in silence, each lost in thought. She went into the hallway and returned with his cap. She leaned forward and kissed him on the cheek as he left.

St. Lô Prison. 9:30 p.m.

Philippe Josse lay on his straw mattress in the cell. He held a Bible in his hand, but he was not reading. He was praying to God for help in what he must do in the night ahead. He looked across at the badly-bruised face of the American, who sat sullenly at the table in the middle of the room. Richter's plan wasn't working, as he'd expected. The American thought he was a stool pigeon and had clammed up. It was probably as well; Richter was sure to have the cell bugged.

Somehow, he had to convince the American of his plan. He grappled with the problem as he reached under the straw mattress and checked on the blanket that he had shredded and knotted together before his taciturn companion had been moved into the cell. They both looked up at the sound of boots on the floor of the corridor outside the cell. It was the German guard. The Germans left the regular French warders to do the day-to-day running of the prison, but they added extra guards.

The boots grew louder as they approached along the first floor corridor. Every twelve minutes, as regular as clockwork. Josse had been counting the paces for the last four hours. Teutonic orderliness, he thought, as he counted the sentry's footfall again. Twenty-seven, twenty-eight, twenty-nine. The German had reached the end of the corridor; there was a scrunch of boot nail on stone as he turned and began to make his way back along the passage, past the cell. Another forty paces, Josse counted, before the pattern of the footfall changed as the guard took the stairs to the floor above, where he repeated the procedure before climbing to the top floor to complete his round, then returning to their floor to start again.

Always twelve minutes, on some occasions a little longer; perhaps the German stopped for a surreptitious cigarette sometimes. Josse turned over the Bible that the French warder had given him earlier. He felt along the spine when he noticed the American watching him.

The Frenchman raised an index finger to his lips. His fingers delved into his pant cuff and emerged with a pencil stub. He opened the Bible, crossed himself and wrote quickly on the inside of the cover in English.

The Germans are listening. We are going to escape. You must trust me.

The American took the book and pencil from Josse and wrote.

No. I am a prisoner of war. They will shoot me.

So, Dalton didn't appear keen about escaping; Josse wanted to ask him if he preferred Richter's torture to being shot, but instead he wrote three words.

Major Dalton. BIGOT.

The American's head went back and his eyes opened wide, wondering where Josse had obtained the information. Josse scribbled again.

You must trust me.

His look, backing up the words, demanded trust. The American held his eyes for a moment and then nodded. Josse looked down at his Bible again, relieved that Dalton had been brought into the scheme. He had not relished the alternative.

His fingers began to pull at the top of the spine of the Bible, his fingernails working at the fabric. When the aperture at the top of the spine was sufficient, he tilted the book and two small steel rods slid into view. He took the rods into his hand. *"Et voilà!"* He whispered. The American's face bore a look of puzzlement.

Suddenly, their heads turned sharply to the cell door. A key was rattling in the lock.

US Naval Headquarters. Dartmouth. 9:30p.m.

Dearest Son,

I hope you are well. I wish I could send you one of your favorite pot roasts, because I'll bet the army chow is lousy.

Your Dad and I are both well, apart from the occasional twinge in my back. Your dad is very proud of you. He keeps saying he wishes he could be with you in the war – you men are all the same – but he contents himself with working on our Victory Garden.

Tom, I hope you don't have to go into the front line. Do you remember Jimmy Streubel? I think he was a year behind you in High School. He's been killed in action in the Marshall Islands. Mrs. Streubel took it hard, but she seems to be proud that she's a Gold Star mother. She's got the service flag with the gold star stuck up in her front window. As for me, it's an honor I never want to have. I'm happy with my blue star service flag, so please keep yourself safe.

I must say, we haven't seen much of Wilma. Your Dad thinks she's going out of her way to avoid us. Mrs. Hafner's daughter Irene says she sees Wilma at the dance hall on Saturday nights, but she hasn't visited us for over two months. I heard from Mrs. Prossner, who lives a few doors down from your apartment, that Wilma may have had Bruiser put to sleep. I know the dog was ill for a while. I'm sorry if this is true – I know that Bruiser was your good buddy.

Well, I promised your Dad that I'd help him put in the Victory Garden, so I've got to go now.

Please behave yourself, be careful, and write soon.

Love,

Mother

There was nothing much about Wilma, but in this case he knew that no news was not good news. He knew he should be grieving for Wilma and for his marriage, but curiously his thoughts were with Bruiser. His great bear of a dog with his floppy ears and, generally, burrs in his coat. Bruiser always had an uncanny ability to gauge his moods; if Tom was sitting on the porch brooding about something, Bruiser would come to him, plop his massive head on Tom's thigh, and heave a great sigh of commiseration. He could see Bruiser's big brown eyes, could feel his breath on his hand. It was strange, but he couldn't quite see Wilma's face, couldn't remember what her voice sounded like. He could remember how she looked in photographs, but he couldn't really remember *her*....

Tears were added to his growing anger. He screwed the letter up and hurled it into the wastebasket. He slouched at his desk, his face resting in his palms. After a minute, the letter was retrieved, his hands smoothing out the crumples. He lit a cigarette and read it again, letting out a long shroud of smoke. Why didn't Wilma at least have the courage to write?

He saw Gwen, a chess piece poised in her hand, smiling as she made a move. How could he talk about courage? He hadn't even had the nerve to tell Gwen about Wilma. Wilma. A stranger back home. He sobbed, but his knuckles whitened as his fist clenched in anger. At least, he hadn't done anything wrong. Not with Gwen. But would he, if the chance arose? If she had... He ground out his cigarette as though he were trying to murder it.

It was the war. None of this would have happened if it hadn't been for the war. There would have been no Gwen, probably no Wilma. Ifs and buts, he thought. He slammed his fist down on the desk.

The phone rang, startling him. He shouted an angry 'yes' into the mouthpiece.

"I'm sorry, sir, but can you come to the radio room, sir?" The voice was urgent. "There's something funny going on."

"What is it?"

"Not sure, sir, but we've picked up a transmission from an unusual source. Seems like it's right here in Devon. And it's not in one of our codes."

"I'm on my way." Tom put down the receiver. He picked up the letter and looked at it for a few moments before stuffing it in his pocket. The war. The damned war.

St. Lô Prison. 9:45 p.m.

Josse barely had time to push the metal rods into his pocket before the cell door swung open, and he was relieved at the sight of the figure of Alphonse Grassin framed in the doorway.

"Enfin, c'est toi." Josse raised a finger to his lips to warn of the German listening devices. The warder nodded and set the food tray on the table. Alphonse Grassin was a Frenchman of the old type. He hated the *Bosches* and all that they stood for. He'd fought them in the last war, just as his grandfather had back in 1870. The defeat of 1940 had struck him hard, but he had had no

way to fight back, until he met Philippe Josse. The mayor of St. Marie de la Croix had taught him how to help – to carry messages, to find out what was going on in the jail, who had been arrested and for what. When Philippe had been arrested, Alphonse knew he could now repay his trust.

"*Eh bien*, what culinary delight have you brought us?" Josse spoke harshly for the benefit of the eavesdroppers.

"It's slop, but it's better than a traitor like you deserves. You and that rat over there." There was venom in his voice, but the American was surprised by the Frenchman's wink. "*Eh bien, au revoir.*" The warder slammed the door shut and locked it. From the inside. He moved quietly towards the American's bed. He handed Josse the key, and crawled under the bed, arranging the blanket to hide himself.

The sound of the German guard's boots could be heard on the stairs. Josse hurriedly pushed the key into his pocket, motioned for Dalton to join him at the table, where they sat eating their food.

As soon as the guard's footsteps began climbing to the next floor, Josse picked up the key and quietly opened the cell door, motioning for Dalton to follow him. As they emerged into the corridor, he held up ten fingers and then another two. The American looked at his watch and nodded. Twelve minutes. Twelve minutes before the German would return.

Josse moved swiftly across the corridor to the window opposite the cell door. There was no glass, only three iron bars, two vertical and one horizontal, forming a lattice to guard against escape. Josse took the first steel rod from his pocket and prayed. At the end of the rod was welded a mold, a mirror image of a six-sided nut. He put it over one of the nuts securing one end of an iron bar, and was pleased to find it made a snug fit. At the other end of that rod was a hole to receive the second rod, which was to act as a lever. He threaded it through and tested it, like a wheel brace.

There was no movement of the nut. He offered up a prayer and increased the pressure. The thread of the nut began to yield, slowly at first, then more readily. Josse panted, pausing to regain his breath as the nut came free. Two more and they could push the bars away, using the unscrewed nuts as a pivot. All the time he was counting, counting the sentry's footsteps even though he could not hear them. He looked up at Dalton, who glanced at his watch and held up ten fingers. It was going well.

But the second nut proved intractable. All the muscles in his arms and wrists strained, the veins at his temples bulging. It would not budge. The American tapped him on the shoulder and took position to try his hand. Still no movement. Sweat began to run from Dalton's brow as he strained and heaved. He was sure there was the slightest give, but he could make no further progress. Suddenly, he went back into the cell and returned with the warder's nightstick. Before Josse could stop him, Dalton slammed it against the nut.

The noise echoed down the corridor. Josse heard stirrings from the other cells, but before he could say anything, Dalton heaved on the lever and the nut moved. The Frenchman finished the work, spinning the nut free.

The American held up seven fingers. Josse was pleasantly surprised when the final nut offered little resistance. He eased it free and began pulling one of the vertical bars, levering it to a position that left the window aperture unobstructed. The second bar proved difficult, but eventually moved. Six fingers. It was going well.

Suddenly he froze. His eyes darted to Dalton, who looked at his watch and shook his head in disbelief. There were footsteps on the stairs coming to their floor.

.

U.S. Naval Headquarters, Dartmouth. 9:45 p.m.

Tom raced to the top floor where the radio room was situated. The guard nodded as he flashed his pass and pushed on the door to make his way past the busy operators toward the duty desk.

"So, what's the story, Jack?"

"Well, sir," the chief petty officer looked tired, but he was agitated, "we've picked up these unusual signals."

"What do they say – what's the message?"

"That's the first thing, sir – we can't break the code. It's not one of ours. We probably will, eventually, but it's not easy."

Tom looked at the code sheets. The patterns of five letter blocks suggested German code. Perhaps Enigma. It could take hours to decode, enough time for the operator to dismantle his equipment and flee. "And the second thing?"

"The fix that our R.D.F. has come up with." R.D.F. Radio Directional Finders were mobile vans with sensitive listening devices. One listening post could home in on a signal source; then another would be called into operation to take a second bearing. Plot the bearings on a map and bingo – the source could be pinpointed. "It's very unusual."

"How so?"

"Well, it's right here, sir." The CPO passed over a map that had two intersecting lines drawn on it. "Right here in Devon. In our zone."

Tom looked at the map; the lines met just outside Blackawton, a small village at the northernmost part of the zone from which all the inhabitants had been removed to make way for the U.S. Army exercises.

"You sure it's not one of ours?" Tom needed to be sure; there were thousands of Americans in the zone.

"Absolutely, sir." The CPO began to count on his fingers. "One, there's none of our people in that place. Two, we don't broadcast on that frequency. And three, Callaghan – he's one of our best operators, sir – he says he's never heard the fist before."

Tom nodded. The fist. Every operator had his own individual way of tapping the Morse key. Some had heavy fists; others a light touch. Skilled operators got to know an individual's hand. Short dashes, pauses, other patterns that gave each operator his own signature, like a fingerprint.

"Okay, I hear you. Thanks for calling me. You say there's none of our men in that area – is there a unit nearby?"

The CPO grimaced. "To be honest, I'm not sure exactly. There's a big exercise going on tonight, so there's bound to be some unit near that area." His brow furrowed. "Trouble is, they're all on the move with long periods of radio silence. I could find out."

"Move on it, Jack." Tom's mind was already racing ahead. "And tell them I want six men to meet me here." His finger stabbed at the village of Blackawton on the map. "Contact me with the details on the walkie-talkie." He hurried from the room.

St. Lô Prison. 9:45 p.m.

It was too soon. But Josse could hear the German sentry's boots climbing the stairs to their floor. Perhaps he had miscalculated. Perhaps the sentry had heard the noise. He pulled on Dalton's sleeve and they slipped back into the cell, closing the door and gently turning the key in the lock.

Alphonse leapt up and was about to speak when Josse raised a finger to his lips and motioned the warder back into the corner of the cell, out of sight of the grille in the door. A quick signal to the American, and they both tumbled onto their straw mattresses, feigning sleep.

The sentry's boots came down the corridor at the usual measured pace. So there was no alarm, thought Josse, still just routine. Josse heard the boots pass the cell and began to count. Twenty-eight, twenty-nine, the turn. It would be forty paces back to the stairs. But the steps stopped outside their cell. To his horror, Josse remembered that he had left the steel rods on the floor under the window. He began to pray.

The German sentry would see the steel rods, he would raise the alarm and... Josse ground his teeth in anger and frustration. He was anticipating the sentry's shouts when he detected a familiar smell: the unmistakable aroma of tobacco. The German had lit a cigarette. Dalton eased himself up on one elbow, but Josse signaled him to lie low. He waited, one minute, two, more. After what seemed an eternity, the footsteps resumed, Josse counting until they went up the stairs to the next floor.

The door was swiftly unlocked and, with Dalton's aid, Josse freed the last nut and turned the bar until its loose end rested on the brick wall. They returned to the cell, Josse pointing to the makeshift rope, signaling Dalton to fix one end to the repositioned bar. As the American left, Alphonse stood up and handed Josse his nightstick; he gave a meaningful look and turned his back. After a second's hesitation, Josse bought the stick firmly down on the back of Alphonse's head and the warder slumped to the floor.

Dalton reappeared in the cell doorway, raised his eyebrows as he saw Alphonse's crumpled form, but said nothing and jerked his head toward the corridor. Josse made to follow, but stopped first to pick up the Bible. Alphonse would be grilled ruthlessly in the morning; leaving incriminating evidence would be fatal.

With one hand on the rope, Josse eased himself onto the window ledge.

The American leaned forward and whispered. "But we're gonna land in the courtyard. We'll still be inside the prison."

Josse gave a half smile. "Trust me, my friend, trust me."

He looked at the yard some five meters below and tested the rope before sliding rapidly down. Dalton followed, landing noisily. Both men backed against the wall, waiting for any reaction. Josse tugged on Dalton's sleeve. "Follow me."

They edged around the yard, their backs to the wall, which was in the shadow of a pale moon. Dalton noticed that the surface of the yard sloped gradually in the direction of the corner to which they were headed. There was still no sound from inside the prison. Josse offered up another prayer.

As they reached the corner, Josse pointed down, and Dalton saw there was the grille of a drain about four feet square. Josse signaled him to stand on one side while he took the other. A fetid smell hit them as they wrapped their fingers around the grille and heaved. There was movement, but one of the corners was stuck. Josse dug in his pocket, pulled out one of the steel rods and began scraping away the debris that had accumulated in the crack. The metal grated against the grille. Voices came from the guardroom at the other end of the yard. Josse scraped frantically. They heaved once more, and the grille came free. Josse's feet reached for the first rung of iron bars set in the wall of the shaft, but the American stopped him.

"Listen!"

Josse lifted his head. He could hear nothing at first and began to resume his descent. Then he heard the noise – a soft purr at first, then a growing drone. Aircraft engines. A lot of them. Josse moved down the shaft and urged Dalton to follow him. The noise was growing louder, as if the very sky were throbbing. As Dalton made a mighty heave to pull the grille back into position, he heard a telephone ring. Within moments, the prison's air raid signal began its screaming wail.

The Evacuated Area. Devon. 10:15 p.m.

Tom showed his impatience by gunning the gas pedal as the guard inspected his pass in the beam of his flashlight.

"Sorry, sir, but you know the drill," the guard spoke without looking up, "no one in the training zone without the proper accreditation." He turned the ID card in his fingers. "For all I know, you might be a German spy." The soldier sensed Tom's growing anger. "Which clearly you ain't, sir. But be careful, sir – there's an exercise going on tonight."

An exercise. Tom thought of the cunning of the man: what better place to hide than in some deserted farmhouse in the middle of a U.S. training ground, the spy's radio traffic hidden among the myriad signals generated by the American army?

Tom drove off in the direction of Blackawton, the village near the source of the signals. The hooded headlights barely picked out the sides of the narrow lanes. The tall hedgerows and tortuous roads made him feel as though he was navigating a maze, and he got lost several times. He tried to contact headquarters, but was frustrated when he found there was no signal on the walkie-talkie.

But suddenly, the village was there. As the moon played hide-and-seek with the clouds, the pale light and the shadows washed over the empty houses, ghostly sentinels of the village's only street; somewhere a door slammed haphazardly in the breeze. He wondered how he would have felt if he had lived in this village. He began to realize how Danny and his family had felt. Thrown out of his house and home so that foreign people could come and leave destruction everywhere.

To his left stood the church, its tombstones losing the battle with the rampant untended grass. Part of the church had been damaged, probably in some previous exercise, and the steeple clock was frozen at ten past six on a day long since gone. There was a light in the church, he was sure. He stopped the jeep, switched off the motor and jumped down.

The bullet struck the pavement about a yard from his feet. For a moment, he froze as the ricochet whistled away, and then threw himself to the ground, rolling to the side of the road, his cap flying away.

The sewer beneath St. Lô Prison. 10:15 p.m.

The wailing of the air raid siren grew fainter as Josse led the American down the rungs sticking out of the concrete wall of the drain. It was a difficult descent. The absence of any light forced Josse to feel with his feet for each rung one at a time, then his hand had to reach up to guide Dalton's feet as he came down after him. Some of the rungs were slippery with the damp of recent rainfall. And, all the time, the overwhelming smell came from below, a growing stench that assaulted their mouths and nostrils.

Down, down they went, step by step. Josse counted. Sixty, seventy, how many more? He felt he was descending into hell as the smell became overpowering. Above him, Dalton coughed and heaved, but followed Josse as he guided his feet. Josse had stopped counting when his foot no longer found a rung beneath him. His massive arms flexed as he lowered himself down until he felt the flow of liquid pull at his feet. The culvert, at last.

"Nous sommes arrivés, mon ami." Josse called to Dalton. "Come, jump."

Dalton dropped the last few feet to join the Frenchman in eighteen inches of flowing sewage. They both hawked and spewed as the foul smell pulled at the contents of their stomachs.

"Merde!" Despite the circumstances, Josse laughed at the irony. It was, indeed, shit. It seemed as if the whole excreta of St. Lô was sweeping around them.

"This way." He turned to his right, his legs moving through the calf-deep filth.

"I can't see. How do you know it's the right way?"

"Because that's the way the shit is going. The other way leads to...," he shook the thought from his mind. "Put your hand on my shoulder and follow me."

After two hundred meters, Josse stopped for breath. Such breath as there was. Despite holding his shirt over his mouth, he felt nauseous; behind him, Dalton was still heaving, although there was nothing left to vomit but his stomach itself.

The first explosion alarmed them. It was little more than a dull thud, but the sewer shook, and then shook again, as another blast forced its way through the earth. Josse felt the American grip his shoulders from behind. There was another blast, then another, followed by a brief pause.

"Your people are bombing the prison." Josse spoke matter-of-factly, without recrimination.

More explosions followed quickly. There was no pattern – just an endless series of powerful bomb blasts that caused the sewer to shudder erratically. Even so far beneath the prison, they could feel the ferocity of the assault above.

"What did you say?" Dalton had to shout to make himself heard.

"Your people – *les Américains* – they are bombing the prison."

"Why are they bombing the pris—" The question died on his lips as he realized the answer. "Jesus!"

"Venez." Josse grabbed his arm as they began to move through the swirling filth. So the American did know about the invasion, he thought. Just as the message Alphonse had brought had said. That's why the Americans were raining bombs on St. Lô prison.

Still the explosions rocked the tunnel. The walls shook, causing Dalton to lose his grip; only Josse's firm grasp on his arm saved him from plunging headlong. The blasts agitated the sewage even more, provoking an even more odious stench.

"Voilà! I can see it!" Josse could barely contain his relief as he saw a small light in the distance. *"Enfin,* the way out."

The explosions began to die away. As they pushed their way toward the growing light, there was a final clump of bombs, then only the sounds of their sloshing feet.

"Not far now." Josse's tone was insistent, driving on the American, who still heaved and retched. The circle of light at the end of the tunnel grew larger as they splashed their way through the filth. They had gone about half a mile, Josse guessed, and it had taken them thirty minutes; a half hour that had seemed a lifetime.

The tunnel narrowed as they approached the exit. There was light, a strange light flickering on the walls of the drain. Spluttering and coughing, they emerged from the mouth of the tunnel to be surprised by the light, which was almost as bright as day. They climbed from the culvert and looked back at the town, engulfed by flames that licked the night sky.

The prison was ablaze, consumed by fire. An image of Alphonse crossed Josse's mind, and he felt a wrench of anguish. His friend was dead without a doubt; it was scant consolation to know he would not have to suffer Richter's torture.

He pointed a finger toward the flaming inferno. "Now you know how highly your generals think of you, *mon ami.*" He looked at Dalton's face, and saw the acceptance there as the flames and shadows drew grotesque patterns upon it. "Every bomb was meant for you."

The American stood dumbfounded until Josse prodded him. Dalton whipped around, eyes glowering.

"Look, Frenchie. I don't know who you are, or who you're working for, but I reckon you're not working for my side. If my guys had sent you instructions to spring me from jail, they sure as hell wouldn't have bombed the place!"

Josse was troubled with Dalton's attitude, but spoke to the American scornfully.

"My friend, I think your options are limited right now. You don't know these parts and you don't speak French. Are you keen to see Herr Richter again? If not, follow me."

The American grudgingly followed as Josse led him to a small copse and rummaged at the foot of a tree, throwing foliage aside until two bicycles were revealed. *"Allons-y."* Josse mounted and urged the American to follow. "First I must send a radio message. And then we must get to the safe house." He sniffed the air. "And get out of these clothes."

Gestapo Headquarters. St. Lô. 10:15 p.m.

Sturmbannführer Richter looked up as he heard the planes' engines. He got up from his desk, walked across the room and opened a window. Below him was the town square and beyond it the prison, but his eyes were looking up at the sky as the distant drone grew louder. Enemy bombers approaching from the north. Richter knew their target and their task. He had no specific information, but he felt it in his bones. The bombers' target was the prison, their purpose to bury Major Dalton and all his secrets. He had been right all along.

As the noise of the engines drew nearer, searchlights began to stab at the sky. He hurried back to his desk and picked up the phone. "I want my staff car at the front door." It was a voice used to giving orders. "Immediately!"

He replaced the receiver and lifted it again. "Connect me with the prison. *Schnell!*" As he waited for the connection, he buttoned his coat and reached for his cap.

"Sergeant, what's the situation?"

"We believe there's been an escape, *mein Herr*. We're checking, but there's an air raid coming."

"I'm perfectly aware of that. I'm not deaf! I suggest you repair to the cellars. *Auf Weiderhören!*"

He clattered the receiver into the cradle and left the room, fastening his coat as he hurriedly descended the stairs. As he emerged into the street, the throb of the engines told him there was little time. His chauffeur saluted him, holding open the door to the limousine. "This is no time for formalities, Helmut. Get us to the outskirts of town – away from this place." He leapt into the car and leaned back in his seat, cursing Josse and the American bombers. They may have outsmarted him for the moment, but he would soon regain the upper hand.

"*Schnell, Helmut, schnell!*" The tires screamed as the driver hit the gas pedal. He must not lose it now, Richter thought. The secret of the *grossinvasion*. It had to be his prize.

Blackawton in the Evacuated Area. 10:30 p.m.

"What the hell's going on?" Tom was aware of a pair of boots approaching him as he lay at the side of the road.

"Sir, as a battle umpire, I have to declare that you've been captured by the Red Force."

Tom leapt to his feet and retrieved his cap. "Captured? I am Major Ford of U.S. Army Intelligence! Why is the U.S. Army firing real bullets at me?"

"They decided to use real ammo for the exercise, sir, to enhance the training." The lieutenant turned on his flashlight, which picked out Tom's epaulettes. "Aren't you part of the invading Blue Force, sir? You're not wearing the armband." The young officer was flustered. "That's against the rules. You could be classified as a spy."

"I know nothing about any goddamned Blue Force – I'm trying to hunt down a possible German spy!" Tom saw that the lieutenant looked dubious, not sure where the exercise ended and reality began. "Look, Lieutenant, I need six men."

"You'd better ask over there, sir." He pointed toward the tombstones.

"In the church?"

"Well, it used to be a church. God knows what it is now." He saluted and walked away. Tom retrieved his flashlight from the jeep and approached the church gates. He struggled with the latch and caught sight, in the moonlight, of a notice hung on the railings of the gate. He switched on his flashlight and read:

To our Allies of the U.S.A.

This church has stood here for several hundred years. Around it has grown a community which has lived in these houses and tilled these fields ever since there was a church. This church, this churchyard in which their loved ones lie at rest, these homes, these fields are as dear to those who have left them as are those that you, our Allies, have left behind. They hope to return one day, as you hope to return to yours. They entrust them to your care, and pray that God's blessing may rest upon us all.

Charles, Bishop of Exeter

"Put that fucking light out!" The shout came from within the churchyard. Tom flicked the switch and pushed on the creaking gate. The church door was open, and a young captain was framed in the light coming from within. "Who are you? What do you want?" The speech sounded slurred.

"I'm Major Ford of U.S. Army Intelligence. I need six men."

"You want what?" The captain's eyes caught sight of Tom's epaulettes as he approached the door; he was unsteady as he saluted. "I'm sorry, sir, but we're in the middle of a big exercise."

"You don't understand, captain," there was anger in Tom's voice, "I'm on a very important mission."

"I'm sorry, sir, but I can't help you." The captain turned to go back into the church.

Tom was beside himself with rage. "I'm ordering you to release six men to me!" Tom's shout echoed along the empty street.

There was a movement behind the captain. "And I'm ordering you to do no such thing, Meisner." The voice came from a full major in combat gear. Tall and well-built, he had a large face that looked young, but there were some flecks of gray in his moustache. He lifted a hipflask to his lips, swilled the liquid in his mouth and swallowed.

"Hell, major, don't you know there's a war going on?" He looked at Tom disparagingly. "Please come inside our grand company HQ," he made a sweep of his arm in a facetious welcome, "before some idiot starts shooting at us."

Tom smelled the liquor on the major's breath as he went through the door. The church was lit by a single arc lamp, powered by a generator humming steadily in the corner. The pews had been pushed against the wall; about twenty men lounged on them or sprawled on the floor, some drinking beer, others shooting a noisy game of craps, barely pausing to look up at the new-comer. A faint but distinct smell of urine hung in the air.

"Major Fonseca at your service." There was a perfunctory salute. "How can I help you, major? As long as you don't ask for men."

"Fonseca, I've never seen such a lack of discipline. Didn't you read the notice on the church gate?"

"Discipline?" Fonseca spat on the church floor. "Don't talk to me about discipline – and don't talk to me about God, either." He turned to a corporal lying on a nearby pew. "Hey, Koswolski, this here major thinks you're not disciplined enough." The dogface smiled, finished his beer and tossed the bottle into a growing pile by the baptismal font.

"Let me tell you something, major." A finger jabbed at Tom's shoulder. "Our great General Staff decided in all their fat-assed wisdom to send us here on some futile exercise, and Americans are shooting at each other – with live ammo, for chrissake – for the sake of *realism*," his tongue lashed out the last word, "while meanwhile the Krauts sit on their asses in France drinking champagne!" His tirade was interrupted by his need for a cigarette, which he lit. "Realism." His voice dripped with venom. "Wish I'd got the brass who gave that order here. I'd show 'em realism."

"Look, Fonseca, I don't care what you think. I need some men." Tom hid his desperation from his voice. "There may be a German spy in the area."

Fonseca guffawed. "Not a single man! I don't give a damn even if Adolf Hitler hisself was in the house over the road. No men!"

Tom decided to force the issue. "I could report you, Fonseca."

Fonseca laughed. "Go ahead. Be my guest. Report all these men, too." His hand waved loosely in the direction of the other men, who were watching sullenly. "Maybe they'll all get stuck in some prison instead of being shipped out to stop German bullets." There was emotion in the voice, and Tom sensed it was not completely liquor-fueled.

"You need to understand, Ford, that in next to no time, these men will be wading up some god-forsaken beach taking everything the Krauts can throw at them," the renewed finger-prodding was slow, deliberate, "while you and the other desk soldiers will be congratulating yourselves on how well *you* did." The jabbing finger fell away as Fonseca breathed deeply to rein in his emotions.

"They'll do the job fine. But maybe in a few weeks most of them – maybe me, too – will be as dead as those under the headstones outside." He pushed his face in front of Tom's. "So don't talk to me about discipline."

Tom was frustrated, but knew he was beaten. All the men fixed him with a sullen stare as they watched him, and he knew he had to back off. "Okay, okay, I understand." He spread his palms wide in front of him in a gesture of submission. "But let me contact my headquarters first. And then I'll be out of your hair in five minutes."

"Sure." Fonseca turned and shouted over his shoulder. "O'Neil, give him a line on the field telephone. And listen to what he says. If he badmouths the unit, let me know."

Tom gave a shrug of the shoulders and followed O'Neil, who took a few minutes to patch him through, but the CPO's voice was clear.

"Major, we were wondering what had happened to you."

"Any news on the transmission?"

"Still loud and clear, sir. The RDF vans confirm the same position. It's a farmhouse just off the road north from Blackawton. About a mile and a half. Pinpoint accuracy. These things are getting better every day. But the vans have got to be withdrawn."

"No, no withdrawal."

"I'm sorry, sir, but this exercise is apparently big shit and we've upset the powers-that-be. A couple of colonels are not very happy that we're pissing on their parade."

"I know, Jack, I found out the hard way. Any news about the men I need?"

"That's negative, too, I'm afraid, major. If I was you, I'd scram right now."

Tom felt angry again. "There's no way I can leave without finding this radio source. Any news about the earlier transmission? Has it been decoded yet?"

"Now that's affirmative, sir. Goddamn strangest transcription. We had to ask the English at Bletchley to help. Seems like he's been talking about the milk production of Devon."

"The milk production of Devon?" Tom's voice was incredulous.

"Yep. Would you like to know what it is?"

"No. Is there nothing else?"

"Afraid not, sir. Hold on, Sergeant Blane is bringing another message. Let's see… Now, this is more like it." Tom could hear a whistle of surprise. "Well, lawdy me, seems like he's talking about our troop movements—"

The line went dead. "Hello, Jack, hello. Are you there?"

There was no response. Tom looked down at the radio operator. "It's dead. What happened?" The young soldier pressed the receiver to his ear and twiddled the dial. "Dunno, sir, but it ain't working." He twiddled some more, then gave up. "Maybe the Blue Forces have captured our communication center. Pops'll be mad as hell."

"Pops?"

"Major Fonseca, sir. " The corporal looked up at Tom. "He's like a father to us." There was genuine feeling in the man's voice. "That's why we call him Pops."

Tom looked away and concentrated on what his chief petty officer had said. Troop movements. Perhaps the spy was transmitting information about the coming invasion. He ran to the church door. As he neared it, Fonseca called out.

"In a hurry major?" He saluted formally. "Come and visit us in France." There was more than a trace of contempt in the voice.

Tom returned the salute and quickly strode to the church door. As he left the building, he stopped to let his eyes adjust to the moonlight that starkly fell across the tombstones. He shook his head, ran from the churchyard and leapt into his jeep.

The outskirts of St. Lô. 11 p.m.

Richter wound down the window of his staff car and watched the American planes depart, the drone of their engines dying as they swung north.

"Well done, Helmut!" He leaned forward and thanked his chauffeur with a hearty slap on the shoulder. "Otherwise, we'd have been fried alive!" He tipped his head toward the inferno that lit the night sky. A ruptured gas main threw huge tongues of flame skyward, casting an unearthly glow over the chaos and destruction beneath them. The prison and much of the center of the town were nothing more than a mound of rubble, strewn with bomb craters; a ghostly cloud of dust, painted red by the flames, hung over the crumpled masonry.

From the top of the hill where the car was parked, Richter could hear the sound of sirens as rescue vehicles tried to pick their way through the devastation. Richter lit a cigarette, inhaled, and blew a smoke ring.

The scene gave him a grim satisfaction. He had been proven right: Major Dalton had the information. The big secret. The bombs had been intended for the American, to shut his mouth forever. But now he had to trust Josse to deliver the goods. Somehow, the words 'Josse' and 'trust' did not sit easily in his mind. But he had little option. By now, Josse and the American could be miles away, if they had escaped. They would have survived, he thought: Josse was a survivor.

But for the air raid, he would have had search parties combing the area. Now, everything was chaos; it would take some time to get his organization back to working order.

"Helmut, drive back as close to the prison as you can. I've got to sort out this mess quickly." He threw his cigarette out of the window as the car lurched forward. As soon as possible, he would have to set his spy ring to work, prodding informers for Josse's whereabouts. He had to find Josse and the American.

The Evacuated Area. Near Old Oak Farm. 11:15 p.m.

Tom was still angry about not getting any support from Fonseca. There was a spy out there, broadcasting troop movements to the enemy, and he had to be stopped. What if he were armed? What if there was more than one? Tom had only his service pistol; even if he'd got no men from Fonseca, why hadn't he asked him for a Thompson submachine gun? He stopped the jeep and breathed deeply, trying to marshal a plan of action.

He took out a map, his hand shielding the flashlight as he pinpointed the coordinates specified by the chief petty officer. The lines crossed at a place called 'Old Oak Farm.' He checked the distance and the bearing. North, about a half-mile farther along the lane on which the jeep stood. He switched off the flashlight, got out of the jeep and made his way forward on foot.

It was not easy. Although the moon still gave some light, he could barely make out the line of the lane. The hedgerows assumed strange, frightening forms in the half light. Suddenly, the hedgerows ended and he came to a stone wall surrounding a farmhouse, gray with a slated roof, the eaves sloping to a tall chimney, sinister in the moonlight. He straddled the gate in the wall, dropped into clinging mud, and squelched free onto drier ground.

For a moment, he thought about brazenly knocking on the front door. If Fonseca had given him the men, he would have done that, to flush out the target into their arms. Alone, he had no choice but to check the back of the house to see if there was another point of entry.

His hands felt the way along the side wall. Suddenly, there was a noise. He flattened himself against the wall and brought out his pistol, his heart racing wildly. He felt a desperate urge to reach for his flashlight, but he fought it off; he must give no sign of his approach. As he got closer to the source of the noise, he picked out the shape of a ramshackle barn set apart from the house. He heard the noise again and sighed with relief as he recognized it as the fluttering of wings. A chicken coop, he thought, his fear subsiding.

The car surprised him. Parked close to the back wall, it was black, short and squat, like most British cars he'd seen. He checked through the rear window to make sure nobody was inside, and then went around to the front. He placed his hand on the radiator grille. It was still warm.

He clung to the shadows as he neared the rear door, cursing as he slipped in the mud. As he picked himself up, he felt sure he had seen a faint light from a lifted curtain in the room above the back door.

He took his pistol from its holster. His free hand tried the doorknob. The door was locked. He pulled the flashlight from his pocket and raised his right foot. At his first kick, the door flew open, the wood splintering as pieces of the lock flew away.

He flashed the light around quickly. He was breathing heavily as his eyes darted left and right, following the beam of light. There was silence. Not a voice, not a sound. Then he saw a light coming from under a door at the head of the stairs. He charged up the staircase, two steps at a time, and flung the door open.

A young man sat at a table beneath the window, his right hand tapping on the Morse key.

"Stop that!" Tom bounded across the room, his right fist slamming down on the operator's hand. "You're under arrest!"

"I'm afraid you're the one under arrest. Put down your gun."

The voice came from the opposite corner of the room. Tom spun around. There was a red-haired British officer standing by the door. In his hand was his service revolver, pointing at Tom's chest.

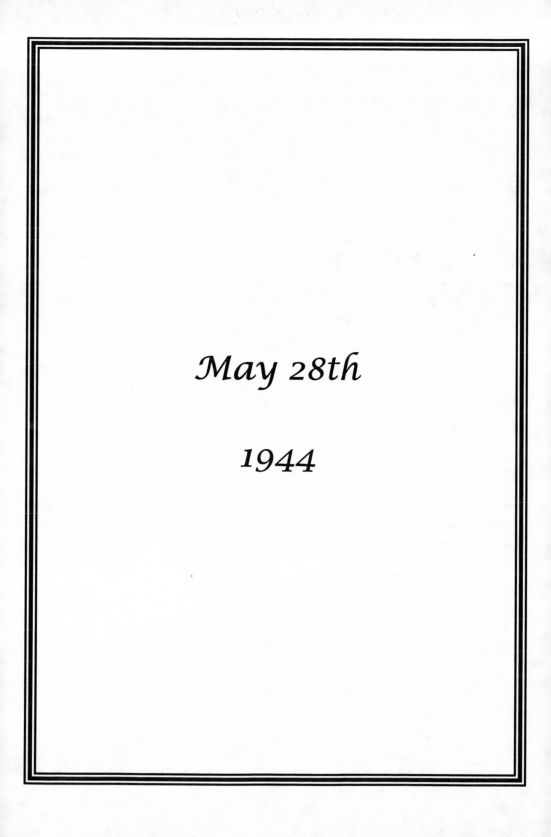

May 28th

1944

"*I* demand to speak with my commanding officer!" Tom's shout echoed along the hallway down which the English officer was leading him.

"All in good time, major." The Englishman spoke for the first time since arresting him, as he opened a door and ushered Tom into a large, well-appointed room. "Kindly wait in here. Please make yourself at ease."

"At ease?" Tom's angry retort was ignored as the door closed, leaving him alone in the spacious room, alone and fighting to control his rage. He was angry and tired. The English officer had bundled him at gunpoint into the car at the farmhouse and the spy had driven them through the night to London. They had sat silent, without uttering a single word throughout the journey.

Tom lowered himself into a large, leather armchair and rubbed his eyes, fighting off the fatigue. The morning sun shone into the room through a wide, east-facing window. It was not the room of an English Army officer; more one of an English gentleman, like the rooms he'd seen in the old films. Two of the walls were lined with mahogany bookcases, the volumes all leather bound. A huge beveled mirror hung over a mantelpiece that bore many delicate china figures. The room was dominated by a massive oak desk with carved panels and claw-and-ball feet; the top was a leather inlay, on which sat an ornate penholder. There was a silver photograph frame – he could not see the picture – and, incongruously, two telephones, one black, one red.

His heavy-lidded eyes tried to take in the framed portraits that hung on the walls. English heroes – Wellington, Nelson – looked down on him. One was more recent. Tom recognized the bulldog face with the piercing blue eyes. Despite his efforts, Tom felt his head fall towards his chest as sleep tried to claim him.

"I'm so sorry to have to put you through all this inconvenience, major." The voice came from the doorway; it was urbane and soft, but it was enough to rouse Tom, who leapt to his feet, shouting. "What's the meaning of all this? I demand to speak with my commanding officer!"

"Please sit down, Major Ford." The tone was soothing, conciliatory. "I have myself just spoken to your Colonel Kessler to explain the situation."

Tom was tired and confused. The man knew both his name and that of his commanding officer. He sank back into the armchair. "Who are you?" He watched the man as he moved smoothly to the desk and sat down, adjusting his black eye patch.

"My name does not matter."

"It matters to me. I capture a German spy red-handed sending messages and I am arrested and dragged here to London. By whose authority?"

"By my authority, major."

"But why me? Why wasn't the spy arrested? He was a spy, wasn't he?"

"You are correct, major." A half smile came to the Englishman's lips. "He is, indeed, a spy. A German spy." The smile broadened at the puzzlement on Tom's face. "Let me explain."

He stood up and moved to the mantelpiece, thrusting his thumbs into his vest pockets. For a brief moment, he looked across at the portrait of Churchill as he gathered his thoughts. He swung towards Tom.

"As a BIGOT, Major Ford, you are already privy to several important secrets." He waved away Tom's attempted protestation. "Yes, I know you are a BIGOT – it is my job to know such things. You know about Operation Overlord – the date of the landing on the Far Shore, and, more importantly, you know the locations of those landings. What you do not know..," he turned and looked at Churchill once more, "...is that we in the U.K. took control of the entire German espionage operation early in the war."

"What?" Tom was incredulous.

"The whole German spy network was turned in 1940. Most of the spies they sent were very willing to work for us. We captured the early ones, and the rest was easy, once they knew the alternative." He drew a silver case from his pocket, pulled out a cigarette and offered the case to Tom.

"Of course, the alternative for them was grim." A thin smile came to his face. "There were a few who refused to play, so we had to, shall we say, put them permanently out of business." He spoke coldly, clinically, as if describing the outcome of a football game. "Needless to say, we made sure Hitler and the Gestapo knew of the executions – it actually helped convince them that the rest of the spy ring was working. Of course, all the turned agents have an officer to supervise and coach them. In the case of the spy you chanced upon, it's Major Priestley – he's the chappie who, shall we say, arrested you and brought you here. He's pretty new to the work. Used to look after agents and was one of the best, so we gave him a new assignment. Perhaps he was a little over-zealous. I do apologize." His fingers reached for the knot in his tie. "As well as giving every turned spy a minder, we monitor every broadcast to ensure there are no problems." He chuckled. "It wouldn't do for a spy to send real information, would it?"

Despite his fatigue, Tom grasped the gist of the Englishman's point. "But, surely, the agents have to give their masters worthwhile information – otherwise they'd quickly be discredited."

"We tell them all sorts of things." He stubbed out his cigarette. "Like the milk production of Devon – more or less accurate, I might add. We even stage acts of sabotage for their benefit. But our main emphasis is on troop movements. The Germans love to know our troop movements."

Tom felt uneasy. "But doesn't that help them—."

"Hear me out, major, and all will be made clear." The Englishman got up from his desk, walked to a display unit fixed to the wall and pulled on a string, drawing down a map of Western Europe. "As a BIGOT, you know vital secrets. Like where the invasion will come."

Tom said nothing. The Englishman smiled. "I respect your wish not to talk of the secret that has been entrusted to you, Major, but there is no need. The invasion will come here." He picked up a pointer and slapped it against the Normandy coast of northern France.

83

"Of course, we don't want the Germans to believe that. That's why we have Operation Fortitude."

"What's that?"

"Operation Fortitude is our plan to deceive the Germans as to the time and place of the invasion."

The pointer moved across the English Channel to Kent. "You've heard of the United States First Army Group?"

"Sure, that's General Patton's outfit." Tom's mind conjured up Patton's bluff figure, with his flashy pearl-handled pistols. The general had been in trouble for slapping a shell-shocked private in Italy, but he still commanded a lot of respect from his men.

"You're correct except for one small point, major." There was a hint of a smile. "The First Army Group doesn't exist."

"Doesn't exist?"

"Well, it exists on paper, and, more importantly, in Hitler's mind." He put down the pointer, returned to the desk and fished a folder from a drawer. "But I'm afraid General Patton is in charge of nothing more than a lot of rubber tanks and trucks."

He opened the folder and passed some photographs to Tom, who was taken aback by what he saw. The aerial photographs showed what seemed to be huge gatherings of tanks, but the close-up images on the ground showed them to be dummies. He chuckled at a picture showing four men carrying a Sherman tank.

"So, there's no First Army Group? General Patton has no men?"

"Some, of course. In particular, scores of radio operators. They work day and night sending fabricated messages, creating the radio traffic of a real Army Group."

Tom saw at once the implication. "So we're pulling a confidence trick on Hitler."

"You could say that," the Englishman looked a little aggrieved at Tom's choice of words, "but I prefer to describe Operation Fortitude as one of disinformation and subterfuge." He returned to the map and picked up the pointer. "*We* know that the invasion is coming *here*." He pointed again at the Normandy coast. "But we want Hitler to believe that the Normandy landing is a diversionary raid and that the main invasion will come *here*." He pulled the pointer eastwards, towards the area of Boulogne and Calais. He tapped the map. "At the Pas de Calais."

The pointer lingered over the area. "If we can get Hitler and the German High Command to believe that, then they will keep the whole of the Fifteenth Army – twenty divisions – in that area, giving us a much better chance to establish a firm bridgehead in Normandy."

Tom gave a low whistle. "Wow! That's some plan."

"Which brings us to your spy."

Tom recalled the unpleasantness of the previous night.

"I'm sure you appreciate, major, that, once we have planted the idea of a Pas de Calais invasion in the minds of Hitler and his generals, we must hammer it home."

The last words were accompanied by the sound of the pointer smacking against the map. "So, we have our tame spies tell their unsuspecting masters of our troop movements."

Tom's eyebrows lifted.

"Not our real movements, of course. We tell them of imaginary movements. Obviously here," he circled the pointer over Patton's non-existent army, "but also *here.*" The stick leapt northwards to Yorkshire, then to Scotland. "Perhaps the Germans might think we're going to invade," the pointer was almost mesmerizing to Tom, as it shifted eastwards, across the North Sea, "here, in Norway. Operation Fortitude covers many possibilities. Do you know how many divisions Hitler keeps in Norway? Nineteen."

In an instant, the pointer traversed a thousand miles, circling Devon, Cornwall and the south-west of England. "But here, where over a million Americans are poised," he pulled the pointer from the map and held it in front of him, "we tell them little, except the milk production of Devon and such things."

Tom leaned forward and placed his chin in his palms. "I understand what you're saying, sir, but why are you telling me all this?"

The Englishman smiled, put down the pointer, returned to his desk and sat down. "You're very perceptive, major, despite what you've been through recently." He tapped another cigarette on his case. "First thing is that you must back off hounding our spies all over Devon." He thrust the cigarette into the flame and inhaled deeply. "Of course, I could have achieved the same end by issuing appropriate orders, but that might have strained Anglo-American relations." He toyed with the cigarette lighter, tossing it up-and-down in his hand. "And, when I saw you were a BIGOT, it made things much easier."

He looked out of the window. "Amazing weather. We haven't had rain for almost a week."

"Will that be all, sir?" Tom tried to keep the impatience from his voice.

"Oh, I'm sorry, major." The Englishman returned to his desk and rifled through a file. "I see that you're aware of the case of Major Dalton?"

"Yes, sir. He disappeared during the operation. We checked and double-checked."

The well-manicured fingers turned another page. "But I also see that you know Major Dalton personally."

"We were at college together."

"Well, I may have some good news for you, Major Ford." He closed the file. "Major Dalton has been freed from the clutches of the Gestapo and is in a safe house in France." He saw Tom's growing smile and returned it. "We're hoping to get him out and back to England as soon as possible."

"That's wonderful news, sir." Tom could not help extending his hand, which was taken and shaken warmly.

"There's one little piece of help I would ask of you, Major."

"Sure – shoot."

"Major Dalton has been through a very traumatic experience." The Englishman stroked his chin thoughtfully. "Being a BIGOT in the hands of the Gestapo can not have been a pleasant experience." Tom nodded his understanding.

"In fact, I have received a radio message from one of my agents this morning that Dalton has told the Gestapo nothing, but he is totally uncooperative with his French hosts – seems as if he doesn't trust anyone." He leaned against his desk. "Probably understandable." He said nothing for several moments and then looked directly at Tom.

"I want you to go to France and help get him out. He'll trust you."

Tom sat back down, dumbfounded. "Isn't it risky to send me? I'm a BIGOT, too."

"Yes, it is risky. But at this stage of the game, with the invasion so close, it's a risk I have to take."

Tom felt he saw a careworn expression on the face of the Englishman, who rubbed a finger and thumb above the bridge of his nose. "What are my orders?"

"For now, do nothing. Go back to your unit in Dartmouth and stand by – I will fix things with your colonel. When we're ready, you will be told. Almost certainly within the next forty-eight hours. I'll arrange for you to be taken to a place where you will receive a full briefing, but, basically it's an in-and-out job. Go in, gain Major Dalton's trust and bring him out."

He pressed a button on his desk to call Priestley into the office. "Above all, do not tell anyone your status or your mission. And that includes Priestley."

There was a knock on the door and Priestley entered; the officer raised his hand to his sleeked red hair in salute.

"Priestley, please take the major back to Dartmouth." The Englishman turned to Tom.

"Thank you for your help, Major Ford. Good luck."

After Ford and Priestley had left, he picked up the red phone and waited for the automatic connection. "Yes sir, he's agreed to do it." He listened for a few moments. "And I'll put the other matter in hand immediately."

He replaced the receiver and reached for the other phone. "Harrison, prepare to launch Operation First Violin. Await my orders for the timing."

On the road back to Dartmouth. 12 noon.

"I'm awfully sorry about last night, old chap." Priestley spoke for the first time since they had left London an hour earlier. Tom grunted. He was tired, his chin untidy with a day's bristle. A shower and a shave beckoned him back to his quarters; he wished away the miles of the Great West Road that eased past the window of the Morris 12 saloon car.

"I'm sure you understand, as an intelligence officer," Priestley insisted on talking, much to Tom's annoyance, "that I had no choice, given the situation."

"Sure." Tom rubbed his eyes. He didn't feel like exchanging pleasantries with a man who had stuck a revolver in his ribs only twelve hours earlier.

"Have you been here long?" The Englishman persisted, intent to strike up a conversation that Tom didn't want.

"Since November last year."

"As long as that?" Priestley sounded surprised, and then relieved. "Well, at least you've learned our customs by now. Unlike so many of your countrymen." The voice combined sarcasm and genteel superiority.

"Yes, I know many of your customs." Tom recalled some of them pleasantly, like Yorkshire pudding, delicious cream teas with those biscuits that the English called scones. His thoughts ran on to Gwen and her long fingers reaching for the sacred English teapot.

"I'm glad you do." Priestley interrupted Tom's pleasant thoughts. "Some of your fellows don't seem to understand us at all. And some of their habits are disgusting. That awful chewing gum."

Tom felt his hackles rise, but bit his tongue. Over a million GI's had come over the Atlantic, to fight the good fight, to defeat Nazism, to help the Brits out. Like him, many would have preferred to stay at home and have a cheeseburger and fries without the fear of a brutal death to follow. Many would die in the coming invasion. Maybe while chewing gum.

"Perhaps I can make up for last night." The car had entered a town. Priestley pulled over to stop by a pub. "Let me treat you to lunch."

"Where are we?" Tom asked sleepily.

"We're at Wells, the smallest city in England."

Tom looked up at the sign proclaiming 'The White Hart' on the front of the pub. He ached to get back to his quarters, but his growling stomach ruled otherwise.

"Don't you need ration coupons for eating at restaurants?"

"No." Priestley got out of the car. "But they'll charge the earth. However, it's on my expense account. SOE looks after us well. Besides, I know the gaffer. Maybe he'll have some bangers and mash for us."

Tom pushed the empty plate away. The soup had been watery; the sausage, as he remembered Danny's expression, was nothing more than 'breadcrumbs in battledress.' At least the mashed potatoes had been tasty. They had eaten in a small, private room at the back of the inn, away from the prying eyes of the public bar.

"Not bad, eh, old chap?" Priestley sipped at his half pint of ale.

"It was very good," Tom lied as he lit a Chesterfield. "You SOE people obviously know how to pull strings. How long have you worked for them?"

"About three years, in various roles." Priestley began to fill his pipe. "I jumped at the chance when it came. If you'd spent six years as an aide in the Berlin embassy, you'd understand why."

"You were in Berlin? Did you see Hitler?"

"Often. I had to observe the Nazi party rallies. The man's a magician."

"Magician? Is that the right word for Hitler?"

"At that time it was. He had the German people eating out of his hand." Priestley applied a match to his pipe and puffed vigorously. "And, I may say, the adulation was understandable."

"How come?" Tom felt uneasy with the conversation.

"Well, he dealt with the people's problems. Unemployment virtually disappeared. Hitler introduced programs that made your President Roosevelt's New Deal look like business as usual." He waved the stem of his pipe to emphasize the point. "Building huge highways and re-armament created jobs, put money in German workers' pockets."

"And he dealt with the troublemakers – the communists and trade unions," Priestley continued. "Suddenly, the Germans had jobs and there were no strikes. Before Hitler, unemployment in Germany was thirty per cent – five million people. Now do you understand why the German people support him?" Priestley emptied his glass.

"But surely he's a madman?" Tom wasn't sure if his anger was directed at the Germans or Priestley. "He started a war that's killed millions – including Germans."

"They'll stick by him, whatever happens, mark my words." Priestley sounded a little smug to Tom, who was both relieved and surprised when the Englishman turned the conversation.

"You must have got quite a dressing down from the boss this morning."

"Dressing down? Boss?"

"The man you met this morning. We know him as 'CD'– the Controller of Deception." He looked down at the bill placed by the waiter on the table. "Good heavens, nine shillings and sixpence – it was half that before the war." He looked up at Tom. "I'm frightfully sorry if the boss ripped into you, old man."

"He didn't. He explained everything about how you operate, Priestley – how you run the German spy ring, feeding the Nazis false information."

Priestley spluttered on his pipe. "My word, you must have priority clearance for him to tell you that. Are you a BIGOT?"

"Are you, Priestley?" Tom shot back the question.

"Yes, of course." The answer came smoothly enough.

"Then you'll know that we shouldn't talk anymore about this matter." Tom saw a hostile reaction come to Priestley's face; his eyes hardened and his cheeks flamed, almost to the color of his hair.

Priestley snatched the pipe from his mouth. "Is impertinence another disagreeable trait in the American character, Ford?"

Tom fought to control his temper. He sighed heavily and waved a placatory hand towards the Englishman.

"Look, Priestley, you've cost me a night's sleep and you've repaid me with a good meal. Why don't we call it a day and get out of here?"

He got up from the table, jammed his cap on his head and made for the door.

The Barley Sheaf Public House, Plymouth. 8 p.m.

Apart from the old men playing dominoes, there was no one else in the bar. Naval personnel didn't frequent the Barley Sheaf, and neither did the bloody Americans. At that moment, it suited Danny fine: he wanted to be alone. He desperately hoped no one he knew would come in. Especially her.

He sipped at his pint of Guinness, and smiled at the advertisement hanging behind the bar, "Guinness is Good for You." Danny's grandfather had been born in Ireland and, like the red hair, the love of Guinness had been passed down. He could see his father with a glass of Guinness in his hand, holding court in The George Inn in Blackawton.

Sally intruded on his memories, and his head dropped. What a mess. When he had first met her... They'd been out a few times. Nothing serious, but it had been fun. The Gaumont Palace cinema in Union Street; how they'd laughed at Cary Grant in *Arsenic and Old Lace*. A few drinks in the Hope and Anchor, meeting her friends.

And then he'd met her father. 'Met' wasn't really the right word. Sally had told him her father was some bigwig in London; he was making a brief visit, and she had asked Danny to meet them for lunch in the posh Royal Castle Hotel in Dartmouth.

It had been a disaster. There'd been a flap on, and he hadn't been able to get off duty. When he arrived at the hotel, they were just leaving. Sally had looked at him reprovingly as he apologized. Her father had looked down his nose at him and shook his hand perfunctorily.

"Nice to have met you." He turned to kiss Sally's cheek. "Must rush. I have an important meeting in London tonight."

Danny had spotted the gold cuff links and watch chain that adorned the other man's Saville Row tailored shirt and suit. He's swaggering, thought Danny, as Sally's father headed for his chauffeured car. As if he bloody well owned the world. Danny had turned to find Sally looking at the pavement.

He called for another Guinness. Class still meant everything in England. Whatever class you were born into determined your life. It affected everything about you – the people you associated with, the schools you went to, even the way you spoke. Danny was aware that, although everyone had the vote, the upper class still ruled England. The aristocracy and the nobility still thrived. Churchill was one of them, despite his pose as a man of the people.

Danny was not enjoying his drink, but he drank deeply. On top of society stood that abomination, royalty. Why should the working class support the richest family in England? How were they different from him? By the accident of birth, nothing more. How he hated them.

He'd joined the Labor Party, but most of the party's leaders were not working class. They'd been to Oxford and Cambridge. There hadn't been any real change.

The working class was its own worst enemy. They lapped up all the royalty stuff. Like his mother and father, God rest his soul. His parents had had a picture of the King hanging in the parlor at the old farmhouse in the evacuated area; Danny always made sure he got the chair at the table that presented his back to it. He'd do anything to get rid of the bastards and all the other self-serving hypocrites.

He was angry. The class issue thwarted his love for Sally. She was strictly off limits. Her father had made that clear with his arrogant look of disdain. He ordered another drink. Guinness was good for you.

A Diary. Somewhere in England.

The invasion of Devon by the accursed Yanks is now complete. The Americans have taken over the Royal Naval College. The holy of holies of the college is the "quarterdeck" (how quaint we English are, to treat naval buildings as ships!). This "quarterdeck" was immediately put to productive use by the Yanks as a storage area for Lucky Strike Cigarettes, under the wistful gaze of the statue of His Late Majesty King George V at the far end of the room. I heard that a G.I., desiring a smoke, lit a match by striking it on the bum of His Britannic Majesty. At last, someone has found a use for royalty!

But of course the only invasion that really matters is the big one, the secret one, the one that shall determine all. Everyone on both sides of the Channel knows it's coming, and probably soon. But the question of when is not really the issue – it doesn't take a genius to figure out the probable dates. One must simply consider: what is needed for the invasion to succeed? First, darkness for the sailings over, followed by brightness for the landing of the first paratroopers – ergo, a late-rising full moon. Second: a low tide at dawn when the first amphibious landings are made so that Rommel's hedgehogs – those spiky devices designed to rip the guts out of the Allied landing boats on the beaches – will be exposed. Third: enough daylight so that there will be another low tide before nightfall for the second landings, for the same reason. Given these considerations, and with an ordinary calendar showing the tides and the phases of the moon, any idiot can see the invasion will take place on June 5th or 6th.

No, the big secret is not when. The big secret is where.

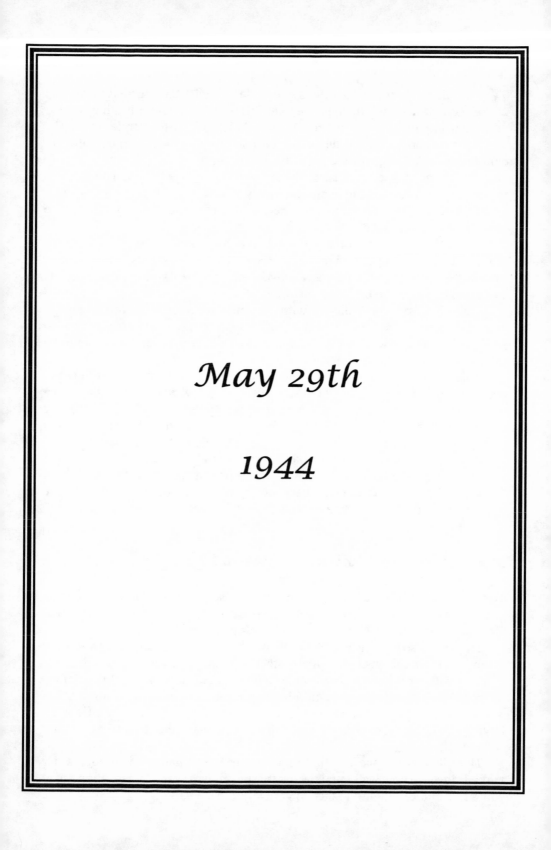

May 29th

1944

The coast of Devon. 2 a.m.

*I*n the three-quarter moon, the agent code-named Blau scurried to the top of the cliff overlooking the cove, pausing for breath before heading for the draw that led down to the beach. Another half hour to the rendezvous. The weather was perfect for the submarine to deliver its valuable cargo. But there could be no delay. Agent Blau ran down to the shore.

The waves slapped against the sand as the agent's eyes searched the sea, from east to west, time and again. Suddenly it was there. A pinpoint of light, briefly stabbing the sky from just below the barely-distinct horizon. The agent's flashlight replied. Once, twice.

Blau's feet shuffled in the wet sand near the water's edge, impatient for the delivery. Why were they taking so long? The agent's eyes looked inland toward the bluff, searching for any movement, and then swung back over the sea, peering across the breaking waves.

There it was: a small dinghy with two men at the oars; an officer sat toward the stern. As the boat beached in the shallows, the two men got out to steady it and the officer reached down, picked up a basket and leapt onto the sand.

"Here it is – as promised." The German officer put the basket on the sand and saluted, formally, his hand rising to his *Kriegsmarine* hat. "What use they will be, I do not know, but good luck. I'm sure you will understand that we cannot hang around." The officer got back into the boat and signaled to the men, who pushed the boat off the beach, jumped in, and rowed away.

Agent Blau picked up the basket. There was a flurry of wings. A finger pushed through the basketwork and caressed one of the birds. "Be quiet, my friends." The path was retraced back up to the top of the bluff. "You have much work to do." The basket swayed. "Later."

Near Hope Cove, Devon, England. 1 p.m.

Tom swung the jeep easily along the narrow hedge-lined lanes. The engine growled as he dropped into second gear for the sharp bend that lead into Galmpton before beginning the descent to Hope Cove.

He had to see Gwen again, to tell her how he felt about her, to tell her about…. His mind went over his mother's letter once more and it became jumbled with what he was preparing to tell Gwen; his lack of concentration on the road caused him almost to collide with a horse-drawn cart coming up the hill. He reversed the jeep, and eased it into a gap at an entrance to a field, allowing the horse to pass along the single-track road; the driver gave him a sullen look.

He killed the engine and lit a cigarette, trying to gather his thoughts. He looked down at the walkie-talkie on the passenger seat. At any moment it could ring and call him to France to get Dalton out.

Then the image of Gwen came to his mind, adding to the jumble of his thoughts. He'd phoned her the day before, and was surprised when she answered; she had sounded happy and had been eager to see him.

He started the engine and pulled on the wheel to get the jeep back onto the narrow lane. He wondered how she would react when he told her about his wife.

She was in the garden when he climbed the path to the cottage gate. Crouched over the vegetable patch, she was brushing aside the earth, her hands ferreting for small new potatoes that she tossed into a wicker basket at her side. She turned her head and saw him, a warm smile coming to her lips as she leapt up.

"There you are, Tom!" She brushed her hands down her apron and, as he closed the gate behind him, he could not but notice that she almost ran towards him. He felt her warmth as she gently hugged him before stepping back to retrieve the basket. "See, I've got some potatoes to go with a sliver of ham I begged off the butcher." She clutched at his hand and urged him toward the door. "Dad's gone down to the pub for lunch. He's going to meet some of his pigeon cronies – men's talk, you know." She winked at him and chattered on excitedly, like a small girl talking of her plans for the day. "I thought we could have a game of chess before lunch." She started for the door, but he held her hand tightly, stopping her.

"Can we go for a walk first, Gwen?" He saw a brief hint of concern hang on the edges of her smile.

"Why not?" Her smile broadened again. "It's a lovely day." Her hand swept up to the sun, hanging in a near-cloudless sky.

Keeping up with her was hard work as he followed her up the steep, narrow path leading to the Bolt Tail headland overlooking the cove. He watched her hips sway with each effortless step, then forced himself to look away as he labored behind her. She gained the peak of the path and reached back, offering a hand to help him up.

"Isn't it just beautiful?" She turned, and they both looked out over the bluff, bathed by a sun dipping in the afternoon sky. A breeze played wistfully with the grass, and fleeting clouds drew random patterns of changing greens on the far hills.

"Come on, race you to the headland!" She turned to set out on the path, but he pulled her back, clutching at the sleeve of her dress.

"I'm beginning to think I should have settled for a game of chess." He was still panting from the arduous climb. "What's the hurry?"

Her eyes held his for a moment, then she freed herself from his grasp and spun on her toes, her arms outstretched. "You're right, Tom. It's a wonderful day." She stopped spinning, her hands dropping to her sides with a sigh. "Why hurry back to the war?"

She came to his side and slipped an arm around his waist. His hand went around her and grasped her upper arm as they began walking to the headland. Some sheep fixed them with a baleful stare before resuming their munching of grass.

Tom's emotions were beginning to pull him apart. He knew he should tell her now. Tell her about his wife. Tell her about the whole goddamned mess. But he was carried away by the joy of the moment. She was right: it was a wonderful day. The waves tumbled rhythmically on the shore below, and a warm breeze caressed them. He caught the fragrance of her hair as she nestled her head on his shoulder. The war, the BIGOTS, the Englishman in London, all seemed so far away. He would tell her later.

They ambled back to the cottage, hand in hand.

"Such a wonderful day, Tom!" Her smile was playful. "But didn't you want to tell me something?"

God, he thought, she knew. She knew. "Tell you something?"

"Yes, you suggested the walk, remember? Woman's intuition, you know."

He drew slightly away from her and she sensed his anxiety. "Is something wrong, Tom?"

"No – yes." He bumbled, then took a deep breath and steadied himself. "Gwen, I think, I think I'm falling in love with you."

The smile returned to her lips. "Is that what's bothering you? My mother, God rest her soul, always said that men found it difficult to express their emotions."

"Gwen, I'm married."

The smile fell from her face. She shook her head, slowly, from side to side; her face took on the anguish of trust that had been betrayed. Denial was her first reaction.

"No, it can't be – it's not true – you don't wear a ring." Her look implored him to tell her that it was not so.

"I never have. I don't like jewelry." He realized the uselessness of what he was saying, but the words came out anyway.

"I see." Her words were the merest whisper, but the glisten in her eyes and the slight tremble of her lower lip belied the composure she was trying so hard to maintain. Tom could feel his heart breaking as he cast his eyes about the garden, desperately seeking somewhere to hide his guilt

"I'm sorry." He felt the lameness of his answer. He wanted to tell her that it was all over between him and Wilma, but he could not.

"Nothing really to be sorry about, is there?" She tried to manage a smile, but her eyes showed only sadness.

The sound of the telephone brought relief and escape to them both, and, as she turned away from him to go into the cottage, she discreetly wiped away a tear. He was not sure what to do and followed her sheepishly into the cottage.

"Yes?" Her voice was tentative, almost reticent. He watched her eyes grow larger, her discomfit giving way to surprise. "Of course." She breathed deeply as she listened. "I'll be there." She nodded at a conversation Tom could not hear. "Goodbye."

She cradled the receiver, looked at it for a brief moment, and then raised her eyes to him. "I have to go to London."

She looked away from him. "It's... it's Aunt Doris – she's had a bad fall."

"Oh." All his instincts were screaming at him to leave, but something kept him rooted to the spot. "Can I see you when you get back, Gwen?"

She stared at him coolly, her tears gone. "Tom, I don't think we should meet again."

He looked at her, seeking any uncertainty in her eyes. There was none; she seemed far away, in another place. He shook his head as he closed the door behind him.

A Diary. Somewhere in England.

I read in the newspaper today that the remaining German soldiers stranded in the Crimea surrendered yesterday – just the latest in a series of catastrophes on the eastern front. What a misadventure it was for Hitler to invade Russia! His blitzkriegs, so brilliantly successful in Poland and France, have deteriorated into a war of attrition in Russia. Such a pity – so many brave German solders enduring winters so cold their piss froze before it hit the ground. Almost 900,000 sons of the Fatherland have starved, frozen, or otherwise been killed in that god-forsaken wasteland. I understand the Wehrmacht are now reduced to shooting their own wounded in the backs of their heads as they retreat.

If only Hitler had pressed his advantage in the Battle of Britain four years ago. If only he hadn't gambled instead on an eastern front. If only he had bombed the British airfields to kingdom come while he had had the chance. He could have then easily invaded. Britain, of course, would have eventually capitulated.

Most importantly, the Americans would not now have a foothold for their planned hop across the channel.

But then my services would not now be required by Herr Richter. There is still hope that Churchill and his American friends can be sent packing.

May 30th

1944

St. Marie de la Croix, Normandy. 1 p.m.

*P*hilippe Josse propped his bicycle against a wall, pressed his frame into a doorway and peered along the Rue de l'Eglise. The street was deserted, save for an old dog stretched lazily on the pavement. The clock on the church tower showed just passed one o'clock, and the late May sun bathed a town religiously observing the ritual of lunch. The shutters on the shops were all pulled down, the silence broken only occasionally by the clatter of plates in some kitchen.

Josse had deliberately chosen this time of day to come back to his town. Perhaps Richter had put a price on his head, and even Frenchmen could be tempted by German gold. Since the escape, he'd hidden the American in the cellar of a farm some kilometers from the town. He grimaced at the memory; Major Dalton had not been cooperative. He'd said openly that he didn't trust the French, had said nothing about the coming invasion, and had become very irritable at being cooped up in the safe house. It had been over two days since the escape, and Josse knew he had to act quickly; he had to contact London again.

He checked the street again and remounted his bicycle. He would have to make his move. It was chancy. Richter would have his spies everywhere and, for the moment, Josse did not wish to be in the company of the German.

The wheels rattled on the cobblestones. He would not have ventured from the farm that was the safe house, but he desperately needed to use Jean-Paul's radio. He heard the noise of a shutter and turned quickly into the alley leading to Jean-Paul's house. The radio was kept in a large shed in the garden. Philippe prayed as he closed the garden gate behind him and leaned the bicycle against the high wooden fence. Please let Jean-Paul be safe, God. And the radio, too.

There was chatter inside the house. He recognized the voices of Jean-Paul and his wife and tapped lightly on the door. The talk stopped; he heard the shuffle of chairs on the tile floor, then silence.

"C'est moi, Jean-Paul," he whispered urgently, "Philippe."

The silence continued for several moments, and then the door opened to reveal Jean-Paul, his anxious face dissolving into a smile as he recognized his old boss.

"Is there any need for that?" Philippe nodded at the pistol in Jean-Paul's hand.

"I'm sorry, Philippe." He lowered the weapon, opened the door wide and quickly ushered Philippe inside. "We thought you were dead in the bombing, and there have been many Gestapo raids lately."

"Eh bien, as you can see, I'm very much alive." He looked across at the slender woman who was picking at the scraps on her plate. Despite the shadows under her eyes, she was still beautiful. *"Bonjour Augustine – ça va bien?"*

"Merde, Philippe," a scowl came with the answer, "what do you want now?" She shuffled off to the sink and rinsed her plate.

100

"I thought you might be pleased to see me again, Augustine." Philippe knew he was on shaky ground. Although she hated the Germans, she was frightened of any danger that might threaten Jean-Paul. That was always her overriding thought.

She threw the dishcloth into the dirty water. "What about Alphonse? He never came home after the night of the bombing. We shall never see him again." Her tone was bitter, and Philippe felt the stab at his heart. Alphonse had been a good friend of them all.

"Yes, I know. *C'est triste.*"

"Sad? That's all you can say? Sad?" Augustine turned to face him, her hands on her hips. "You play your stupid spy games and what happens? Alphonse dies. Hundreds of people die in the bombing." She choked on her words, unable to speak further; her hands went to her face to brush away the tears. "To hell with you!" She ran to the door, slamming it behind her, her shoes thudding angrily on the stairs as she climbed to the bedroom.

Jean-Paul gave the older man a rueful look. "I'm sorry, Philippe, but we're all upset. The bombing has changed everything – the Germans are raiding the towns more frequently. Augustine's frightened – we all are."

"I understand, *mon ami.*" Philippe patted Jean-Paul on the back. "But now is the time to be brave." He sat down at the table. "And trust in God."

"God has not been good to us, Philippe." Jean-Paul spoke sullenly, but he sat down and poured two glasses of wine. "What is it that you want?"

"I need to use the radio." He sipped at his wine. "It's urgent."

Jean-Paul looked down at the table. "I'm afraid we have a problem. The battery is dead."

"Can't it be recharged?"

"I've tried." There was a shake of the head. "But it's no good."

"Then we've got to find a replacement." Philippe thumped the table.

"That's easier said than done." There was a hint of resentment. "The bombing has virtually wiped out our organization in St. Lô. We have no communication. Maybe we could get a replacement from Valognes, but it's fifteen kilometers away, and we haven't got a car. Perhaps I can persuade Augustine to cycle over there."

Philippe got up from the table, his face contorted with frustration. "It's possible – if she can get back in time. If not, we'll use the main power supply and alter the frequency by changing the crystals every so often."

"We have only one set of crystals." Jean-Paul raised his head to see the shock on the other man's face. "And if we use the main power supply with only one set, there's a real danger of—"

Josse waved the protest aside. "It's a risk we have to take." He looked at his watch. "In six hours. My message is expected at seven o'clock tonight."

The road from Valognes to St. Marie de la Croix. 6:30 p.m.

Augustine pedaled quickly, the tires of her bicycle humming on the road. She looked up at the cloud-flecked sun beginning to edge its way down into the western sky and shook her head. She was late; there was less than an hour for her to deliver the battery back to their house in St. Marie de la Croix. If she didn't get it back in time, Philippe would use the main power supply, with all the danger that implied.

She was tired and her legs felt heavy. Her breath came in gasps as she neared the brow of the hill on the southern outskirts of Valognes. She had to rest; reluctantly, she climbed down and began pushing the bicycle to the peak, as she struggled to recover her breath.

The crystals were safely hidden in her underwear, but she was worried about the battery. She checked on the wickerwork basket strapped to the rear pannier of the bike. The battery was wedged into the base. A false bottom lay atop it, then there was some bread and finally a napkin. She knew the conceal-ment would not survive anything more than a cursory inspection, but there hadn't been much trouble so far. The guard at Valognes had waved her through with no more than a casual glance at her papers; a German truck had passed her on the road, the soldiers in the back leering at her, but she had seen such looks before on the faces of many men: they were not interested in security.

Her twenty-five year old body was not unattractive, she knew. Her breasts strained at her blouse as she continued to breathe deeply. Jean-Paul was always attentive, always seeking to coax her into what he called his *'dessert favori.'*

She smiled at the memory, and looked over the countryside as she crested the top of the hill. It looked little different from the vista she and Jean-Paul had seen as they traveled to Portbail for their honeymoon five years ago. She looked out over the haphazard quilted pattern of fields. In some, the crop was still ripening; in others, contented cows munched the lush grass. *Was it really five years ago*? She had been barely twenty, but her family had long known she was destined for Jean-Paul. They had been close friends since childhood.

She remounted the bicycle and began coasting down the far side of the hill. The land looked the same; the fields, the hedgerows had not changed. But it was different, she knew: ever since that June in 1940, when the Germans had come, it had been different.

How she hated them. For others, life seemed the same: the seasons came and went, the farms were tended, the harvests gathered in. But, for her, the oppression was always there. The Germans did as they liked, requisitioning their produce, or whatever they wanted, for few miserable *sous*. Her main fear was the dreaded labor law – the *Service Travail Obligatoire*: men were con-scripted and then just disappeared – shipped to Germany to work as slave labor in the German armaments industry.

Jean-Paul had so far escaped the draft. But it could happen at any time. Her grip on the handlebars tightened in her fury. Jean-Paul had vowed that if the Germans did come for him, he would do what hundreds of Frenchmen had already done: flee, and join the growing bands of armed *resistants* hiding in the woods and forests.

She swung around a bend and quickened her pace as she saw that the long, straight road ahead was empty. Maybe she could get back in time. Perhaps it would be better for Jean-Paul to join the *maquis*. The work he was doing with Philippe Josse was much more dangerous. Josse was devious and ruthless. They were all pawns in the vast game of chess he played. Pawns could be sacrificed.

Only at the last moment did she see the huge pothole in the road. The front wheel fell into it, and she was almost thrown over the handlebars. She toppled to one side, a cry of pain coming from her lips as her knees scraped the road surface. The rear wheel of the bike was perched in the air, spinning. Despite her pain, she was relieved to see the basket containing the battery was still strapped in position.

She winced as she gingerly got back to her feet and gathered the bread scattered across the road. Hastily, she stuffed it back into the basket and tried to pull the bicycle from the hole. After a few moments, she stopped and sobbed. The front wheel had been twisted out of shape, the tire ruptured and pulled from the rim.

She squatted down on her haunches, the heels of her hands pressing into her eyes in despair. She had failed. She could not deliver the battery and the crystals in time, and she would probably be out after curfew. She felt things could not be worse. She heard a rumble and looked up. A German staff car, a swastika pennant fluttering on the hood, was coming down the road towards her.

St. Marie de la Croix. Jean-Paul's house. 6:45 p.m.

The huge shoulders of Philippe Josse hunched over the table, his hand hovering above the Morse key. On a shelf in front of him sat the radio set and a small table lamp, its feeble light giving scant illumination to the shed in Jean-Paul's garden. Beside the lamp was an old battered alarm clock, its hands approaching seven o'clock.

"God, it's stifling in here." Jean-Paul pulled a handkerchief from his pocket and ran it across the beads of sweat on the back of his neck. It was not yet June, but the whole of May had seen nothing but hot, cloudless skies. The small shed was like an oven, heat pervading everywhere. A tiny shaft of sunlight came through a small hole in the roof, playing with the billowing smoke rising from a cigarette in the ashtray.

"Let's hope the *Bosches* are tired by the heat, too. At least for the next half-hour." Josse pulled from his pocket the message he had encoded earlier and placed it on the table, ironing it with the palms of his hands.

103

Jean-Paul swatted vainly at an annoying fly. "I'm worried about Augustine. She should be back by now."

"She knows how to look after herself." Josse looked impatiently at the clock. "Perhaps she ran into a checkpoint, but she can handle that. As long as she's back by curfew, she'll be all right." Josse checked the wiring of the radio. "But without the battery and the crystals, we'll have to use the main power supply." He picked up the plug and reached for the socket.

"You realize the risk you're taking? If the Germans—"

"Of course I know the risk. Please be quiet, Jean-Paul. I need to concentrate." He flicked a switch, his eyes checking all the indicators as the dials lit up. He pushed the receiver of the headset to his ear and tapped out his call signal. He received an acknowledgement immediately, and was about to transmit his message when he was surprised to hear 'QXLR' – stand by for immediate message.

His hand pulled back from the key, picked up a pencil and wrote down the letters as they came through the earpiece. After five minutes he received the 'message ends' code. He tapped out a rapid 'stand by,' reached for a code sheet and began to decipher.

Jean-Paul lit a cigarette, opened the door a crack and listened for any sound in the street. Relieved at the silence, he closed the door and turned to Josse. "I thought you had an important message to send."

"Quiet!" Josse spoke harshly as he struggled with the decoding.

Jean-Paul shook his head at Philippe's impatience. He watched as the pencil scratched across the paper, and was surprised when the older man suddenly stopped writing, the pencil dropping from his fingers and rolling across the table.

"Well, their message is obviously important." Jean-Paul drew on his cigarette. "What do they say?"

Josse picked up the message and read it again. He tapped a cigarette from the packet, lit it and applied the flame of the lighter to the piece of paper; he ground the ashes in the palms of his hand before blowing them away.

"It means I have to act quickly." Josse stared at the radio. "They're coming to get an American I have in hiding. They arrive tonight."

"Is that all? Jean-Paul's nose wrinkled. "Okay, it's risky," he shrugged his shoulders, "but it's almost routine for you."

Josse looked at his watch. "I have only six hours to prepare." Josse went back to the radio, his stubby fingers showing remarkable agility as the key tapped out his message.

Jean-Paul walked up and down fretfully, looking anxiously at his watch, willing the minutes away. Where was Augustine?

"What's taking you so long, Philippe? Let's get out of here, now."

Josse ignored him, his fingers still tapping on the key. Suddenly, the hum of the radio fell away and the table lamp died. "*Mon dieu*, we need God's help now."

"*Merde.*" Jean-Paul produced a flashlight and flicked vainly at the lamp switch. "They're on to us!" There was panic in his voice. "We must get out now."

"Wait." Josse knew the danger. The Gestapo had picked up his signal. Richter was not stupid. The Germans shut down the electricity grid, area by area; if the signal stopped, they knew roughly the area from where it originated. Then they'd restore the power, await the resumption of the message and send in the radio direction finder vans. And then....

"Jean-Paul, you must get out of here now. The *maquis* group in the forest of Lessay – join them!" He opened a cupboard and pulled out some folders which he thrust into the younger man's hands. "Take these code sheets."

"But what about Augustine? I can't go without her." A vein on his temple throbbed. "She could come back at any time and walk straight into the arms of the Gestapo."

"I'll tell her to follow you."

"But aren't you coming with me?"

"Later, I must complete the transmission."

Jean-Paul's eyes widened. "But that's suicide, you fool!"

As he spoke, there was a hum, and the indicators on the radio's dials flickered. The power had been restored. Josse hunched over the key and began tapping.

"Philippe, I don't trust you – you'll kill us all."

Josse's fingers continued to caress the key. "Go, Jean-Paul. In the name of God, go!"

The road from Valognes to St. Marie de la Croix. 6:45 p.m.

The German's perfect French surprised Augustine. "*C'est n'est pas sérieux, j'espère?*" The officer stepped down from the large staff car and saluted.

"No, it's not serious, just a scratch." She rubbed her bruised knee, and she could see that his eyes looked beyond her hand at the glimpse of her thigh.

"But my bicycle..." She moved across to the wrecked machine with a silent prayer. "And I have to be back in St. Marie de la Croix before curfew." She saw that his eyes were wandering over her body.

"*Quelle chance!*" His eyes at last found hers. "I am going that way." He spoke authoritatively to the driver, who stepped down from the car and opened the trunk. He walked towards the bike. Augustine's heart jumped; surely he would feel the extra weight? She made as if to help him, but he picked up the wrecked machine and placed it in the trunk without a word.

"*S'il vous plaît, ma'm'selle?*" The officer, a cocksure look on his face, was holding open the rear door. She stepped in and settled back on the leather seat, catching his self-assured smile from the corner of her eye. Such an arrogant bastard. God, how she hated him and all the Germans.

105

"Such a beautiful country!" He waved his hand expansively at the countryside passing by. Yes, she thought, it would be, if it weren't for bastards like you. The car sped along the highway and hurtled through a village, scattering chickens. Augustine prayed to God that no one she knew would see her. Thankfully, there were only a few more kilometers to go.

She was horrified when he put his hand upon her thigh. But she dared not risk a scene; the outskirts of St. Marie were not far away, and she would soon be safe. She decided to humor him.

"M'sieur!" She flashed her eyes at him, affronted, but not without a hint of allure.

"I'm so sorry, *Ma'm'selle.*" But there was no contrition in his look, and he did not remove the hand. "Perhaps we could meet tomorrow? I'm staying at the *Hotel du Lion.*"

"Why not?" She looked at him from the corners of her eyes, smiled and lifted his hand from her thigh with a gentle squeeze. She could almost feel the expectant surge run through his body.

"Perhaps, *ma'm'selle*, you will do me the honor of dining with me? Shall we say eight o'clock?"

"Mais bien sûr." She affected another smile. "But I must get out here." She welcomed the sight of the outskirts of the town; it would not do to be seen getting down from a German car in the center. "I live nearby."

The officer tapped his chauffeur's shoulder. The car stopped, the bicycle was pulled from the trunk and she took it from the driver.

"A demain." He gave a polite salute as she carried her wrecked machine away.

She waved, waited until the vehicle had disappeared and spat on the ground. The words hissed from her mouth. "Over my dead body."

St. Marie de la Croix. Jean-Paul's house. 7:15 p.m.

Josse tapped feverishly with the Morse key, glancing anxiously at his watch. Two minutes, three minutes since the Germans had reconnected the power supply. The back of his free hand mopped away the beads of sweat from his brow. Please God, he prayed, a few more minutes.

He forced himself to concentrate on the task in hand, but he had half an ear listening for the radio detection vans. He knew he ought to leave at once, but what he had to do was of vital importance. The next message he received would give him all the answers. He sent his call sign and waited for the reply, his fingers drumming on the table. He looked at the receiver, begging it to show life. Reply, damn you, reply.

As if it could read his mind, the receiver began to pulse with the signal. His left hand pushed the earphone tighter into his ear as his other grabbed the pencil stub and scurried across the notebook. Just a few more minutes, please.

Suddenly, the staccato beat of the radio stopped. He tossed the headphones aside and thought he heard another sound: the growl of a truck engine at the end of the street.

The code sheet. His fingers grasped it from the shelf and he began to decode the message. His jaw fell slack as he read the unfolding words; his hands shook, the incredulous look on his face fading only when he heard the sound of rifle butts crashing against the door of the house. He had only a few moments before they smashed the door down; the house would be searched, and then they would come into the garden....

He breathed deeply, trying to keep his mind focused. He screwed up the message and the code sheet into a small ball and pushed it into his mouth. His teeth champed quickly, generating the necessary saliva before he moved the ball to the back of his mouth and swallowed.

There were German voices outside in the garden. His fingers reached once more for the Morse key. He had to send the message – QVP, QVP; it was a simple code: I am in immediate danger of capture. He was too late. The latch rattled and the door flew open. Framed in the doorway was the figure of Richter. His Luger pistol was pointed directly at Josse's head.

Special Agents' Headquarters. Somewhere in England. 8 p.m.

"I'm here to see Captain Baldwin." Jeanne showed her pass to the soldier at the entrance to the camp. So young, she thought. Virtually everyone over eighteen was conscripted by now. She was only in her mid-twenties, yet she felt a generation apart from the soldier whose youthful eyes looked at her face and checked it with her ID card before reaching for the guardhouse telephone.

The memories of the disastrous visit to France came back, nagging her again. She should have killed Josse. Priestley had said the Frenchman was a double agent in the pay of the Germans, and the ambush she'd walked into had proved it. But she still harbored doubts. Why had Josse allowed her to escape from the Germans? Now Priestley was gone and his replacement had summoned her for a briefing. Was it to reprimand her?

She was still trying to square the circle when the soldier handed back her ID card. "Captain Baldwin is expecting you, miss."

Jeanne strode along the path, feeling the warmth of the late spring sun. May had been such a wonderful month: warm and comforting, as if heralding not only summer, but a whole new world.

But what did the new world hold for her? Thoughts of him came to her mind, and an ache nagged at her heart. He would not be part of it. She sighed and lifted the latch to the hut, not caring too much what the future held for her.

"Pleased to meet you, Jeanne." The young officer shook hands with a limp grasp. "I'm Baldwin, but please call me Ralph." He had a posh accent nurtured by years of private schooling and university, and the self-assured mannerisms to match, as his outstretched hand indicated where Jeanne should sit.

"Thank you for coming so promptly, Jeanne. I know it's very short notice, but there's a vitally important mission for tonight." He flicked through a dossier on his desk. Jeanne was stunned; surely he had already seen Priestley's report about the terrible botch she'd made of her last mission?

Baldwin closed the dossier and leaned forward. "I cannot overstate the importance of this mission, Jeanne." He was trying to be casual, but she sensed he was tense. "We want you to escort a courier into France. The messages and instructions he carries are vital to the plans for...," he checked himself, "...are vital to our plans."

Her head lifted. She knew it was the invasion. The plans for the French Resistance when the invasion came.

"Why can't I take the messages myself? I've been to France many times. I know the ropes, the people, everything."

Baldwin raised his eyebrows, taken aback by her eagerness. "Really, Jeanne, you know the rules – it's a need-to-know basis. I was told you were difficult to handle." He looked at her reproachfully.

Jeanne's head dropped slightly. "I'm sorry. It's just that I'm so keen to go back to France. To do something useful."

"And so you shall go, Jeanne." Baldwin's calm manner returned at the sight of her contrition. "And now, I'd like you to meet the courier you're going to escort." He opened the door and a young, fresh-faced officer came into the room.

"This is Lieutenant Wainwright, Jeanne." They shook hands.

"Is this your first drop?" Jeanne asked. The lieutenant brushed his fingers through his blond hair and nodded.

"Well, there are side benefits to the job." Jeanne sought to put him at ease. "You'll get a slap-up dinner before we go tonight." She smiled, but knew she herself was usually too nervous to eat anything before the departure: it made her feel like a condemned prisoner eating the last meal.

Baldwin cut across the small talk. "You are to take him and his messages to Philippe Josse."

Jeanne's mouth half-opened, but she caught any words lingering there and said nothing as she turned for the door. On her last mission, Priestley had ordered her to kill Josse. Now she was to deliver the invasion plans to him. She felt confused; hadn't Baldwin read Priestley's debriefing about her last mission? And why would she be asked to help deliver the plans to Josse, of all people?

St. Marie de la Croix. Jean-Paul's house. 8 p.m.

Richter lowered his pistol when he saw Josse was alone and unarmed. "I thought it might be you, Josse," there was a smug smile on his face, "which is why I came myself." He shouted orders, and there was the sound of army boots as guards took their position outside the door.

Josse did not get up from his seat. "I'm surprised it took you so long, Herr Richter."

Richter's smile vanished for a moment before he guffawed loudly. "You never fail to amaze me, Josse. You seem to have an alibi for every occasion."

Josse leaned back in the chair and lit a *Gitane.* "You didn't expect me to walk into Gestapo headquarters with half of France watching, did you?" His voice had a light, sarcastic edge.

"Really, Josse, you test my patience." Richter's boots creaked on the floor of the shed as he moved to the table. "So, Josse, perhaps you have more fairy tales to tell me?" He took a cigarette from his case and tapped it against the silver lid. His casual manner belied the sharp movements of his mind. "You have the American?"

"No, he is dead." Josse spoke evenly, without hesitation. If he revealed the major's existence, Richter would soon have troops raid the countryside and flush the American out.

"Dead? He died in the bombing?" Richter asked sharply, probing. Josse knew he had to parry quickly: if the American had died in the bombing, then Richter would know that the major had said nothing, and that would be curtains for him.

"No, he was badly wounded. He died some hours later."

"Where did you bury him?" The simplicity of Richter's question almost caught Josse unaware. If there'd been a death, then there'd have been a burial. Josse ground out his cigarette, the ash from the full ashtray spilling onto the table.

"I'm afraid there wasn't time for a burial. Your men were everywhere." Josse sensed the German's eyes analyzing his every reaction. "His body was dropped into the old disused well by the side of the Valognes road, about five kilometers south of the town."

Richter said nothing, but opened the door and barked an order. Immediately, there was a clatter of hobnails, followed by the starting of a car. So, the sly fox was checking everything, but Josse was not unduly worried. He'd used the well as a rallying point for some Resistance raids. It was over three hundred feet deep, the bottom cluttered with collapsed masonry and the rubbish of ten years; it would take a long time to get to the bottom, if that were possible. Long enough for his purposes, Josse hoped.

Richter resumed his position at the table, his face unable to conceal a grin. "Well, Josse, we shall soon find out if your story is correct."

The Frenchman shrugged his wide shoulders. "It is the job of all cops to check details. But I sometimes wonder if you trust yourself." Richter bristled, and Josse hastily moved on. "Anyway, you are wasting your time. Before he died, the American talked."

"He knew the secret, didn't he Josse?" Richter leaned his haunches against the table. "That's why the Americans bombed the prison, eh?"

"He spoke of the big secret."

Richter's laugh surprised Josse. "So, a dying man tells you the secret." The German pulled out a handkerchief and blew his nose noisily. "Forgive me, Josse, you are such a comedian. I can hardly contain myself."

"I can't believe you can treat this information so lightly, Herr Richter." Josse stood up. "It could change the course of the whole war. Germany can yet win. The American told me about the invasion. When and where."

"Josse, you disappoint me." Richter idly watched a smoke ring climb through the hot, humid air. *"Wenn und wo, eh?"* The German stood and motioned for Josse to sit again; he looked at him patronizingly, as if speaking to a tiresome boy.

"I have no need of your information. I know when." He loomed over Josse. "It's either early June or mid-July – the moon and tides must be right. Otherwise, the invasion will not come before next year, by which time, Germany, with its new…." He stopped, realizing he was saying too much, and continued to lecture Josse disdainfully. "As to where, the answer can be whittled down to three options." He raised three fingers in front of the Frenchman's face. "One, the Pas de Calais." He ticked off his index finger. "Two. Normandy." Another finger disappeared. "And, three – although I think this unlikely – Norway." He smiled the indulgent smile of a superior intellect. "You see, Josse, not only the Führer understands military strategy."

"But don't you think the Führer would like to know *exactly* where and when?" Josse watched for Richter's reaction. "And maybe yourself, *Sturmbannführer*. On the other hand," he shrugged, "if you're not interested—"

"I could shoot you right now, Josse." Richter's hand reached down into his pocket; the Frenchman tried hard not to betray his emotions, but a thousand prayers flew heavenwards. Richter caught Josse's reaction, and he laughed loudly as his hand emerged from his pocket clutching a hip flask. "But I'm in need of some amusement." He looked at the swastika engraved on the flask before removing the cap slowly. He raised the flask to his lips and savored the liquor as it danced sharply on his tongue. "Please tell me the fairy tale of the American."

"It is no fairy tale. If it is, you're probably the author." Josse dared a reproachful look toward Richter.

Richter's brow furrowed; he was nonplussed for the first time in the encounter. "What do you mean?"

Josse sensed the German's discomfort, but suppressed a smile as he walked over to a well-worn map of northern Europe pinned untidily to the wooden wall of the shed. "Because you are right, Herr Richter. Your analysis is correct." He pointed to the north-east. "Norway is not an option. A small diversionary raid, perhaps."

Richter assumed an air of indifference. "Is that all the American told you?" He affected a yawn, but Josse could tell he was avid for more.

"He told me much more." Josse's hand ran over the map, along the coast of Normandy, from Ouistreham in the east, through Arromanches and Port-en-Bassin; the hand completed the sweep on the coast of the Cotentin peninsula.

"The Allies will land here." He tapped the map. "In Normandy. On June 5th."

A penthouse in Kensington, London. 8:15 p.m.

"And how are things in Dartmouth?" The disembodied voice of her father came from behind *The Times* newspaper that he was reading in his armchair after dinner.

"Much the same, Daddy. Everybody's waiting for the big day." Sally had come up to London the day before to enjoy a spot of leave. She'd been surprised that the Germans had renewed the bombing of the city.

"It will be soon, Daddy, won't it?" She sipped at her cup and was surprised at the taste of real coffee, unlike the chicory essence they had on the base. Somehow, the rationing rules didn't seem to apply to her father.

"Soon." The noncommittal grunt came from the other side of the newspaper. She knew her father wouldn't say any more, even though he worked at the top level of the government. He'd spoken of his meetings with Churchill, of how Eisenhower was, as he said, 'amazingly polite for a bloody American.' Her father probably knew the date of the invasion, but he would say nothing, not even to his daughter.

She got up from the table and went over to the large window of her father's penthouse apartment, looking down over Kensington, relatively untouched by the war. She sat down on a Chippendale chair and surveyed the lavishly-furnished apartment. How different it was from her one-room digs in Dartmouth, different from the modest terraced house of Danny's uncle and aunt in Plymouth.

Danny had taken her there for lunch one day. The house had been clean and tidy, but was small, sparsely-furnished, and unheated; there was no bathroom, only an outhouse in the yard. Danny's aunt had gone to great lengths to put a fine meal on the table, but Sally had been sure that they had sacrificed their whole monthly ration allowance of meat to provide it.

Danny. Her thoughts kept coming back to him. He was so different from all the stuffed-shirt, stiff-upper-lipped men that she had met in the society her father inhabited. A little shy, but genuine. Why did she keep thinking about him? She wasn't in love with him, she knew. He'd always been correct with her, never made an improper advance. And he was handsome.

"I hope the invasion comes soon, Daddy. And the end of the war. Then we can start to build a new life."

"A new life?" The newspaper dropped, revealing her father's silver hair and black eye patch. "What new life?" he asked sharply.

111

"Well...well...," she stammered before his cold stare, "we can reward the people – the ordinary people – who fought and will win the war."

"Reward ordinary people?" Her father folded the newspaper and stood up. "That's socialism." He contained his anger and sighed. "I suppose you've been talking to that Irish friend of yours."

"What if I have?" Sally bristled defensively. "You may not have noticed it, Father, but I am twenty-three."

"Because he's not our sort," he spoke coldly but without anger, "whatever age you are. Your mother would turn in her grave if she knew you were going out with that oik."

"He's not an oik." Sally leapt to her feet. "He's a lieutenant in the Royal Navy. Fighting to win the war – like millions of the ordinary people you seem to detest." She flashed a look of contempt at her father, who tossed his napkin onto the table.

"What's more, he's a socialist. A member of the Labor Party. Not only an oik, but a dangerous oik."

"You've been checking up on him!" Sally's mouth fell open in astonishment. "You've been using your position with the government to spy on him!"

Her father ignored her. "Now, if you will excuse me, I have urgent work to do. I'll be in my study."

He turned in the doorway. "He's not our sort, Sally." The door closed behind him.

Sally was close to tears in her rage. Her father had been spying on Danny. Perhaps Danny was right. He'd said that society was ruled by an upper class that cared little or nothing about the lower orders, just their hold on power and privilege. Her hands were trembling as she lit a cigarette. She'd thought Danny had been a bit like a preacher, but she'd just seen evidence. From her own father. The upper class ruled and controlled society. She drew heavily on the cigarette, angry at something she had never thought of before. She had been born into that upper class. Maybe that was why Danny had avoided her since the disastrous meeting with her father. She was not his sort.

St. Marie de la Croix. Jean-Paul's House. 8:30 p.m.

"So, Josse, you know the '*wo*' and the '*wenn*'." Richter eased back in his chair, and lifted his hipflask to his lips again. "Where? Normandy! When? June 5ᵗʰ! Remarkable!" The irony in his voice was heavy. "I shall inform *Reichsführer* Himmler immediately." The smile on his face disappeared, replaced by menace. "Do you take me for a fool, Josse?"

Josse ignored the barb and drew deeply on his Gitane. "The American told me more." He allowed himself a half smile. "With this knowledge, you will certainly be able to impress Herr Himmler. Maybe the Führer himself."

"Tell me how I can impress the Führer, Josse." The German's tone had a world-weariness encouraged by the schnapps from his hip flask. "Before I throw you in Coutances jail when my guards return."

112

Josse could feel his sweat-sodden shirt clinging to him like a second skin. "The American told me how the Allies intend to fool you."

"Fool us? Fool us?" Richter laughed, but Josse could sense the German was more attentive. "Please tell me how, Josse."

"Because the landing in Normandy is just a ruse. To draw Hitler into a trap." Josse got up and walked back to the map. "The main assault will come later." He tapped the map. "Here, at the Pas de Calais."

Richter snorted, but he could not hide his interest. "How can you know this?"

Josse sat down, the chair creaking from his weight. "The American told me that across the English Channel in Kent the United States First Army Group is preparing – under General Patton."

Josse was disappointed that Richter showed no surprise. "General Patton's presence is known to us. We are not idiots, Josse." He looked at Josse and shrugged. "You are really telling me nothing new, apart from the Normandy ruse. And why should I believe you about that?"

"The American told me."

"Ah, the conveniently dead American again." He looked at his watch. "My men should be back soon. Then we shall be able to see if your story holds up."

"But he also told me how you can verify the time of the invasion by listening to the radio."

Richter looked at the Frenchman incredulously. "Perhaps the BBC will broadcast the invasion to the world?"

"You are absolutely right, Herr Richter." Josse fixed the German's eyes. "The BBC will announce it." Josse tapped on the radio. "I have just received the message. They will broadcast, through their *messages personnels* to France, the onset of the invasion with two couplets from Verlaine."

Richter's face cracked into a smile. "That preposterous French poet?"

"Whatever you think of its literary merits, his poetry will tell you when the invasion – the diversionary invasion – is to come."

"Tell me," Richter's spoke wearily, "tell me of this poetry."

"The first couplet reads *'Les sanglots longs/ Des violons de l'automne.'* If I may translate: 'The long sobs/ of autumn's violins'." Josse leaned forward over the table. "When the BBC broadcasts these lines, they are telling all the French *Maquis* and *resistants* to prepare, that the invasion is coming soon."

"What exactly do you mean by 'soon'?"

"Within five days. Later comes the second couplet, which reads: *'Blessent mon coeur/ D' une langueur monotone.'* Which means: 'wound my heart/ with a monotonous languor.' When that message is broadcast by the BBC *messages personnels*, it means that the landings in Normandy will take place within forty-eight hours." Josse studied the long ash on his cigarette as if contemplating when it would drop to the floor. "The Führer can then make his plans and dispositions accordingly."

113

"So that's the pathetic tale you have to tell, Josse." Richter looked disdainfully at the Frenchman. "Based on a conversation with a conveniently dead American – and a message you purportedly received from London." He slammed his fist down on the table. "Frankly, I don't believe you." He picked up his cap and spun it on his finger. "Perhaps it will be better to transfer you to Gestapo headquarters. With a little persuasion," he looked at Josse menacingly, "we can find the real truth."

"But I can tell you the real truth now – there is no need for, as you put it, persuasion. There will be a plane coming tonight. A courier is to arrive with the detailed plans for me and all the Resistance on what to do when the diversionary landings in Normandy take place. Similar courier drops are being made in the Pas de Calais to prepare for Patton's arrival, but I know nothing of these. But the drop in Normandy, I know, is coming tonight." He emphasized the last word as his finger searched on the map. "Here."

"Now, at last, what you have to say becomes interest—" Richter's head snapped around at the rattle of the latch.

"I've got the batt—" Augustine dropped the bag in shock. Her eyes darted from Josse to Richter, then back to the Frenchman. The expression on her face spoke both of fear and betrayal. Time seemed to hang for several seconds until she threw her head back and hurled her spittle at Josse's face.

"Salaud!" She spat again. "Swine! Traitor!" In an instant, she turned and ran, slamming the door behind her. Richter broke from his stunned surprise and leapt to his feet to follow her, his right hand bringing his Luger from its holster.

"No!" Josse lunged forward and grabbed Richter's sleeve. "Let her go. She can't harm your cause now that you have what you've been looking for."

They both heard the clattering of Augustine's heels on the pavement. Richter smashed Josse's hand aside with his pistol and raced into the street.

'Run, legs, run!' Augustine fled down the street, arms pumping, breast heaving. Fear drove her. The stark fear of a noise behind her, the fear of the click of an automatic weapon, the crack of a gunshot. She felt her lungs screaming, urging her to slow down, insisting she should stop. Still she ran, her shoes clipping on the cobbles, her fear defying her body's protests.

Richter's experience took charge as he kicked aside the garden gate. 'Think clearly, don't rush.' He looked down the street she had taken. He could not see her. The sun hung low in the western sky, dazzling him. Then he saw her, running down the hill. He began to run after her, realized the futility of an uneven chase, and stopped. He needed her alive; she could tell him so much. His hand came up, leveling his Luger at the fleeing figure. The shot had to be accurate.

'Where to run? Where?' She had heard the sound of his boots; she had to get out of his line of fire. There was a road to the left, sixty feet away. She had to make it. A desperate message to her legs. Not far now.

Richter dropped onto one knee; he must aim to wound only. He carefully took aim and squeezed the trigger. Crack! The report of the shot echoed back to him from the walls of the houses lining the street.

Augustine had almost made the corner when she heard the shot. Immediately, there was an intense pain in her right shoulder. She staggered, clutched at the corner of the building as she rounded it, then fell on the steps of a house.

'Got her.' Richter stood up and began to walk down the street. He took a few steps and then stopped, cursing himself. Josse. He had completely forgotten Josse. He hesitated for a few moments, looking down the street, then retraced his path hastily, careening through the gate, his pistol raised as he entered the shed. Nothing. Josse had gone.

Augustine reached for her shoulder, feeling blood seep through her fingers. She tried to get up, but almost fainted and fell in a heap. Richter would have her soon. She felt consciousness drifting away. There was a pale shaft of light as the door to the house opened. *"Viens."* The whisper hung in the air as unknown hands pulled her inside.

Tempsford, a Royal Air Force Base in England. 10 p.m.

"The briefing is simple." The Royal Air Force officer looked across the table to where Tom sat in flying gear. "The Flight Lieutenant," there was a nod toward the pilot sitting next to Tom, "will land you in France – there's no need for you to know where – just after midnight." He paused to ensure that he had the American's full attention. "You will be met by a unit of the French Resistance." He saw the alarm on Tom's face and smiled. "It's all right; there'll be someone who speaks English." He continued in a matter-of-fact way. "You will be taken to the safe house where Major Dalton is hidden, and which he steadfastly refuses to leave. Because you are his friend, you will be able to convince him that the escape plan is not a trap. Exactly twenty-four hours later, the plane will return to pick up you and your friend. It will be a squeeze, but we think we can do it."

"Squeeze?" Tom was mystified.

The officer gave a half-yawn, as he realized he had to explain the technicalities of the plan. "We'll be using a Lysander aircraft – there's room for only two passengers."

"Couldn't we use a bigger plane?"

"The Lysander can land in a very short distance. Any larger aircraft would need a landing strip in excess of one thousand yards. Given the situation and the urgency, we have no choice. So we've rustled up a Lysander. It's a very reliable aircraft."

115

Tom somehow did not feel comforted by the officer's words. The pilot was asked to wait outside; as the door closed, the officer spoke to Tom again.

"Although this mission looks simple, it's still highly dangerous. Do you have your service pistol?"

Tom pulled aside his overcoat to display his holster.

"Good. These items may help." The Englishman opened a desk drawer and pulled out a wad of used French franc notes and a little square tin. "They're Benzedrine tablets – useful to combat tiredness. As will these bars of chocolate."

Tom started to get up.

"Wait – there's one more thing." The officer pulled out a slightly larger tin and pushed it gingerly across the desk.

"What is it?" Tom picked up the tin and turned it in his hands.

"There's an L-pill inside."

"L-pill?"

"If you're about to fall into the hands of the Gestapo, you're advised to use it." The officer looked somewhat uncomfortable. "The 'L' is for 'lethal.' It's cyanide. Just take it out and bite it in half. Death is almost instantaneous."

Tom put the tin in the breast pocket of his shirt and felt a stab of fear; perhaps he was taking on more than he had bargained for.

"Good luck. Bradshaw will look after you from now on. He's a fine pilot." The officer offered his hand. Tom shook it firmly and hoped the officer did not notice the sweat on his palm.

The light was beginning to fail as the truck pulled out of the hangar and made its way across the tarmac to the plane, sitting squat on the runway. It looked small and frail.

"Don't worry, sir." The pilot at his side seemed to sense his anxiety. "It may look like a string bag, but the Flying Carrot's a damned good aircraft."

"You call the plane a flying carrot?"

"Because of its shape, sir. Not a very nice name, I know, but at least we pilots are called 'The Pimpernels of the Air'."

The pilot seemed pleased with the title, but it brought visions of the guillotine to Tom's mind, images fortunately dispersed by the pilot's incessant chatter.

"I wouldn't fly anything else. I think we've only ever lost one."

Tom grimaced. Perhaps this would be the night when the averages evened out. He glanced at his watch. It was past ten o'clock, but there was still a glimmer of light in the western sky. The moon was pallid, awaiting the full darkness of night.

"Everyone's always a bit nervous, the first time, but it'll be a piece of cake." The young man shrugged his shoulders when Tom did not reply. "Don't want to talk, eh? Okay, I'll shut up."

Tom didn't hear him. Even the anxieties of the night ahead could not stop his thinking of her. Her hair, her face, her lips. Then the pained smile when he'd told her that he was married; her tears, brushed quickly away. He'd wanted to hold her, to tell her that everything was all right, that his marriage was as good as over, that.... But he'd said nothing.

It took an effort of will to push her image from his mind, to concentrate on the task that lay ahead. He'd meet Glenn Dalton, persuade him that the escape plan was genuine, and within twenty-four hours, they'd be back in England, the BIGOT secret safe. It seemed so simple.

As Tom jumped down from the truck with the pilot, he heard the insistent beat of the propeller at low revs. The pilot took him around the back of the aircraft and guided him to the fixed ladder that led up to the passenger seat.

Tom strapped himself in as the pilot settled into the cockpit in front of him. As the pilot gunned the engine, the propeller blades screamed and the fuselage shuddered, awaiting its release. Tom was pushed into the back of his seat as the aircraft was launched down the runway, its speed increasing as the pilot pulled back on the stick and the plane climbed effortlessly into the sky.

Tom saw the faint orange glow on the horizon as the sun surrendered to the night. The mission would be easy. They would be back within twenty-four hours. He relaxed and breathed more slowly; but he felt the tin containing the L-pill press against his chest. Yep, the mission would be easy. A piece of cake.

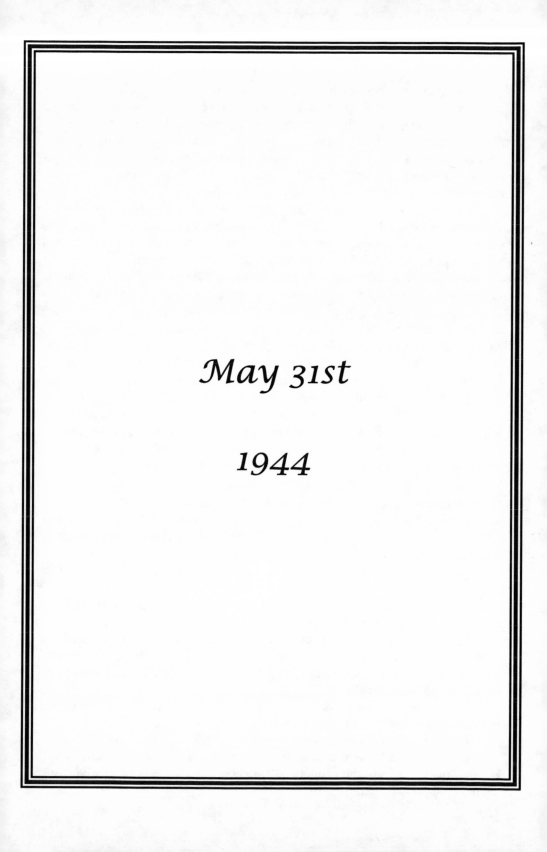

May 31st

1944

Somewhere over Normandy. 12:30 a.m.

*T*he plane began to fall from the night sky like an owl seeking a hapless mouse. Tom looked down from the cramped compartment, but could see nothing. He did not like flying. His stomach lurched and his heart hammered against his rib cage. And he was cold. He squeezed his gloved hands together, hoping to press some warmth back into his fingers. He wondered how the pilot saw anything. There were only sounds – the droning engine and the rushing wind outside the aircraft; all else was a gray void.

The pilot waved his hand, his right index finger pointing downwards. Tom craned his neck but could still see nothing. However, his perspective changed as the pilot gunned the engine and banked the aircraft, forcing Tom to clutch instinctively at the side of the small compartment.

Below, he detected three pinpricks of light in the shape of an 'L', marking the landing position. The shape of the letter on the ground reminded him of the L-pill nestling innocuously in the breast pocket of his shirt, at times pressing against the fabric when he moved. The pill was supposed to be for his benefit, when death became preferable to the agony of torture and possibly betraying the secret. He thought it perverse that there were men on his side, fighting for the Allied cause, who, in certain circumstances, would prefer him dead.

The plane leveled off, the pitch of the engine falling away. He pushed the thoughts of the pill from his mind. He didn't want to die. Even though, at that moment, his life didn't amount to much more than a row of beans. Perhaps he could straighten things out with Gwen, convince her that his previous life now meant nothing, tell her that he hadn't meant to treat her badly.

The machine plunged quickly towards the earth. Branches of trees sped by his window, so close he felt he could reach out and touch them. A fierce jolt slammed his rear end into his seat, as the aircraft fought for a safe embrace with the earth. He was thrown against both sides of the compartment as the plane lurched left and right.

Finally, the plane came to rest. The pilot brought the revolutions right down and turned to him. "Welcome to France."

Despite the cold, sweat ran into Tom's eyebrows. He opened the canopy and made his way down the ladder where a heavily-built man awaited him.

"See you tomorrow, same time." The pilot gave a cheery wave, shut his canopy and waited until the two figures were beyond the wingtip before gunning the engine. After three hundred yards, the plane lifted, bounced once and vanished into the night sky.

"Major Ford?" The Frenchman offered his huge hand. "I am Philippe Josse. We must hurry to the safe house where Major Dalton is hidden."

Tom withdrew his hand from the vice-like grip. "Call me Tom."

"Eh bien, Tom," Josse looked at his watch, "we depart *immediatement."* He led Tom to a gap in the hedgerow. Tom could see little as he looked along the moon-speckled road.

120

"Where's the car?"

"Car?" Josse laughed. "Here is our transport." He pointed to two bicycles leaning against the fence. "*Allons-y, mon ami Américain.* Follow me." The Frenchman threw himself astride his bicycle with an athletic leap.

Tom searched his memory for skills learned many years before and wobbled a little before he measured the pace of the pedals.

An aircraft over France. 2:30 a.m.

It was always the moment Jeanne dreaded. The wind roared through the open aircraft door, almost drowning out the steady drone of the engines. She checked her parachute and tested the fit of the webbing under her arms before her hands went up to the static line where she double-checked her hook-up, which would automatically open her chute when she leapt from the plane. There was the time when one agent hadn't checked...

Jeanne felt the fear. Her breathing was deep and slow as she fought to maintain her composure. She had made many drops, but the feelings were always the same. Her stomach muscles were steel hawsers, droplets of perspiration dropped from her brow to her cheeks and her heart raced.

She looked at Lieutenant Wainwright and silently cursed his calmness. "Did you enjoy the dinner?" She tried to ease the tension. Wainright's blond head nodded, but he said nothing. He held on his lap a briefcase, from which ran a chain linked to his wrist. In the case, she knew, were the final instructions to be given to the Resistance leaders, yet he looked as if he were delivering the daily newspaper.

Ironically, the instructions were to go to Josse; the man she had been ordered to kill was now to be handed all the plans. But, despite her fears and doubts, she did not question her orders this time. Like all agents, she had to know only a small piece of the puzzle; those at the top knew where all the pieces fitted together.

The light over the open door still showed red and she became impatient for it to change. She would do her job. Guide the lieutenant to the right people, support and protect him, then get them both out of France.

The invasion could not be far away. Soon the fields of France flashing below the plane would echo and crash with the might of the Allied army coming to grips with the German war machine. To see the Nazis beaten and crushed, driven out of France: that was why she was risking her life.

"Stand by!" The RAF crewman's shout brought her back into the realm of fear. The wind howled through the open door, above which the light still shone red, the color bathing her face a harsh blood-crimson. Almost by instinct, she checked her chute again, and made sure that the lieutenant's hook-up was sound. She moved towards the open door, felt the slipstream pulling at her, tensed her body and grabbed the door frame. In a moment, the red light died, replaced by green.

"Go, go, go!" the dispatcher behind her shouted.

She took a deep breath and hurled herself through the hole, her eyes shut tight. She felt herself falling, her body twisting in the wind. She counted; every time she jumped, she counted. One. Two. She knew that, by the time she reached five, the chute would automatically deploy. Three. If it didn't.... Four. She heard the snap as the parachute opened, grasping at the air. There was the sudden jolt of pain as the harness webbing dug into her groin. She began to laugh hysterically; it was the only form of pain she ever welcomed.

Her body swayed gently beneath the chute, and she looked up to see the comforting billow of silk, ghostly in the light of the moon. She looked for the accompanying chute of the lieutenant, but saw only the emptiness of the night sky. She looked down and saw the fields of Normandy drifting slowly up to meet her.

The moon spilled off her chute onto the fields enclosed by the hedgerows below. The landing was the second worst part of a jump. Throwing herself out of an airplane was terrifying, but now the ground began to rush up to her. Perhaps she might spear herself on a tree, or land awkwardly in a ploughed field and break a leg. Missions had failed because of a broken limb or a sprained ankle.

Besides, she had other worries. Surely there should be the sight of the lieutenant's chute. But there was nothing. Where was he?

The ground was almost upon her. She pulled hard on the left harness to guide the chute, barely missing a large tree. The landing was hard, but she rolled with it over her shoulder, as she had been taught in countless exercises. She was winded; her lungs gasped for air. She got to her feet, gathering the chute towards her. She folded it and looked for someplace to bury it, to hide evidence of her arrival in France.

She made for a tree at the edge of the field, pulled a small spade from her pack, and cleared the earth from its base. The silk of the chute ran through her fingers as she began to stuff it into the hole. She thought of the thousands of Frenchwomen who would sell their souls for the chance of making underwear from the precious fabric.

Where was the lieutenant? She had to link up with him quickly, deliver him and the plans to the *maquis*. Philippe Josse came into her thoughts, a confused jumble of doubt and half-belief. Jeanne shook her head and pulled off her jump suit, straightening her coat and skirt. She felt for the comforting shape of the pistol in her pocket.

She jumped as the beam of a flashlight pierced the darkness. Her heart raced as she tried to discern the figure behind the beam. The man was short and squat. Philippe?

"Bienvenue à France, ma'm'selle."

From the crude accent, she knew it was not Philippe, nor the voice of any Frenchman. There was the click of an automatic weapon.

"Sturmbannführer Hermann Richter. Gestapo." There was a low chuckle. *"A vôtre service."*

Normandy. A safe house. 2:30 a.m.

The farmhouse looked foreboding as Tom followed Josse's bicycle through the gateway into the yard. The stone façade, large and dark, cast a menacing night shadow across the yard; the moon played with the slate roof, making a ghostly aura that seemed to hang above the house.

A dog barked, followed by a voice ordering the animal to be quiet. Tom followed Josse as he pedaled to a large wooden barn some twenty meters from the house. "In here, *les bicyclettes.* Your friend, the *Américain*, he is in the house." Josse led Tom on foot across the yard.

A man stood in the doorway, framed by the light of an oil lamp behind him. Josse greeted the farmer, who pulled the stub of a cigarette from his mouth and tossed it into a bucket by the side of the door.

"I'm glad you're back." The man looked at Tom sullenly. "Another one?"

"Yes, but they'll both be gone this time tomorrow."

"About time. The Germans have been stepping up on their raids."

"They've been here?"

"No, but they did a big search in town."

Josse prayed that Richter didn't have any leads to him yet. When Richter captured the plans at the drop that night, the pressure would be off, and he wouldn't have to provide any more alibis.

Josse shepherded Tom through the doorway. The animal smells of the yard were replaced by the mixed odors of stale tobacco and burnt garlic. The light of an oil lamp flickered over the tired furniture, but there was no sign of Dalton. Tom looked across at Josse and raised an inquiring eyebrow.

Josse pointed downward and motioned to Tom to help move the table. He pulled aside the tattered rug to reveal a trap door. He tugged it open and beckoned Tom to follow him as he pulled out his flashlight and descended into the cellar. Tom took care as he went down the steep set of steps, following Josse's light.

The cellar was small, barely ten feet square, and there was a pervading smell of damp and decay. Josse played the beam around, revealing old boxes and newspapers; a few dozen dust-covered bottles of wine lay in a rack; there was nothing else but a cupboard set into the far wall.

"Where's Major Dalton?" Tom asked. Josse did not answer, but stepped across the floor and opened the cupboard. Josse knocked once and bent down, depressing a hidden lever and easing the cupboard away from the wall.

Tom could see nothing until Josse pointed his flashlight. There was a small recess, barely big enough to hold the straw mattress that lay along its length. On top of the mattress lay a man dressed scruffily in traditional blue French overalls, rubbing his eyes to adjust to Josse's light. Tom knew it was Dalton, but did not recognize him until he spoke.

"What's up? Is there a raid?" The frightened voice was directed at Josse.

Tom stepped forward into the light. "We've come to get you out, Glenn."

Dalton rubbed his eyes again and swung his legs down from the recess. "Holy Mother of God! It's Tom Ford." Dalton's eyes widened in surprise. "What on earth are you doing here? Are you on the run from the Krauts, too?"

"No, Glenn, as I said, I'm here to get you out. This coming night." Dalton's smile turned to a scowl as the Frenchman spoke.

"I'll get you some food, but it's better you both stay here until morning." Josse took out some matches and lit a rusty oil lamp hanging from a beam before making his way back up the steps, closing the trapdoor behind him.

"You can't trust these Frenchies." Dalton's whisper was harsh. "Particularly that guy."

Tom wondered if Dalton's mind had been affected by staying in the cellar. "Have you been in this hole all the time?"

"Hell, no. Only when there's danger of a Kraut raid. But I have to sleep in the hole." Dalton shook his head. "And it can sure drive a man crazy. So I sure am glad to see you, Tom." He slapped Tom on the back and pulled him over towards the light. "You are one hell of a mother-fucking sight for sore eyes."

"It sure is good to see you, too, Glenn." Tom grasped Dalton's upper arms. Haven't seen you since that end-of-season game against…" His memory struggled for the name.

"Clemson!" Dalton leapt as the memory returned. "Remember your throw? How I turned the defender? Touchdown! Victory for the Blue Devils."

Tom recalled the ball heading towards the end zone as if it were yesterday, but it seemed so long ago. A war ago. He shook the memory from his mind. "We've got to get you out of here, Glenn. Pronto. There's a plane coming for us tonight." He found an old wooden box and sat on it.

"Why don't you trust Josse? Didn't he help you escape from the jail at St. Lô?"

Dalton went to the steps, listened for any noise above, and then pulled Tom into a corner, his voice dropping to a whisper. "Yes, it's true he did. But I wouldn't trust him as far as I could throw him. He's been trying to pump me about…."

The subject wasn't mentioned, but both men understood. The invasion.

Well, I'm here now, Glenn. I can tell you that it's all right." Tom gave Dalton a reassuring pat on the back. "We'll be getting out of here within twenty-four hours."

"Now that I've seen you, I'm ready to go." There was a creak as the trapdoor opened above them." Dalton leaned towards Tom. "But we can't trust Josse. We have to be very careful."

A field in Normandy. 3 a.m.

Jeanne tried to break the paralyzing grip of fear. The beam of the German's flashlight held her like a rabbit caught in a car's headlights. Her body screamed at her to move, to run, as if knowing the pain awaiting it at the hands of the German.

A bird, disturbed by the flashlight, flew up with a frightened cry breaking the silence and the paralysis of fear upon her. Her hand moved slowly towards her pocket. She stared into the beam as her fingers inched into her coat pocket.

"Well, *ma'm'selle*, have you nothing to say for yourself?" There was another chuckle from the darkness behind the flashlight.

Her hand grasped the butt of her pistol inside her pocket, her index finger reaching forward to the trigger. Just a few more seconds—

The stock of a rifle slammed between her shoulder blades and the breath rushed from her body. She fell to the ground, winded. Before she could recover, two pairs of hands seized her roughly, dragging her upright and pinning her arms to her side. She saw the German soldier's helmet in front of her and kicked backwards at the shins of the soldier holding her from behind. He grunted, yet tightened his grip. Her head flew back as the other man slammed his knuckles into her cheek.

"Don't kill her! Don't kill her!" The man with the flashlight barked as he moved towards Jeanne, hanging loosely in her captors' arms. "Search her! Thoroughly!"

Jeanne caught the features of the face in the harsh light. It was the Gestapo chief in the photos Priestley had shown her, the one talking to Josse. Josse! Her mind reeled. She should have followed Priestley's orders. Josse had betrayed her.

Calloused hands ran over her body. The pistol was soon found. Another pocket revealed her false passport. Both were handed to Richter.

"I said search her thoroughly."

The soldiers' hands returned, opening her coat, pressing into her flesh, her groin. A leering face looked down at her as hands came inside her coat and cupped her breasts. She turned her head away, but the hands were insistent and found what they were looking for. The leer was replaced by a knowing grin. A hand rose to the collar of her blouse, tugging sharply, tearing the blouse asunder, before plunging into her brassiere, lingering as it grasped the small tin box hidden there.

The hand emerged, triumphant with its find. The soldier handed the box to Richter, who captured it in the flashlight beam as he snapped it open to reveal her L-pill.

"Well, we have her pistol and her suicide pill. She can neither kill us nor herself." He placed the items in his tunic pocket and flipped open her false passport. A smile creased his face. "Dairy worker? Perhaps your cows will also drop by parachute?" Richter's face hardened. "Now, *Ma'm'selle* Busson – if that is your real name," Richter brought the flashlight up to her face, "perhaps you can help us by answering a few questions. Please come with me." He nodded to the soldiers and began to walk across the field to the gate in the corner.

The soldiers released Jeanne, and she pulled her coat over her exposed breasts, willing some warmth into her body, her spirit. One of the soldiers pushed her forward, and she followed Richter. She could not get warm. Her body shivered from fear of what was to come. She knew what the Gestapo did to captured agents.

No. Not for her. Not that. She began to run blindly, half stumbling on the grass. She could see nothing, did not know where she going, yet still she ran. Anywhere. Not that. She heard the sound of a rifle bolt. Click. Click. Yes, yes, she thought, shoot, please shoot.

There was no rifle shot, nothing to spare her. Only Richter's voice.

"Don't shoot, you fools! After her!"

Her legs moved instinctively, her lungs gasping at the thin night air. The sounds of the cursing Germans grew closer. She saw a gap in the hedgerow ahead. If she could make it, perhaps—

The hand grabbed at her shoulder. She tried to shake it off, but it was persistent, clutching at her until she lost her balance, stumbled and fell. The soldier fell on top of her. She struggled briefly, but the soldier hit her with his fist, and her head fell onto the earth. She could fight no more. Despair enveloped her as she heard Richter's voice.

"Hold her! Tie her hands!"

She felt her arms pulled in front of her, then the twine cutting into her flesh. The soldiers hauled her to her feet, and one tied a rope to her bound wrists, like a leash. He half-dragged her, like a dog, to the gate.

Richter strode along the road towards his staff car. Jeanne looked at his cropped head, sitting neckless on his shoulders, and feared the cruelty lurking there.

As he approached the car, an aide thrust a piece of paper into his hand. He read the message and then he let out a cry of triumph. He folded the paper and looked at Jeanne.

"Well, *ma'm'selle*, now that you have finished with your foolish behavior, I have some questions to ask you at my headquarters." He took the rope leash from the soldier, opened the car door and pushed her inside.

"But first I have something to show you."

In Richter's staff car. 3:30 a.m.

The moon was masked by thick clouds and Jeanne could barely see the hedgerows dancing past the car window. She was afraid. Richter would torture her, she knew, but she didn't have any secrets of great value to give him. She knew the name of Josse, of course, but it was certain that Josse was in Richter's pay. He had betrayed her; Priestley had been right all along.

But she didn't possess the real secret, the one which Richter was undoubtedly seeking. Of the invasion, she knew nothing. She glanced across at the Gestapo chief ensconced in the leather seat, a smirk upon his face. Despite his uniform, he looked very ordinary. Yet she knew he held the power of life and death over her. She pulled her bound arms close to her and shrank back into the seat.

The light surprised Jeanne. She looked through the driver's windshield, and saw they were still in the countryside, the tall hedgerows towering at the side of the road. A searchlight had been set up; its beam was focused into the field beyond the hedgerow, but the light lit up a platoon of soldiers lining the road. Richter spoke to the driver; the car came to a halt.

"*Ma'm'selle*, perhaps you will follow me?" Richter's tone was gentle, even polite, but Jeanne pulled away from him. He grabbed the leash tied to her wrists and dragged her from the car. She staggered, recovered her balance, and saw the soldiers. They stood at attention, as if on parade, their rifles at their shoulders.

Jeanne's head fell. There were to be no questions; it was one of Richter's sadistic tricks. An execution squad in the middle of a field. Richter pushed her past the soldiers into the field.

Jeanne heard the soldiers and Richter follow her. She looked down and was acutely conscious of her feet walking across the soil. Why were they moving like that, moving so normally, yet they were walking her to her death? Had Yvette walked the same way to her death in Holland? She resolved to be brave, or at least to appear so. She raised her head and moved with measured pace.

The searchlight pointed to a far corner of the field. There was something there – it looked like an animal, hunched on the ground. She stopped, but Richter prodded her forward. As she neared the spot, she could see the shape was the body of a man, crumpled and broken, the face embedded in the soil. On his back was an unopened parachute pack. An arm hung grotesquely askew from the body. At the wrist was fastened a handcuff; attached to it was a chain, and at the other end of the chain was a briefcase.

So Lieutenant Wainwright's parachute had failed to open. That's why she hadn't seen him floating in the air above her. Her eyes dropped to the briefcase and she grimaced. Now Richter would have the secret. There was nothing she could do.

Richter signaled to one of his men, who reached down and turned the body over, revealing a face with sightless eyes.

"*Ma'm'selle*, who is this man?"

Jeanne looked at the face for a few seconds.

"I don't know. I've never seen him before in my life."

Richter lashed the back of his hand across her face and she crumpled at his feet. He turned away and barked orders at two of the soldiers.

"Get that body to the Forensic Unit immediately. I want every test and a complete search carried out." He looked at his watch. Almost four o'clock; there was a hint of dawn in the sky. "Tell Colonel Schumann that I need a full forensic report by ten o'clock."

He turned back to Jeanne and tugged on her leash.

"We'll see if we can jog your memory back at headquarters."

Jeanne felt the stinging of the bruises on her face and knew it was a pinprick compared with what was to come. Yet she had told Richter the truth.

127

She looked down at the body as it was carried past her on a stretcher. She had never seen the face before. The hair was dark, not blond. It was not the body of Lieutenant Wainwright.

Richter's Gestapo Office. Coutances. 10:30 a.m.

"My dear Richter, there can be no doubt about it." Although Colonel Hans Schumann's forensic team had had only limited time, the autopsy had been performed methodically and meticulously, as had the analysis of the clothing and the documents. "The man was a British agent who died because his parachute failed to open." He sipped his coffee and looked over to the Gestapo chief.

"You don't look happy, Hermann." Schumann set his coffee down on the table. "With the discovery of the documents in the briefcase, I'd have thought you'd be ecstatic."

"Could he have been dead before he hit the ground?" Richter's question stunned Schumann for a moment.

"Absolutely not! Let's see," his hand turned the pages of the report on his lap, "rigor mortis had begun to set in only after you shipped the body to us. He could have been dead for only two to three hours. Your men did well to find him so quickly."

"Perhaps he could have been killed in the plane and thrown out?" Richter finished his coffee.

"Certainly," Schumann's voice was heavy with sarcasm, "if there were someone in the plane who could rupture his spleen and have the strength to break his rib cage with such force to drive a broken rib into his aorta. That was the cause of death. Really, Hermann, you have to trust the forensic evidence."

"I trust nothing and nobody." Richter smiled. "That's why I'm Chief of the Gestapo in Normandy. It's all too simple. I'm told by an informer of the drop and then one of the agents arrives conveniently dead." He offered Schumann a cigar before taking one for himself. "Did you check the parachute?"

"Don't you ever let go, Hermann?" There was a mild annoyance in Schumann's voice. "Actually, my department did not check the chute, as we have no expertise in that area." Before the Gestapo man could intervene, Schumann continued, "So I contacted Hauptmann Blucher of the 9ᵗʰ *Fallschirmjäger* Division, and he examined it closely."

"And?" Richter spoke through a smoke ring.

"He said that the parachute had failed to deploy properly. It resulted in what he called a 'Roman Candle,' when the parachutist falls to earth at a great speed. The Hauptman said that the parachute may not have been packed correctly. Apparently these things happen from time to time. He told me of an incident in the Crete campaign—"

128

"Yes, yes," Richter cut in brusquely, "and what have you found out about the man?"

"Ah, now that is much more interesting." Schumann lifted his lanky frame from the seat and walked over to the table, looking down on an array of articles: the dead man's blood-stained clothing, his shoes, his briefcase with handcuffs still attached; cigarettes and matches, some other exhibits in small cellophane wrappers, and, finally, carefully stored in folders, a number of documents.

"All the clothing is French made, and, as you can see, the cigarettes and matches are also French. He was all dressed up by the British to pass as French." Schumann waved a hand at the items. "But the man is, without a doubt, a British army officer."

"Your evidence?"

"Not only a British officer, but an officer on an urgent, important mission." Schumann's fingers tapped on the folders holding the documents.

"My dear Hans, I have already read the transcript of the invasion papers."

"Then you will know that the man's name is Wainwright. Lieutenant Wainwright."

Richter walked around the table, picked up the documents and weighed them in his hand. It was exactly as Josse had said. Normandy. June 5th. There was only a brief mention of Patton's army, the First United States Army Group; but the documents indicated that he would come later, in the Pas de Calais.

Richter turned sharply to Schumann. "How do we know it's not a plant?"

"Hermann, I may detest the English, but I hardly think they're barbarous enough to throw one of their officer class out of an airplane." He chuckled. "And it's not the sort of mission for which they'd call for volunteers."

He picked up the briefcase. "Besides, there is other evidence. This briefcase is British-made. The stitching is unique to England. In fact, one of my experts is almost prepared to stake his reputation that it was made within ten miles of Birmingham." He warmed to his task as he picked up one of the small cellophane wrappers. "We found this in the cuff of his pants. It's the seed pod of a plant found only in England."

"So, this man, this body originated in England." Richter was not yet satisfied, his mind still shredding the facts, looking for an irrefutable conclusion. "But how do we know it is really – what was his name – Wainwright?"

Schumann picked up one of the man's shoes from the table. "It looks like a normal shoe, doesn't it?"

Richter feigned a yawn. "Don't tell me – it has a false heel."

"Of course," Schumann continued. "But do you know what we found in the compartment?"

"I'm beginning to tire of this game, Hans. I presume you found his L-pill."

"Yes. But we also found something much more significant. It turns out that Lieutenant Wainwright was a naughty boy!"

"Naughty boy? Hans, have you become as puerile as the English Public Schoolboy?"

Schumann ignored the slight. "No, but perhaps Lieutenant Wainwright was." He picked up a wrapper and tipped out a tightly-folded letter.

"Wainwright broke the rules. And this letter will dispel all your doubts."

He slid the envelope and letter across the table. "It is addressed to Lieutenant Wainwright at The Army and Navy Club in Pall Mall, London. We've checked the address."

"But why should he keep the letter? And why did he hide it?"

"Ah, why, indeed." Schumann pulled out a typewritten sheet. "This is the translation. I have to say that the junior officer who transcribed it became very embarrassed."

"What could embarrass a German officer?"

"Its contents are amusing. It is written by Wainwright's wife – or girl-friend." He put on his glasses and looked at the translation. "We can only know her as Mary, for such is her signature. But this Mary is neither meek nor mild. The letter shows she is obsessed with only one thing."

Schumann pulled out a handkerchief, took off his glasses and cleaned them. "There are graphic accounts of what the genteel Mary intends to perform upon Lieutenant Wainwright the next time she has his body to hand, so to speak. Not to mention detailed descriptions of her bedtime activities when Wainwright is away."

He handed the transcript to Richter. "I'll not bother you with the details, Hermann. You can, if you wish, read them for yourself. Presumably, Lieutenant Wainwright secreted the letter away," he smiled, "for, shall we say, his future enjoyment?"

Richter tossed the transcript aside. "I'm not interested in the sordid details. The envelope? It's genuine?"

Schumann folded his spectacles and stood. "It's genuine. The address is genuine; the English one-penny stamp is genuine; and the English watermark on the paper is genuine.

He picked up the folder that contained the operational documents found in the briefcase. "And now, Hermann, you have the secret that can win the war. The first invasion comes in Normandy, but it's a ruse. Then Patton's group strikes in the Pas de Calais three weeks later and that will be the genuine invasion. The BBC will even announce it for you!" He picked up one of the documents. "Verlaine's couplets: *'Les sanglots longs/ Des violons de l'automne.'* 'The long sobs/ of autumn's violins.' The diversionary invasion will come in five days. *'Blessent mon coeur/ D' une langueur monotone.'* 'Wound my heart/ with a monotonous languor.' Invasion imminent."

Schumann gave a congratulatory slap on the Gestapo chief's back. "Well done, Hermann. I wish I could see *Reichsführer* Himmler's face when you tell him."

Richter pondered the significance of the evidence. It was all as Josse had said: the plan, the timings, all delivered into his hands. Yet still he harbored doubts.

"I shall need more corroboration." He spoke tersely.

"More corroboration?"

"Yes, and I know where to get it." Richter smiled at Schumann's confounded look. "There is the woman we have in the cellar. I shall ask her about Lieutenant Wainwright." He ground out his cigar. "In my own way."

The Farm. 11 a.m.

The noise from the road startled Josse. He glanced at the tall case clock as his hefty frame moved quickly to a window at the southern end of the farmhouse. Eleven o'clock. Dominic wasn't due back until three in the afternoon. He motioned quickly to the Americans, who leapt from their seats, pushed the table aside and disappeared down into the cellar.

"What's going on?" The farmer's wife shuffled in from the kitchen, quickly re-arranging the carpet and table over the trapdoor.

"I heard a noise, Bernadette." Josse spoke without turning his head from the window.

The old woman listened for a moment. "It's only Dominic. I'd know that squeaky bike anywhere."

At that moment, Dominic appeared at the gate on his bicycle, pedaling furiously. The dog ran forward, barking his greeting to his master and Josse threw open the door as Dominic leaned his bike against the farmhouse wall. "Are you being followed?"

The farmer shook his head, still panting to regain his breath. He beckoned Josse out into the yard.

"What's the matter?" Josse clutched the farmer's upper arms.

"It's something," Dominic pulled the air into his lungs, "it's something I don't think the Americans should hear."

"They can barely understand you anyway. What is it?"

"I'm nearly sixty." The farmer spat on the ground. "I shouldn't have to race around like that."

"What is it? Tell me!"

"I met Henri, as you asked." The old man thrust a Gauloise into his mouth, his hand shaking as he lit it. "Or, rather, Henri met me. He ran toward me as I rode into the Place de l'Eglise. He shouldn't do that – the *bosches* could have been watching."

"What did he say?" Josse shouted, his impatience turning to anger.

"He told me the Germans had found a British agent last night." His words came quickly. "Parachute failed to open. Dead."

Josse nodded, saying nothing. Richter had acted upon his information.

"You are not upset?" Dominic's eyebrows lifted. "Henri said the Germans found some messages. In a briefcase."

Josse turned away. Richter had the confirmation he needed.

"Wait, there's more." Dominic tugged on his sleeve. "The Germans also captured another agent. Alive."

"And?" So Richter had another capture.

"Henri said she was taken to Gestapo headquarters this morning."

"She?" Josse turned to face the old man.

"Yes, it was that young woman who has been here before." Dominic drew on his cigarette deeply. "What was her name? I forget. My mind is like a colander nowadays."

Josse stood rigid for a moment before speaking her name. "Jeanne?"

"*Oui!* Jeanne! *C'est ça!* Jeanne. You remember her. Jeanne Busson."

"Yes, I remember Jeanne Busson." Josse's stomach lurched. Jeanne. Of all the agents that could have been sent…. "Come, Dominic, we have work to do. And we need to act fast!"

The Gestapo Prison. 12 noon

Jeanne awoke and opened her eyes. All was darkness. She could see nothing. Her nose twitched at the damp, dank smell that hung in the fetid air and her hand clutched at the hard earth on which she lay. Her mind tried to drag her back into the sleep that had comforted her, but the burning pain on her cheek kept her awake.

He had hit her face. The memory of the German's hand smashing into her cheek jolted her back to full consciousness. She sat up, wishing she had some way to penetrate the darkness. How long? How long had she slept? How long had she been in this dark hole? An hour? A day?

She reached behind her and felt the rough brick of the wall, wondering why it comforted her to feel something solid in the dark dungeon. Was this how sanity was surrendered, finding false security in danger? A scurry of tiny feet came from the darkness and she instinctively wrapped herself into a fetal position. Rats. She heard them again. They couldn't see her, but they could smell her.

No, no, please God, let me out, let me out. She stood up, her arms flailing uselessly before her as she staggered across the darkness. She crashed into another wall and fell down, her body and mind reeling. The thought of the pain to come invaded her, touching her fingers, her feet, her breasts. She fought against the sob that came to her throat; breath followed deep breath as she sucked air into her body. She stared into the unseen void, squatting on her haunches, her nostrils flared. Like an animal, she thought; they're dehumanizing me. No, don't let the darkness hem you in, don't let it crush your spirit. Think of light, think of warmth, think of happier times.

Her mind searched and found him: his face, his hands, his smile. The sun behind him, the cry of the birds, the smell of the grass beneath their feet, the touch of his hand. The light, the bright light shone in the darkness.

The door to her cell creaked and the images vanished. She lifted her hand to hide from the stark electric light coming from the entrance to her cell. She turned to the light, her eyes struggling to focus. There was a shadow in the doorway.

"I think it's time we had a talk."

It was Richter. She struggled to recapture the earlier images: the sun and him, his touch. But they were gone.

The Farm. 1 p.m.

Josse's pen scratched across the paper. He took the last drag from his cigarette and tossed it toward the hearth. The butt fell short onto a rug; Bernadette rushed forward, scooped it up and tossed it into the fireplace.

"You'll kill us all, one day, Philippe." She walked to the stove, took the lid off a pot and stirred.

Josse folded the letter and stuffed it in an envelope. "Where's Dominic?"

"He's in the barn, tending the cows. They don't know there's a war on." She lifted the lid again and sniffed. "He'll be back soon." She looked at the clock and started to lay plates on the table. "His stomach will tell him it's time for lunch."

As if on cue, the door latch rattled. Dominic sat down on the stool by the door and began to take off his muddy boots.

"Dominic, we have to act quickly." Josse licked the envelope and sealed it with a thump of his huge fist. "Where did you put the radio I brought from Jean-Paul's?"

"It's hidden at the back of the bottom drawer." He pointed to a large dresser under the window. "There's a new battery, and we have several of those little things," he thought for a moment, "crystals. *C'est ça.* Crystals. These contraptions are beyond me."

Bernadette lowered a ladle into the simmering pot and sipped at it. "The stew's ready. I'll get the Americans. Please help me move the table."

"No, not yet." Josse spoke sharply. "There are things to do first." He thrust the letter at Dominic. "Dominic, I want you to take this to Henri."

The farmer looked up angrily. "But it's lunchtime." He waved his hand to the table where Bernadette was setting the plates.

"I'm sorry, but it's urgent."

Bernadette slammed the utensils on the table. "Why can't you take it yourself?"

"Because I must use the radio." He lowered his eyes from her stare and walked across to the dresser.

Dominic grumbled under his breath, and retied his bootlaces before putting on his coat and stuffing the letter in his pocket. The latch rattled as he closed the door behind him.

"Merde." The oath hissed through the old woman's lips as she removed the pot from the heat.

"Ça va." Josse carefully put the radio back in its hiding place. "Now let's give the Americans their lunch, Bernadette." He smiled at the farmer's wife.

"You can't get around me with one of those smiles, Philippe." She scowled at Josse as she put the pot back on the heat. "What about Dominic? When will he eat?"

"He'll be back soon. Don't worry, Bernadette." He pulled the carpet aside and reached down for the latch on the trapdoor.

"I never worried before you came into our lives." She dug a ladle into the pot and filled the dishes. "Now, I worry all the time."

"It won't be long now, Bernadette." Josse heaved on the trapdoor. "Soon, we – and all of France – will be free."

"Free?" There was scorn in her voice. "Free to have another army rob our farm? Take all that we have?"

"The *Amis* will be different."

Her derisive laugh was drowned by the enthusiastic voices of the Americans as they came up the steps from the cellar.

"At last!" Dalton's head popped up from the hole. "That beautiful smell has been driving me wild, ma'am."

Bernadette did not move from the stove.

"Tell her, Josse, her food smells good."

The Frenchman translated and a beam came to the old woman's face. *"Merçi, m'sieur."*

Dalton attacked his large bowl while Tom awaited his portion. It was a simple stew of potatoes, carrots and beans; a few bits of fatty garlic sausage added flavor.

"Just twelve hours and we'll be out of here." Tom picked up his spoon and dug into the stew Bernadette placed before him. "What are the plans, Philippe? How will we get to the landing field?"

"There are no plans. He ripped open a crust of bread and dipped it into his stew. "Unfortunately, the whole operation has been delayed for twenty-four hours."

"Delayed?" Dalton almost shouted, a look of incredulity on his face.

"The weather is changing." Josse spoke through the bread he was chewing. "Too much cloud is forecast." He wiped the stew's juices from his mustache. "Now, please excuse me, but I must go. There are things I must attend to."

He got up from the table, pulled his coat on and made for the door. "You must stay here. It's safe. Don't leave the farmhouse."

Tom looked out of the window. There was not a cloud in the sky. He felt the pressure of Dalton's foot on his own under the table and recalled his words. 'We must not trust Josse.'

Gestapo Headquarters. 2 p.m.

Richter looked at the woman sitting in the chair in front of his desk.

"It is quite a simple situation, *Ma'm'selle* Busson. You answer a few questions and," he tapped a cigarette on his silver case, "we avoid, shall I say, unpleasant things."

Jeanne tried hard to focus on the German's words. Her mind was still numb from her solitary confinement, her eyes still adjusting to the desk light shining in her face. She shook her head.

"There is no need to be negative, *ma'm'selle*. Just a few questions and there will be no problems. Who was the other agent who came in with you last night? The one we found dead? Was he a friend of yours?"

Jeanne shook her head and felt her body shiver. Was it cold? Or fear?

"But you do know his name?" Richter pushed the desk lamp closer to her face.

Again, she shook her head.

"I see you are shivering. Perhaps you would like a cognac?" He went to a cabinet and pulled out a bottle. "Cognac is a very good for banishing the cold."

And for loosening the tongue, she thought, declining the glass he offered.

"As you wish. Shall we start with his name?"

Jeanne raised her head defiantly and brushed her hair from her face. "I do not know. I told you I had never seen him before."

"Perhaps *I* am cold." Richter raised the glass to his lips and sipped at the amber liquid. "You disappoint me, Jeanne." He rolled the cognac over his tongue and swallowed. "I advise you to answer my questions. Who was he?"

"I've told you, I don't know." She knew it was the truth; she had never seen the man.

Richter looked disappointed. "Really, Jeanne, you are making things very difficult for yourself."

She crossed her arms and hugged herself, trying to stop the shivering. She saw Richter get up from his chair and she tensed. "You're going to torture me, aren't you?"

Richter did not answer, but twirled his cigarette in his fingers, looking at the burning tobacco. Jeanne's eyes were drawn irresistibly to the red glow. Richter slowly touched the end of the cigarette on the ashtray, gently brushing the metal. He looked at Jeanne and thrust the cigarette down sharply, his wrist turning as he crushed the red hot ember against the metal.

"I am not going to torture you. I would not soil my hands with such sordid trade."

Jeanne looked at him incredulously, trying to stifle what she knew was a false glimmer of hope.

Richter pushed away the ashtray and drained his glass.

"No, I do not torture. I have others to do that work. I have a system that works remarkably well. I give the orders, but I don't see the result of my orders. I don't wish to see. I need only the information. So I sleep soundly in my bed."

Jeanne pulled her arms around her shoulders. She felt the chill of fear for the monster before her.

Richter got up and walked to the door. "On the other hand, the man who performs…," he paused at the doorway, searching for the correct words, "the man who follows my orders knows he is doing just that: following orders. He does his job dispassionately, coldly, because he is merely following orders. And, thus, he, too, sleeps soundly. It's a good system."

Jeanne shuddered. She felt herself in the presence of great evil, an evil that enveloped her like a fetid cloud. There was no trace of emotion on his face as he spoke. "But we can avoid all this unpleasantness. Just tell me the name of the other agent."

Jeanne dropped her eyes and shook her head.

Richter went to the door. "Müller!" His shout echoed along the corridor.

Jeanne felt the perspiration break out on her brow as she looked up at the doorway. The man was insignificant, a sparse frame on which his uniform hung shabbily. His face was without expression. He looked like a doorman at a hotel waiting to carry her bags. Jeanne looked at the hands that would carry her bags, hanging from the coat sleeves. The fingers were squat and huge, the knuckles flexing.

"Sergeant Müller will talk with you now." Richter closed the door behind him as he left.

The huge hands came toward her.

Gestapo Headquarters. Two hours later.

"I have come to report, as ordered, *Sturmbannführer.*" The sergeant clicked his heels and saluted, no trace of emotion on his face.

"What is there to report, Müller?" Richter tapped impatiently on his desk. "Did she talk?"

"They all talk, sir." The sergeant smiled. "Of course, she was at first reluctant, but after I introduced her to the *bagnoire*—"

"Spare me the details, Müller." Richter cut him short. He knew all about the *bagnoire*. The victim's head was pushed into a bucket of water for a long, long time, over and over again, almost to the point of drowning. Only an expert torturer knew the precise moment to pull out the head, just a few seconds before the victim drowned. "What did she say?"

"Not much, at first. It's strange, sir, but I have always found that men show less fear, but in the end, it is always the women who can stand more pain. During the *bagnoire*, she said just one thing. She screamed, over and over again, that someone called Philippe Josse had betrayed her."

Richter eased back in his chair and gazed at the ceiling with an air of contentment. The woman's statement was better than any confession: if she knew Josse had betrayed her, then it was guaranteed that the Frenchman's information was to be trusted. It was the corroboration he needed.

"And that was it, Müller? That's all she said?"

"Not exactly, sir. I tried a different approach…."

"And what did she tell you then?"

"On the fourth toenail, she told me that the other agent was a Lieutenant Wainwright."

"Excellent!"

"And that he was carrying plans to be delivered to the Resistance, plans to be put into operation at the time of the invasion."

"Did she know anything of the invasion?"

"Nothing, except it is coming soon."

"Is that all? You're sure she knows nothing?"

Müller's face was impassive. "I'm sure. Absolutely sure."

Richter's eyes narrowed. The treasure he had received was huge. He had confirmation that the information he had received from Josse was correct. He now knew the big secret; he knew where and when the invasion would occur: first, in Normandy, a ruse, then the real invasion, with Patton, in the Pas de Calais. And, as an added bonus, he knew the plans for the sabotage activities for the French Resistance.

He was jubilant, but he kept his composure in front of Müller. He reached out and picked up the phone. "Get me a connection to *Reichsführer* Himmler as soon as possible."

He replaced the receiver and looked across at the sergeant. "Where is she now?"

"Back in the isolation cell. If you want further information, I'm afraid it will be difficult. She's in bad shape. It's not just her feet. She appears to be in a fever, a delirium. It sometimes happens after the *bagnoire*. I don't think I could question her again for quite some time."

"No matter, she's served her purpose. We'll ship her back east in due course."

The sergeant nodded. Shipping her back east meant sending her to a death camp. If she survived long enough to get there.

"May I go now, sir?" He saw that Richter was pacing around his desk, his mind clearly on what he would say when the call came from Berlin.

"Yes," Richter waved him away, "you have done well, Müller."

The sergeant pocketed his notebook, saluted and smiled as he left. It had been a job well done.

Berlin. The Reich Chancellery. 10 p.m.

"Well, Heinrich, what is so important that you need to tell me at once?" The Führer sat at his desk, sipping at a cup of tea. The huge room, with its marble columns and stark Aryan art, seemed to dwarf the two men, but the man with the burning coals for eyes who flicked his dark hair back from his forehead dominated it with his personality. "I have to meet those idiot generals in half an hour."

137

He proceeded to launch a harangue against the failings and inadequacies of the German General Staff. *Reichsführer* Himmler, in the black garb of the S.S., stood still, peering through his rimless spectacles, waiting for the tirade to end.

"*Mein Führer*, I have received an important report from *Sturmbannführer* Richter, the head of the Gestapo in Normandy."

"Ah, Richter." The Führer smiled and gently placed his teacup in the saucer. "I remember him well. One of the *Alten Kämpfer*, you know. You must remember Richter, Heinrich – he was with us in Munich in '23. A most reliable man. Solid. A true National Socialist."

Himmler waited patiently. He had long become accustomed to Hitler's lengthy expositions about the past. It was necessary to humor him, to curry his favor, in order to keep ahead of that fat bastard, Goering.

"Well, what does Richter have to say?" Hitler surprised the *Reichsführer* by coming straight to the point.

"He has obtained ironclad evidence from British intelligence that the Allies are preparing an invasion in Normandy in June."

"Good!" Hitler jumped to his feet and slapped a hand against his thigh. "I welcome the invasion! It will be our chance to deal the Allies a decisive blow. I have waited for this moment. The British and the mongrel Americans will be given a nasty surprise! I will tell von Rundstedt to put the 7th and 15th Armies on alert.

"But of course, *mein Führer.*" Himmler was surprised at his leader's optimism, but was always prudent enough to agree with him. "Richter says that his information suggests the landings in Normandy will be a ruse."

"He's right!" Hitler pounded his right fist into his left palm. "I've always known it! The main thrust will come in the Pas de Calais – with Patton. That man is a genius! If only I had generals like him!"

The Führer swung on his heel and turned to a huge map of Europe on the wall. "Patton will hope to take the direct route to the Reich. From the Pas de Calais, through Belgium to the Ruhr." He dragged his hand across the map. "It is what I would do myself. But we'll be ready for them!" He slapped his hand against the map.

"I'll tell Rommel and von Rundstedt that I shall retain personal control of the Panzer divisions in France. There will be no movement, no change in their dispositions until I say so. With the landing in Normandy a diversion, I must keep the armored divisions flexible. Rommel and von Rundstedt would throw them in at the first whiff of grapeshot. We must make some provision for Normandy, of course, but my inclination is not to commit them in Normandy, but to keep them ready to meet Patton's arrival. Ready to smash him in the face! That's the way to do it, *ja*, Heinrich?"

"The officer corps are no match for you, *mein Führer*. They were wrong in '40 and '41, and they're wrong now." Himmler saw the light of previous triumphs return to his leader's eyes.

Hitler continued to pore over the map. "Of course, all intelligence needs to be taken with a pinch of salt. It needs a mind of genius to assess every nuance." His finger again traced the northern coast of France. "But Richter's report has endorsed my own strategy. I am convinced that the main thrust of the Allies will be at the Pas de Calais. I cannot trust that old fool Rundstedt to deal with this situation.

Himmler smiled, gently nodding his agreement that Rundstedt, the arrogant Commander-in-Chief of the German forces in France, was a fool. He hated the aristocratic officer corps, who looked down their noses at him. "I know you're right, *mein Führer.*"

Hitler turned from the map and fixed Himmler. "Richter has done good work. You should promote him." He began to pace back and forth. "I must keep control of the Panzer divisions. Then, when Patton comes, I shall be ready to strike." He smashed his fist down on the desk. "The Pas de Calais. I knew I was right!"

June 1st

1944

The Guardroom of Coutances Prison. 3:30 a.m.

*T*he German guard cursed as a black Citroen came to a halt at the perimeter gate to the prison. What the hell was up now? He slid the half-empty
bottle of schnapps into the desk drawer and looked at his watch. A long time
before dawn and the arrival of the relief guard.

He peered through the window of the guardroom, bespattered by the incessant rain. He cursed again. It was the first day of June, but a storm was
blowing in. He'd had enough of France; three years of occupation duty, just
sitting on his butt. He got up from his seat and slung his rifle over his shoulder. Still, he shouldn't complain. At least it was much better than the Eastern
front. He'd heard some terrible tales about Russia....

He saw a black-uniformed figure slide out from the driver's door. A sergeant in the *Milice*. Nasty piece of work. The *Milice* were the French
equivalent of the Gestapo, only worse. Betraying their own French countrymen. Many of the inmates in the jail were there because of the *Milice*.

He opened the guardroom door and looked into the wet darkness; the
headlights of the car probed through the rain. *"Entrez, entrez!"* The guard
urged the sergeant indoors. *"Que voulez-vous?"* He knew his French was bad,
but it was understood by the *Milice* man, who saluted.

"We have come to collect the prisoner."

"Prisoner?"

"Yes, the prisoner, Jeanne Busson."

"I have no knowledge of it." The German returned to his desk and shuffled through his papers. "There's nothing here."

"It's a special order."

"But I have no record. There is nothing in the duty log."

"I have the order here." A deep voice came from the doorway, and the
German looked up to see a burly figure in the uniform of a *Milice* colonel,
waving a piece of paper in his hand.

The guard saluted, took the order and shook his head. "But I have no instructions about the release of a prisoner."

"Perhaps you should look at the signature." The colonel brushed his hand
across his mustache in a gesture of impatience as the soldier looked at the signature and blanched. "Yes, it is the signature of *Sturmbannführer* Richter."

The soldier swallowed. Richter. Head of the Gestapo in Normandy. He
recognized the authority behind the order, but knew he had to cover his ass. "I
shall have to contact the duty officer."

"But of course." The colonel nodded. "But do it quickly. I'm sure the
Sturmbannführer would not like to hear of any delay."

The soldier picked up the guardhouse phone and made the connection.

"Forgive me, gentlemen, for taking so long." The duty officer took off his
rain-soaked raincoat and hung it on the guardhouse door. "It's a foul night."
He looked from one *Milice* man to the other, detected the colonel's rank from
his epaulettes and saluted.

"I understand, Colonel, that you have a special order for the release of a prisoner?"

"Yes, the guard has it."

The duty officer took the paper from the soldier and raised his eyebrows when he saw Richter's signature. "It looks in order, but it's most unusual."

"Unusual?" The *Milice* colonel chuckled as he lit a cigarette. "Not when you've been on the job as long as I have, captain. Once Richter has got the scum to squeal, he gets rid of them." The smoke drifted up from his mouth, adding to the brown stain on his gray mustache. "As you can see from the order, this one's headed to Fresnes, the jail outside Paris. It's the usual way. Then they disappear to the east. God knows where. Who cares?" He shrugged his shoulders. "They never come back."

The captain gave the Frenchman a disdainful look. "I am aware of the procedures. And now, if you will excuse me, I have to make a telephone call." He reached for the receiver.

"You're going to call *Sturmbannführer* Richter?"

"I would not dream of calling Herr Richter at three in the morning." The duty officer smiled. "It wouldn't enhance my career. But I need to find out where the prisoner is located."

Consciousness tugged at her mind. She opened her eyes and found the same black impenetrable void. Her hands pressed against the damp earth of the cell floor as her memory tried to find the last page that had been turned. Then the pain hit her. Searing, knife-cutting pain. Screaming pain, screaming up from her feet, clawing at her body, thrusting hot needles into her brain.

The memory's pages turned quickly. She remembered the German's unconcerned face as he brought the pincers towards her toes. Pain stabbed again, twisting its knife. She beat her head against the floor in the vain hope that new pain would deflect the old. Her memory thrust other images upon her: her body hog-tied to a stake, turned so her head was totally immersed in a bath of water, her lungs screaming for oxygen. The moment of release, the frantic gasp for air before being plunged down again. Again and again.

The serrated blade of pain racked its path across her body again, but she remembered the longer break from the water, when her lungs sucked greedily. And she remembered the questions. Who was the other agent? Where will the invasion be coming?

Still the pain burned at her flesh. What had she said? Had she given a name? The pain told her that she didn't care, that the answers didn't matter. For a moment, a brief moment, she held the vision of a man, looking over the sea, holding her hand, but the agony soon snatched it into the darkness.

She longed for another blackness, the deep shadow of unconsciousness to free her from the pain. The freedom came. Her body continued to shake with the fever, but the welcome darkness claimed her. She did not feel the arms of the German soldier who tossed her over his shoulder.

The *Milice* colonel pushed the peak of his képi high onto his forehead. "It's good that we're getting rid of this scum. Communists, Jews, and the British agents that would help those bastards take over France. It's good that we see eye-to-eye on this matter, Hauptman."

"Quite so, Colonel, but, on this occasion, it hardly seems worth your effort." He replaced the receiver and picked up the prisoner's file from the desk. "I'm told that the Busson woman is barely alive. She has been interrogated," he paused, "shall we say, in depth. The guard says she's delirious, and has lapsed into unconsciousness."

The colonel shrugged his shoulders. "But I have my orders. I must carry them out."

"I am aware of the importance of all *Sturmbannführer* Richter's orders. The guard is bringing the prisoner to the guardhouse." The officer produced a notepad from the desk and wrote upon it. "You'll have to sign for her. After that, she's your problem."

He pushed the pad across the desk and yawned. "If you'll complete the paperwork?"

As the colonel reached across to sign, he looked through the window of the guardhouse and saw a German soldier; across his shoulder hung what seemed to be a sack of potatoes. He put down the pen and turned to his aide. "Sergeant, put that heap of garbage in the car and let's get away."

He pushed the signed docket across the desk and saluted the officer. *"Auf wiedersehen, mein Herr."*

The German soldier lifted the guard rail at the perimeter fence and the Citroen slid away from the prison, the rain beating on the windscreen.

"How is the prisoner, Henri?" The *Milice* colonel took off his hat and mopped his brow.

"She's not well." The sergeant did not take his eyes from the windshield and the flailing wiper. "She's unconscious and has a fever. It doesn't look good."

"Then step on it. We need to push on. There's not much time."

"But what will happen when the Germans find out that the order is a fake, Philippe?"

"Hopefully, they won't find out. But we don't want to be around if they do. *Vite, vite.*" Josse slumped back in his seat and began to undo the buttons of the hated *Milice* uniform.

The safe house. A farm in Normandy. 7 a.m.

Glenn Dalton sipped at the cup of coffee and grimaced at the bitter taste. "God, don't these French know how to make java?"

"Quit your bellyaching," Tom chided as he broke open the bread, fresh and still warm from Bernadette's oven. He savored the aroma and the taste as he crunched on the crust.

"Is this all the French have for breakfast?" Dalton looked at the meager display before him. "Coffee and bread? I'm fed up with it. I'd give my right arm for some ham and eggs."

"You'd probably have to." Tom took a swig of his coffee and looked in vain for a sugar bowl. "The Germans requisition anything and everything from the French. Count your blessings. At least the butter's real. And delicious."

"Okay, so I gripe." Dalton tugged at a piece of bread. "But I've been here a week, sleeping in that hole. These farm folks are nice, but I can't understand a word they say." He wiped the back of his hand across his mouth. "But that Josse is a bastard. He promised us he'd get us out last night and we're still stuck here."

He looked at the clock. It was only seven, but the night storm had passed, and the sun had already clambered into the summer sky, casting the criss-cross shadow of the window frame across the table. "Say, what date is it? I've lost all track of time."

"Me, too. Let's see," Tom tried to construct a calendar in his mind. I came over yesterday." He turned to Bernadette, who was carrying a fresh pot of coffee to the table. *"Quelle date est-il?"* Tom knew his French was bad, but prayed for a response.

"C'est le premier Juin."

"It's the first of June." As he spoke Tom looked at Dalton. There was a silence, but each knew the other's thoughts. In four days it would come.

The quiet was broken by the farmer's bicycle rattling across the yard with some urgency. The door flew open; the old man slumped down at the table and poured himself a coffee. A heated exchange with his wife followed, conducted at a machine-gun pace that Tom could not hope to understand.

Tom stood up and spoke slowly and loudly. *"Où est M'sieur Josse?"* The couple stopped talking, the farmer looking surprised at being addressed in his own tongue by the American.

"Il vient, il vient!" Dominic pulled Tom toward the window and pointed down the road leading to the farm. *"Cinq minutes, cinq minutes."* He waved five fingers in front of Tom's face. *"Il y a une jeune femme dans la voiture – blessée, gravement blessée."* Then his voice again became a machine gun and Tom could no longer understand, although he heard the words 'German' and 'prison' several times.

"What the hell's he going on about?" Dalton's angry drawl cut across the French babble.

"I don't fully understand. Seems like Josse is going to arrive in five minutes."

"About time. Maybe he'll tell us when we're going to get out of this lousy hole."

"But there's something else. The old man said that Josse is bringing a young woman. He says she's badly wounded."

"Jesus H. Christ!" Dalton's loud curse brought an alarmed look from the farmer's wife. "As if we haven't got enough trouble on our plate! First he cancels last night's escape flight and now he turns up with some injured broad. I told you, Tom, I don't trust this guy."

"It sure is fishy, I've got to admit." Had the English called off the escape flight, or had Josse done so himself? Now there was an injured woman to contend with. What was Josse's game?

Dominic tugged on his sleeve. Tom looked through the window and saw a black Citroen limousine making its way through the mud at the entrance to the farm. His eyes caught the black uniform of the driver. Cursing that he had left his pistol in the cellar, Tom leapt across the room to seize the knife on the table.

"Non, non," the farmer confronted him, *"c'est Philippe et Henri."*

Tom felt relieved, but watched anxiously as the two men got out of the car. Henri opened the trunk and pulled out two bundles of clothing tied with string. Josse opened the rear door and lifted out what to Tom at first appeared to be another bundle of clothes. But he then detected a human form, a head and a body almost completely enveloped by a blanket. The lower part of the legs hung below the blanket; the crudely-applied bandages on the feet were red with blood.

"Stand clear, stand clear!" Josse called out as he reached the doorway. Bernadette had quickly made up a cot in the back room, and Josse gently lowered the blanket-shrouded woman onto it. The old woman put her hands to her face in shock as she looked closely at the bloodstained bandages; she shook her head and at once put a large pan of water on the stove.

"She's been badly tortured by those Gestapo swine." Josse returned to the main room and began to take off the *Milice* uniform. "She's unconscious most of the time, or in a delirium." He caught the bundle of clothes tossed to him by Henri and began to put them on. "She's ill as well as in great pain."

He spoke rapidly in French to the farmer's wife, and then turned back to Tom. "There'll be a doctor coming, but he can't get here until eleven o'clock."

Dalton's voice came from the corner of the room. "I suppose this means we're not leaving tonight?" The question had a laconic, world-weary edge.

"No, it doesn't, my American friend," Josse spoke sharply as he buttoned up his shirt, "it's essential that you leave tonight. The plane will arrive soon after midnight."

"Who is she?" Tom sat down at the table and pulled at the remnants of the loaf.

Josse thought for a few moments before he spoke. "Her name is Jeanne and she is a British agent. That is all you need to know."

"She coming with us?" Dalton nodded towards the back room.

"No, that is not part of the plan. Besides, there's no room – the plane has only two passenger seats." He put on his coat, pulled out his cigarettes and lit one. "Bernadette will look after her here until she's ready to travel." His eyes turned to the doorway of the back room and he spoke softly. "If she pulls through."

"She seems in bad shape. If you can't get her out with us, how will you get her out?"

"There are many ways." Josse was non-committal. "Perhaps a fishing boat from a village on the coast. It's done often – sometimes for American airmen who have been shot down. Are you ready, Henri?" He headed for the door, where he stopped and turned.

"After the doctor has visited, stay here in the farmhouse. Henri and I need to dispose of the car and cover our tracks. Henri will come to collect you before midnight and take you to the big landing field at the *Ferme des Hirondelles.*"

"Aren't you coming back?" Dalton's question was pointed, and Tom had half-expected it.

"I have a lot to do." Josse seemed unconcerned. "There are men to be organized, and the landing strip to be prepared. I shall see you tonight. *Au revoir.*" He turned sharply and was gone, with Henri in tow.

Tom looked at Dalton and sensed his buddy's suspicion, but, before he could say anything, a moan came from the cot in the other room. He looked through and saw Bernadette applying fresh bandages to the agent's bloodied feet. He went to the doorway; the old woman raised a finger to her lips to command his silence.

He looked to the head of the bed, but could see little in the darkness; the curtains had been pulled tightly. There was another moan, followed by an incoherent rambling. Her body twisted and turned. *"Non, non."* The whispered word came from her lips again and again. The head shook from side to side, shaking itself free from the blanket, the face coming into a patch of light from the kitchen.

"Oh, my God!" Tom moved toward the bed. "Gwen! Gwen!"

Sally's Quarters, Dartmouth, Devon. 1 p.m.

Sally pushed the plate aside; she really wasn't hungry.

The words of her father kept coming back to her. *"Your mother would turn in her grave if he knew you were going out with that oik."*

All her life she had defied her father, even if unwittingly. Her mother, daughter of the Duke of Malpass, had died when Sally, an only child, was just a baby, and her metamorphosis into a genteel young woman of society had been entrusted to Aunt Agatha, a doughty woman who preferred the company of the Cliveden Set to that of a little girl. So, left to her own devices, Sally began discovering the world on her own terms.

Like the blissful summer when she was ten, spent at her father's country house, mainly in the company of Fred, a boy of about seventeen who helped out in the garage. Fred was like an older brother: he showed her the best tree for climbing in the woods, the stream where waterfowl dived for fish, and the hollow log where she could hide her special treasures. Once Fred had shown her a vixen with her cubs; the sight of the elegant creature caring for the cuddly balls of fur took Sally's breath away.

That fall, Sally, who rode well, was deemed ready for a formal hunt. It was exciting at first – the rising before dawn, the party dressed in their pinks, the adults sipping brandy from silver cups, the hounds barking, the sound of the horn, the charge of the horses. But when she saw the dead fox dangling from the mouth of the hound, her eyes filled with tears: she remembered the beautiful vixen; somewhere there were cubs who were orphans. She recoiled when her father tried to dab her with the fox's blood in the traditional first-hunt initiation rite. In disgust, she had turned her horse and ridden away.

She preferred to watch Fred, puttering with cars in the garage, his hands, black with grease, manipulating the mysterious metal parts of the engine like a surgeon performing an operation. He explained them to her and taught her to change plugs and tires, skills she would later find more useful than the tea-pouring lessons of her aunt. Fred came from Cheapside in London – an official Cockney, born within earshot of the bells of St. Mary-le-Bow – and he taught her Cockney rhyming slang. She loved its lighthearted logic: the last word in a common phrase rhymed with the word it was to replace. So "tit for tat" was "hat," and "trouble and strife" was "wife." But the best part was that you usually dropped the rhyming word and used only the first words, so "your wife's hat" became "your trouble's titfer." She picked the argot up quickly from Fred and it became their secret language.

That blissful summer came to an end when, in the presence of her father and his friends, she accidentally used some Cockney slang. The stunned silence was suddenly sliced asunder by Aunt Agatha's patrician voice: "Well, really, if Sally is to speak a foreign language, shouldn't it be French?" Soon after, she was packed off to Haberdasher's School for Girls.

As she grew older, she learned to fit into her father's world. She had been groomed for high society, but she never felt comfortable in it. Then came the war. Strangely, for her it had been wonderful – a liberation that had taken her away from an artificial world to do something useful. And, had it not been for the war, she never would have met Danny. Whatever her father said about him, she knew he was a positive force in her life.

But she hadn't heard from him for nearly a week, and he usually called every day. Was he deliberately avoiding her?

The Farm. Normandy. 2 p.m.

Gwen an agent? Tom found it difficult to believe. He remembered the walk across the headland; he saw again her spinning on her toes as she reached for the happiness of the spring sky, so far from war. But now she was lying in the next room, broken in body and mind. He recalled the sadness of their parting, after he had told her about his estranged wife. Now she was so close to him, but he could not tell her what he needed to say.

148

The visit of the French doctor had been brief. He had felt her forehead, taken her temperature and pulse, and had shaken his head. His hand had dipped into his bag, emerged with syringe and ampoule, and proceeded to give an injection. Tom had tried to ask questions, but his French was not good enough, and the doctor had cast his eyes about him, clearly anxious to leave such a dangerous spot. All Tom had found out was that Gwen – or Jeanne – would sleep for at least twelve hours. After that... the doctor had shrugged his shoulders as he left; he would return the next day, if possible.

Suddenly, the door flew open and Dominic burst into the room. He rushed to the window, and an incomprehensible babble of French ensued as he shouted at his wife. Bernadette threw her hands to her cheeks, her face suddenly a grim mask of panic and fear. Tom moved quickly between the couple and grasped the man's shoulders.

"Parlez lentement, m'sieur." Tom looked into the terrified eyes of the Frenchman, who spoke as slowly as his fear would let him.

"Les Bosches viennent. Ils pillent toutes les fermes dans le voisinage."

"There's a problem?" Dalton leapt from his chair.

"The Germans are coming. Apparently they're raiding all the farms in the neighborhood."

Dalton needed no second bidding. He rushed to the trapdoor leading to the cellar, heading for his secret hiding place.

Tom whipped around to see Dalton beginning to go down the steps. "But what about the woman? Shouldn't we put her in the—?" His question went unanswered as Dalton slammed the trapdoor closed behind him. Tom heard the bolt go home.

Before Tom could do anything, Bernadette shuffled quickly across the floor, rearranged the rug over the trapdoor and pushed the table over the rug, all the time gabbling at her husband so fast that Tom could not grasp a word.

He tried to overcome the grip of panic. He had to get Gwen to safety. His hands reached out and grabbed the old woman's shoulders. "What about Gwen? What about the woman?" She looked at him, her face frozen in incomprehension and fear.

He struggled to find the French words. *"Mais la femme?"* He nodded to the cot in the next room.

Tom could see the petrified look in the woman's eyes. Once the Germans found they were hiding agents, it would be all over.

"La grange." Dominic pointed to the barn across the yard. *"Portez-la à la grange!"*

The barn. Tom knew he had no option. Even if he had not left his pistol in the cellar, he could not fight off a German platoon alone. He raced into the bedroom and hurriedly slipped his hands under Gwen's blanket. She was no lightweight, he thought, as he lifted her from the cot. He remembered how she had powerfully pulled him onto the headland at Hope Cove. There was no protest, no sound as he placed her across his shoulder. Dominic waved his arms, hurrying him out of the door.

Tom's feet slipped, but he kept his balance as he ploughed his way through the mud toward the barn. His lungs heaving, he glanced quickly over his shoulder down the road. There was still nothing in sight. How long did he have? His free hand yanked on the barn door. Before him was a floor, strewn with straw. Ahead, a wooden ladder leaned against a rafter, leading to an upper level with many bales of hay.

Tom shifted Gwen's frame to his other shoulder and began to climb the rungs, his ears listening fearfully for any sound coming from the road. The sweat broke out on his brow as he clutched at the last rung with his free arm, feeling the ladder shake with the weight it bore. For a second, he felt he was losing his balance, but he leaned forward and the ladder steadied, groaning against his efforts.

Then the sounds came: the urgent screaming of the motor cycle, the lower drone of a truck, the guttural German shouts. He heaved Gwen onto the floor of the loft, jumped up after her, and was about to kick the ladder away when he realized that, if it lay on the floor, it would be as good as a calling card to the Germans.

The noises came closer. There was the piercing screech of brakes as he lifted Gwen over the closely-packed bales. The sweat of exertion and fear glued his shirt to his back; his breathing was heavy as he lowered her into a small alcove between the bales and a small open window that overlooked the farmyard. He resisted the temptation to close the window, and hurriedly scooped armfuls of loose hay over Gwen until she was covered to a depth of three feet.

The sounds coming through the window were confused. Angry German shouts, frightened French voices. Then the creak of the barn door. Frantically, Tom heaped more loose hay into a space by Gwen's side and burrowed his way under it. He fought to lie completely still, to bring his breathing under control.

The ladder creaked under a soldier's boot. Suddenly, he felt Gwen begin to stir. Not now, Gwen. Sleep, for God's sake, sleep. He gently edged closer to her, and felt the L-pill tin box press against his chest.

Canterbury, England 2 p.m.

The three stars on each shoulder of the general's jacket glinted in the sunlight as he stroked his bull terrier, Willie, behind the ears. General George S. Patton knew that his entire existence had been propelled by destiny toward one single, shining moment in history: the most important military operation the world would ever see – the invasion to liberate Europe. But at the last minute, fate had pulled the rug out from under him. His official role in the invasion was essentially the same as the part played by a carved wooden decoy in a duck hunt. When the invasion took place, he'd be sitting in England on his ass making believe, for the benefit of the Germans, that the real invasion was coming in another month, maybe another year. Pretending the real invasion would be targeting the Pas de Calais, not Normandy.

A year ago, when he liberated Sicily, he had been hailed as the boldest war hero of all time, so it was a knock-out blow when Omar Bradley, his former junior officer, was given command of the invasion forces by Ike. Maybe it was some sort of schoolboy punishment for his having slapped that coward in the hospital, that mental case private whose so-called nerves kept him off the battlefield. Then things got worse. He had made some off-the-record remarks which the newspapers had got hold of and had blown all out of proportion. Supposedly, he had slighted America's charming comrades-in-arms, the Ruskies, whose Commie bastard leader Stalin was even worse than Hitler. Ike almost sent him packing over that incident.

Whatever the cause, his once ascendant star had taken a nose-dive. His official role in the great event, the event for which his entire life and career had been a preamble, was pretending that he commanded the phony 'First Army Group,' a force supposedly poised to attack the Germans at the Pas de Calais. The 'First Army Group' was bogus, nothing more than a film set and props. The irony made him want to puke: he, a fighting man's man, Old Blood-and-Guts himself, was now the commander of a bunch of set designers and fake radio units. Jesus, Mary, and Joseph.

True, he admitted, these guys were effective at what they were asked to do. They'd built a vast army post that was little more than plywood and canvas, around which tanks and jeeps moved with all the strategic purpose of the cleverly-designed balloons they actually were. But they looked great from the air, which is where the Germans would be seeing them. Dumb Kraut bastards.

Okay, so the fake radio units were good, too. Working from a script eight inches thick, they created the illusion of a huge invasion army and kept the wires buzzing with all sorts of bogus communications. He could barely suppress a chuckle at the thought of the Germans analyzing all that meaningless crap.

Still, he itched to get into the real fray. Okay, he was training the Third Army group which would go in after the invasion forces gained a foothold. But goddamn – he'd miss the event that really meant something – the cross-channel invasion, the watershed of the whole war.

Balls. He reached for his bottle of bourbon.

The Farm. 2:10 p.m.

One by one, the rungs of the ladder creaked as the German soldier's boots scraped against them. Tom fought to keep his breathing slow. Gwen's face was close, a few wisps of hay separating them as they lay under the mound of straw he had built over them. The bruises on her cheeks were purple and angry, but she had stopped stirring and now lay still. As he looked at her, Tom remembered other days, and vowed to himself that they would survive this horror, that they would get back to England, that—

A German voice called out from the top of the ladder; a guttural response came from below, from the floor of the barn. Tom knew that he and Gwen could not be seen because they were behind a wall of bales of hay. He prayed that the soldier would make nothing more than a cursory search of the loft before going back down the ladder.

Suddenly his body tensed. Despite her drug-induced sleep, Gwen moved slightly. There were more angry shouts coming from the yard. Gwen stirred again and her lips began to move, but soundlessly. No, Gwen, please don't speak. Tom pressed himself to her, feeling her warm body against his.

He heard the soldier speak again to his mate below. Perhaps he would go back down the ladder, drawn to the commotion in the yard. Tom reached into his pocket and pulled out the L-pill.

Gwen moaned, and Tom pushed his lips to hers, kissing her to stifle the sound; there was no response. The German came on; Tom could feel the boards of the loft floor buckle under the soldier's weight. There was the swish of his bayonet as he thrust it into the loose hay. Tom thrust the L-pill between his teeth and again pressed his lips to Gwen's. One bite, and it would all be over; for him, for Gwen.

The bayonet came through the hay, pushing and prodding. The cold steel came closer, ever probing. Tom saw it in a brief flash, and then it was gone. One more thrust and…. He clenched his teeth on the pill.

Suddenly, there was uproar in the yard below. Orders were barked out, and Tom realized the German soldier had stopped his search. There was a shout from the man below, and the soldier began to retrace his steps down the ladder.

Tom waited until he heard the barn door slam shut before slowly removing his lips from Gwen's and carefully pulling the pill from his mouth. He looked at her still face, calm and unknowing, as his body shook involuntarily with relief. He breathed deeply to regain his self-control, but there was a new fear. Perhaps they had found Dalton! There were still noises from the yard. He edged noise-lessly to the wall of the loft and put an eye to a crack in the planking.

Dominic and Bernadette were being brutally manhandled into the back of a truck. An officer came from the farmhouse carrying a wooden box. Tom's heart sank; they had found the radio. He watched with a sick ache in his heart as the couple was thrown into the truck. Despite the extreme threat to them, there had been no betrayal. They had helped him and Dalton, offered the hos-pitality of their home, despite the danger, when they could have kept their noses clean and stood apart from a war that would now claim their lives.

The officer put the radio in the cab of the truck as the soldiers climbed into the back and closed the tailgate. As soon as the officer lowered himself into the sidecar of the motorcycle, he gave the signal and the small convoy headed for the gate. Tom watched as the vehicles swung onto the road and waited until the noise of the engines died away. The only sound coming from the yard was the incessant barking of Dominic's dog, pining for his master.

Tom looked over at Gwen. She was resting peacefully again, her breathing deep and even. It was nearly three o'clock, at least seven hours until dark, when Henri would come to get them. If he came. Word of the Germans' raid would spread very quickly through the neighborhood; it was more than likely that Henri would not come back.

He moved the straw from Gwen's sleeping form and tried to form a plan of action, but was distracted by the plaintive yowling of the dog in the yard. Perhaps he could find the airfield himself; he wasn't sure of its exact whereabouts, but he knew it wasn't far. Above all, he had to take Gwen. But how? He had no transport and he couldn't carry her alone. He wasn't sure about Dalton. His time in the Gestapo prison had soured him; he was unreliable. He slumped down on his haunches, his hands clamped over his ears to shut out the yapping of the dog, trying to think.

His head fell onto his chest. The task was impossible. He didn't know where to go, how to get there, how to take Gwen. He looked at her, seeking an inspiration that did not come; the weight of his helplessness bore down upon him.

A shot rang out in the yard. He leapt to his feet. There was an agonized howl and the barking stopped. Tom rushed back to the gap in the planking. Dominic's dog lay in the yard, twitching in its death throes. His eyes moved to the farmhouse door. A soldier propped his rifle against the wall and lit a cigarette. The Germans had left a sentry behind.

A restaurant in Carteret, Normandy. 2:30 p.m.

Despite his success, Richter was not content, although he had every reason to be so. He had captured one of the greatest secrets of the war; Himmler had been effusive with the Führer's praise, and had promoted him with immediate effect.

Obersturmbannführer! Another feather in his cap. But still the doubts nagged him. Again, he thought through all the evidence that Colonel Schumann had laid before him, detail by detail, but could find no fault. Müller's interrogation of the woman had confirmed what Josse had said.

Richter emptied his wine glass and looked out of the restaurant's window to see the street bathed by a sun past its noon-time high. His chauffeur had driven him to Carteret for lunch, to a favorite bistro. The waiters were sometimes surly, but prudently deferred to the rank his uniform proclaimed. And the food was excellent; for the head of the Normandy Gestapo, there was no rationing. The butter-rich *soupe à l'oignon* had been followed by a delicious *gigot d'agneau* stiff with garlic, all washed down with a smooth Medoc. He smiled as the waiter brought the chocolate soufflé he'd ordered at the start of the meal.

Why was he worrying? Everything was going so well. He picked up a spoon and poked into the soufflé, watching it deflate. Perhaps Schumann was right. Perhaps he was paranoid.

But the doubt returned and grew. His men had not found the body of the American. Their report had stated that the well was derelict and too deep for immediate investigation; specialists would be needed, and they would have to come from Caen. But why had there been no mention in the report of smell? Surely a decomposing body would produce enough stench to disturb even the roughest soldier's nose? He tried to dispel the image by savoring the bouquet of the cognac *digestif* placed before him, but he made a mental note to question the soldiers again.

But he knew where the real answers lay. Josse. Apart from the dead American, everything the Frenchman had said to him had been proved correct. The master plan of the Allies, the agent's landing with the proof of the plan, the date, Verlaine's couplets, all verified by the captured documents. But Josse had disappeared. Why? Of course, the Frenchman always worked in devious ways. Yet he took the bribe money easily enough, and his information was generally reliable and worthwhile.

But Richter's gut feeling told him not to trust Josse. It irked the Gestapo chief that he could not confirm this emotion with reason, and that at the moment of his greatest triumph, he still harbored doubts.

The door to the bistro flew open. The chauffeur looked flustered, but came to attention and saluted.

"Yes, what is it?" Richter was angry that his enjoyment of the final moments of his lunch had been disturbed.

"There is a call for you on the field telephone, *mein Herr*. The commandant of the prison at Coutances."

Richter scowled, threw some banknotes onto the table and made his way to the car. The chauffeur handed him the telephone.

"*Ja*, Humboldt? Richter here."

"*Obersturmbannführer*, I fear there has been an irregularity."

"Irregularity? Be precise."

"Two *Milice* men arrived in the early hours with a warrant to collect a prisoner. The duty officer complied with the warrant."

"Why are you bothering me with these petty bureaucratic details? Can't you run a prison on your own?"

"I checked with the local *Milice* this morning," there was a touch of fear in the commandant's voice, "regrettably, they had no record of sending a patrol to collect a prisoner."

"Why didn't you check at the time, you fool?" Richter shouted into the mouthpiece. "Who was the prisoner?"

"The young woman. Jeanne Busson."

"*Mein Gott!*" Richter's face reddened with his growing fury. "Are you all idiots? You let a prisoner go without checking?"

154

"It seems that the duty officer was convinced that the warrant was authentic, *mein Herr.*"

"Why didn't he check? Why didn't he call the signatory to the warrant?" Richter spat his question at the telephone.

"It was three o'clock in the morning."

"That's an excuse? I want the duty officer court-martialed!" Richter was screaming with rage. "He should have dragged the signatory from his bed, whatever the hour." He angrily pummeled the car with his fist. "And which *Dummkopf* signed this warrant?"

There was a brief silence at the other end. "According to the duty officer, you did, *mein Herr.*" There was a hasty addition. "Obviously, it's a forgery."

Richter bristled, trying to contain the last vestige of self control. "Josse. It can only be Josse's work. Put out a full alert for him. At once. I want him arrested. Alive." He slammed the receiver down.

The Farm. 3 p.m.

Tom kissed Gwen's forehead. She did not stir from her drug-induced sleep. Yes, my love, he thought, sleep. Sleep well. Please sleep until we're safe. He remembered her, looking out to sea from the Bolt Tail headland, then peering down at the chessboard, stealing glances at him between moves.

The sound of the sentry's cough brought him back sharply to the immediate, dangerous present. There could be no hope of safety until he had dealt with the German and released Dalton from his hiding place. He went down the ladder slowly and pressed his back to the wall of the barn, edging his way toward the door. There was an opening where the hinges were set and he looked through it. He saw the sentry prop his rifle against the wall and go into the house. Tom tensed. Perhaps this was his chance – he could sprint across and grab the rifle. But the soldier emerged from the house with a chair and a bottle of wine; his head went back as he drank deeply.

Tom weighed the situation. The German's pals could come back at any time. He needed five seconds, a diversion of five seconds so he could cross the yard and get around the back of the farmhouse. Then he could move through the house and tackle the sentry from behind.

He leaned back against the wooden wall of the barn and was alarmed when it creaked. He put his head quickly back to his peephole. The German had got up from the chair and was picking up his rifle.

Tom fought the grip of panic. He could go back quickly to the loft. Or he could wait until the sentry came into the barn and pounce on him. He had almost decided on the latter when he watched the German sling the rifle over his shoulder, lift the bottle to his lips and empty it, before walking to the wall that enclosed the yard.

The soldier was trying to balance the empty bottle on the uneven wall. At the first attempt, the bottle fell into the mud at the foot of the wall. Perhaps this was Tom's chance to run, but the sentry succeeded at his second attempt, pulled his rifle from his shoulder and returned to his chair.

Tom froze when the soldier raised his weapon, but then realized he was taking aim at the bottle. He was bored! The Kraut was bored and was amusing himself with target practice. Tom jumped instinctively at the sound of the first shot. Then a second, a third. He was about to chance running across the yard, but the shattering of glass held him back. He peeked again and saw the German get up from the chair and go back into the house.

Tom moved quickly across the yard to the side wall. Ducking beneath the windows, he began to make his way to the back of the house, his breath quickening.

When he reached the back door he paused. All the nervous tension in his body urged him on, but he held back. Patience. He had to wait, wait for the shots from the sentry's rifle. He strained his ears, but there was no sound except the trilling of a bird basking in the afternoon sun.

A German curse cut across the birdsong, then the sound that Tom was waiting for. Crack! He moved as soon as he heard the shot, pulling open the door, making his way swiftly through the kitchen. Crack! He cast his eyes about him frantically. He needed a weapon to deal with the German. Crack! There was the sound of broken glass and a cry of triumph from outside. A weapon, he needed a weapon. His eyes lit upon Bernadette's cheese cutter, a long thin wire between wooden handles. Tom grasped it quickly. At any moment, the German would come through the door looking for another bottle. He breathed deeply, formed a loop with the wire and stood behind the door.

The latch rattled. The German lurched into the room, half turning as the loop dropped over his head and beneath his chin. Tom's arm muscles bulged as he pulled the wire tight.

The Farm. 3:30 p.m.

Tom vomited into the kitchen sink. He picked up a towel, wiped the spittle from his lips and dabbed at the blood that soaked his coat. He looked across at the German's body lying in the doorway, the head half severed. His stomach heaved again, but it was empty. He turned on the tap and thrust his head under the flow of cold water.

He'd never killed before, not even when his father had taken him on hunting trips. There were those in the army, he knew, for whom killing was routine, no more unusual than shaving in the morning. But the killing wasn't always done close up. A bomb dropped from a great height, a rifle shot from a hundred yards. Impersonal. The push of a button, the pull of the trigger. They did not smell their victim's fear, nor feel the writhing of his death throes.

Tom ran his hands through his wet hair and looked across at the body. The German had a mother, perhaps a wife. Tom rationalized to dispel his guilt and to preserve his sanity. The German would have done the same to him, shot him as he had shot the poor dog. Kill or be killed. That's what they said, wasn't it?

Gwen. She was still out there, in the barn. He had to work out a plan to get her onto the plane to England. He wiped his face again on the towel and then tossed it over the German's head.

The chair groaned as he flopped into it. He was exhausted and drained. The Germans could come back at any time. Why would they leave a sentry, unless they intended to return? And Henri, who was supposed to come back later to lead them to the aircraft landing field – surely the grapevine would tell him of the Germans' visit, of Dominic and Bernadette's arrest? He'd avoid the farm like the plague.

He searched desperately for any crumb of comfort. He remembered Josse's mentioning '*Le grand champ à la Ferme des Hirondelles.*' But where was the big field at Swallow Farm? And even if he knew, how was he going to get Gwen there, locked as she was in deep sedation?

He decided to get Gwen back to the farmhouse before checking out Dalton in the cellar. He looked through the windows before racing across the yard to the barn. By the time he returned and lowered Gwen from his shoulder onto the cot, he was sweating and breathing heavily. He would need help to get her to the field where the plane would land. If he could find out where the field was.

Tom moved the table to one side and tried the trapdoor. It was still bolted. Dalton hadn't moved. Tom banged on the trapdoor.

Crack! Tom rolled away as the pistol shot rang out. Crack! Another shot followed.

"Glenn, it's me, you fool! Stop shooting!"

There was silence for a few moments before Dalton's face emerged.

"I'm sorry, Tom. I heard shooting and footsteps. I thought the Germans were coming to search the cellar."

"They've gone now." Tom got back to his feet and pointed at Dalton's pistol. "You need to be careful with that thing. Where did you get it?"

"Josse gave it to me." Dalton was already climbing the steps to the kitchen. "We gotta get out of here. He stopped short when he saw the German's body.

"What the hell is that?"

"It's a sentry the Germans left behind. I had to kill him."

"Well, you sure did a good job." Dalton moved to the sideboard, reached for a half empty bottle of wine, lifted it to his lips and drained it. He slumped into a chair and began to reload his pistol.

"Let's scram!" Dalton's gun was shaking so much it seemed to have a will of its own.

"Glenn, we don't know where to go. Josse told us that the plane would land at Swallow Farm, but we don't have the slightest idea where it is. Henri's supposed to come back later to pick us up, but after the German raid," he shrugged, "who knows?"

"Josse. That son of a bitch. Have you noticed how he left and within a couple of hours the Germans arrived?"

Tom's head dropped. Perhaps they could not trust the Frenchman. But would he really betray Dominic and Bernadette, his own countrymen?

"We gotta go." Dalton slammed home the pistol's magazine and headed for the door.

"But where are we going to go?"

"We'll have to take our chances. Anything's better than staying here. The Krauts are sure to come back for him," he cocked a thumb over his shoulder towards the body, "and they're gonna be a bit pissed off when they find him."

Tom placed himself between Dalton and the door. "We're not going anywhere without her." He inclined his head to the bedroom.

"What's she to us?" Dalton shrugged the argument aside. "Whoever finds her, German or French, they'll look after her."

"Glenn, she's a British agent. She's already been tortured. We can't leave her behind." Tom hesitated, wondering if he should say more. "Besides, I know her. We met in England."

"Big deal, Tom. But we gotta think about the secret we know. A lot of our buddies depend on us. What if the Germans caught us? And tortured us?" There was fear and panic in Dalton's voice. "I say we go now."

"We don't leave without her." Tom squared up to Dalton.

"Tom, you're a fool. The Krauts could be back at any minute." He tried to go around Tom, whose arms barred the doorway.

"You heard what I said, Glenn...."

There was a noise from the road. They both spun around.

"They're coming back!" Dalton pulled his pistol from his pocket and rushed to the open window. Tom peered around the doorway. There was movement behind the farm wall, but he couldn't be sure what it was. He looked down the road. There were no vehicles.

Crack! Tom looked across the room. The shot came from Dalton's pistol. "They're coming! They're coming!" Crack! Crack!

Tom looked out of the door again and saw a movement of white fabric. "Oh, my God!" For a moment he was paralyzed with shock. Crack!

"For Christ's sake, stop shooting!" He hurled himself across the room at Dalton, pulling him from the window and throwing him to the floor.

"You idiot, it's a little girl!"

The Farm. 3:45 p.m.

The child lay awkwardly by the wall just beyond the gate to the yard. About eight years old, Tom thought. He approached her slowly. She looked like a stricken butterfly, her arms flapping spasmodically. Her white pinafore was bespattered with mud, but Tom offered thanks to Heaven that he could see no blood.

Tom looked beneath the cloche-shaped hat and could see she was sobbing and simpering, her lower lip quivering as her lungs clutched unevenly and raggedly at the air.

"Non! Non!" She kicked out at him as he squatted beside her. A trace of mud came to her cheeks as she wiped away her tears. *"Non!"* She kicked out again.

Tom raised his hands slowly, palms towards her. *"Il est bien."* She sobbed again, but her frightened eyes looked at him.

"Il est bien, il est bien." Tom repeated, his mind desperately searching his limited French vocabulary for other words to allay the fear in the terrified eyes that seemed to occupy most of her face. He reached out and offered his hand to the child. *"Venez, venez avec moi."*

There was a vigorous shake of the dark curls that hung down behind the hat. He realized that his blood-stained uniform frightened her. Tom reached into his pocket and pulled out a small chocolate bar. She looked at him, then to the chocolate, the eyes undecided between fear of him and desire for the treat. With a sudden movement, she snatched the bar from his hand, and then withdrew as she unwrapped the chocolate and popped it into her mouth.

Tom watched the mixed feelings on the child's face as the chocolate melted on her tongue. She picked herself up.

"Où est ma grand-mère?"

Tom knew he must not tell her what had happened. He grappled with the French words and told her that her grandparents had gone to get groceries as he took her bicycle and led her to the farmhouse. Suddenly, she dropped his hand and ran towards the door.

Tom raced after her. She mustn't see the dead German! He grabbed her by the sleeve. The girl spun around and he could see the fear return to her eyes. Another piece of chocolate appeared in his hand and a brief smile came to her lips. He was glad the Brits had given him the chocolate. He knelt down beside her so she wouldn't feel intimidated.

"Comment vous appelez-vous?" He smiled.

"Je m'appelle Céleste." She held the chocolate to her lips. *"Et vous?"*

"Tom."

"Tom?" Her eyebrows lifted. *"C'est un nom drôle."* She tossed the chocolate into her mouth.

Yes, Tom thought, a funny name. The door opened and Dalton stuck his head out.

"Oh, it's her."

"You know her?" Tom's brow creased in surprise.

"She comes around some evenings. Josse told me her father was killed early in the war and her mother went nuts and was put in some loony bin." Dalton forced a smile to his lips as he looked down at the girl. "Some kinfolk or friends look after her in town. The old folks are her grandparents."

"Well, she's the German you shot at." There was acid in his voice as he comforted the girl, who had become frightened again with Dalton's presence.

159

"How the hell was I to know?" Dalton ran his fingers through his unkempt hair. "And now we got another damned problem." He scowled. "First Josse dumps an injured broad on us, and now we've got a sniveling brat. We don't know where to go and the Krauts could be here at any minute to find their buddy has been relieved of his head." His hand shook as he lit a cigarette. "Any ideas, buddy?" He flicked the match away. "After all, you were the quarterback."

"At the moment, no, but I'm looking for a Hail Mary pass." Tom didn't look at Dalton as he spoke, but smiled at the little girl as he gazed into her eyes. "But your first play is to move the body to the cellar and cover up the mess. We don't want this child to see it, do we?"

"Jesus H. Christ!" Dalton pushed on the door and went into the farmhouse.

Tom felt the little fingers grab at his hand.

"Un autre chocolat, s'il vous plaît?"

The Farm. 5 p.m.

Tom felt Gwen's forehead; there was no change in her condition. At least she was still sleeping. He tucked the blankets around her on her cot and made his way back to the living room.

"Jesus, I'm clean out of cigarettes." Dalton crumpled his packet but didn't get up from his seat in the window alcove, from where he was watching the road. He shaded his eyes against the sun. "No sign yet. Maybe the Krauts aren't coming back today. Or maybe they'll come back after dark. Either way, we're in a jam, Tom, and all you do is jabber in French with the kid."

"Here." Tom tossed a pack of Gitanes across the room. "My talk with Céleste," the girl looked up at him at the mention of her name, "has given us an outside chance of getting out of here." He returned to the doorway of the back room, listening to Gwen's regular breathing.

Dalton drew on his cigarette and coughed several times. "Jeez, this French tobacco is crap. So, how's the kid gonna get us out of here?" He coughed again. "She got a magic wand?"

"In a way, yes. She knows where Swallow Farm is – where the airstrip is located."

Dalton's eyes widened as he jumped down from his perch at the window. "Why didn't you say so earlier? Let's blow this joint!"

"Later, when it gets dark. The plane isn't scheduled to arrive until after midnight, remember?"

"No, let's go before the Germans get back. Which way do we go?"

"I'm not sure. I can't translate the directions. It seems we have to go through some woods. I'll tell the girl we're going to meet her grandparents there." He cast his eyes downwards. "Okay, it's a lie, but she'll hear the bad news soon enough. In any case she'll show us the way."

"Surely there'll be some barn near the field where we can hide and wait for the plane?" Dalton pulled on his coat.

"We're not leaving without her." Tom spoke quietly but firmly, his jaw set as he pointed to the other room.

"For chrissake, Tom," Dalton became agitated, "she's at death's door."

Dalton reacted to Tom's angry look. "And what if the Germans capture and torture us? Forget about us, what about the invasion plans? Isn't your mission to get me out of here? Who said anything about a British agent?" He shouted in his desperation, and the frightened girl looked at him with eyes agog.

Tom waited until the tirade had ended. "Glenn, we've already discussed it. She goes with us. We can't go until the sun has almost gone. Think what it would look like – a young girl and two men with hardly a smattering of French carrying an injured woman along the road in broad daylight." He shook his head. "We'd be lucky to get half a mile without the cover of darkness."

Dalton realized he had little choice but to accept the plan, but still snorted his exasperation. "So how we gonna get her there? The woman's no light weight, you know. You gonna hail a cab?"

There was a noisy clatter as Tom upended the dining table, causing Dalton and the girl to jump.

"Break the legs off this table while I look around for a hammer and nails. We'll leave at dusk."

The Farm. 9:30 p.m.

Tom looked down at the little girl dozing in the armchair, her limbs akimbo like a rag doll. He wished to God he had no need to disturb her, but he knew that soon he must; there was no other way out, except for her to lead them, hopefully to safety. He decided she could sleep a little longer as he looked through the doorway to see the sun touch the horizon. When the sky began to darken, that would be the time to move. Until then, he could leave her with her dreams.

"Well, I hope that works." Dalton looked at the table top lying on the floor; the legs had been removed and fitted crudely to the corners, to act as stretcher handles. "I think it's time to go, Tom."

"Yep, you're right. Help me put her onto the stretcher."

The two men lifted the makeshift stretcher, took it through to the next room and laid it next to the cot.

"Before we lift her down, help me with these." Tom produced the four leather reins he had found in the barn. They lifted the tabletop and slipped two of the reins underneath.

There was no movement from Gwen as they lifted her from the cot and lowered the mattress to the stretcher. Tom put his ear in front of Gwen's mouth, buried in the sheets. He felt the warmth of her breath on his cheek and felt easier.

"I'll tie her down with the reins, Glenn; you tie the other reins to the handles and then we'll drape them across our shoulders to help ease the weight. And then we'll get out of here."

Tom fastened Gwen down, then returned to the armchair and gently shook Céleste. The child stirred, opened her eyes and jumped in fear at first when she saw Tom's face. After a few moments, she recognized a friend, but her voice was anxious. *"Où est ma grand-mère?"*

Tom winced inwardly. He didn't want to cause the child any hurt; he lied, telling her that her grandparents were waiting for her at Swallow Farm.

Her hand reached forward for chocolate. Tom's hands went for his pants pockets, but came up empty. He shook his head, put on a sorry face and showed her his empty palms. He pointed to the door.

"Allons-y!"

Céleste looked apprehensive, but she tightened the ribbon of her bonnet, before speaking to Tom at length.

"What'd she say? What's she jabbering about?" Dalton lifted his end of the stretcher as Tom gave the command.

"She said we leave the farm, go about half a mile to the crossroads and then turn left." Tom ensured that the stretcher safely negotiated the narrow doorway. "Then it gets a bit complicated. Seems we have to go off the road and through some woods. But she says it's only two miles to Swallow Farm."

The strange procession made its way through the farmyard gate: the little French girl leading the two American officers, who carried an injured English woman strapped to a makeshift stretcher. There was still a fading gray light, enough to discern the road and the hedgerows, but Tom knew they would soon need a flashlight, and he had given one to Céleste to use when it was too dark to see.

He adjusted his stride to fall in step with Dalton, who was holding the front poles. Gwen rocked as they walked, restrained by the straps and still unconscious. What if Dalton was right? What if Josse was a double-dealing traitor? Suppose he'd arranged for a German squad to meet them?

Tom did his best to shrug off the thoughts. There was no option but to go on. He looked beyond Dalton's heaving shoulders to Céleste, who strode forward like a little soldier. He realized that their safety and the security of the whole invasion were entrusted to a little French girl.

They would need the luck of the devil or the intervention of the Almighty to get them home safely. Either would do.

On the road to Swallow Farm. 11 p.m.

The night was warm. There was not a whisper of wind; a few wisps of cloud hung like a lace curtain in front of a moon not quite full. And it was quiet; there was no sound along the road, apart from the footfalls of the strange group making its way to Swallow Farm.

Céleste was tired, but she felt as if she were in some big adventure. She looked over her shoulder at the men carrying the woman on a stretcher. Strange men, from a foreign land. Perhaps the woman was a princess who was being rescued. *Oui, une princesse!* And the handsome man who had given her chocolate was a prince! She wasn't quite sure about the grumpy man. Maybe he was the prince's faithful friend, a knight.

"Jesus Christ, Tom, we gotta rest soon;" Dalton spoke with labored breath, "it's like hauling the Statue of Liberty."

"Keep going, Glenn," Tom muttered encouragingly, although he, too, was sweating. "We'll rest as soon as we get off the road." Céleste had said it was necessary to avoid a village where there were Germans.

They followed the girl as she left the road and followed a path leading to the woods. The leaves shaded the moonlight, and it became very dark. They slowly lowered the stretcher by the side of the path.

"Céleste, *venez.*" Tom took the flashlight from her and checked Gwen. She was still unconscious, her pulse slow but regular.

Céleste looked at Tom. She was sure he was a prince, even though he came from America, and Madame Lyons, her teacher, had told her that there were no princes in America. But he was brave and handsome, and she no longer felt frightened.

Suddenly, there was noise from the road they had just left.

"Hit the deck!" Tom hissed. Dalton threw himself to the ground. Tom killed the flashlight and grabbed Céleste, sheltering her under his arms as he lay beside the stretcher.

The engine noises came nearer – the headlights of two vehicles were coming along the road.

"*M'sieur, m'sieur!*" Céleste whimpered.

Tom had not realized that he was almost smothering the girl. He eased his grip. "Ssh!" She lay silent in his arms. He felt pressure on his fingers. The squeeze of a small hand. He squeezed back.

The first vehicle was a staff car, caught in the headlights of the second. The other vehicle seemed to be a half-track, a troop carrier. Tom tensed himself for the squeal of brakes, but the headlights of the German vehicles swung around the bend in the road, drew abreast of them and sped past.

After they had disappeared back into the darkness, Dalton raised his head. "They're going to the farm!" He leapt to his feet. "And when they find their dead buddy, all hell will break loose. The Krauts will be all over everywhere."

"Stop panicking, Glenn," Tom said calmly as he hauled himself upright, "we can still make it." He switched on the flashlight again and looked down at Céleste.

"*Ce n'est pas loin?*" He spoke slowly.

"*Trente minutes.*" She pointed down the path leading through the woods.

"What are you chattering about?" Glenn rubbed his shoulders where the leather straps had cut in. "I can't believe we're putting our lives in the hands of a French brat!"

"You got any other suggestions?" Tom reached down and held Céleste's hand. "She says the farm is only a half-hour away. Let's go." He gave the flashlight to the girl and motioned her to lead the way before taking his position at the rear of the stretcher. Dalton shrugged sullenly, but bent down to put the harness over his shoulders and, at Tom's signal, they lifted Gwen from the ground.

"Suivez-moi!" The girl set off along the path with her flashlight.

"She said to follow her."

There was an element of truth in what Dalton had said. They were entrusting their lives to the tiny speck of humanity that walked before them, guiding them they knew not where.

Céleste was unaware of this burden. She moved forward with a determined look on her face. She would help the prince save his princess.

Dalton slipped, and cursed as he tried to keep the stretcher level. "Tom, we ain't got a snowball's chance in hell. We're probably walking into one of Josse's traps."

"It's the only chance we got."

Céleste turned and called to them. *"Vite, c'est pas loin."*

They were going downhill, and the end of the wood was in sight. Beyond the trees, the moonlight bathed a grassy knoll that dropped quickly to a road lined with hedgerows. On the other side of the road was a vast field.

"Arrêtez la lumière!" Tom called in a hoarse whisper; Céleste switched off the light.

"We'll take a rest here, before we leave the woods." Tom heard a thankful sigh from his colleague as they lowered the stretcher.

Dalton breathed heavily as he squatted on the grass. "Next time you fall in love, buddy, pick someone like Shirley Temple instead of Mae West."

Despite the hopelessness of their situation, they both chuckled, to the amazement of Céleste, who perched herself on a log and looked at them wide-eyed. She pointed down the slope to the field. *"C'est la Ferme des Hirondelles. Nous sommes arrivés."*

Tom saw the puzzled look on Dalton's face. "She says we're there;" he nodded to the field beyond the road, "that's Swallow Farm."

It was nearly midnight. The plane would come soon. If it came at all. He peered down at the field. Was Josse there? He narrowed his eyes: he was almost certain he could see some activity – a movement in the moonlight. Or was it just the shadows of trees? Even with the lack of certainty, he knew they had to act.

"Glenn, we should make tracks." He checked the restraints holding Gwen and stood up.

"Why don't we wait for the sound of the plane? That way, we'll know we've got half a chance."

It was a good point, Tom thought. As he weighed the options, the problem solved itself. Dalton leapt to his feet. The sound came from the north, the faint, but steady drone of a single aircraft. They lifted the stretcher and got back into harness.

The strange column, almost ghostly in the moonlight, made its way down to the road. Céleste trudged sleepily at the front, followed by the weary Americans.

Tom was now sure there was movement in the field. Shadows flitted across the grass, but to some purpose, perhaps preparing their lamps to guide the pilot in. But French or German? There was no sound as the figures silently moved into position.

"D'ya hear that, Tom?" The stretcher lurched as Dalton stopped and looked skywards. Tom staggered, but recovered his balance. The noise of the aircraft's engine had changed, lowered to a soft purr. It was coming in to land. He looked down briefly at Gwen. England, Hope Cove, safety were only a few yards away.

They reached the road and Dalton hesitated, looking left and right. "Which way?"

Tom called out to Céleste. *"Quelle direction allons-nous?"*

She waved her hand. *"Suivez-moi."* She made a turn to the right and the Americans followed her as surely as if she had been General Patton.

The sound of the aircraft grew louder as it drew nearer. It was all or nothing. Either they would all be back in England or...

"Shouldn't we check that we're not walking into a trap?" Dalton echoed Tom's thoughts. The revolutions of the engine eased; the plane was coming into land.

"If we are, it's too late now." Tom felt Céleste's tug on his arm. She spoke quickly and pointed down the road.

"She says there's a gate down there. Let's go."

They moved along the road, the stretcher swinging between them. Céleste ran ahead, her white ankle socks catching the moonlight. They reached the gate and stopped. Not far now, Tom thought. Almost there. Just a few more yards.

He stiffened as he heard the click of an automatic weapon and felt the muzzle press into the base of his spine.

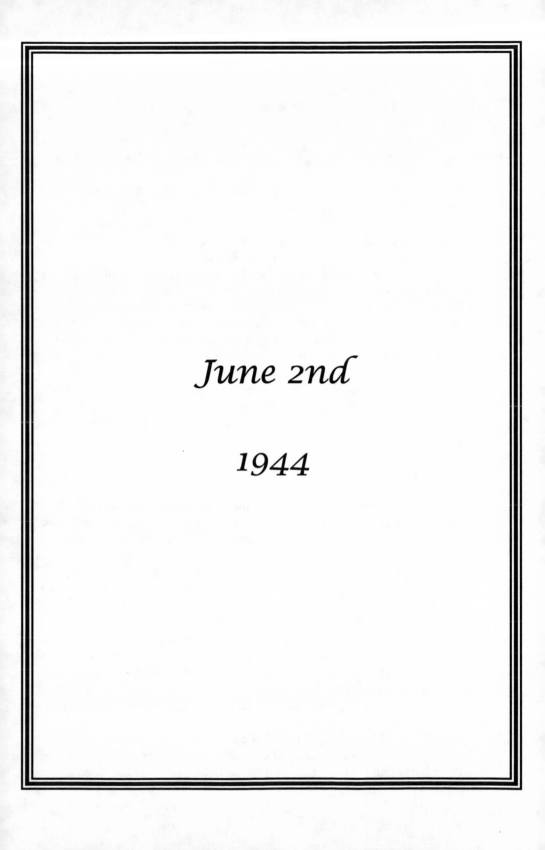

June 2nd

1944

"*Arrêtez!*"
Tom felt his fear ease a little at the sound of a French voice, but the weapon still pushed firmly into his back.

"*Nous sommes Américains.*" Tom said quickly, his mind desperately searching for more words to explain. Before he could, Céleste looked from under her bonnet.

"*Oncle Jules!*" She ran past the Americans to the man with the gun.

"Céleste!" There was surprise in the man's voice. "*Comment? Pourquoi?*" A rapid conversation in French ensued, beyond Tom's ability, although he was bewildered to pick up the word 'prince.'

"What's going on?" Dalton's voice was fearful.

"It seems this guy is our little friend's uncle. We're damn lucky we brought her along. Otherwise, we could be dead meat now."

"Okay, it was a good call. But is he going to let us get to the plane?"

Tom cast his eyes around the sky. The plane was very close now. The pressure of the gun was removed. The man came from behind him, looked at Gwen on the stretcher and shouldered his firearm. His eyes met Tom's and he smiled.

"*Eh bien, Votre Altesse le Prince.*" He threw his head back and laughed. "*Suivez-moi.*" He took Céleste's hand in his and led them to the gate.

"What'd he say? What'd he say?" Dalton shouted as they followed him into the field.

"I'm not sure. My French isn't so hot. But it sounded like he thinks I'm the Prince of Wales!"

The Americans and the girl followed the Frenchman into the field. Several men were running across the grass, seeking their designated positions. There was a muted cry and each man switched on a flashlight and pointed it to the sky.

They lowered the stretcher and looked skywards. Suddenly the plane appeared, hovering like a huge black moth before dropping swiftly to earth. The aircraft slithered and shuddered to a halt, then turned to make its way back to the other end of the field, ready for an immediate take-off.

The unmistakable figure of Josse hurried towards the group. "How on earth did you get here?" He wore a look of genuine surprise. "Henri just got back from the farm. He said the place was crawling with Germans. We thought you'd been arrested."

The girl emerged from the shadows behind Tom; Josse looked at her incredulously.

"Céleste!" He picked the girl up and hugged her.

"She's all right." Tom spoke reassuringly. "If it weren't for her, we wouldn't be here. She led the way." He paused before whispering. "You know about Dominic and Bernadette?"

Josse was silent for a moment. "Yes."

"The little girl doesn't know. I couldn't tell her. You do understand?"

The Frenchman said nothing, but nodded. Despite the poor light, Tom felt sure he saw tears well up in Josse's eyes. Suddenly, he put Céleste down.

"But you are here, that's the main thing. The plane has brought important messages for me, and I was going to send it back empty. Quickly," he urged the Americans forward, "you must board the plane!"

Dalton set off towards the end of the field, but Tom did not move.

"She comes with us." He pointed down to Gwen's sleeping form.

"Jeanne? Ce n'est pas possible!" Josse became exasperated. "You have my eternal gratitude for saving her from the Germans, but she must stay here. There's no room for her. There are only two seats on the plane!"

"Then she will take mine." Tom shouted. "Glenn, take her with you."

Dalton came back across the field, found himself looking at the muzzle of Josse's pistol and stopped. Céleste started whimpering and ran to her uncle.

"This is not the time for heroic gestures, Major Ford." He turned the pistol in Tom's direction. "Both of you know the details of the invasion. If either of you were captured, you could betray it. You both must go."

"Make's sense to me." Dalton beckoned to Tom. "Let's get outta here!"

"No, we've got to take Gwen." Tom moved towards Josse, but stopped when he heard the Frenchman cock the pistol and level it at his chest.

"My orders are..." Josse stopped. "I shall not hesitate to shoot you – both of you – if you don't get on the plane. If the Germans capture and torture you, you will betray the secret and thousands of American soldiers will die. Is that what you want?"

The noise of the aircraft rose as the pilot gunned the engine; he had risked his life to fly in with the conditions less than perfect, and he was anxious to get away.

"Jesus, Tom, we gotta go!" Dalton called out plaintively.

Tom's eyes went from Gwen to fix Josse. The Frenchman lowered his pistol.

"I swear to God that she will be safe." He lowered his head. "She's become like a daughter to me." His voice trembled. He raised his head and fixed Tom with a stare. "I swear to you that she will return to England. Now, go!"

Tom felt Dalton pull at his sleeve, but he held Josse's stare.

"I trust you, Josse. I don't know why I should, but I do." He knelt briefly by the stretcher, kissed Gwen's forehead and turned to go to the aircraft.

"Mon prince, mon prince!" There was a flurry of arms and legs as Céleste clasped Tom around his waist. He bent down, picked up the little girl and looked into her eyes. In the midst of the war, the treachery, the violence, there was still innocence in the world. He kissed her on the cheek and lowered her slowly to the grass.

"Go! Go now!" Josse shouted above the engine's roar.

Tom stole a last glance at Gwen and sprinted across the field.

A Safe House. Normandy. Noon.

Jeanne awoke. There was no darkness, no dank odor of the cell and its floor of sodden earth. There was light, the dull light of a rainy day, but it was a welcome light. The rain pattered against the small window of the bedroom; the sheets around her were crisp.

Her mind thrust unwanted memories upon her. The last thing she could remember was being tossed back into the cell after...

The pain. The pain was still there in her feet, but it didn't consume her whole body as it had. It gnawed at her toes, but there were no longer red-hot needles thrusting into her very fiber. She tossed back the sheets, wondering whose floral-patterned full-length nightdress she was wearing. She lifted the hem and saw that her feet were bandaged, as only a nurse could do.

Where was she? She could tell by the huge armoire against the wall that she was still in France, but where? And who had brought her here? She eased her legs over the side of the bed and tried to stand, but, after a few moments, the pain was too much, and she flopped back onto the pillow, searching the ceiling for answers. She could vaguely recall rain and a car; the smell of hay came to her.

Jeanne shook her head on the pillow as these half-images tried to penetrate the clouds of her memory. Perhaps the torture had deranged her mind. She struggled to recall other things, but there was nothing. Nothing except the pain and the knuckles on the hands of her torturer. The memories she didn't want to recall relentlessly pushed their way in.

She cried out, and then jumped as the bedroom door opened. A child's face peered into the room, breaking into a happy smile when she saw Jeanne. The girl's shrill French voice cried down to the foot of the stairs.

"She's awake! The princess is awake!"

Princess? Had Jeanne heard correctly? Perhaps it was all a dream and she would soon wake up back in the prison cell. But she could hear the girl's shoes as she skipped down the stairs.

"The princess is awake! The princess is awake!"

Jeanne's head fell back on the pillow and she closed her eyes.

The Safe House. 2 p.m.

Footsteps on the stairs awoke her again. They were heavier this time, not those of the little girl. Jeanne hauled herself into a sitting position with the pillow propped behind her. With the footsteps came an aroma of food, chicken perhaps, and the unmistakable scent of onions. The smell of coffee lurked in the background.

The bedroom door opened and a young, pretty woman came into the room. About her age, Jeanne thought, perhaps a little older. She was carrying a tray with a large soup bowl, some bread, and a mug of coffee.

"Good to see you awake. I thought you'd like something to eat." The woman smiled and set the tray down on Jeanne's lap.

"Who are you? Where am I? How did I get here?" Jeanne's need to find answers had overpowered her usual good manners. "I'm sorry. I know I'm in safe hands. I didn't mean to sound ungrateful."

"Not at all." The woman pulled a cigarette from a pack and lit it. "My name is Augustine. I live – or used to live – in St. Marie de la Croix. But now we're in Les Bois Olives, a safe house just outside the village of Hamelin, about thirty kilometers from St. Mâlo."

Jeanne nodded; she had been involved in an action in the Breton port the year before. She tore a piece of bread off the small loaf and took a tentative bite.

The woman got up and went to the window, checking out the approach road that led up from the village to the house. She sensed Jeanne's anxiety and turned to her.

"It's okay. You can't be too careful. But it's quite safe."

"I see you've been in the war, too." Jeanne pointed at a bandage on the woman's arm, just below her ruffled sleeve.

"I was shot while escaping from the Gestapo. It's healing." The woman sat down on a small chair in front of the window. She had an aura of calmness and self-assurance.

"You're in the Resistance, Augustine?"

"No." She shrugged her shoulders. "Well, I do things from time to time. Many of us do. My husband, Jean-Paul, is in the Resistance." She nodded towards the barely-touched soup bowl. "Please eat. You must regain your strength"

"I'll try." Jeanne had no appetite, and felt that she never would again, but took a sip. "Is your husband here?"

"No." She opened the window and tossed out the cigarette. "The Gestapo was after him. He's with the *maquis* in Lessay forest. Waiting for the invasion."

"Invasion?" Jeanne put the spoon back down on the tray. "You know about the invasion?"

"Not much, except that it's coming soon. Please God, let it come soon." She raised her eyes to the ceiling as anger crept into her voice. "Then we shall be rid of the *Bosches*, the *Milice*, and all the other swine." Her knuckles whitened as she clenched her fists in rage. After a few moments, she relaxed and sighed longingly. "Then we can get back to normal."

Jeanne mulled over Augustine's words. What was normal? She remembered her childhood, when her parents took her every Sunday to the beach. That sort of 'normal' would never return. Then she thought of Tom, the American, of the snatched games of chess, of Hope Cove, of the walks on the cliff. Would that memory ever be normal, something she would take for granted?

"Please tell me how I got here."

"It's a long story. Apparently, after Philippe had rescued you from Coutances jail—"

"Philippe?"

"*Oui,* Philippe. Philippe Josse." Augustine looked puzzled. "I thought you knew him. He saved me, too, after I had been shot by Richter, the head of the Gestapo."

The name sent a chill through Jeanne's body. "You must be mistaken. Josse is in the pay of the Germans. He betrayed my landing place. I had orders..." Jeanne realized she had said too much and stopped.

"I shouldn't jump to conclusions. I did, when I found Philippe with Richter. But he saved my life and brought me here. I'm sure he's playing some sort of double game. And I trust him now."

The effort of trying to put all the pieces together was making Jeanne's head ache, but at least it was holding the shrieking memories at bay. "I'm still not convinced."

"Look at it this way." There was emotion in the Frenchwoman's voice. "Philippe saved both of us, you and me. If it hadn't been for him, we'd both be rotting in a Gestapo prison, or maybe..."

The last word went unsaid, but Jeanne understood. Had Josse now rescued her twice? The images of the time in the field at Labouchère's farm came to her, when, with the Germans swarming around, he had tossed her into the plane. Now there had been a second time, when, according to Augustine, he had snatched her from under Richter's nose.

But she felt uneasy. Something didn't ring true. Why had Priestley ordered her to shoot Josse?

She dropped the bread onto the tray. "I'm sorry, I can't eat any more."

Augustine came to the bedside and placed her hand on Jeanne's forehead. "You're still feverish." She took the tray away. "Get some rest."

A Diary. Somewhere in England

I read in the Daily Express – a Churchill-supporting rag fit only for toilet paper – that Monte Cassino has finally been taken by the Allies.

I once visited the thousand-year-old monastery where St. Benedict first established his famous Rule – it was a glorious sight, filled with splendid and ancient treasures. Of course, they were reduced to rubble during the Americans' first bombing raid in January. They thought the monastery was filled with German soldiers, but – so much for Allied intelligence – all they managed to wipe out were a few monks. However, the Allies did Germany a great favor: the Germans found the rubble of the monastery an excellent place to hide and dig in. And so they did for almost five months, wiping out over 50,000 Allied soldiers during their stay.

Hitler's taking on Italy as an ally was a big mistake. If General Rommel had been let loose on the Russian front instead of having had to bail out Mussolini in North Africa, Operation Barbarossa – the invasion of Russia – might have had a very different outcome.

Barbarossa. "Red Beard." I understand that the operation was named after Frederick Barbarossa, the emperor of the First Reich. I feel an affinity for him – like me, he had red hair!

If Germany loses Italy, it means little, of course. What is of much more importance is that the German High Command be able to throw the coming Allied invasion back into the English Channel. And, I think I shall soon be privy to the whole secret. What fun I'll have then!

June 3rd

1944

The Safe House. 9 a.m.

"I hope you're feeling better." Augustine carried a tray of bread, jam, and coffee.

"Yes, much better. Thanks for all you've done for me, Augustine." Jeanne hungrily tore at the bread. "Was that your little girl I saw yesterday?"

"Céleste? No, she's not my daughter." She lit a cigarette. "Her father was killed in the early days of the war. Her mother couldn't deal with his death." She inhaled deeply. "Her mother took to her bed, into which she had piled all his clothes. They found her mother naked and embracing his things, as though they were the real man. Eventually, she had to be committed to the asylum near Valognes. Céleste is now looked after by some relatives, but they find an extra mouth to feed, even a small one, a burden. I have just heard that her grandparents have been taken by the Gestapo. She doesn't know that yet. "

"Oh, dear God, how sad. The little girl seemed so happy yesterday. How do you suppose she's managed to keep up her spirits?"

"Who knows? Perhaps she's shut it out of her mind; perhaps she lives in a world of her own. Do you know she calls you princess?"

"Yes, I heard her use that name, but I can't imagine why."

"Céleste played a big part in your rescue." Augustine adjusted Jeanne's pillows. "If it hadn't been for her and the Americans—"

"Americans?"

"Oh, of course, you wouldn't know." Augustine poured more coffee into Jeanne's cup, pleased that she was eating at last. "You were heavily sedated to ease your pain."

"So that's why I can't remember anything."

"I only know what Philippe told me. It seems that, at the same time he rescued you from the jail, he was trying to get two Americans back to England. It was Céleste who led them – they were carrying you on a stretcher – to the airfield where the rescue plane landed. The girl insists that one of the Americans was a prince," Augustine smiled, "and that you were the princess he came to save."

"But why wasn't I put onto the plane?"

"There wasn't enough—"

The door flew open and Céleste bounded into the room.

"You're awake again." She clapped her hands together in joy. "I'm so happy."

She came to the side of the bed. Jeanne offered her cheeks for the girl to kiss, and then patted the mattress, inviting her to sit on the bed beside her.

"Will your prince come back for you?" The question caught Jeanne unawares.

"Céleste," Augustine turned from the window, "stop playing that silly game."

"No, it's all right." Jeanne reached out to take the girl's hand. "I'm not sure, Céleste. Perhaps. What was the prince like?"

176

Jeanne looked into Céleste's big eyes. You're so young and innocent, she thought, clinging to fairy tales to escape the woes of your world. Even the loss of your parents has not yet cured you of believing in happy endings.

"He was big and brave and handsome." A dreamy look came to the girl's face. "I didn't know that Americans were so handsome. He rescued you just like the prince in my book. And he was so strong." Céleste warmed to her story. "He carried you all the way to Swallow Farm. There was another American who helped him, but he wasn't nice – he didn't have any chocolate."

Jeanne caught Augustine's glance as the Frenchwoman lifted her eyes to the ceiling in an exaggerated expression of disbelief at the child's tale.

Céleste jumped down from the bed, excitedly. "But the prince did, and he was so handsome. Will you marry him?"

Augustine came forward to shepherd the child away, but Jeanne lifted her palm to stay her.

"How can I marry this prince, when I don't know his name?"

"He told me his name! He told me his name!" Céleste jumped up and down, and then suddenly stopped. "But I can't remember it." Frustration furrowed the child's brow. "It was a strange name, not a French name."

"That's enough, Céleste." Augustine winked at Jeanne. "The princess must rest now."

The child beamed a smile at Gwen and went through the door that Augustine was holding open. Jeanne's eyes welled up and her throat caught as she saw the door close behind the child. She was just a little girl, but soon she'd have another heavy burden thrust on her slight shoulders. When she knew she had lost her grandparents, would she keep on believing in happy endings?

"The princess will marry the prince!" Jeanne could hear Céleste sing-songing as she went down the stairs.

Jeanne brushed away a tear. "I hope there's not much for me to do tomorrow. There's still a lot of pain, and I can barely walk."

Augustine closed the door so the child couldn't hear.

"Philippe will need to solve that problem. He told me that it was absolutely essential that you get back to England within the next two days. He's gone to Carteret to find a small fishing boat for the job. You must leave here tomorrow at the latest."

"Why then? What's today's date?"

"Today is the third of June."

Jeanne tried to sort things out. She closed her eyes. Josse, Wainwright, Priestley, Richter. The characters merged, disappeared and then reformed in her thoughts. Then, for no reason, the image of Sherlock Holmes appeared. She opened her eyes and sat up with a start. 'Eliminate the impossible...'

"Augustine, do you have a radio here?"

"No, there's no radio here. You'll have to ask Philippe about it. He won't be back until this afternoon. He has to move very carefully. The Gestapo has posted a reward for his capture. Try to get some rest." She closed the bedroom door behind her.

Jeanne lay back on the pillow. She went over the events once more and became convinced that there was only one answer to the question that had been vexing her. She began to compose in her mind the message she had to send to England. Suddenly, she bit her lip; she had no code book, no code sheets.

The Safe House. 5:30 p.m.

The rattle of the latch downstairs drifted into her slumber. She was still drowsy and sought to rediscover her dream. She had seen Tom, his slender fingers grasping the white queen, looking at her, smiling as he made a decisive move. There was another noise, but she ignored it as she drifted between sleep and consciousness. It was a wedding, and Céleste was there, clapping her hands and shouting. "The prince is marrying the princess!"

Then there was a deep voice coming from below. "We have to leave at dawn tomorrow." It was Josse's voice and suddenly she was fully awake.

"Philippe, Philippe!" She shouted, and heard his heavy tread on the stairs.

"Ça va, ma petite singe?" Josse gave one of his rare smiles as he entered the bedroom. "You look much better. Augustine's food is good, eh?"

"Delicious! I'm fine, Philippe. But there's still a lot of pain. I can't walk more than a few steps."

"Merde!" The smile fell from his face. He shouted down the stairs. "Augustine! Please come up." He pulled up a chair to the side of the bed and sat down as Augustine came in.

"I'm afraid we have a serious problem. We have to leave for Carteret early tomorrow morning. The *Bosches* are making organized raids throughout the area. Patrols have been intensified in St. Hilaire, and one of our houses in St. James was raided today." His hand tugged nervously at his mustache. "Fortunately we had enough warning, but it's becoming dangerous out there."

Augustine sat on the edge of the bed. "But Jeanne can barely walk – she needs more time to heal."

"We don't have that sort of time." There was a harshness in his voice that caused the two women to recoil. "I'm sorry," he spoke more softly, "but there is no margin for error. We must leave tomorrow, before Richter's men sweep the area. I've arranged a boat with René LeGrand, but the tide gives us only a two-hour window, from six until eight the morning after tomorrow."

There was silence for some time as he weighed his course of action. "I will arrive with my horse and trap at six tomorrow morning. We will need to travel most of the day." He looked at Jeanne. "I can carry you to the trap here, but there is no way I can do the same to take you from the road to the mooring point in Carteret – it will look too obvious – even the dumbest German would be suspicious."

"Perhaps I could lean on your shoulder." Jeanne tried to look hopeful

"It's at least two hundred meters." Josse gestured Augustine to get off the bed and pulled back the sheets. "Let's see how far you can manage now."

"Is there a need for—?" Augustine's words were cut off by Jeanne as she swung her feet down to the floor.

"I'll try." Jeanne reached for the Frenchwoman's shoulder and hauled herself up onto one foot. Despite all her effort at self control, the pain showed on her face. With her other arm, she held onto Josse as she tried to take another step.

She could not help the cry that came from her lips; she felt like she was walking on broken glass.

"That's enough!" Josse's strong arms swept her up and put her back on the bed. "No matter how brave you are, Jeanne, you cannot do that."

He lowered her down onto the pillow and sat down. Jeanne looked resigned. "I'm sorry to be so much trouble."

Josse gave her a reassuring look. "Don't worry, we'll find a way." He turned to Augustine.

"I think it would be better if you came with us, Augustine." The women's eyes widened as he continued to spell out his plan. "You will be Jeanne's sister. She has been an invalid all her life. You will be going to visit your mother – René LeGrand's wife – in Carteret."

He glanced at his watch. "Give me your ID papers, Augustine."

"ID Papers?"

"Yes, we need to get you a new set. I need the photograph. I've already had several different versions for Jeanne since she first started coming to France."

He looked again at his watch. "I can get back to St. James on my bike before the curfew, but I've got to hurry." He turned to go.

"What about Céleste?" Augustine asked anxiously.

"We'll drop her off at her uncle's on the way." He was about to descend the stairs when Jeanne called out.

"Philippe, I need to send a radio message right away."

Josse frowned. "There's no way to get you to a radio tonight. Besides, it's very dangerous – the Germans took your code sheets, remember?"

"But it's very important – it's about—"

"I have to go." He cut her short. "We'll talk about it tomorrow."

Headquarters Allied Expeditionary Force. 10 p.m.

The Supreme Commander of the Allied Expeditionary Force hurried through the rain lashing at him and his entourage of senior officers. The three-quarters moon was almost covered by the gathering clouds sweeping in from the north-west. He thought of June in Abilene, Kansas where it didn't rain for days on end.

179

The whole invasion was threatened by the vagaries of the damned English weather. May had been a beautiful month, bathing England in warm sunshine, day after day. And now this gathering storm. The general looked up at the darkened sky and racing clouds. Ships were already at sea, carrying tens of thousands of troops around to the southern coast of England and the Isle of Wight, gathering to unleash the invasion onto the Far Shore on June 5th.

He cursed. The last thing he wanted was a storm, with troopships wallowing in the ocean. An aide raced from the doorway of Southwick House, carrying an umbrella.

"What's the latest news on the weather?" the general asked urgently.

"The weather people aren't happy, sir."

"Neither am I. What are they saying?"

"The storm is worsening. They think they'll have a clearer picture later."

The Supreme Commander's mind ran through the invasion schedule, calculating quickly the latest time he could postpone H-hour.

"Arrange a conference in six hour's time. 0400 hours. I want Tedder, Montgomery, Bradley, the whole bang shoot." He shouted above the wind. "And I want a full report from the weatherman, what's his name?"

"You mean Captain Stagg, sir?"

"Yes, that's him. Full report. 0400 hours. In the map room."

Gestapo Headquarters. St. James. 10:30 p.m.

"Thank you *Reichsführer*, thank you." Richter waited for the line to go dead. It would not do to hang up on Himmler.

So the promotion was confirmed. *Obersturmbannführer* Richter. He allowed himself the pleasure of uttering his new rank. At least Bertha would be pleased; his wife would revel in her new status amidst the soirées over which she presided in Berlin. He grimaced. She would want more money, to buy a wardrobe worthy of the wife of an *Obersturmbannführer*.

He sighed and began to pore over his papers. A report on a tap of a noted general's phone. He made a note of the salacious details; it might come in useful later. An execution warrant for a French terrorist caught placing explosive charges; he signed with a flourish and tossed it aside. His eyes widened as he picked up the next report.

'Radio Report. May 31ˢᵗ. The following message, broadcast by the BBC, was received at 2030. *Les sanglots longs des violons d'automne.* The long sobs of autumn's violins.'

Richter looked at the date and grabbed the phone. "Connect me with *Hauptmann* Schreier."

The exchange was heated.

"Schreier, I told you to report to me personally immediately when the first of the Verlaine couplets was received. The report I have received is three days old! Three days old, Schreier!"

"But, sir, you told me to concentrate all resources on finding Josse."

"Isn't it possible to do more than one thing at a time? I am told even the whores on the *Wilhelmstrasse* can do that!"

"I wouldn't know, sir. But you may be interested to know that Josse has been spotted."

"Why didn't you tell me this before, you *Dummkopf?*"

"Because I've only just found out, sir."

Richter breathed deeply, struggling to bring his temper under control. "Where is he?"

"We're not exactly sure. My men haven't seen him in person, but informants say he's been seen in the St. James area."

"Raid every farm within ten kilometers of the town. Josse is clever enough not to hide in the towns. And make sure all Army checkpoints have a Gestapo officer in attendance to keep the soldiers on their toes."

"I've barely got enough men, sir."

"Don't make pathetic excuses, Schreier!" Richter shouted into the mouthpiece.

"Very well, sir. Is there anything else?"

"Yes. Tell your men it is almost certain that Josse will be traveling with a woman," he remembered what Müller had done to the Busson woman, "and she will have great difficulty in walking."

"Difficulty walking, sir?"

"Yes, you idiot. And so would you if you'd had your toenails pulled out!" There was silence at the other end of the line.

"Finally, Schreier. I want you to report to me as soon as there's a sighting of the Frenchman. Or if there's a broadcast of the second Verlaine couplet. No delays, no excuses, this time. Do I make myself clear?"

"Yes, sir."

Richter slammed the receiver down and pinched the bridge of his nose. He couldn't trust Schreier to do the job. That was why he had moved his headquarters to St. James. Capturing Josse was too important; he would have to take personal command of the operation.

He made an immediate assessment that the Frenchman would attempt nothing overnight; Josse would know that there were increased patrols. Richter went to the window and looked at the sky; there was heavy cloud cover, threatening rain. There could be no air operation; nothing would happen that night, Richter decided; he would leave a message with his chauffeur, Helmut, to call him just before dawn and they would set out early.

He picked up the report and read the Verlaine couplet again. It meant the invasion would come in five days from the date of the message. He looked at his desk diary and made the calculation. June 5th. Just as Josse had said.

A Diary. Somewhere in England.

Rome has fallen, I hear on the BBC. It's bad news, but no matter. Tomorrow I shall attend a briefing on Operation Overlord. I shall know everything at last.

Of course, the invasion is already underway. I cannot stop it, but when Richter receives the full operational details, the whole operation will be mincemeat.

Everything is prepared. The pigeons are ready. Tomorrow I shall have the secret – and then my birds will fly!

June 4th

1944

Supreme Headquarters. Map Room. 4 a.m.

The Supreme Commander ground out his third cigarette of the meeting and lit another.

"So, Captain Stagg, how bad is the forecast?"

"I'm afraid it's rather bad, sir." The captain's rounded vowels had a somber edge. "A depression off the north-west coast of Ireland is moving southeast. And it's deepening."

"Please spare us the meteorological details, captain. What's the impact on the invasion?"

The captain hesitated. Eisenhower's civility and diplomacy were well-known; his present testiness showed the pressure upon him at that moment.

"The rain and wind will continue—"

"Let me ask you a direct question, captain." His fingers rapped impatiently on the table. "I have the lives of thousands of men dependent on my decision. Can the four weather conditions necessary for a landing be met?" He ticked them off on the fingers of his hand as he called them out. "A wind of under fifteen miles an hour on the beaches, under twenty miles an hour at sea; visibility of at least three miles; and cloud ceiling no lower than three thousand feet."

The British meteorological officer did not answer immediately. On his answer rested the fate of thousands of men; two years of strategic planning hung on his words.

"For June 5th, sir, I can answer with certainty. The answer is no."

Hushed mutterings went around the room. Every general and admiral knew that the invasion force was already on the move. Ships from as far apart as Wales and Norfolk were steering for the gathering point in the English Channel. The huge concrete caissons that would form artificial harbors had been slipped from their moorings.

"I see." The general spoke calmly, hiding his disappointment. "Then I must order a postponement for twenty-four hours." He ground out his cigarette and pulled another from the pack.

"I'm sure we can handle a delay of one day, gentlemen, although it will be difficult for those men already in the boats." He lit his cigarette and turned again to the weatherman. "Can you offer any improvement for the sixth? You see, captain, the invasion is not like an automobile – I can't stop and start it at will. At the moment it's like a coiled spring: once I release the catch, it will be impossible to stop." He drew heavily on his cigarette.

"If I have to stop it, I have to do it within the next twenty-four hours, and that means returning all troops to base. And if I do that," he opened his palms, "the invasion will need to be postponed for a month, maybe two, and we'll be plagued with serious problems of security and morale of the troops. So, what about the sixth?"

184

The officer paused, thinking out his answer carefully. "I'm afraid it looks like more of the same." He could see the disappointment on the faces in the room. "There is a chance – a slight chance – that the storm will abate by the sixth. But at the moment, we can't be sure."

"When will you be sure?"

"About this time tomorrow, sir."

"Very well." The general spoke calmly and evenly, although the weight of his great responsibility showed in the dark shadows under his eyes. "Your office is to keep me informed throughout the day. Gentlemen, we shall reconvene tomorrow," he looked up at the clock on the wall, "at three a.m."

As the meeting broke up, the general gestured the head of the British SOE to his side.

"I'd like to congratulate you on the job you did getting that BIGOT out of France. It was a great relief to me. For a while I thought I'd have to call off the invasion."

"It was nothing." The man with the eye patch replied with typical British understatement. "In fact, much of the success is down to one of your own chaps, a Major Ford."

"Ford, eh?" The general pulled a small notebook from his pocket and jotted down the name. "Now, what about the other operation – Operation First Violin isn't it?"

"Yes, sir, the operation has gone more or less according to plan. However, we haven't heard from our French agent for two days. He's constantly on the move to escape the Gestapo."

"Keep me informed. You know how much depends on the operation."

"Of course." Fortescue proffered his lighter as the general pulled out a cigarette. "It'll be over soon, thank heaven." The Englishman gave a smile. "Then perhaps you can indulge in a little golf."

The American chuckled. "A bit like Sir Francis Drake playing bowls while waiting for the Armada, eh? I don't think I could do it."

"Certainly not in this weather, sir."

The general's smile vanished. "Don't talk to me about the weather."

Between Les Bois Olives and St. James. 7 a.m.

The hooves of the horse made a brisk clip on the road as the trap breasted the hill on the outskirts of Hamelin and made its way westwards to St. James. Josse sat on the buckboard, slapping the reins along the horse's quarters to urge her on. The old mare responded, pulling hard. Josse knew he could trust Florence. He had to. It was one thing driving a stolen car at night dressed as Milice officers, but ordinary Frenchmen driving cars in the daytime would attract every German for miles; gasoline in rural areas was reserved for the occupiers.

In the back sat the two women, Jeanne with a blanket wrapped around her legs, Augustine with Céleste on her lap. The sun hung low in the cloudy early morning sky.

"It's good that we got an early start," Josse spoke out of the corner of his mouth to the back seats, "it's a long drive, and we must get to Carteret before curfew tonight."

"Where did you lose your moustache *M'sieur* Josse?" Céleste's childish voice chirped. "And why has all your hair turned gray? And when did you become a priest?"

The two women tried in vain to stifle their chuckles. They had been amused when Philippe had arrived to pick them up. He had obviously disguised himself, so well that they needed a second look at his ill-fitting suit and clerical collar.

"Céleste, you ask too many questions. Did you know that curiosity killed the cat?"

"But I am not a cat, *M'sieur* Josse. Or are you now to be called *M'sieur Le Pré?*"

"My hair has gone gray worrying about you, *ma petite*," Josse sighed his answer, "and I have become a priest to do the work of God."

"Why do you worry about me? And what is the work of God?"

"Enough!" Josse snorted. "Can't you two find something to amuse her? I have enough to worry about." He pulled on the reins as the trap began its descent into St. James.

The women laughed, and Augustine began to engage Céleste, talking about her classes at school. Within moments, the girl was back on the subject of princes and princesses; it was Josse's turn to laugh, but his humor was stifled as he looked down the road. Half a mile ahead was a German checkpoint.

"Merde!"

"Priests shouldn't swear, *M'sieur* Josse."

The Frenchman ignored the child. "The checkpoint wasn't here yesterday. Richter has stepped up his security. We cannot go into St. James. Even with the disguises and new ID cards, we dare not risk it." In one movement, he pulled on the reins and guided the horse down a side road. "I know another way to Avranches."

"But what about Céleste?" Augustine's voice was anxious. "We need to get her to her uncle."

"It's too dangerous," Josse flapped the reins, "we'll have to take her with us."

Richter's Headquarters. St. James. 7 a.m.

The *Obersturmbannführer* pushed away his half-eaten ham and eggs and finished his coffee. Through the window, the early morning sun still lay hidden behind the clouds, but the pale gray light had dispelled the night.

Richter weighed the situation. It was critical that he put himself into Josse's mind, to predict what the Frenchman would do.

He still wasn't sure of the Frenchman. Much of what Josse had told him had turned out to be correct: Allied drop zones, arms consignments and the like. Apart from such tactical information, his latest contribution had been of immense strategic value. It had been confirmed with the discovery of the agent Wainwright's body with the plans and the broadcast by the BBC of the first line of the Verlaine couplets.

That Josse had betrayed the British had been confirmed by the prisoner, Jeanne Busson, under torture. But despite everything, he still had his doubts about Josse. He had hoped for a message from Agent Blau embedded in England, but there had been nothing for a month; communication by pigeon mail was difficult and slow, but Blau would trust no other form.

Josse. He had given him the benefit of the doubt over the American Dalton; perhaps Josse had got information from him and perhaps the American was now dead. But there could be no rationale behind Josse's rescue of the Busson woman, the British agent. It was because of Josse's information that the woman had been captured. Did he feel guilty about it? Why?

Perhaps there was a romantic relationship between the two? Richter shook his head. Josse was almost old enough to be her father. But why should he put his life at risk to rescue her? Did she still have some strategic value he, Richter, could not fathom?

Whatever the reason, Richter knew he had to capture Josse and his English friend before they flew the coop. He donned his tunic with the new *Obersturmbannführer* flashes, picked up his cap and strode out into the entrance hall of the *Mairie*. Josse would need to get her out quickly. Before June 5th. Before the Allied decoy landings on the Normandy beaches. The weather forecast for the next few days showed clouds and rain. There could be no airlift out. Josse would have to get her out by boat.

Richter realized he had to make a vital calculation. Would Josse go for the fishing villages along the north Brittany coast? Or would he choose somewhere on the western coast of the Cotentin peninsula – maybe Granville? Perhaps he would swing east, go through St. Hilaire and head for the ports on the north Normandy coast. Richter shook his head. Too risky, especially with the ten-kilometer exclusion zone along the Calvados coast; too many checkpoints, with special passes needed.

Besides, it was too far. Josse would be mad to use a motor vehicle: he might as well carry a sign announcing his presence. Perhaps they might use bicycles, but even then it was too far to go in one day; besides, the English agent was injured. No, it was Brittany or Cotentin. But which? Depending on his choice, Josse would have to go through either St. James or Avranches.

He hurried out the door. His chauffeur, Helmut, was holding open the door to his staff car. Behind the car, Schreier sat in the passenger seat of a truck with a platoon of men in the back. He made his decision. He had ordered the security around St. James to be strengthened yesterday. He walked back to the truck and spoke to Schreier.

"Have you ensured that all checkpoints between St. James and Avranches will report any vehicle with a man and a crippled woman?"

Schreier nodded. *"Jawohl, mein Herr."*

"Take the road for Avranches, Helmut!" He sank back into the leather seat as the convoy set out.

Between St. James and Avranches. 7:45 a.m.

The trap eased off the road onto a rutted path that led down into a wooded glade. Jeanne, Augustine and Céleste jolted around like pebbles in a can, and were relieved when Josse brought the vehicle to a halt. The horse neighed her relief, her quarters heavily flecked with foam.

"Oh, my aching back." Augustine opened the door and lurched from the trap.

"Please can I get out, now?" Céleste's voice was insistent. "I need a pee-pee."

"Yes. We're stopping for half an hour while I feed and water Florence. Augustine, there's a bucket hanging under the trap. Could you fill it from the stream at the bottom of that path, please?" Augustine took the bucket and disappeared.

Josse gingerly lowered his hefty frame down from the buckboard and looked at his watch. They had made good time. After evading the checkpoint at St. James, he had swung north, managing to drive around all checkpoints.

Josse opened the bag of oats he had taken from the trap and filled the horse's nosebag. Florence dropped her head willingly as he threw the bag over her ears and secured it to the bridle. There was a brief neigh of thanks before the mare began eating hungrily.

The way ahead would not be so easy. He had to go through Avranches to get to the coastal road leading to Carteret. There would be a checkpoint that could not be avoided. And it would be heavily manned.

Augustine returned with the bucket of water. "Would anyone like some breakfast?" She pulled a picnic box from the trap.

"Oui, Oui!" Céleste had returned from her call of nature. *"S'il vous plaît."* She added as an afterthought. Augustine gave her a sandwich.

"We've got some *rillettes*, and a *morceau de saucisse*. There's plenty of bread, and I've got a bag of apples."

Josse turned to Jeanne. "Are you all right, *ma petite singe?"*

"Yes, I'm fine," she smiled, "but I feel so useless, not being able to walk."

"Don't worry, we'll get you back to England." The Frenchman offered her a cigarette but she declined.

"I don't know how to thank you for rescuing me from the prison, Philippe. I owe my life to you."

"It was nothing. You know you are like a daughter to me. You should never have been...." He stopped, knowing he had said too much.

Jeanne's eyes narrowed. Was it true? Is that how Richter had found out? She probed gently. "I was astonished Richter knew of my drop zone."

"So was I." Josse averted his eyes and looked down at the ground. "But Richter's very clever." He hesitated. "Or very lucky."

"Yes, very lucky." Jeanne decided not to push the point as Josse turned away to water the horse.

But a picture began to form in her mind. It was vague at first, indistinct, a skeleton that needed flesh. But she began to build on it. There was a plot, a scheme so incredible as to defy belief.

Not all the pieces had fallen into place, but Jeanne knew something that no one else knew, not even those who had devised the grand plan. She knew that there was someone working to destroy the plan, someone on the inside. And she knew who that someone was.

Richter's Staff Car. On the road to Avranches. 8 a.m.

Richter had forgotten that it was market day in Avranches. The narrow road leading down to the town was cluttered with farmers' carts and traps taking produce to the market place. The horses, heads down, laboring between the shafts, snorted steam into the morning air, like tired locomotives.

Heaven knew where they got the produce, Richter thought. Probably hidden from the army's requisitions. He had always found the French peasants slow and surly, but he knew they were possessed of great cunning. Living in the countryside during wartime was not as difficult as living in the city. Despite raids and requisitions, the farmers always managed to feed their families.

Richter cursed. His early morning start was working against him; the farmers had been on the move from the moment the curfew had ended. At least there had been no American air raids.

"Stop, Helmut!" The chauffeur braked, bringing the car to a halt on the wheel-rutted road. Richter checked through the rear window that Schreier's truck with his platoon of men had stopped. He beckoned the officer to join him as he got down from the car.

"Helmut, can you get past these carts?"

The chauffeur looked at the road ahead and shrugged his shoulders.

"It's possible, but the road is very narrow. I'll have to go slowly or we'll wind up in the ditch on the other side. But Schreier's truck..."

"We'll try, sir." Schreier tried to appear optimistic. "But the truck has a wider wheelbase—"

"Yes, yes, I know that, you idiot!" Richter tried to control his temper.

Schreier looked sheepish. "It will be difficult, but we shall try our best. But the congestion is going to get worse."

"Worse? Worse?" Richter became agitated. "Why?"

"Because I passed on your orders, sir. Every vehicle going through the Avranches checkpoint is being searched thoroughly. All papers are being meticulously checked."

Richter thought he heard a hint of insubordination but ignored it.

"We shall go on without you, Schreier. You must follow as best you can." Richter did not like the decision to separate himself from Schreier's platoon, but he saw no option. Delay might allow Josse to escape. He leapt back into the car. "Drive on, Helmut."

The chauffeur steered the car to the outside of the line of carts and inched forward slowly. Richter looked at the horse-drawn carts as they passed. Most of the drivers did not look at him, their faces fixed steadily on the road ahead. Those that did had the unmistakable look of hatred in their eyes.

Richter ignored them. He was used to the hatred of impotence. He cast his eyes carefully over every cart and trap they passed. Any one of them could be carrying Josse and the Englishwoman.

On the road to Avranches. 8:30 a.m.

Josse cursed under his breath. He had known it was market day, and had hoped to profit from the anonymity of being just one vehicle among others. But he had not expected such a delay; he had been waiting in the slow-moving line of carts for nearly half an hour. As Florence pulled the trap slowly forward, she whinnied fractiously in frustration. Josse tucked a finger into his clerical collar, trying to get some relief from the chafing on his bull neck.

The reason for the delay came into view as Florence rounded the bend: there was a German checkpoint ahead, about two hundred meters. He had expected it; this one was unavoidable.

"Are we there yet?" Céleste sang out from the back seat.

"Not yet, my child." Josse spoke calmly, despite the growing pressure on his nerves.

"When will we be there?"

"Soon," Josse sighed, "but you must be quiet."

"Why?"

"Because, if you are not, the princess will be in danger."

He heard the barely-suppressed giggles of the women, but there were no more questions.

"Look!" Augustine stood behind the buckboard and pointed along the road toward the checkpoint. A cyclist was coming the other way, shouting to all the carts as he passed. He drew alongside the trap. "The Germans are searching everything thoroughly. They're after somebody."

Me, Josse thought. Richter had increased security. But the Frenchman knew he had to continue. There was no alternative; to pull Florence out of line and turn would be bound to attract suspicion. He prayed that the forged papers would get them through.

Florence moved forward without bidding as the cart ahead entered the checkpoint, the driver cursing the delay. An officer checked the driver's papers as two soldiers climbed into the back of the cart and began searching through the boxes of produce, probing everywhere.

Eventually, they got down, shaking their heads. The officer nodded, handed the papers back and shouted an order. The barrier rose and the farmer, still cursing, shook the reins at his horse. Florence moved forward slowly, her shoes scraping on the cobbles as she pulled the trap into the checkpoint.

"Your papers, please, Father." The German officer spoke fluent French and, for a brief instant, Josse hesitated, forgetting he was a priest. He reached into his pocket, cursing inwardly. Such a mistake could prove fatal. The officer showed no reaction and nodded to the two guards, who began to search under the trap. One pulled down the bucket holding Florence's feed and thrust his bayonet into it several times.

"Where are you going, Father?"

"Périers," he lied. "I'm taking these women to see their mother. She's very ill." Josse adopted a somber look, leaned forward to the officer and whispered. "She's not expected to last this day." He crossed himself.

"And the child?"

"Granddaughter."

The officer looked at the papers again and walked to the door of the trap.

"And where are you going," he looked down at the papers again, "Céleste?"

Josse could sense the cunning in the question to the child and offered up a prayer.

"To save the princess."

The German raised his eyebrows.

"It's all right." Augustine lifted Céleste to her lap. "She lives in a dream world, a world of her own. Her father was killed at the start of the war and it has made her unbalanced." She looked at the officer beseechingly. "These things happen. Whatever country you belong to."

The German shook his head in sympathy and handed the papers back to Josse. "Go on, Father." He signaled and the soldier raised the barrier.

Josse put the papers away and picked up the reins. Florence stirred, ready to go.

"Wait!" The order was shouted in French, but with a heavy guttural accent.

Josse turned to see a man emerge from the guardhouse by the checkpoint. He saw the black leather coat and knew at once: Gestapo.

"Let me see those papers for myself."

Josse feigned confusion as he handed the papers to the Gestapo man. "What is the problem?"

"No problem at all, Father." He flipped through the papers, walked to the rear of the trap and looked up at the women. "Which one of you is *Ma'm'selle* Busson?"

Jeanne half opened her mouth but realized the trap. She looked at Augustine; both women shrugged their shoulders. "You must have misread the papers, *M'sieur*. There is no one of that name here."

The Gestapo man looked at the papers again. "And what is your name, *Ma'm'selle?*"

"It's Dubois. Charlotte Dubois."

"She's a princess!" Céleste shouted.

"Very well, Princess Dubois. Please step down and follow me. I would like to ask you some questions."

The pain in Jeanne's feet had troubled her little during the journey. Now she felt hot needles probing at her toes; she knew she would be unable to stand.

The Checkpoint. 8:45 a.m.

The sound came from the northern sky, a steady drone of aircraft engines, growing louder with every second. All heads, French and German, swung towards it, scanning the sky. For a moment, all was still. Then a horse whinnied and reared. A voice broke the silence.

"American bombers!"

Several people jumped down from the carts and began to run aimlessly. The scream of a woman pierced through the growing noise of the bombers' engines. The Gestapo man and the German soldiers hesitated for a moment, and then fled, seeking shelter.

Josse knew that the bombers were aiming for the railway yard about a half mile from the road. He slipped the reins through his fingers; he could feel Florence's fear, her anxiety to escape from the noise. There was little time before the bombs came raining down.

"Quick, Augustine. Get the gun hidden below the floor. If anybody follows us, shoot." He flicked the whip on Florence's rump. She needed no second bidding, shooting forward through the still-open gate. Augustine was thrown to her knees as she grappled with the floorboards. Jeanne grabbed Céleste and held her tightly.

Crump. Crump. The sound of the first bombs fueled Florence's fear, driving her forward. Within a few strides she was at the gallop, the wheels rattling on the cobbles. There was an explosion to their left, crumbling a building, hurling masonry and glass everywhere. Josse fixed his eyes on the road ahead. He had little control over the crazed horse. The trap clipped a curb, tipped onto two wheels, and then righted itself.

Jeanne pulled Céleste to her and looked behind. A bomb hit the checkpoint, blasting the road. She could feel the child whimpering at her breast. Another bomb fell and agonizing screams came from the road behind. For some reason, Jeanne could feel the damp earth of her prison cell. She hugged the child and wept.

The Checkpoint. 8:45 a.m.

The blast of the bomb lifted Richter's staff car into the air. It fell with a shudder, one rear wheel in the ditch. Richter picked himself up from the floor, cursing.

"Damn the Americans! Where the hell is the Luftwaffe?" He picked up his hat and jammed it on his head. "That fat tub of lard Goering needs a kick in the ass! He couldn't organize an orgy in a brothel! Drive on, Helmut!"

His order was answered with a groan. The chauffeur turned, his face a bloody mess from its collision with the steering wheel.

"Are you all right, Helmut? Can you drive?"

"I think so, sir." He took a handkerchief from his pocket, wiped his face and was frightened by the amount of blood staining the white cloth. He resisted the urge to look in the rear-view mirror.

"You don't look very pretty, but you'll live, Helmut. Let's go!"

The chauffeur engaged a gear and revved the engine, but there was no response.

"I'm afraid the car is in a worse state than I am, sir." The words were ill-formed by a tongue that searched for teeth that were no longer in place.

"Damn!" Richter leapt down from the car, looked at the wheel stuck in the ditch and kicked the tire in frustration. There was chaos all around him. Horses reared, screaming with fear, desperately seeking escape from the straps and reins that held them. Ahead of him was a crater where a bomb had destroyed the road. An animal mutilated by the blast lay in the road, its hooves flailing futilely in the throes of death; by its side stretched the body of its owner, oblivious to his horse's final agony.

"Where is Schreier?" Richter looked back down the road, his face impervious to the tragedy around him. He regretted his decision to separate from the support platoon. Now he had to rethink his plan. He tried to dismiss the acrid smell of the bomb, intermingled with the odor of burning flesh; he had to think clearly.

If Josse and the woman had been killed in the bombing, it would be a disaster. Everything Josse had told him about the decoy invasion had been confirmed. Yet the Frenchman had rescued the very woman he had betrayed. Something did not add up, and, with the invasion only two days away, he needed to capture Josse to get an explanation of the contradictions.

If they had escaped, Richter felt sure they would be heading north. Josse would avoid Granville: too many Germans for his liking. But the Frenchman had to make for a port. Which one?

Unless he got out of his present predicament, there would be no chance of catching Josse. He heaved uselessly at the rear fender; even with Helmut's help, lifting the wheel from the ditch proved impossible. Richter cast about in desperation for help. An old man ran across the road, seeking escape from the mayhem and danger. Richter called to him, but the man ignored him, his fear of American bombs greater than that of the German. Richter pulled out his pistol and fired, and the Frenchman fell dead by the side of the road.

"Look out, *mein Herr!*"

Richter turned at Helmut's cry and saw a young French peasant coming towards him. The German briefly saw the eyes burning with hatred. Then he saw the small hand sickle in the man's fist. The man was almost upon him, the steel blade held above his head. "You swine – you've killed my father!"

Crack! The pistol jumped in Richter's hand. Still the man came on, his hatred defying the wound. Crack! Crack! The man faltered, reeling, but his hand came down as he fell against the German, the blade cleaving into Richter's left arm, just below the shoulder. Richter staggered back as the man fell against him; the odor of Calvados came from the Frenchman's mouth.

Richter emptied the pistol's magazine into the man's head. The blood spurted over Richter's tunic as his assailant fell dead at his feet, the sickle rattling on the cobblestones.

"Verdammt! Verdammt!" Richter pushed his pistol into the holster and clutched at the wound on his left arm.

"Can I help? Let me see." Helmut tugged at the rip in the sleeve caused by the sickle, exposing the wound.

Richter winced with the pain and looked down at the blood seeping from the gash in his flesh. "It's not too bad. I've seen worse." He remembered when a communist bastard of the Red Front had smashed his jaw with an iron bar in a street fight.

"Maybe, but it needs treatment, sir. We need to get you to a hospital."

"No, you treat it, Helmut." Richter nodded towards the car. The chauffeur ran to the vehicle and pulled the first aid kit from the glove compartment. Richter cursed his luck. Every wasted minute helped Josse. Where was he? Where was the Frenchman going?

He clenched his teeth as Helmut applied a stinging antiseptic to his arm and bound the wound. Josse had to head for a port. But which? Richter knew he had to pick up the scent quickly, or Josse would slip the net.

"That's patched you up for the moment, sir, but you must go to the hospital."

"There isn't time." Josse had to be caught. "Let's find the *Kommandantur* and get some transport."

"But there's a danger of infection, sir." Helmut pleaded.

"There are bigger dangers than that facing us, Helmut." Richter strode off through the chaos around them, his uninjured arm beckoning the chauffeur to follow. It was nothing more than an inspired guess, but he felt he knew where Josse was heading. Then the darkness of unconsciousness enveloped him and he crumpled to the ground.

The road from Avranches. 9:30 a.m.

As they left the northern outskirts of Avranches, Florence became more ame-
nable to restraint. The mare's mouth sawed through the bit, but Josse brought
her back to the trot.

Josse looked over his shoulder. Jeanne and Augustine were comforting
Céleste, who was sobbing, the fear still in her eyes. The aircraft had gone, but
the evidence of their cruel visit still hung in the sky: a pall of black smoke
drifted over the town. Josse grimaced. Yet more French people had died as the
Allies pursued their plan of bombing the railways to cut the German lines of
communication in preparation for the invasion.

He took consolation that there was nothing on the road behind them. No
one was following them. But Josse knew that fate did not always deal the
right cards. When Richter got news of the events at the checkpoint, he'd use
all his resources to hunt them down.

A stream ran alongside the road; he halted Florence and jumped down
from the buckboard. He ran his hands over the mare's fetlocks. There was
some warmth, but the horse was sound.

"I'm going to get some water for Florence." He looked under the trap and
was relieved to find the bucket still swinging on its hook. To water the mare
would take valuable time, he knew, but Florence was their passport to escape;
a tired, thirsty horse would mean inevitable capture.

Josse leaned over the stream and dragged the bucket in the water. He
would have to leave the coast road soon. Much as he would like to go that
way, it would take them too close to Granville: the pre-war fashionable resort
was now a honey pot for German officers.

Florence gulped noisily, emptying the bucket quickly. Josse returned to
the stream for more. For the next few hours, he knew that the horse was the
most important creature in the world. He looked at his watch. Nearly ten
o'clock in the morning. They could still make Fierville before curfew, given
good luck.

The mare almost drained the second offering and raised her head, replete.
Josse poured the remainder over the horse's head to cool her off and reached
under the trap to place the bucket on the hook. Augustine called out to him.
"Please give me the bucket, Philippe."

He looked up. "What on earth do you want with the bucket?"

"It's Jeanne, you fool. She can't get down, and she needs to..."

Dartmouth. Devon. 5 p.m.

Sally swung the car around the tight corner at Clarence Street onto College Way. She was late. She had been told to pick up an officer, but the whole
of Dartmouth was one massive traffic jam of military vehicles. The big day
was near, she was sure.

As she tried to get past a truck, she saw him walking on the pavement. He was in civilian clothes, but there was no mistaking the red hair.

"Danny!" Sally shouted through the open window.

He half-turned, recognized her, made to continue walking, then stopped again.

"Danny, please get into the car." There was a pleading in her voice that she tried to disguise but couldn't. He shrugged his shoulders, opened the door and sat beside her.

"Where have you been hiding, Danny?" She looked at him, but he averted his eyes.

"I haven't been hiding anywhere." There was an edge to his voice. "I've been on duty. There's a war on, you know."

"I know, but I haven't heard from you since…." She stopped; she hadn't seen him since he'd met her father.

"Sally, I'm sorry, but…." There was a hint of guilt in his voice.

"Yes?"

"I don't know how to say this, Sally," he looked ahead through the windshield, "but you're not my sort."

"Not your sort?" Her reaction was angry; she felt hurt.

"I knew I'd get it wrong. What I meant to say was…." He turned his head and looked at her. "Sally, I like you – in fact, I like you very much – but it's just…."

"It's just what?"

"We come from different backgrounds, perhaps even different worlds. Maybe we shouldn't meet. Your father….It's so difficult." He lit a cigarette; she noticed the match shaking in his hand.

"Are you saying that it's because we come from different classes?" She spoke sharply and went on before he could answer. "You sound just like my father – you're just as pompous as he is."

The traffic began moving and she shifted through the gears.

"What he – and you – don't realize is the war has changed – is changing – everything. Everyone's had to muck in together to get through this nightmare."

"Some people – ordinary people – have had to muck in more than others," Danny replied sullenly. "Did your father have to move out of his house and home like mine did?"

"You're missing the point, Danny. Things will never be the same again. There'll be no going back to the days before the war. Do you think ordinary people will allow that to happen? Or have you no faith in ordinary people anymore?" She looked at him sharply, angrily, and cursed as she was forced to hit the brakes to avoid the truck in front as the traffic slowed again.

She breathed deeply, trying to control her conflicting emotions.

"Danny, do you realize if it hadn't been for the war, we wouldn't have met? I'd probably be cosseted on my father's country estate, unaware of the real world. The world that the war – and you – have shown me."

Danny hung his head at the impact of her words.

"Has it ever occurred to you, Danny, that I might like you?"

He raised his head and looked at her, his face showing his inner torment. His eyes broke away from hers. "I'm sorry, Sally, but it won't work out." He opened the door quickly and jumped out. He looked at her once more, shrugged his shoulders, and was gone.

Sally began to pound the horn. Again and again.

The driver of the American truck ahead stuck his head out the window and looked back at her. "What's up with you, lady?"

The Village of Fierville. Normandy. 5 p.m.

Fierville greeted the trap in the quiet of a cloudy, showery afternoon. The small village lay away from the main route, nestling in a rural backwater of the Cotentin peninsula. The small harbor of Carteret was five miles away; Cherbourg was within an hour's drive, but that bustling seaport could have been in a different world from the almost-deserted square that welcomed Josse and a tired Florence.

The Frenchman let the mare find her own pace – no more than a weary walk as she made her way past the few cottages that hugged the side of the road leading to the village square.

He glanced behind him. Augustine was still alert and vigilant, her hand grasping the sub-machine gun that lay on the seat beside her, although there was no need for it: there was no German presence in Fierville. On the seat opposite, Jeanne, wrapped in a blanket, looked into the distance, preoccupied; Céleste, covered by a cape to protect her from the rain, slumbered obliviously on her lap.

Florence's pace quickened as she spotted the horse trough in front of the *Mairie*, a stone building with shuttered windows that formed one side of the square. Opposite was an old Romanesque church. Between the two buildings, on a third side of the square, was a bar that had seen better days. Josse looked beyond the wizened customer sipping his *vin rouge* on the terrace and saw Danielle, the owner of the bar since her husband had become a prisoner of war. They acknowledged each other as Josse jumped down and worked the hand pump, bringing water cascading into the trough. Florence drank deeply.

"*Bien fait*, Florence." Josse stroked the horse's neck and mane. The mare had done well indeed, bringing them along all the back roads without complaint. There had been one checkpoint, but the soldier wasn't even a German, probably some Slav in the uniform of the Third Reich; he had waved them through.

"Are we there yet?" Céleste rubbed her eyes, awakened by the cessation of motion.

"Oui, ma petite, we're there!" Josse gave Florence's neck a final pat and went to the rear of the trap. Danielle strolled over to join them and the women introduced themselves.

"We'll be staying here overnight." Josse opened the door to the trap. "Danielle has prepared rooms for us. René LeGrand will pick us up just after dawn tomorrow. As the captain of the fishing vessel, he'll have the necessary papers." He offered his hand to Augustine as she got down. "Augustine, I need you to come with us tomorrow, to help with getting Jeanne to the boat."

"Et toi, ma petite," he lifted Céleste down from the trap, "you will stay here, at your *maison de vacances."*

"A vacation?" The girl skipped around him. "I haven't had a vacation since…"

Her voice trailed away; she seemed to slip away into another world. Augustine bent down and scooped her up, kissing her. "It'll be a good vacation, Céleste. Aunt Danielle will take you on walks in the country."

"Another aunt." Céleste pouted. "I love my aunts, but…" She stopped and bit her lower lip. The three women looked at each other.

"Let's get out of the rain." Josse lifted Jeanne from the trap, his brawny arms tightening as he carried her to the bar.

Outside the Royal Naval College. Dartmouth. 6:30p.m.

"I'm awfully sorry I'm late, Major Priestley." Sally brought the car to a halt outside the Dartmouth Royal Naval College, now the headquarters of the U.S. Navy.

The red-haired officer climbed quickly into the passenger seat and placed his attaché case in the foot well. "I was getting a little anxious, Sally. You're usually so prompt." He looked at his watch, clearly in a hurry.

Sally eased the car onto the hill leading out of the city and immediately ran into traffic congestion. "Sorry about this, Major," Sally moved the car forward in low gear, "but the whole American army seems to be on the move."

"Damn the Americans." Priestley slapped the dashboard impatiently. "I've had my fill of the Americans. I have to liaise with them twice a week now. Orders from the top. Such arrogant b—" He caught himself quickly. "Sorry, Sally, but our friends from across the Atlantic do try one's patience. They think they're running the show, now."

Sally smiled at him, but said nothing. As she inched her way up the hill behind the convoy of trucks, she thought of her meeting with Danny. He was so pig-headed. When he'd told her earlier that he was not her sort, she'd exploded. Perhaps she shouldn't have been so angry with him; she'd only reinforced his opinion. She tried to thrust the thought of him from her mind, as she maneuvered around a truck. She didn't love him – she was sure of that. But he was so different, so refreshing with his ideas. But so stubborn.

"You've missed the turn." Priestley spoke angrily.

"I'm sorry, major." Sally cursed herself for allowing Danny to occupy her mind.

Priestley kept looking at his watch. It had taken over an hour to get out of the city, but eventually Sally swung the car west, and they began to crawl in the direction of Halwell. There was still a lot of U.S. military traffic on the road.

"I'm sorry about the traffic, Major – obviously something special going on." She dropped down a gear to overtake an American truck; the GI's in the back whistled at her and blew her kisses.

"The Americans will soon be gone, Sally. Thank Heaven."

"You mean it's coming soon – the invasion?"

"Perhaps I've said too much already, Sally, but yes, it's coming soon."

"You know?" Sally could barely contain her excitement. At last everything she'd worked for, in her own small way, was coming to fruition.

"Look, forget what I said, Sally." Priestley looked anxious. "Mum's the word, eh?"

"Mum's the word, sir." Sally looked for the side turn that would take them off the main road towards the farm where Alistair Priestley lodged. She was sure that he was involved in some hush-hush business, but she wouldn't ask, just as she wouldn't ask her father about his work.

Priestley looked at his watch again. "Have you ever thought what may happen if the invasion doesn't succeed?"

"Doesn't succeed? Of course it will succeed."

"But suppose the Germans have found out the plans, and throw the invasion back into the sea?"

"How can they have learned? Spies?" Sally waited for a gap in the traffic and swung the car south towards Blackawton.

Priestley laughed briefly, and then looked serious. "Have you ever considered what may happen if the invasion fails with a huge loss of American life? Suppose the Americans throw in the towel? What if public opinion forced Roosevelt to bring their soldiers home, or to concentrate on the Japs, their real enemy, leaving us on our own?"

Sally was stunned. She'd never thought about it. For her, the coming invasion was a beacon of hope, its light leading to the end of the war. The thought of having to fight on for years against the Nazis – without the Americans – was too depressing. "Pray God it doesn't come to that!"

"Yes," Priestley spoke softly. "Perhaps prayer is necessary." He looked at the line of trucks ahead and glanced again at his watch. "Damn these Americans."

The Bar at Fierville. 7 p.m.

Danielle ladled out the last of the rabbit stew, the aroma mingling with the smoke coming from the wood fire in the hearth. It had suddenly turned cold for June. A shutter clattered in the growing wind; Danielle hurried to secure it.

Josse cleaned his plate with a crust of bread, got up from the table and went to the window. The weather was deteriorating. The wind was gathering; the sky was covered with clouds scudding from the north west. He could almost smell the coming storm. It did not augur well for what had to be done in the morning.

"And now a special treat for Céleste." Danielle pulled a dish from the oven. "Raspberry tart!"

"Mon favori!" Céleste cried excitedly.

"Philippe," Jeanne turned to where he stood at the window, "I need to talk to you."

"What is it?"

Jeanne looked at the two women. "I need to talk privately."

Josse shrugged his shoulders, then lifted her, still sitting in her chair, and carried her through to the deserted bar. Danielle followed with an already-lit oil lamp, set it upon a table and left the room, closing the door behind her.

"What is it, Jeanne?" He drew another chair to the table and lit a cigarette. The lamp cast shadows on his face, exaggerating the care that lined it.

"I need to send a radio message."

"Impossible." He smacked an annoyed hand on the table. "I've already told you so. It's too dangerous. Besides, you have no code sheet."

"Perhaps I could use your code?"

"Out of the question. I'm not scheduled to make a broadcast until tomorrow evening – by which time you'll be well on your way to England."

"But it's vital." Jeanne ignored his tirade and spoke quietly. "It could prevent your plans from being betrayed."

"What plans? I have only one plan at the moment – to put you on a boat to England tomorrow and to get back to St. Marie before—"

"Before the invasion?" She interrupted. "That's the real plan, isn't it, Philippe? Something to do with the invasion?" She fixed his brown eyes and he held her stare for a while before speaking.

"The invasion is coming, of course, and it will come soon. We all have our tasks to do." He shrugged his shoulders. "There are, as you say, plans for the Resistance. But that's all."

"But didn't Wainwright have those plans? They were supposed to be delivered to you."

"I never received them." He spoke in an offhand manner. "Anyway, the plans have been changed."

"Why did you rescue me from jail, Philippe? It would have made no difference to the plans."

The question took him aback. She was right. Her rescue was not part of the plan. If he had followed the plan as he'd been instructed to, she would have been rotting in some German concentration camp and he wouldn't have jeopardized Richter's confidence. But he had known that it was partly his fault that she had been captured.

"Because I wanted you to live, Jeanne. Even in all the horror of this war, people have emotions, become fond of one another." He looked away in embarrassment. He could not tell her how he had really felt about her since he had first met her. "I've told you before that you're like a daughter to me."

A spattering of rain brushed the window, and Josse went across to peer into the night at the gathering storm. "I just want to get you back to England, Jeanne. Besides," he turned and smiled, "I promised your prince that I'd get you back safely."

"My prince?" Jeanne smiled mischievously. "Perhaps you and Céleste have called for my pumpkin coach?"

"Céleste doesn't always live in a dream world. Your prince is very real. And he's American."

The door flew open and Céleste skipped into the bar room.

"Princess, princess, I came for a kiss before I go to bed."

Danielle appeared in the doorway. "I'm sorry; I took my eyes off her for a moment."

"It's all right." Jeanne kissed the girl on the forehead. "Sweet dreams, *ma petite.*"

Céleste looked at her earnestly. "You will find your prince, won't you?"

"Of course." She patted the girl on the back. "Now you must go to bed."

The girl made to leave, but turned in the doorway. "Now I remember the prince's name. It was not a French name." She took a few seconds to get her lips and tongue around the word. "It was Tom!"

Dartmouth, Devon. 8 p.m.

A chill ran down Sally's back. Her hand shook as she lit a cigarette; she drew deeply on it, trying to steady her nerves. Her palms felt clammy; a fine perspiration beaded on her forehead. Her eyes looked down to her lap, on which sat a small leather-bound book. She picked it up and read it through again, her fingers trembling as she turned the pages. Her breathing became rapid and she felt her pulse pounding in her forehead. Surely it couldn't be Danny's?

Sally tossed the book onto the passenger seat as if it had been a red-hot coal. It couldn't be true. She shook her head. It was someone's sick idea of a joke. She'd found it half an hour before, as she was returning the car to the pool at the end of the day.

201

There had been the usual check she made – officers often left umbrellas, even briefcases in her car – and then she'd found it, under the passenger seat. She'd read it and found it to be a diary – a diary of someone who was extremely dangerous.

The words had been etched on her mind as she had read them.

'What they have done to me and my family can never be forgiven...' 'When I get the secret of the invasion to Richter...' 'When the Germans get the full operational details..."

The diary was full of hatred for Churchill and the Royal Family, words that reminded her of things Danny had said. Something was wrong, dreadfully wrong. The diary was clearly that of a spy. She jumped down from the car and stamped out her cigarette, her mind racing through the people whom she'd driven that day. The three lieutenants she'd collected in the early morning, who'd talked about baseball all the way to Plymouth; one had tried to flirt with her. Rear Admiral Melchett. Surely not; no, he'd sat in the back seat as if he were royalty, not condescending to talk to her. Then Alistair Priestley, out beyond Blackawton, worried about threats to the invasion. And Danny.

She opened the diary again. 'Like me, he had red hair...'

No, no, it couldn't be Danny. Her mind rebelled against the thought. He hated Churchill, despised her father and all he stood for, but surely he wasn't a spy.

Her father. He would know what to do. She'd never been allowed to probe into what he did, but she knew he was a big shot in the Intelligence Service. Yes, he would know what to do. She put the diary in her pocket and ran to the office.

The young Wren at the duty desk looked up as Sally approached. "You look as if you've seen a ghost! Are you all right?"

"Yes, no, er...." Sally was flustered.

"Can I get you a cup of tea?"

"No, I'm fine." Sally pulled herself together. "Look, I need to make an urgent phone call."

"You know making private telephone calls is against regulations." The clerk looked doubtful for a moment and then smiled. "Use the phone in that room." She pointed to a small annex to the office. "I won't tell anyone if you don't." She winked. "Boy friend trouble, is it, dear?"

"Not really." Sally hoped desperately that it wasn't as she made her way to the annex.

The phone at her father's Kensington home rang unanswered. She tried four times without reply. Sally was desperate, flicking quickly through her personal address book, searching for her father's special office number. She'd never used it before – he'd told her to use it only in an emergency. In her haste, she misdialed, cursed herself, then dialed slowly and deliberately.

There was an answer after only three rings. It was not her father.

"Brigadier Fortescue's office."

"This is Sally Fortescue. May I speak with my father, please?"

There was a brief pause; the aide was not used to such calls. "I'm sorry, miss, but the Brigadier is in conference with the prime minister in Whitehall."

Sally cursed her luck. At the one time she had needed her father, he was deep in the bowels of Churchill's bomb-proof bunker below Whitehall.

"Do you know when he'll be back?"

"I'm afraid I can't say, miss. Knowing the prime minister's methods, I would say the conference could go on until the small hours of the morning." The voice was dryly patronizing, eager to get on to other, more important matters. "Can I take a message for him, miss?"

Sally glanced at her watch. It would be hours before her father got a message. And what message could she leave? That a dangerous traitor was on the loose? That she didn't know the identity of the spy, except that it might be Danny? The aide might think that she was drunk or mad, or both.

"Hello, hello, miss. Are you still there?"

"Yes. Tell him I'll try to contact him later."

"Very well, miss." The line went dead.

Sally hung up and looked at the diary lying in her palm, feeling as if it were burning her hand. She thought for a moment and bit her lip. She knew what she had to do.

The desk clerk looked up. "Everything all right now, dear?" The question went unanswered, so she opened the vehicle log book. "Shall we check in your car until tomorrow?"

"No, I've got another pick-up to make." Sally made for the door and turned. "Thanks for letting me make the call."

"That's all right. Take care."

Sally got into the car and made a quick calculation. She reckoned that she could get to Plymouth in an hour, maybe a little more. She fired the engine and turned out of the gate onto the road. Perhaps it wasn't the right thing, but she knew she had to do it. She would confront Danny with the diary.

Fierville, Normandy. 10 p.m.

Jeanne gazed absently into the fire, watching the flames lick at the wood. Philippe had gone to bed and had soon been followed by Augustine, who had urged her to get some sleep because of the early start the next morning. But she was still stunned by what Philippe had told her: how Tom had saved her from the Germans, how he had wanted to give up his place on the plane for her, how he had made Philippe promise to get her back to England.

She saw Tom's face in the flames of the fire and she regretted what had happened at their last meeting. Of course, he should have told her earlier about his wife back in the States. But he'd been kind. He hadn't tried to take advantage of her, he hadn't treated her cheaply. A sharp ache tugged at her. It could have been so different. Damn the war, she thought, damn it to hell.

"It's going to be rough weather for you tomorrow." Danielle looked up from the dish-washing and saw the rain running down the window. "I think you should get your head down soon." She plumped the pillows on the cot on which Jeanne sat.

"You're right." She returned her gaze to the fire. She wanted a little more time to look at his face. At least he was safe back in England. She wondered what he was doing at that moment. Was he thinking about her? She conjured up the time they had first met at All Saint's Church, then how shy he had been at the Bach concert afterward. The memories flooded back: meeting again at The Hope and Anchor, their walks on the headland, the games of chess, the way she had invited him to tea by using—

"Danielle, I have to send a message before we go to bed. It's to confirm the departure tomorrow. The Navy will need to know when and where to meet LeGrand's fishing vessel. I'd forgotten."

The Frenchwoman looked at her curiously. "Philippe said nothing to me about it."

"He must have forgotten, too." Jeanne smiled disarmingly. "Where is the radio?"

"It's hidden in the cupboard by the side of the hearth." Danielle hesitated. "I think I should check with Philippe."

"No, don't bother him. He's probably asleep by now. Please rig the aerial. Let's get it done and go to bed. We have a busy day tomorrow."

Plymouth, Devon. 9:50 p.m.

Sally shifted down a gear as she crossed the bridge over the River Plym and entered the city. Nearly ten o'clock. She realized that she hadn't thought out her plan very clearly. If Danny was working a night duty, she'd have little chance of seeing him. She couldn't just roll up to the shore base and demand to see him. At best, she'd be laughed at; at worst, the Provost Marshall would have her thrown in the brig.

But if he wasn't on duty, she knew where he'd be. The Barley Sheaf, the pub where Danny once told her that he could find the finest pint of Guinness in Plymouth. The car approached the outskirts of the city. Sally saw the evidence of the German bombing raids of the previous month, adding to the ruins made back in 1940 and 1941. The rubble of demolished houses had been bulldozed into heaps. She thought about the people who had lived in those houses until the bombs rained from above. All had lost their homes, some their lives.

Sally was incensed. After all they had gone through, battling on to survive – now all their sacrifices were being betrayed. She turned onto King Street, looking for the pub Danny frequented.

No, it couldn't be Danny who was committing this foul deed. Yet the words of the diary kept hammering in her head: "the German High Command can throw the invasion back into the channel…", "when I get the secret of the invasion….", "red hair…" Did he really hate his own people so much that he would betray them?

Suddenly, she saw the pub on the left, on the corner of King Street. Sally parked the car and walked along the street, her low-heeled Wren shoes clipping on the pavement. She peered through the crack in the curtain of the pub bar. There were not many in the bar, but it was nearing closing time. Through the window, she heard the barman ring the bell behind the bar. "Last orders, please, gentlemen, last orders."

Then she saw him. He was alone in a corner of the bar, looking down at his pint of Guinness, ruffling his fingers through his red hair

Maybe it is you, she thought. You hate Churchill, the Royal Family, my father and everything they stand for. She thrust aside conflicting emotions and opened the public bar door.

"Danny!" Sally shouted over the noise of the bar, which suddenly died away. She saw his face as his eyes lifted to hers. At first there was consternation, then a half smile, followed by fear. He turned his eyes away. Sally made her way over to his table.

"Danny, I need to talk to you."

"I don't think there's much left to say, Sally." He avoided her eyes.

"It's not about us, Danny – or maybe it is. It's about this!" She brought the diary from behind her back, her eyes keenly watching his face for any reaction.

He looked at the book. His brow furrowed; there was a look of surprised puzzlement on his face. "What's all this about, Sally?"

"You wrote this, didn't you – this is your diary, isn't it?" There was anger in her raised voice. The gentle hubbub of people in the bar ordering their last drinks fell away; eyes turned toward them.

She dropped her voice to a whisper. "Let's talk outside in the car." She turned and headed for the door. Danny pushed his drink aside and reluctantly followed.

"Sally, I didn't write this." Danny skimmed the diary by the interior light of the car. "It's not even my handwriting."

"How do I know that?" Sally's question was sharp. "I've never seen your writing."

Danny's head fell to his chest. He remembered that he once had decided to write to let Sally know how he felt about her, but had lacked the courage to see it through. At that moment, as he looked at her angry face, he wished he had.

"This is not my diary. I don't keep a diary." He tried to speak convincingly, but he sounded desperate.

"But the bit about not being able to forgive what had been done to the writer's family – that's you, isn't it?" Sally snatched the book from him and read the relevant passage. "Your family were thrown off their farm, weren't they? And your father...." She paused, as she detected the look on his face. "And all the stuff about hating Churchill – I've heard those words from your own lips many times." Sally was almost hysterical, a hysteria brought on by the damning evidence she did not want to believe.

"Sally, stop it!" The vehemence in Danny's voice caused Sally to move away from him. "I did not write it!" He shouted, then shook his head and spoke more gently.

"Sally, whatever you think about me, I am not a spy. Yes, I want to change things and get rid of the old order, but I am not a traitor to my country."

Sally shook her head, not knowing what to believe.

Danny flicked through the book again. "Whoever did write this diary," he spoke urgently, "is a dangerous menace who must be stopped at once. You understand what this is all about, Sally?" He moved the book in front of her. "It's about the invasion. Although we don't know the secret, we know it's coming soon – you've only got to look at all the American activity going on. But the person who wrote this diary knows the secret, he knows the where and when, the full details. And if that information fell into the Germans' hands, it could delay the Allied victory for years."

Danny looked through the diary again. "Where did you find it, Sally?"

"Under the seat where you're sitting – where you sat this afternoon." She looked away from him, as he bridled against the lingering accusation.

"Who else has been in the car today?"

"I ran three naval lieutenants from Dartmouth to Plymouth, but it couldn't be any of them – they were American, and the diary is obviously written by an Englishman."

She continued to recall her day. "Then there was Rear Admiral Melchett. He sat in the back seat and never said a word. I doubt that he dislikes Churchill."

"Anyone else?"

"Yes. After I dropped off the Admiral, that's when I picked you up." She cast him a sideways glance.

"And that's it?"

"No, I had one final assignment, late in the afternoon. Major Priestley. My God, Danny," she gasped, "could it be him?" She stopped, remembering where she had heard about what would happen if the invasion failed.

"Who is this character, Sally?"

"I don't know, really. He's involved in some big hush-hush work. Liaison with the Americans in the Dartmouth headquarters. I have to bring him in and take him back to some farmhouse twice a week. Heaven knows what he does there."

"Where is this farmhouse?" Danny asked.

"It's north of Blackawton. Right on the edge of the American zone." She screwed up her eyes as she tried to remember. "Old Oak Farm, that's it!"

"Heavens!" Danny could not contain his amazement. "John Witherspoon's old place."

"You know it?"

"About a mile from where my family live." Danny shrugged. "Or used to."

"I'm sorry. I didn't want to remind you." Sally felt the guilt of her accusations and now felt she was rubbing salt into Danny's wounds.

"Have you told anyone else about this?" Danny held up the diary. "Did you report it?"

"No. I tried to call my father, but he's in conference with Churchill." Sally bit her lip. She shouldn't have told Danny. His look said everything: so your father rubs shoulders with the old devil himself. Her voice began to waver. "Oh, Danny, I've been such a fool…"

Danny pushed the image of Sally's father from his mind. What should he do? Of course, he knew what he ought to do: he should report it to his superior officer. But what then? He'd probably not be believed at first, even with Sally's evidence. Then there'd be an enquiry, reporting through the usual channels, the whole issue grinding through a bureaucracy that, at that time, was occupied with the imminent invasion.

He made his decision.

"Do you trust me, Sally?" He looked into her eyes and searched her face for the slightest trace of doubt.

"Yes, I trust you, Danny." She began to sob, and put her face in her hands. "How could I ever…"

Danny reached up and gently took her hands from her face, his fingers lightly brushing away her tears. "Don't upset yourself about it." He leaned forward and brushed her forehead with his lips.

Sally looked up at him. "But what are we going to do?"

"Start up the engine. We're going to have a talk with Major Priestley."

On the way to Old Oak Farm. 11:35 p.m.

Sally swung the car off the Plymouth-Dartmouth road and turned down the single-track road heading to Blackawton from the north. The moon, hiding behind scudding clouds, offered her no help.

Danny looked at his watch. "Coming up to midnight. At least the rain's eased off." The windshield wipers flicked at the intermittent drizzle.

Sally slowed as the hedgerows on either side brushed the sides of the car. "Are you sure we're doing the right thing, Danny?" There was anxiety in her voice as she peered at the road ahead, barely distinguishable in the meager light from the hooded headlights. "Shouldn't we go back and report it to the authorities?"

"No. Haven't you noticed something, Sally?"

"What?"

"Where are the Americans? Last week, this whole area was teeming with them." He waved his hand across the landscape. "Now, there's nobody. Not a single GI. Not one. You know what that means?"

"The invasion?"

"It's under way." Danny held up the diary. "We don't know where it's going to be, but whoever wrote this diary knows both when and, more importantly, where. If it's Priestley, we have to tackle him now. If we go back and report it, it'll be too late."

Danny ran his fingers over the leather cover. "Remember what it says in here?" He quoted from memory. "Soon I shall have the secret..."

"But how's he going to get the information to the Germans? Radio?"

"No. The last diary entry says he's going to use pigeons. And if he hasn't sent the messages already, he won't be able to send them before dawn tomorrow."

"Why?"

"Because the birds can't home without the sun."

"But what if he's already..." Her voice trailed away as their eyes met, their stunned silence expressing their worst fears.

Old Oak Farm. 11:45 p.m.

Agent Blau was in sight of his goal, but he felt frustrated. It had taken him hours to transpose the six messages he had copied from the Top Secret file that morning. It had not been easy. Great care was necessary in their preparation; there could be no mistakes.

He rubbed his tired eyes and brought the oil lamp closer as he painstakingly finished the final message. He looked down at the six pieces of paper. Just six messages to send and he would be done. Six messages. One for each of the five landing beaches in Normandy: Gold; Juno; Sword; Utah; and Omaha. And the most important – to warn about Operation Fortitude, the General Patton-led deception plan. Just six messages and the invasion would be destroyed. Churchill would fall, and the despicable Americans would lick their wounds and pull out of the war in Europe.

He carefully folded the pieces of paper. There would be no radio message that could be intercepted or jammed. Just the steady beat of pigeons' wings, undetectable by radio, heading for Richter's headquarters in Normandy.

He regretted that the stupid little Wren had been late picking him up and had made the wrong turn in the damned American traffic. The delay had cost him vital hours, as the birds could not find their way to France without the sun in the sky. There was no way to stop the invasion, he knew – it was already underway. But once Richter passed on the message, the German army would be able to respond tactically; when they knew there was no threat from Patton, that the Normandy invasion was not a ruse, the Panzer divisions could be released from the Pas de Calais and leveled against the invaders.

He slipped the messages into the rings that he would attach to the pigeons' legs and arranged them in a straight line. Six little rings. The fate of the world. The downfall of Churchill. Revenge.

He was about to scoop up the rings, but stopped. There was a noise outside. Agent Blau opened the drawer of the bureau and pulled out a Mauser 45.

Outside Old Oak Farm. 11:45 p.m.

"We're nearly there, Danny. It's about a quarter of a mile, off to the right."

"I know." Danny thought of happier days, when he was a lad and when he used to come over to Old Oak Farm to play hide and seek in the barn with Bill, Mr. Witherspoon's son.

"Danny, I don't think we should announce our arrival." Sally flicked off the lights and killed the engine.

Danny was jolted from his reverie. "Sorry, I was thinking of other things. You're right. Let's go the rest of the way on foot." Danny got out; he pulled his naval hat down over his eyes, poor protection against the persistent drizzle. Sally pulled her naval cape around her and joined him. They stared into the darkness of the night; the moon promised a glimpse, then surrendered once more to the clouds.

"How are we going to handle this, Danny?"

"I gave it some thought on the way out." He opened the trunk and brought out the lug wrench. "Here's what I think we should do. He'll open the door for you since he knows you." He looked at her anxiously. "But it'll be risky."

"I'm up to it, Danny. It's got to be done." Sally tried to make herself look taller than her five-foot-two. "Besides, you're right – he won't see me as a threat. He'll wonder what I'm doing here at midnight, but he won't feel threatened."

"When he answers the door, show him the diary. You'll see from his reaction whether it's his. If he reacts, drop it."

"Drop the diary?" Sally furrowed her brow.

"It's important to him. If it's his diary, he'll step forward to pick it up." They made their way toward the farm. "I'll be hiding by the side of the door. When he steps forward, I'll knock him out with this." He brandished the lug wrench.

Sally stopped. "I'm not so sure, Danny." She hesitated at the thought of violence. "Perhaps we should go back and let the authorities know."

"We haven't time, Sally," he whispered, "the invasion's about to happen. Thousands of soldiers' lives are at risk. Maybe the whole war. Come on, let's go."

As they approached, they could see the gate and the farmhouse beyond.

Suddenly she stopped. "I'm frightened, Danny."

He put his arms around her and hugged her tightly. "So am I."

Old Oak Farm. Midnight.

As soon as he heard the sound, Priestley moved noiselessly across the room and climbed the stairs. He left the light on; the blackout curtains were drawn, but he didn't want to give the slightest clue that he had been alerted to a presence outside.

The upstairs floor was unlit, but he felt his way along the landing and opened the door to the radio room. It was empty. The turned German spy that he had minded was back in Portsmouth jail, his mission over. Priestley allowed himself a chuckle. If only the spy had known that he had been supervised by a top agent for the Germans. And that all the misinformation sent about Patton and the FUSAG was about to be undone within hours.

He pulled back the curtain and looked down onto the farmyard. The rain had almost stopped and the moon, not quite full, sought a way through the clouds. There were two figures in the yard. He recognized one at once: it was the Fortescue woman who chauffeured him from Dartmouth. His eyes swung to the other figure, a tall man in a naval uniform; he did not know him.

What were they doing? He looked back at the woman. There was something in her hand. Priestley's eyes widened. He dropped the curtain and raced down the stairs, reaching for his briefcase. His hand searched inside. The plans for the invasion were there, but the diary was missing.

Of course, he should not have kept a diary. But, after the war, he would be able to publish it, to claim the credit, to show his role in the upcoming victory. It had been wrong to keep the diary, he knew, but all would be well. The foolish Fortescue woman and her companion were about to deliver the damning evidence back into his hands.

He picked up the silencer for the Mauser and screwed it onto the muzzle. There was a knock. He held the gun behind his back and opened the door.

"Sally! What on earth are you doing here at this time of night?" Priestley's figure appeared ghostly, caught eerily by the oil lamp within. Sally could see little, but she noticed his eyes drop briefly to the diary in her hand.

"I, er, found this diary in the car. I thought it might be yours." She had a feeling things were going wrong.

"No, it's not mine. I'm sorry you made the trip out here for nothing." Priestley spoke offhandedly, but tightened his grip on the Mauser behind his back. He knew the man who accompanied her was to his right, pressed against the farmhouse wall. "But why don't you come in and have a drink? You must be soaked." He beckoned her to enter the farmhouse.

"That's very kind of you." Sally tried to act normal, but there was anxiety in her voice. She caught Priestley's eyes glance once more at the book in her hand. It was his diary. She knew it. She stepped forward a pace and let the diary slip from her fingers, forcing herself not to look at Danny crouched by the wall.

"Leave it. It's of no importance." Priestley was ready for the trick. If he leaned forward to pick up the diary, the man would attack him. He had to lure the unknown man on; he tensed himself, ready for the attack. "Come in, it's warm inside."

"No, no—" Sally backed away from the door.

The attack would come at any moment, Priestley thought. The shock of it still surprised him. The lug wrench smashed into the door, splintering the wood. For a moment, he saw the attacker's eyes, wild with desperation. The lug wrench rose again. Priestley pulled the Mauser from behind his back and fired hastily. He heard the woman scream "Danny! Danny!" The bullet clipped his attacker's shoulder. The wrench dropped, clattering on the stone floor. Priestley pushed the wounded man aside and swung his arm under Sally's throat. He turned her so that her body was between him and the young man, and pushed the Mauser against her temple. "Enough of this silly game. Get inside."

June 5th

1944

Southwick. Headquarters Allied Expeditionary Force. 3 a.m.

"You're sure, Captain Stagg – you're saying that we have a chance to go on the sixth?" Eisenhower tried to curb his excitement.

"To be honest, sir, not one hundred per cent," the Englishman tugged at his tie, "but the storm definitely shows signs of abating. The wind will drop, for sure. I think the conditions can be met. Of course, the sea will be choppy on the approaches to the beaches, but it'll be within the requirements."

"And the day after?"

"Much better. The weather will improve right through to the weekend. I'm afraid I haven't enough information to go beyond that."

Ike looked at the others in the room. "What are your opinions, gentlemen?"

"It's a bit dicey, sir," General Bradley offered, "but I think the odds are just about in our favor."

The British Admiral Ramsey got up from his chair. "I'm sure the fleet can handle the conditions, but I can't speak for the beaches. The improving conditions will be of help to us as we put the artificial harbors into position."

There was a slight pause as the admiral's words were weighed by the others in the room. Monty rapped his knuckles on the table sharply. "I say go!"

Eisenhower thought for a few seconds. "Very well, gentlemen, we go. I don't like it, but it's an acceptable risk. D-day will be June 6th."

U.S. Naval Headquarters, Dartmouth. 3 a.m.

Tom had drawn night duty. He was tired and on edge. All through the past day, despite the bad weather, the harbor of Dartmouth had emptied its vast armada of ships into the open sea. Everyone knew that the time had come. The occasion had been almost festive; there had been cheering from the dockside and some pretty Wrens, in their navy blue uniforms, had blown kisses to the departing men.

It had been a day of anxious hope. Hope, that the greatest invasion the world had seen would triumph and sweep the Nazi curse from Europe. Anxiety, because the men on the ships would soon be facing mortal danger.

Tom felt these emotions, too, but other feelings tugged at him. He'd not heard anything about Gwen since he'd left France. He cursed himself. He should have forced Josse to put her on the plane. Why had he been so foolish to trust the Frenchman?

Through the window of his office, he could just make out a vessel belatedly slip her moorings in the darkness of night. He slapped his hand against the window pane in frustration. The great day was at hand, yet he could think of nothing but Gwen. Where was she now? Was she safe?

He walked back to his desk and slumped in the chair, swallowed by his powerlessness. He'd been to the Wrens' headquarters at the Royal Dart Hotel in Kingswear, hoping to find Sally in case she had news of Gwen, but she couldn't be found. He'd visited Hope Cove, but Gwen's father had little to tell him. According to him, Gwen was away, visiting her aunt in Gravesend. Tom had said nothing. Obviously, Gwen could not tell her father about her role.

Tom restlessly went back to the window and was alarmed to see the flags and pennants stretched taut in the wind. The men at sea were in for a rough time.

In his desperation for news of Gwen, he'd thought of contacting the mysterious Englishman with the eye patch who had asked him to go to France, but it had been impossible; he couldn't just pick up the telephone and ask to be connected to the head of the British SOE. The thought of driving up to London to seek him out had crossed his mind, but the whole of southern England had been cordoned off as a security measure prior to the invasion.

He'd hoped that being on night watch would help him take his mind off Gwen, but it hadn't. He was angry that he could do nothing but wait for news of her. He had to see her, to put things right, to tell her why he hadn't told her about his wife, to tell her his marriage was as good as over. And to tell her he loved her.

He resented the intrusion into his thoughts as the door opened.

"Yes?" He spoke sharply to the sergeant who came into the office.

"Sorry to disturb you, sir, but the Brits received a message they can't decipher." He held out a piece of paper in his hand.

"What is it?" Tom's brow furrowed. "Where's it from?"

"They're not sure what it is, sir. Except that it comes from France."

"I'll look at it." He took the message from his hand. The sergeant began to leave, then stopped and turned.

"It's very strange, sir, but I was told the operator who took the message said she recognized the fist. Swore it was a known British agent that she used to deal with, but she's not heard from her for some time. Monkey was her codename. Good luck with the decoding, sir." He saluted and closed the door.

Tom looked down at the message transcript, his mind and heart racing. He didn't know Gwen's codename, but it was possible. He forced himself not to jump to conclusions; it could be any of a hundred agents. But perhaps the piece of paper on his desk was proof that Gwen was alive. He tried to contain the growing hope in his heart, but his hand shook as he picked up the coded message.

He read the transcript, the tidy groups, each of five random letters shouting their challenge at him. If Gwen had sent this message, why hadn't she used a regular code? Why hadn't Josse supplied her with a code sheet?

There was only one answer: to decipher the message. He picked up a pencil to begin a frequency analysis, but, after a few moments, he put the pencil down. The possibilities played across his mind. Gwen knew that his job was to decipher unknown codes. Perhaps it was a message for him specifically, designed to ensure it came before his eyes.

215

He knew the code! His hand reached down and opened the drawer in which he kept his personal things, rooting around until he had it in his hand: the Sherlock Holmes book. He flipped the pages, pulling out the letter with her coded invitation to tea. On the back was the solution he had made at the time.

Five minutes later, he read the complete message, his jaw agape in shock. He knew he should report the message, but someone would ask for confirmation, and he knew there wasn't time. He had to act there and then. He reached for the phone. "Sergeant, I need a jeep immediately. Front door in five minutes."

He replaced the receiver, picked up his service revolver and checked the chambers. His hand reached into another drawer and came out with a box of cartridges that he stuffed into his pocket.

He left the office and raced down the stairs. He knew Gwen was alive, but he still didn't know whether she was safe. But one thing was certain: the invasion was in danger.

A military hospital in Avranches, Normandy. 4 a.m.

The light forced its way through Richter's eyelids. He opened his eyes to a shimmering white canvas on which vague shadows danced. His hand came up to rub his eyes; he felt the pain in his arm and the memories came. The man, the sickle... he focused his eyes and the white resolved itself into the electric light above his head. The shadows became a German uniform. Helmut.

"Thank God you're all right, sir."

"Where am I? What's going on?" Richter struggled to get upright on the bed; he regretted his action as the pain stabbed at his arm again.

"You're in the hospital, sir." The chauffeur leaned over the bed. "You passed out after the attack on you. I had an ambulance bring you here. The doctor has sewn up your wound and bandaged it."

"What time is it?"

"Just after four a.m., sir. You were on the operating table for some time—"

"Four o'clock in the morning?" Richter cursed and swung his legs off the bed, his mind trying to force his body to ignore the pain in his arm. Josse had stolen fifteen hours' start. "Where is my uniform? Where are my boots?"

"But, sir, the doctor said—"

"A curse on all doctors! We have to get moving. Now! Did you get the car repaired?"

"No, sir, I thought it more important—"

The chauffeur was spared more of his boss's anger as the door opened. An officer entered, followed by a white-coated doctor.

"Heil Hitler!" The officer raised his hand in salute. "I am pleased the *Obersturmbannführer* is recovering."

"Cut the bullshit, Colonel. Who are you?"

"I am Colonel Hunstmann, *mein Herr,* Commandant of the Avranches garrison."

"Well, Huntsmann, I need a uniform and transport. Within half an hour."

"I really must protest—" The doctor came forward.

"Go to hell!" Richter turned to the officer. "Well, colonel?"

The officer looked dubious. "The air raid has had a devastating effect upon us. Perhaps in two hours I can provide a car and an escort. But in half an hour…"

Richter looked at his watch and grimaced as the pain struck again. Josse had too big a start. "There is not enough time. Get me a uniform and transport within thirty minutes. Now, move!"

"But, *mein Herr,* I regret we don't have the uniform of an *Obersturmbannführer* —"

"This is no time for protocol. Any uniform will do – just get it to me now!"

"Jawohl, mein Herr! But before I go, I have been asked to give you this important message. It was broadcast on the BBC this morning." The colonel handed a piece of paper to Richter, saluted with a click of his heels and hurried from the room.

Richter read the message.

'Blessent mon coeur avec une langeur monotone.'

The second Verlaine couplet. The landings would come in the next forty-eight hours.

Slapton Sands. South Devon. 4:15 a.m.

Tom sped through the narrow roads of Strete before swinging down the steep descent to Slapton Sands. He shook his head. Gwen's message was preposterous; it couldn't be true. And then he thought of the Sherlock Holmes she had quoted. 'My dear Watson, when you have eliminated the impossible, whatever remains, *however improbable,* must be the truth.'

He raced the jeep along the coastal strip. It looked so different. On that day but two weeks ago when so many lives had been lost, the sun had shone on the horrific scene that had greeted him. Now, the first glimmer of the pre-dawn picked out the dark scudding clouds. The beach now was quiet; all the men taking part in the invasion had been shipped to their embarkation points, and were perhaps already heading for the Far Shore.

And they could all be in far more danger than they knew. If the message Gwen had sent was correct, the whole invasion was threatened by betrayal. He turned right, wove the jeep through Slapton village and took the road to Blackawton.

Old Oak Farm. 4:30 a.m.

Priestley pulled a bottle of brandy from the bottom drawer of the desk and poured himself a large measure. He felt pleased with himself as he sipped at the drink, savoring its flavor. Soon. He looked down at the six rings on the desk. They were all that was needed to bring Churchill and his aristocratic friends to their knees and send the Americans home with an almighty bloody nose.

He felt the warmth of the liquor wash his stomach and, for some reason, an old saying came to mind. 'Revenge is a dish best enjoyed cold.' He filled his pipe and tamped it down. He'd waited a long time, many years for this moment. He raised his glass. "Here's to you, Dad."

He'd been a young lad when his father went off to war; he hadn't waited to be conscripted – he'd volunteered to fight 'for King and Country' at the outbreak in 1914. And his King and country had deserted him in his hour of need. It was five years before Priestley had seen his father again. He was broken in body and probably in spirit. In the last few weeks of the war, a shell splinter had left his right arm almost useless.

The Welsh windbag Lloyd George had promised the soldiers – what was it? –'a land fit for heroes.' Instead, his father had received nothing, not even a pension. While Churchill and his cronies lounged about their gentlemen's clubs, Priestley's father had called himself lucky to find a job as a grounds man at a minor Public School for the sons of gentlemen.

His father, who had given five years of his life in the war, had to tip his cap at those who had lived off the fat of the land. Priestley slammed his glass down in anger. He bit hard on the stem of his pipe. How he had hated those days. The toffs used to mock him, call him names because of his red hair.

Priestley recalled his revenge. There'd been a short fat boy, much younger than himself, the son of an American Jewish banker – how he hated those people. He'd caught the boy alone one day, and had taken great delight in beating the daylights out of him.

There'd been an inquiry at the school. His father had been sacked and they'd been evicted. His father never blamed him, but he was a broken man and he died soon after. Priestley clenched his fist. Bastards.

His mother had received a modest legacy when her uncle died and they managed somehow. She had been proud of him when he worked hard to win a scholarship to a provincial university. The snobs there never liked him, but he ignored them, working hard to graduate in German and French. He was surprised when his application for the Diplomatic Service had been accepted.

Berlin. Priestley emptied his glass and refilled it. How he'd loved the German capital. The parties. Those blue-eyed German boys with blond hair and smooth skin. And the Nazis, so powerful, dealing with the Jews and the communists. And Konrad. Priestley smiled at the memory. His lips so soft, his tongue so powerful.

He'd met Hitler, who emanated power. And Himmler, who suggested he could be of service to the Reich. There had really been no need for Himmler's aide to produce the secretly-taken photographs of him with Konrad. Blackmail hadn't been necessary.

Priestley put down his glass and saw again the image of his father going off to war. He looked down at the six messages that he knew would condemn thousands of men to their deaths. He did not care.

He looked at his watch. Almost five o'clock. Soon it would be dawn, and the birds could be released.

Near Old Oak Farm. 5 a.m.

The jeep hurtled through the deserted village of Blackawton. Tom briefly looked across at St. Michael's, the church where he had met Major Fonseca and his men. He wondered where they were now. Probably cramped on some landing ship in the English Channel. And a possible disaster awaiting them.

He went over Gwen's message in his mind. Priestley was a traitor. He had told her to kill Josse because he knew how important the Frenchman was to the Allies' plans. Tom headed north, up the hill out of the village. What if Priestley knew the details of the invasion plans? Tom knew there had been a delay for a day, until the 6th, because of the weather. Did Priestley know?

The rain had abated; the storm was blowing itself out, the almost-full moon seeking, and finding, a gap in the clouds.

If Priestley knew the secret.... Tom shuddered at the consequences. The whole invasion would be compromised. The Germans would know that Patton was not commanding an army in Kent and East Anglia, that there would be no invasion at the Pas de Calais. Tom realized the implications. Hitler would shift his armored divisions to Normandy: the men already heading for the Far Shore would be slaughtered, pushed back into the sea.

Perhaps Priestley had already made contact with his paymaster. Tom's heart sank, and then recovered. How? How could Priestley pass the secret to the Germans? He couldn't use the turned German spy Tom had seen when he was last at the farmhouse. The spy chief in London had told him that all messages were monitored. Priestley couldn't send a radio message.

But then how could Priestley get the message out? There was a hint of light in the eastern sky; the fingers of dawn were beginning to claw at the night sky. Tom saw the oak tree at the entrance to the farm and stopped momentarily to check his revolver. He spun the chamber to check the bullets and snapped the weapon shut. How could Priestley get the message out?

Old Oak Farm. 5:15 a.m.

Priestley picked up the rings holding the six messages and pulled aside the blackout curtain, looking at the eastern sky. He needed the dawn before he could release the pigeons. Without the daylight, the birds could not find their bearings; their journey to Richter's headquarters in Normandy depended on the sun.

Priestley smiled. The whole fate of the war depended on the miraculous homing instinct of an animal with a brain little larger than a pea. All his work of the last four years waited on the rising of the sun. At sunrise, his revenge would be complete. Churchill would eventually fall. The Americans would inevitably be beaten.

There was a noise from below. Priestley put the rings in his pocket and checked the door to the cellar. The lock held firm. He would have to kill them, of course – the stupid Wren and the foolish naval lieutenant. It would be weeks before anyone would find them in this God-forsaken hole, and by then he would be back in the Berlin he had loved in the 'Thirties. He would use their car, drive to Slapton Sands – no one would dream of using that place as an escape route. The U-boat would send ashore a dinghy and he would be away, his mission complete.

Priestley looked again at the eastern sky: there was a slight glimmer of light. He would kill them later, after he had sent the messages. He opened the farmhouse door and made his way across the yard to the barn where the wicker basket holding the birds lay.

Just half an hour, he thought, thirty minutes, and it would all be done. Then he saw the lights of a vehicle and reached for the pistol in his pocket.

Old Oak Farm. 5:15 a.m.

Tom swung the jeep into the farmyard and saw Priestley immediately. The figure was shadowy, running towards the barn, but there was no doubting the red hair picked out by headlights.

The Englishman gave a brief look of surprise and his right hand moved quickly. The windshield in front of Tom shattered, the bullet zinging away. Tom instinctively threw his upper body down onto the passenger seat, grabbing his revolver as he did so. He heard another bullet thud into the front of the jeep.

Priestley had the drop on him; he dared not raise his head. He quickly drew a picture of the yard in his mind: Priestley was in the doorway of the barn, roughly twenty yards ahead. From his crouched position, Tom eased his feet across to the pedals, slipped the gear shift into first, let out the clutch and hit the gas pedal.

The jeep leapt forward. Tom braced himself for the crash. There was a loud splintering of wood as the vehicle hit the barn door. He heard the headlights shatter. The doors of the jeep flew open with the impact and Tom rolled out onto the muddy ground, clutching his revolver.

He saw nothing as he looked from ground level under the jeep. Only the shattered barn door, not a glimpse of Priestley's legs. After the mayhem, there was only the sound of steam hissing from the broken radiator. Tom leapt up and raced to the barn, looking around him for any sign of Priestley; Tom's back was against the wall of the barn, his elbow cocked, his pistol by the side of his face.

He decided to wait. Priestley was in the barn; he had nowhere to go. The light was improving, and soon the sun would inch its way above the horizon. Then he heard another noise. A noise he had heard before, when he had come to the farm searching for the source of the radio signal. It was a gentle noise: the cooing of birds. Pigeons! Priestley was using pigeons to send his messages to his German friends.

Old Oak Farm. 5:15 a.m.

"Danny, Danny where are you? Are you all right?" Sally jumped as she awoke from a fatigue-induced sleep. She pushed her arms in front of her, trying to find him in the darkness of the cellar in which Priestley had locked them.

"I'm down here." Danny flicked his Zippo lighter. He was sitting on the floor, his back resting against a wall green with damp. The left shoulder of his tunic was torn apart by Priestley's bullet, the sleeve matted with clotted blood.

"Danny!" Sally stooped close to the flame, her eyes moving rapidly between the wound and his face; his teeth clamped on his lower lip.

"Get the coat off quickly. I shouldn't have fallen asleep." She took the lighter from his hand and he struggled from the coat, a muted cry coming from his lips as he pulled the left sleeve free. She unbuttoned his tunic and gently helped him to remove it.

"Oh, my God, Danny." She reached into her pocket, pulled out her handkerchief and pressed it against the wound.

"It's not really bad. It looks worse than it is." He looked at her face, her anxiety accentuated by the flickering light. "Ouch, it's hot." Danny dropped the lighter, plunging them back into darkness.

Sally dropped to her haunches, her hands feverishly searching for the metal casing of the lighter. Her left hand felt his fingers; he gripped her hand, his other flicked the lighter and restored the flame.

"Danny, I'm so sorry. I feel like such a fool." Sally pushed her handkerchief against his wound.

"No, I'm the fool." Danny grimaced. "I should have listened to what you said. We should've gone for help." Danny tried to put on a brave face, but failed to hide his helplessness. They both looked upwards as the sound of Priestley's feet rattled on the floorboards above. "I'm going to save the lighter fuel, okay?" He snuffed the flame as she nodded. "You realize he has to kill us?"

"What can we do?" Sally returned the squeeze of his hand.

"We have to try to escape." Danny's voice had more than a hint of desperation.

"But he'll shoot us!"

"He'll shoot us anyway." Danny flicked on the lighter to check the position of the stairs leading up to the cellar doors. There were more sounds of creaking floorboards above as Priestley moved about.

"He's got to do something soon, Sally." Danny stood up, his bloodied left arm hanging at his side, his right hand holding the lighter aloft. "From what I read in that diary, he's got the most valuable secret of the war." He looked at his watch. "It'll soon be light. He's going to release the birds. And we've got to stop him."

"But how, Danny? He's got a gun, and we're unarmed."

"That might be useful!" He nodded toward a long-handled hoe on the floor, its head rusted with disuse. Sally picked it up.

"I'm going to kick the door down. Here, hold this." He handed her the lighter and began to climb the stairs, but stumbled.

"Danny, it's madness! You're in no fit state – he'll kill you."

Suddenly they both stood stock still. There was the noise of an engine in the farmyard. They heard Priestley's footsteps racing to the door, the door slamming behind him. Danny and Sally looked at each other, puzzlement on their faces. Sally jumped at the sounds of gunshots. They heard the engine scream, followed by the crash of glass and the splintering of wood.

"What's going on, Danny?"

"I don't know, but it gives us a chance." He moved to the top of the stairs and began kicking at the lock.

The jamb splintered and the door flew open. The parlor was empty.

Danny swung around and helped Sally up the last few steps. His breathing was labored; sweat ran down his brow from his efforts; his white shirt sleeve was red with blood.

"Sally, we have to—" He did not finish. His eyes rolled and he fell in a heap at her feet.

"Danny!" She put down the hoe and knelt at his side. She put her fingers on his wrist, desperately searching for a pulse.

Priestley breathed heavily in the darkness of the barn, looking at the smashed jeep in the doorway. He had managed to jump aside at the last moment, but his heart still raced. He'd caught a glimpse of the driver's face as the jeep came into the yard. It was Ford, the damned American who'd been snooping on the farm a week ago. This time, he had to be eliminated.

The steam hissed from the radiator. Priestley trained his gun over the doorway as his other hand felt the six rings in his pocket. He kept the gun trained on the wreck of the jeep as he moved into the shadows of the barn. The rings seemed to burn like fire as he held them in his palm. He had to get the messages onto the birds and send them on their way to Richter in France.

From outside the barn, Tom pressed his eye to a crack in the wooden wall. The light in the eastern sky grew; within the next few minutes, the sun would rise. More light entered the barn door, slowly piercing the shadows. He could see the floor of the barn, strewn with moldy straw.

The broken jeep radiator hissed its last. Of Priestley, there was no trace. Tom knew he was lying low, waiting to jump him. But where? He cast his eyes over the shadows at the far end of the barn. Nothing, not a glimpse of movement.

But Tom clearly heard a noise. From the dark, far corner of the barn came the cooing of the pigeons. Tom couldn't see the basket that held them, but he knew the birds were essential to the traitor. He peered carefully around the doorway; if he could kill the birds, Priestley would be helpless, unable to complete his mission.

The sounds of the birds continued to come from the deep shadows. Tom made his best guess of the basket's location. He leaned around the doorway, leveled his pistol and fired blind.

The cooing was replaced by squawks of fear. Tom caught a movement from the corner of his eye. Priestley was breaking cover. Tom leapt into the doorway and swung his pistol toward the movement.

Priestley would let nothing stop him now. He crouched, unmoving in the shadows of the barn, his right hand fiercely gripping his pistol. After all his planning, the years of waiting, he was not going to let some Yank spoil it. He could see Tom's shadow to the right of the smashed door and the crumpled radiator of the jeep.

His shadow! The sun was up! He could release the pigeons. He glanced over to the wicker basket. The birds had sensed the sun and were stirring. Damn the American bastard. He felt his way towards the basket, taking the rings from his pocket. He jumped as the American's bullet thudded into the wall of the barn. The echoes of the gunshot and the squawking of the birds rang in Priestley's ears.

No, no, not the pigeons, he thought as he leapt up and swung his pistol toward the figure in the doorway of the barn. He pulled the trigger at the same moment that a flash came from the American's weapon.

Sally's fingers found a pulse. Danny stirred for a moment, his eyes rolling as he half-opened his lids. His fall had restarted the bleeding. No, no, Danny, don't die. She had to stop the loss of blood. Kicking off a shoe, she hiked up her skirt, pulled off one of her stockings and tied it tightly around Danny's arm, just below the shoulder.

He winced at the pain and then looked up at her hazily, half-conscious.

"You must stop him, Sally." His head fell back to the floor.

Anger seized Sally. She took off her coat and put it under Danny's head. Her face burned with fury as she picked up the hoe and made her way through the farmhouse door to the yard.

Someone had hit his thigh with a sledgehammer. Tom felt the pain of the bullet tearing into his flesh. He fired into the darkness and then took a step forward. His leg screamed at him, refusing to obey. He fell, his pistol spinning away from him as his elbow hit the floor.

His arms tried to pull him forward, his fingers reaching for his gun. The pain in his thigh told him to stop. As did the cold metal of Priestley's revolver pressed against his temple.

Priestley was overjoyed. The arrogant American was in his power. "Don't try anything foolish, Ford." He kicked Tom's pistol into the shadows of the barn, and stood up, his pistol still pointing at Tom's skull.

"You came at an opportune moment, Ford." The Englishman retrieved the basket of pigeons from the shadows. Tom tried to move, but his leg failed him. "You are about to witness the moment when Churchill becomes doomed."

Tom looked into Priestley's wild eyes. "I'm surprised you didn't shoot me when you had the chance."

"But I will old chap." Priestley smiled smugly. "Later. And the others, too."

"The others?"

"A charming Wren and her boyfriend," he nodded over his shoulder, "locked up in the cellar over there."

Priestley pulled the six rings from his pocket and opened his palm, showing them to Tom. "But before I kill you, I want you to know what I'm doing. See these six rings, Ford?" There was the rattle of metal as he shook them in his hand. "They're going to change history. Everything Hitler needs to know about the invasion. Every landing beach. All five of them." He held up a ring. "And then there's the ridiculous nonsense of Patton's nonexistent Army Group. Once the Germans find out about this deception, the game will be up for the invasion."

"Why are you doing this, Priestley?"

"I'm settling a score for what Churchill's friends did to my father and me. And money, of course. The Germans have paid me handsomely since 1936."

His hand reached into the basket and emerged with one of the birds. He attached a ring, went to the open window of the barn, and released the creature. It flew up, circled the barn and headed south.

Priestley turned from the doorway to face Tom. "And now, my American friend, you are watching the downfall of Churchill. And soon all of you bloody Americans will go back home with your tails between your legs."

"You're mad, Priestley." Tom's face was contorted with frustrated rage and the pain from his leg wound. He tried to lift himself up, but fell back in agony. "You're condemning thousands of Allied soldiers to death."

Priestley laughed. "I prefer to think I'm making history." He thrust his hand back into the basket.

Sally stepped out into the farmyard and stopped short as she saw the wrecked jeep lodged in the smashed door of the barn. So that was the cause of the noise and the shots she and Danny had heard. Who had driven it? Where was Priestley?

Her thoughts were distracted by the flutter of wings; she watched as a pigeon left the window of the barn and climbed into the sky. She made her way quickly to the barn, the hoe held tightly in her hands. There were voices, one American, the other distinctly Priestley's. She edged her way along the wall of the barn and peeked through a gap in the wood. The light was improving as the sun breasted the horizon, but the shadows in the barn revealed only shapes. There was a man on the floor, wounded in the thigh; he was wearing an American uniform. He lifted his face and she caught her breath. It was Tom.

Then she saw Priestley. He was laughing as he stooped beside a basket full of pigeons, his back to her. Sally felt caught between rage and fear; she hesitated for a moment before moving quietly into the gap between the wrecked jeep and the door that hung loosely on its hinges. Tom had seen her, she was sure. He dragged himself toward Priestley and the basket, yelling at the top of his voice.

The Englishman cursed. "You've played the hero for the last time, Yank." He lifted his pistol and aimed it for Tom's head.

Sally raised the hoe above her head and with all her might smashed it down on the back of Priestley's skull.

The traitor fell to his knees, stunned. He tried to turn, but Sally hit his head with the hoe again and he fell limply to the floor. She saw the blood running through the red hair. Sally was consumed by rage; she raised the hoe again.

"No, Sally, no!" Tom's voice startled Sally. She lowered the hoe, her body shaking. "Get the rings, Sally, get the rings!"

"What about your wound?" She moved towards him.

"No, Sally, get the rings!"

"Rings? What rings?" Sally cast her eyes about the barn, confused.

"They'll be near him, somewhere." Tom dragged himself across the floor. "He probably dropped them when you hit him. Get them!"

Sally went over to Priestley's limp form, crouched down and ran her hand through the rotten straw. She picked up Priestley's gun and then her fingers found the metal bands; she scooped them up and handed them to Tom, together with the gun. She looked down at his wound.

"I'm going to get an ambulance for you and Danny. Right now."

"Danny?" Tom asked in vain; she was gone.

Tom fumbled with the rings that contained the messages.

Sweat ran down his forehead. Priestley had managed to get one message away. There were five rings left. He forced his trembling fingers to free the message from the rings and unfold them.

The first was headed 'Utah' – the codename of one of the American assault beaches in Normandy; as a BIGOT he knew the name. Beneath the heading was the detailed disposition of American troops.

Tom hurried through the rings. 'Gold.' The beach towards the eastern side of the landing; the message showed where the Canadians would land. The next two rings: 'Juno' and 'Sword.' The British beaches, where Montgomery's soldiers would go ashore.

The pain in his thigh screamed at him, but he did not hear it. He realized what would have happened if the messages had reached the Germans. He picked up the last ring and smoothed out the message with his hand. 'Operation Fortitude.' He knew what it was: the whole plan of the deception – a message that would have told the Nazis that Patton's army did not exist: that the invasion in the Pas de Calais was a fraud.

Tom heaved a sigh of relief. The Germans would still believe that the invasion in Normandy was a diversion. Hitler would keep his main forces miles away.

His euphoria gave way to alarm. He realized there was one message that Priestley had managed to get away.

'Omaha.'

On the road from Avranches to Cherbourg. 5:30 a.m.

"Can't you go any faster, Helmut?" Richter thumped the dashboard impatiently and regretted the action as the pain seared into his arm.

"Not in this weather, sir; we'd end up in a ditch." The chauffeur peered through the rain-lashed windshield, the flip-flop of the wipers just able to cope with the deluge. Richter looked at the road ahead, barely lit by the car's subdued headlights. The night sky was completely covered with cloud; the wind whipped at the passing trees.

The Gestapo chief allowed himself a smile, despite the pain in his arm. No plane could have landed in such weather to spirit Josse and the Englishwoman away. No plane. Perhaps a boat; yes, surely a boat. He had issued orders for extra security at all harbors. But which port, which harbor would Josse choose?

The tightness of the uniform distracted him as he tugged at the collar. His own uniform had been bloodstained, hacked by the assailant's blade. The look in the Frenchman's eyes as he came toward him flashed into his memory and he shuddered. The colonel had apologized that the only uniform available was that of a corporal. He was sure he looked foolish, wearing a corporal's uniform but with the cap of an *Obersturmbannführer*, but he did not care. He had to catch Josse.

"There's some coffee in the flask on the back seat, sir." Helmut nodded over his shoulder. Richter began to reach for it before the pain stopped him.

"Stop the car and get it for me, Helmut."

The car slid to a halt and Helmut retrieved the flask. Richter inhaled the aroma and savored the sharp taste. The chauffeur made to re-engage the gear.

"No, wait a few moments, Helmut, I need to take a leak." He also needed time to think. The effects of the anesthetic still wore on him. He climbed out of the car; the wind and rain, together with the coffee, cleared his mind.

Perhaps Josse had given him the correct information about the invasion. The last Verlaine couplet had confirmed that the decoy invasion was on its way. It was already June 5th, the date that Josse had predicted. Perhaps the rescue of the woman was something not in Josse's plan. Maybe a personal loyalty? Love?

The thought of Josse being in love with the Englishwoman amused him. On the other hand, Josse could have told him a pack of lies and he could have walked into the trap.

But from which harbor would Josse depart with the Busson woman? And when? He chuckled at the irony of the situation. Another big secret. Where and when? Surely not that morning? The day of the invasion?

Yes! A masterstroke by the Frenchman. He'd get her out in the confusion of the landings. Early. Before the Allied troops hit the beaches.

"Shall I drive on, sir?" The chauffeur took the flask as Richter got back into the car.

"In a minute." Richter took a map from the glove compartment and turned on a flashlight.

Where? Where? He ran his finger over the map. Josse, Josse, where will you go? Not Granville; too heavily guarded. Cherbourg was out of the question. No, Josse would go to some small port on the west coast. He snapped the map shut.

"Let's go, Helmut. Turn left at the crossroads at La Haye. Take the road for Carteret."

Richter settled back in his seat. He felt content, despite the pain in his arm. He knew where Josse was heading. And he would be there to meet him.

On the road to the port of Carteret. 6:30 a.m.

"For the sake of God, René, calm down." Josse looked across at the driver of the truck. René had the hard, weather-beaten face of a man who had spent most of his life at sea, but he looked anxious.

"But the security, Philippe. The Germans have increased the security." He spoke through the cigarette clamped between his lips. "I know I promised you to get the woman out, but I'm scared."

"Relax, René. The *Bosches* have seen you take your fishing boat out on the tide for four years. It's routine for them. It's part of their day."

"Yes, I know, but I was told last night that they're going to search every vehicle at the checkpoint in the harbor." He pulled the truck over. "It's madness, Philippe, madness. Perhaps we can try tomorrow."

Josse recalled the message he had heard on the radio the night before. *"Blessent mon coeur avec une langeur monotone."* The invasion was imminent; the next day would probably be too late.

"Listen, René, it'll be easy." Josse brushed aside the skipper's objections. "I'm one of your crew members." He looked down at the blue overalls, the traditional garb of a trawler man. "Augustine and I are covered as crew members on the papers I gave you."

"And what about the agent?" The skipper thrust his thumb towards the back of the covered truck. "Not to mention the guns you are carrying."

Josse pondered for a moment as the wipers brushed the rain from the windshield. The Sten gun strapped to his body was well-hidden, but would not get past a body search. He looked over his shoulder into the back of the truck. Amidst the fisherman's tackle of nets and buoys was Augustine dressed in overalls, also with a concealed gun; Jeanne sat on the floor.

He cursed the extra security. Richter's work, without a doubt. Normally, René would wave his papers and go through the checkpoint as a matter of routine. Now, one look at Jeanne by a German guard and the game would be up.

"How far is it from the checkpoint to your boat?"

"About a hundred meters, maybe a hundred and fifty."

"Right, we'll take advantage of the weather." Josse looked out at the heavy rain falling. "This is what we'll do."

Josse spoke for a minute, outlining his plans. René nodded and slipped the truck into gear.

The entrance to the harbor. 6:45 a.m.

The rain lashed against the truck as it turned into the harbor entrance. Although the sun had just risen, there was no hint of it in a heavily-overcast sky that looked more like November than June.

"It's a relief to see that the checkpoint is under the control of good old Sergeant Steinitz." René pointed to a rotund German soldier supervising the searching of the two carts in the line ahead. The drivers were cursing; they were used to being waved through to their vessels.

"You know him?" Josse raised an eyebrow.

"I have a drink with him most nights in the bar. How else do you think I know about the increased security? Or the garrison strength? Or the hundred other things you send back to London? He's not a bad sort, for a German. Just wants the war to be over, like most of us."

"*Now*, René. Do it now." Josse spoke softly and the skipper deliberately pulled out the choke button.

The first truck pulled away from the checkpoint. René pressed hard on the gas pedal to flood the carburetor, and the engine quickly died. "Let's go!" Josse pulled down his cap over his eyes and jumped down, heading for the back of the truck.

René got down cursing, and beat his fists angrily on the hood before opening it. The rain sizzled on the hot engine manifold.

"What's up? What's the matter?" The sergeant came huffing towards René, leaving the other two soldiers to search the cart in front. The rain ran down his face onto his sodden cape. He peered over the skipper's shoulder into the engine well.

"*Merde! Merde!*" The Frenchman fiddled with the plug leads. On the other side of the truck, his crewmembers carried the large fishing net, slung between their shoulders like a hammock.

"René," the German twisted his tongue around the French name, "you're the last one. Sort it out, quickly. Then we can all get out of this infernal rain."

The Frenchman threw up his arms in despair. "It's no good, Sergeant – I have to go, or I'll miss the tide." He pulled his papers from his pocket and thrust them at the German; he saw that the net had been carried through the checkpoint, where the other soldiers were still searching the truck at the front of the line.

The sergeant gave a cursory glance at the papers. "But I have to search your truck, René."

"Be my guest. It'll be there all day. I'll get it fixed when I get back from fishing." He hurried after the crew with the net, who were walking along the long wooden pier to his boat.

"Wait!"

They all stopped at the shout. The skipper turned slowly to face the sergeant.

"A drink in the bar when you get back, René? And perhaps…?"

René laughed. "You shall have the best of the catch, Sergeant Steinitz!"

June 5th 1944

The entrance to the harbor. 7 a.m.

"Damn this rain! It can't be far now." Richter looked at the rain obscuring the windshield and thumped his fist on the dashboard in his impatience. "There! There it is, Helmut!" He pointed to the entrance to the harbor about two hundred meters along the road. The car turned off the road to find a deserted truck by an unmanned checkpoint, the gate open.

"The fools, the idiots!" Richter fumed. "Didn't they get my orders to tighten security? The whole American army could walk through here!" He leapt from the car. "Where is everybody? Idiots!" He grabbed for his hat, but it was swept away with the wind.

"I'll get it for you, sir." Helmut opened the car door, pushing against the wind.

"No, we haven't time. I'll deal with these fools later." He jumped back into the car. "Drive on, Helmut. Down to the pier."

The Pier at Carteret Harbor. 7 a.m.

"Hurry, hurry!" René urged them on as they carried the net along the pier, their shoes slipping on the rain-sodden wooden boards. Despite the protection of the breakwater, the waves slapped against the pier, throwing spray over them. Josse looked beyond Augustine, who was carrying the front of the net; René's boat was pitching at its moorings, as if seized by a madness to confront the angry waves outside the harbor wall.

"We're coming, *Belle Époque,*" he shouted at his boat. "Philippe, this is insane. How on earth did I let you talk me into this nonsense?"

"You've done it many times before, René." Josse glanced behind him; the German guards had disappeared. "We're nearly home and dry."

"Dry?" LeGrand snorted. "You joke at a time like this?"

Suddenly, the front of the net fell, as Augustine dropped to one knee. "I can't hold on. My hands are cold and wet, and she's so heavy!"

LeGrand leapt forward and took the net from her hands. "Josse, you send a woman to do a man's job!" He raised the net to his shoulder and headed to the boat. Josse said nothing, but recalled what Augustine had done to get a new battery to him in St. Marie de la Croix. He saw the world-weariness in her eyes.

They reached the stern of the boat, which heaved at the pier like a bucking bronco.

LeGrand and Josse lowered the net to their waists and waited for a favorable moment before lowering the net containing Jeanne to the deck. There was a thud, the net spilled open, revealing the tarp that was wrapped around Jeanne. An arm fell out.

"*Mon Dieu,* she is unconscious." Augustine's hands went to her face.

"She'll be all right." LeGrand jumped into the cockpit. "Cast off!"

Josse grabbed Augustine by the arms. "You can go, too, Augustine."

She looked into Josse's eyes, the tears mingling with the rain on her face.

"Jump, woman!" LeGrand shouted up from the boat.

"No, I can't leave. France is my home. I'm going to join my husband and fight the *Bosches.*"

"Philippe, for God's sake, cast off."

Josse tossed down the bow and stern ropes from the dock as LeGrand pressed the starter. The engine coughed twice, but did not respond. LeGrand took off his sou'wester hat and lashed it against the wheel. *"Belle Époque,* you are like a stubborn old woman!"

As if goaded by the insult, the engine roared an angry answer. The skipper cranked the gear and spun the wheel. The boat slid away from the pier, brushing aside the waves as it made for the harbor mouth.

"Look!" Augustine pointed toward the stern of the boat. A head appeared, then an arm, waving. "It's Jeanne, she's all right." The boat left the harbor and pointed into the wind, ready to battle the storm.

"Grace à Dieu!" Josse crossed himself. "Now, let's get away." He wiped the rain from his face and pulled down his hat.

They ran back along the pier. Suddenly, Josse threw out his arm across Augustine. "Stop!" He looked back to the entrance to the pier, about two hundred meters away. Two German soldiers. One a private, the other, hatless, a corporal. He looked at the corporal, his hair plastered to his head by the rain.

"Get out your gun, Augustine."

Why was he wearing a corporal's uniform? Josse thought. It was Richter.

"It's Josse, Helmut, I'd know him anywhere." Richter watched as the Frenchman and the woman at his side pulled Sten guns from beneath their overalls.

"What are we going to do, sir? We can't match their machine guns. We've only got our Walther pistols." The chauffeur brushed the rain from his face.

Richter pointed to the boat, now well beyond the harbor wall. "The main priority is to have that vessel intercepted. The Englishwoman is on that boat. We must go back to the checkpoint and get a message through to the *Kriegsmarine.*"

The wind tugged at his coat as he ran back to the car. "Josse can't get far. He can't come back through the checkpoint – he knows we'll be waiting for him there. He'll go up the coastal path, up the headland, to the lighthouse. But the only way out is through here. He can't escape." Richter jumped back in the car as Helmut engaged the gear and let out the clutch.

"We'll send the message, get help and then go after Josse."

The chauffeur opened the throttle and headed back to the checkpoint, longing for a warm, dry bed in his hometown of Potsdam.

"Why have they left?" Augustine shouted over the wind. "Why didn't they come after us?"

"They've gone to get help." Josse realized that Richter had out-foxed him. He'd try to get the boat intercepted, and then come back with a platoon to pick up Augustine and himself. They couldn't go back through the harbor entrance; Richter would be waiting to pick them off. They could go only up the coastal path toward the lighthouse. The path was a dead end, unless they tried to scale down the dangerous cliffs on the other side. There was no choice. "Let's go." He headed up to the coastal path; Augustine followed, her submachine gun slung over her shoulder.

Richter was angry. The guardhouse at the checkpoint seemed deserted. Rain gushed from the spouting; the door was shut, but smoke came from the chimney. The barrier was erect, open for all traffic. Not a soldier in sight.

"Incompetent fools! If this is how we are going to meet the invasion, God help us!"

He leapt from the car, ran across and tugged at the handle. The door was locked.

"Open up! Open up!" Richter hammered on the door. There was a noise, barely audible above the wind; he was sure there was the clink of glass, a bottle perhaps. His knuckles beat upon the door again.

"Hold your horses, I'm coming!" The voice was gruff. The key turned and the door was opened by a tall, heavy sergeant with a look of annoyance. Richter pushed on the door, but the soldier resisted the movement.

"What's up, Corporal? You're not supposed to come in here. Push off."

Even in the uniform of a corporal, Richter still found it difficult to contain his outrage. "I'm not a corporal – I am *Obersturmbannführer* Richter of the Gestapo!"

The sergeant looked at the bedraggled, soaked uniform. "Yes, and I'm Field Marshall Rommel."

"I am the Head of the Gestapo in Normandy!" Richter could smell the schnapps on the sergeant's breath.

"You don't say. Push off, Corporal." He made to close the door.

"Perhaps you will understand this!" Richter thrust his pistol into the man's belly.

The soldier looked surprised and backed off. "Corporal, you're making a lot of trouble for yourself."

"It's you who are in trouble, Sergeant. Your name?" Richter was angry that there was no fear in the man's eyes, just a wary concern.

"I am Sergeant Steinitz."

"Well, Steinitz, you should know that I'm going to have your balls ripped off. I'll have you court-martialed!" Richter looked around the deserted guardhouse. "Where is the guard? Where are your officers?"

"The guard has been stood down because of the storm. As for the officers, you'll find them up in the town. Probably in the bar of the hotel."

"Doesn't anybody know there's an invasion coming?"

"In this weather?" The sergeant shrugged his shoulders. "Even a corporal should be able to see there's no chance."

Richter struggled to contain his temper. He would court-martial every officer and every soldier in the unit, but his rage was costing him time. He brandished the pistol in the soldier's face.

"Where's the telephone?"

Steinitz pointed to the small office at the back of the guardroom. Richter felt relieved. At last, he could get out a message to the *Kriegsmarine* to apprehend the boat.

"But it's *kaputt.*" The sergeant made a sour face. "Since this morning. Lots of Resistance actions lately – railway lines blown up, telegraph poles brought down, even telephone exchanges being attacked."

"It can't be…" Richter's mind reeled. He had seen the Resistance plans, taken from the agent Wainwright's briefcase, and he had issued orders to counter them. But the sabotage had happened elsewhere.

His eyes widened. The captured plans had been false. Josse had fed him a pack of lies. The whole thing was nothing more than a trick, a big lie. Patton was not going to attack at the Pas de Calais.

Richter felt the anger rising in him. He had fed Josse's lies to Himmler and the Führer. The Frenchman had to be captured. Richter's rage exploded.

"Sergeant, you will come with me. Bring two extra Schmeissers for me and my driver."

"No. I don't take orders from corporals."

"No? You dare to defy my order?" Richter was at boiling point, the veins in his temples bulging. He shot the sergeant in the head, picked up two Schmeissers and rushed out into the rain.

Josse struggled to get his breath. The steep path up the headland rose before him. Above stood the lighthouse, defying the wind. Sweat mingled with the rain on his face as his feet struggled to find purchase on the sodden ground. Augustine climbed in front of him, the Sten gun strung across her back; how he envied the young limbs that drove her up the hill.

"Wait a moment, Augustine." The path had reached the dirt road that led from the harbor to the lighthouse. The rain had reduced it to a quagmire; the mud clung to their feet.

"Are you all right?" Augustine shouted into the wind.

"Yes, I just need to get my breath." He turned into the wind to look out to sea. René's boat was being tossed like a cork, but ploughed ahead toward the horizon, disappearing into a trough before rising to breast the next wave. Josse offered up a prayer for its safety. If anyone could get a boat through a storm, René could. If he wasn't intercepted by a fast German E-boat.

Josse looked down the muddy track, beyond the trees on the lower slopes, to where it led to the harbor. There was no sign of any activity, but he knew Richter held all the cards. The German wasn't stupid. He'd probably worked out the ruse about the captured plans. The Gestapo man had to make only one phone call and the whole plan would be in danger. Then Richter would get an E-boat dispatched, and return with a squad of soldiers to kill them. No, he wouldn't kill them. He'd take them alive. Josse looked at Augustine and shuddered, as much from fear of what Richter could do as from the sodden clothes that clung to his body.

Against Richter's power, all he had was Augustine and two Sten guns. He wished she had gone on the boat.

"Philippe, let's get to the lighthouse – at least it will give us some shelter."

Josse knew the lighthouse was an illusion of escape. Once cornered inside it, there was no way out. Only upwards. Richter wouldn't hesitate to order his men to make suicide attacks. He and Augustine could only hold on until the ammunition ran out and then…

He felt despondent. All his work for the last year had been wasted. One phone call by Richter would destroy all he had done. Jeanne would be captured by a German boat; even worse, the coming invasion would be defeated on the beaches.

"Look, Philippe, look!" Augustine pointed down through the trees on the lower slopes. There was a solitary black Citroen skidding to a halt at the entrance to the muddy road that led up to the lighthouse. Richter. Josse cast his eyes beyond the car to the checkpoint and guardhouse. Nothing. No trucks carrying troops, not a solitary German soldier. Perhaps Richter had met a problem.

"Okay, Augustine. Head for the lighthouse."

Richter looked up at the two ant-like figures scrambling up the hill beyond the trees towards the lighthouse, a quarter mile away.

"Drive on, Helmut, take the road to the lighthouse. We'll soon have them!"

"But sir—"

"Drive on!"

The driver gunned the engine and launched the Citroen forward off the tarmac of the harbor. Within ten meters, the wheels were spinning uselessly as the car sank axle-deep into the mud.

Richter cursed. Josse must not escape. The Frenchman must be tortured until he begged to tell his secrets. His arm reached to the rear seats, grabbed the two machine pistols and handed one to the driver.

"Follow me, Helmut." He opened the door, recoiling before the wind and rain.

"I am not a combat soldier, sir. I have never been under fire."

"We are National Socialists, Helmut." He looked up at the figures nearing the lighthouse. "Combat is our destiny!"

"Get off the path, Augustine! Get out of the mud!" Josse looked back down the track. Richter's car was abandoned in the mud, its doors hanging open like useless wings. There was no sign of Richter or his driver. He looked at the clump of trees that straddled the first hundred meters of the track, searching for any movement; he could see none. The sea fret blown up by the wind hampered his view.

Augustine was ahead of him, heading for the gate in the waist-high stone wall that girded the headland. About twenty meters beyond the wall stood the lighthouse; fifty meters inland of the tower was the keeper's small cottage.

Josse's breath was labored as he followed Augustine to the gate. Why? Why had Richter come after them with just one other man? There was no exit other than the path they had just climbed. Surely there had been enough time for Richter to gather a platoon of soldiers. The German still held the upper hand, but what had driven him to make a rash decision? Perhaps revenge? He had been outfoxed and wanted revenge. Maybe Richter had an Achilles heel after all.

"Philippe!" Augustine's shout made him turn. The lighthouse keeper had emerged from his cottage and was running toward them. His eyes widened with fright as he saw the weapons in their hands.

"We need your help!" Josse yelled, but the man continued to run.

"No! No! I'm just a lighthouse keeper – I want nothing to do with you!" His stocky frame thrust Augustine aside as he rushed through the gate and started to run down the muddy track.

"No, stop!" Josse shouted after him. "There are Germans down there."

"They know me – I'm the lighthouse keeper." He ran down towards the trees.

Richter signaled Helmut to continue up the headland under cover of the trees. Josse could not escape this time. The Frenchman had trapped himself; there was no way out for him. Why had he taken such a route? Richter had no answer to the question, but knew he had to remain alert. Josse had escaped from him before; there was no limit to his cunning.

The Gestapo man stumbled over a tree root, pitching his left shoulder against a tree. He cried out with the pain of the wound he had received at Avranches. Helmut looked across at him, but Richter recovered his balance and waved his chauffeur on. Josse had to be taken. Alive.

Suddenly, there was a noise from ahead. Richter glimpsed a stocky man, coming through the trees. Josse had cracked, Richter thought; the Frenchman was reduced to desperation, trying to rush him. Richter swung his machine pistol toward the running figure and fired a quick burst at the man's legs. The man hung in the air for a moment and then fell to the ground.

"Got him!" Richter was elated.

Josse heard the burst of fire and crossed himself; he should have stopped the lighthouse keeper. He felt the anger grow within him and vowed to make Richter pay.

"What do we do, Philippe?" Augustine looked at him, her eyes wide with fright.

Josse's eyes ran from the lighthouse to the cottage. He had seconds to make a decision, a decision of life or death for the two of them. "They'll come up one on either side of the track. Go to the cottage – the second floor window. I'll try to draw their fire. If you see any movement, fire!"

As Josse took cover in the entrance to the lighthouse, Augustine scurried into the cottage, relieved that at least she was out of the wind and rain.

The wounded lighthouse keeper looked up at Richter with terror in his eyes.

"Verdammt!" Richter cursed and brought the butt of his machine pistol down hard on the Frenchman's skull, incensed that it was not Josse.

He peered through the last of the tree cover. There were about twenty meters of open ground to the wall, with the lighthouse beyond. Josse would split his forces, he knew. The German's eyes scanned the windows of the cottage. Nothing. Quickly, he looked upward to the balcony at the top of the lighthouse, but that, too, was deserted. Richter was puzzled. If he had been in Josse's shoes, he would have made for the balcony. There was little cover up there, but it was a perfect position to cover the exposed area between the trees and the wall.

Perhaps Josse was heading up the lighthouse stairs at that moment. Richter knew he had to act quickly. "Helmut!" he shouted across to his driver, at the edge of the tree cover, ten meters to his right. "Make for the base of the wall to the right of the gate. I'll go to the left. As fast as you can. And keep low. Go!"

As Helmut set out, Richter waited a few seconds. He could provide cover if the driver drew fire. He dropped to one knee and took general aim at the cottage, moving the sights of his gun from window to window.

Augustine pushed the bed aside so she could get to the window. She was afraid, but held her weapon tightly as she pulled the curtains aside to improve her view. She looked down from the window over the small exposed strip of land between the trees and the wall. She saw nobody; the wind howled at the window, the rain running down the pane, but there was no movement below.

The image of her husband came to her mind. She wanted to be with him, to build a new life after the war, after the *Bosches* had been driven from France; they would have the child they had postponed when the Germans invaded.

Her eyes caught a movement, to her left, just before the wall. A German, crouching, heading for the gate. The field of vision was not quite right. She opened the window, swung up her weapon and leaned forward.

Helmut was afraid as he crouched and ran through the rain to the wall. In all the war, he had never fired a shot in anger. He'd always been a driver, ever since he'd passed his test and had driven busses around the streets of Potsdam. How he wished that he were back there, driving the number twelve route.

He heard a noise and looked up. There was a woman framed in the window of the cottage. He swung his machine pistol upward. There was another noise and he wondered who was hitting his chest with a hammer.

Richter heard the burst of fire and saw Helmut stagger, his arms flailing the air. The Gestapo man's eyes moved rapidly from the lighthouse to the cottage. He saw the woman in the window, leaning forward to get a better shot.

His machine pistol chattered as he emptied half a magazine into the window frame. The woman's body jerked in a macabre dance as the bullets hit her. She flopped forward, her shattered body hanging over the window sill, her Sten gun clattering as it fell onto the roof of an outhouse.

There was another burst of fire from the lighthouse and Helmut pitched lifeless to the ground. Richter sprinted the last few meters. He could not see Josse, but knew he was in the lighthouse doorway. He threw himself into the mud at the foot of the wall.

Josse felt as if his heart must burst. From the doorway of the lighthouse, he saw Augustine's body hanging from the window and tried to curb his emotions. The wrong decision. He should have gone to the cottage; or he should have raced to the observation platform to give better cover for her.

His heart was heavy. Alphonse, the warder at the jail, the farmer Dominic and his wife Bernadette; now Augustine. How many more lives would be claimed before the operation was over? 'You must ensure the success of Operation First Violin at all costs.' That had been the message of his London taskmasters. Were they aware of the costs? Did they care?

His grief gave way to a rage that focused on one man, the man he knew was responsible for the deaths of his friends. Richter. Suddenly, a spray of bullets pinged off the stone surround of the doorway. The Frenchman swung his gun and returned the fire before quickly withdrawing to safety.

"Josse, Josse, listen to me." It was Richter's voice, calling from the other side of the wall. "Your resistance is useless. Surrender now. I promise you, on my word of honor, that you will not be harmed. I will grant you immunity, a pardon."

Josse heard the words and spat on the ground. They were the words of the man who had killed Augustine, who had tortured Jeanne, who had caused the death of so many French people. Josse felt himself consumed, not only with hatred, but with an emotion he had never felt before: a blood lust ran through his veins. Richter had to die; his odious life had to be snuffed out.

Josse breathed deeply, struggling to bring reason through the red mist that had seized his mind. Richter must die. But how? The Frenchman checked his ammunition. The magazine was almost empty. He pulled out the last magazine from the pocket of his overalls and clipped it into position.

"Josse, come out now. I promise you a pardon."

The Frenchman knew the stand-off position was to Richter's advantage. Eventually, the Germans would send someone to find out what had happened to the Gestapo chief. He looked at the stairs spiraling around the inner wall of the lighthouse, leading up to the observation platform. He calculated that it would take about thirty seconds to get to the top. If he could get up there, Richter's position behind the wall would be exposed. He could pick him off at will.

"Okay, Richter, I'm coming out." He turned and ran for the stairs.

Richter lay prone at the wall, his Schmeisser leveled at the doorway of the lighthouse. He hadn't expected Josse to be so foolish to fall for such a trick. The moment the Frenchman emerged, he would cut him down. He waited, peering over the gun sights. Five seconds. Ten. Nothing. Suddenly, Richter realized that Josse was setting his own trap. He looked up at the observation platform. Josse was heading there. If the Frenchman reached the platform... Slowly and deliberately, Richter stood up. There was no gunfire. He ran through the gateway, against the wind, his legs pounding the wet grass as they raced for the doorway to the lighthouse.

Only one more flight to the platform. Josse's legs were leaden, only his will driving him on. Richter must die. He looked up at the door to the platform, his hand pulling on the stair rail. He reached out for the doorknob, inches away. Suddenly, his muddied boots slipped from under him. He crashed against the rail. The Sten gun slipped from his shoulder. Josse watched it as it careened off the walls until it fell with a clatter onto the floor of the lighthouse.

Richter was there, looking down at the gun, then upwards. Josse hurled himself at the platform door as bullets pinged off the stonework. He threw himself onto the platform, kicking the door shut behind him.

Richter looked down again at Josse's weapon and smiled. The Frenchman was helpless. He had no defense. The German checked his Schmeisser; the ammunition was low, but enough to deal with an unarmed Josse. The game was over. He began to climb the stairs.

Josse clung to the rail of the platform. The rain had eased, but the wind still tugged at his overalls. He looked down. Below him, at the foot of the lighthouse, the cliffs of the headland fell away ninety feet to the sea crashing against the rocks. There was no way to escape. Soon, Richter would come through the door and that would be the end.

Rational thought deserted him. The need to save his own life was thrust aside by the red mist that demanded he kill Richter. He looked down at the seas pounding on the cliffs below. At all costs. He leapt back as a burst of bullets came through the door. He heard Richter's boot kick and splinter the wood. The German came out, brandishing his Schmeisser.

"So, Josse, your foolish game is over at last." Richter leveled his gun at the Frenchman's chest. "You made me look a fool with your lies, Josse, and now you will pay for it. You will come back to my Headquarters. After I have made a call to the High Command, telling them that your whole story about the decoy invasion is a pack of lies, we shall beat the truth out of you."

Josse was stunned. Richter had not yet spoken to the German High Command! Operation First Violin was not yet in jeopardy.

"Look, Josse, it is the fifth of June," Richter waved his Schmeisser out over the stormy sea. "Where is the invasion you promised?"

Josse seized the moment as the gun pointed away from him. He threw himself at Richter. The German quickly brought his gun down but had time only for a single shot. Josse felt the bullet hit him, but he grabbed Richter, pinning his arms in a bear hug. The German let out a cry of pain as the pressure of Josse's grip reopened the knife wound. The gun clattered to the floor. Josse kicked it over the edge of the platform; it fell onto the rocks, ninety feet below.

Josse could smell Richter's sweat as the two men grappled on the platform. The Frenchman could feel the weakness stealing into his arms. The pain of the wound began to hit him; he could feel the warm blood seeping through his overalls. His body was driven by will and hatred, hatred for the odious man still locked in his grip. He pushed Richter's back against the waist-high guard rail.

Richter kicked hard at the Frenchman's shins, and then found enough leverage to work his right hand up to Josse's face. The Gestapo chief knew he just had to survive for a minute, maybe a little more before the bullet in Josse's gut would take its eventual toll. He pushed his fingers into the Frenchman's eyes and managed to turn, so that Josse's back was against the guard rail. Only moments now, Richter thought, as he felt Josse's grip loosen slightly.

239

Josse offered up a prayer. He could see nothing as Richter's fingers gouged in his eyes; the guard rail pushed into the small of his back. Please God, give me the strength. He saw the faces of Dominic, Bernadette, Augustine. And Jeanne. With a supreme effort, he pulled Richter to him and threw himself backward over the rail.

Richter's scream of terror was the last thing he ever heard.

In the English Channel. 4. p.m.

The rain had stopped. Jeanne used her arms to lever herself to a bench that ran around the stern. The wind had lost most of its anger, although there was still a chop on the sea, causing the boat to pitch. The late afternoon sun tried to force its way through the thinning clouds.

She prayed that he had received her message. Jeanne looked behind her. France had disappeared over the horizon some hours before, but Jeanne knew that part of her was still there. She thought of Philippe and Augustine, who had made her escape possible and prayed they were safe. Céleste's face appeared to her and she felt a pang in her heart.

"Look, Jeanne, look!" René shouted from his position at the wheel.

Jeanne swung her head to the northern horizon. A motor torpedo boat was making towards them, throwing up a fierce bow wave as the prow cleaved through the water. As René swung the helm, Jeanne looked beyond the approaching vessel, but the English coast was not yet in sight. But she knew it was there. Home, England. Jeanne would be sloughed off, Gwen would emerge again. A sense of happiness overwhelmed her, unlike any since she had been in Hope Cove, playing chess with...

Tom. She had to see Tom, to thank him for saving her. To tell him that... she smiled wryly. To tell him that she wanted to play chess with him again.

The deafening roar of the torpedo boat's engine eased to a throb as it came alongside the fishing boat. Two sailors swung ropes over the cleats to hold the vessels together. A lieutenant bounded along the deck of the naval vessel.

"Hurry, hurry!" he shouted urgently.

Jeanne clutched at the side of the fishing boat and tried to stand, but the pain would not let her. "I'm sorry, but I'm injured. I can't walk."

The lieutenant nodded to a sailor, who leapt into the well of the fishing boat. "Excuse me, ma'am," his legs braced against the sway of the boat, "but this is the only way." He put his hands under her arms, lifted her and tossed her over his left shoulder.

René started to shout as Jeanne was transferred to the torpedo boat, his arms waving.

"What's up with him?" The lieutenant helped lower Jeanne down to the deck.

240

"He wants you to cast off. He wants to get back to France." Jeanne explained.

"I'm afraid that's not possible. He'll have to come with us. Tell him to leave his boat and come aboard."

She translated. René flew into a rage. *"Jamais! Jamais!"*

"Tell him if he doesn't come, he leaves me with no alternative but to sink his boat."

"Why? How can you? What's the panic?"

"If you could see what's behind us over the horizon, you'd understand."

Jeanne understood at once. The invasion. The invasion was under way. She shouted down to René. *"René, je t'en prie, le débarquement s'approche!"*

The Frenchman's eyes grew large, looking at her incredulously. A sailor leaned down and offered a hand. René looked at the sky for a moment, then embraced the boat's wheel and kissed it. *"Adieu, Belle Époque, ma Cherie."* He grasped the sailor's hand and climbed onto the naval vessel.

"Cast off! Half speed ahead. Steer zero-two-zero." The lieutenant shouted the orders as he carried Jeanne aft toward the small bridge. Jeanne felt the surge of the boat's power and saw René looking back wistfully as his vessel drifted away.

Jeanne marveled at the sight. Ship after ship. Hundreds of them, all heading south-east across the bows of the torpedo boat. The lieutenant swung his binoculars along the horizon. "We'll never see anything like this again in our lifetime." He handed the glasses to Jeanne.

She saw the vast array of ships, and then looked beyond them to the Devon coast. Please let him be safe. If he had acted on her message, she prayed he was unhurt. She looked again at the ships. A great armada, all heading for the Far Shore. Please, God, let France be free.

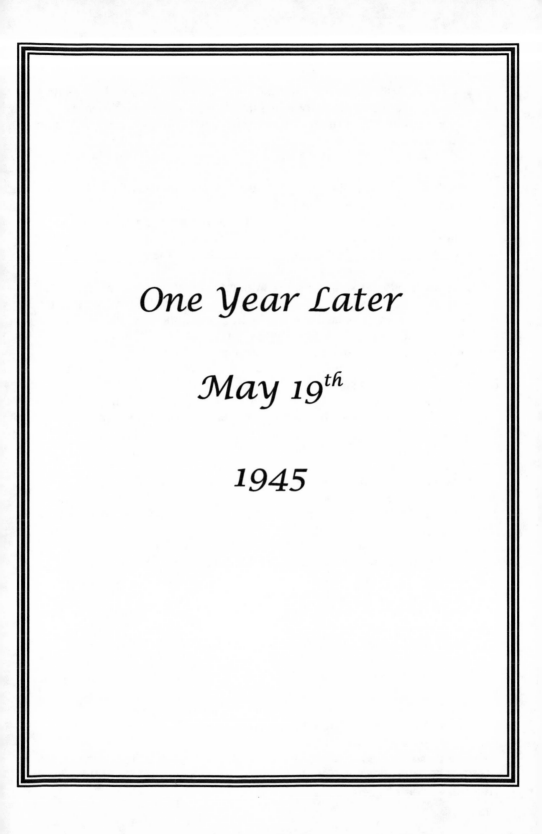

One Year Later

May 19th

1945

Blackawton, Devon, England.

"**D**oesn't Sally make a wonderful bride?" Gwen smiled at Tom as they followed the bridal party down the path from the church that he had seen a year ago in very different circumstances when it had been used as an army headquarters.

"Not half as wonderful as the matron of honor." He offered his arm; she slid her hand through.

"It's like a never-ending party." Gwen lifted the hem of her long silk dress with her free hand to swing it clear of the uncut grass by the side of the path. She walked a little unevenly, although the pain had long since gone.

Tom tightened his arm against Gwen's. She was right. A never-ending party. Only twelve days before, they had celebrated the end of the war in Europe. There had been dancing in the streets; everyone was drunk, embracing strangers like long-lost friends, joyful that the nightmare was at last over.

And his – their – nightmare was over, too. Gwen had recovered through the winter, although he sensed she had been scarred not only physically. But they had shared many concerts and many games of chess. They had fed off each other, needing each other to erase the pain of the past.

"What's up, Tom?" Gwen's eyes had anxious corners. "You're looking as if you're about to lose a game of chess!"

"Oh, it's nothing." He pulled her to one side as the photographer lined up the bride and groom by the church gate. "Gwen, I've met him before. I know what he does."

"Who?"

"Sally's father."

"You know what he does?" There was genuine surprise in her voice. "I don't think even Sally knows what he does. He's some big-wig in intelligence. It's all hush-hush, even now that the war's over." Gwen turned at the photographer's shout.

"Bride's father, best man, and matron of honor, please."

"Wait a moment." Sally turned her back and threw her bridal bouquet over her shoulder. Tom reached out instinctively and caught it. Sally turned again and gave out one of her infectious laughs.

"You're not supposed to do that, Tom. Or is it another strange American custom we don't know?"

Tom looked embarrassed and handed the bouquet to Gwen. "I think this was meant for you." He looked back to Sally. "Sorry!" His eyes were drawn to her father standing by her side. It was the man who had asked him to go to France.

"To the reception, everyone." The best man waved his arm toward The George Inn across the road from the church.

"We're so pleased you could come." Danny grasped Tom's hand, his beaming smile complementing his pristine dress whites. "If it hadn't been for you, we wouldn't be here."

244

Tom looked abashed, and Gwen compounded his embarrassment. "Neither would I."

"Let's not forget," Tom kissed the bride on the cheeks, "that if it hadn't been for Céleste, not one of us would be here."

"Ah, the little French girl you told us about." Sally smiled. "Have you found out anything about her yet?"

"No, not a thing." Tom shook his head. They all knew the story. He had made enquiries through channels. They all knew that Josse was dead, killing Richter to protect the big secret. Augustine had given her life, too. But of Céleste, his contacts in France had come up with nothing except a polite reminder that searching for a little girl wasn't high on their list of things to do.

"Well, it's good to see you both." Sally broke the silence. "And is it going to be wedding bells for you two soon?"

"Who knows?"

Gwen looked up at Tom. They had spent a lot of time together since her escape from France, helping each other to repair the wounds, both of the body and the mind. He had encouraged her to walk again; the first time they had walked together on Bolt Tail headland at Hope Cove had been a triumph for them both. And they both talked through the other scars, the scars on their minds. The torture, the killings: even now Tom could not slice cheese without seeing the German soldier's face and sobbing. Gwen could not take a bath without thinking of the *bagnoire*.

"But you have cleared the deck, Tom?" Danny used the naval metaphor to skirt around a difficult subject.

"Sure." The American nodded. Yes, Tom thought, his divorce had come through. He looked at Gwen again. There was love in her eyes; in his, too. But they were not ready. Not yet.

"Damned good do!" Gwen's father appeared, a glass of beer in his hand. "Good show! Here's to the bride and groom." He drank deeply from his glass, and turned to Tom. "I suppose you'll be coming to talk to me soon, old boy."

"Why?" Tom looked astonished.

"Why? You know, keeping her in the manner to which she has become accustomed, and all that stuff." He nudged his elbow into Tom's arm.

Tom looked to Gwen for help.

"Dad, Tom's an American. I'm not sure they go in for that sort of thing nowadays. You're so old fashioned."

"A table, à table." The best man summoned the group to the wedding banquet. Tom saw Sally's father staring at him.

The George Inn had been refurbished especially for the wedding. Heaven knew, Tom thought, where they had got the paint to cover the dereliction of the year's abandonment. Some people had moved back into the area that the U.S. Army had used as a training ground, but there was still much work to be done. The tables buzzed with talk as the guests tucked into the wedding feast. Tom saw the Yorkshire pudding and turned to grin at Gwen. "Like old times, isn't it?"

Gwen's father shouted across the table. "I don't suppose there's Spotted Dick to follow?"

Sally laughed and looked at Tom and Gwen. "I hope you two aren't going to get out a chessboard!"

Tom pushed away his empty plate and looked through the window back across the road to the church. He wondered briefly where Major Fonseca and his men were, how many had survived the war.

"Pray silence for the best man."

It wasn't a fancy reception. About twenty people sat at the tables, many of them Sally's Wren friends and Danny's Royal Navy colleagues.

"We won't mention where we got the roast beef you have just enjoyed." The best man began his speech to laughter; everyone knew it came from the black market. He went on to make the ribald speech that best men always make. From time to time, Gwen leant forward to translate the heavy West Country accent for Tom.

After the best man sat down to prolonged clapping, the bride's father stood. Tom saw him fiddling with his gold cuff links. His rounded vowels seemed out of place in the public house saloon; he spoke of the war and duty and Tom sensed the other guests did not want to hear of the war. For them, it was over: time to move on.

The man whom Tom knew as a spymaster seemed aloof, distant. He spoke in a manner more suited to the corridors of power than the wedding of his daughter.

Gwen whispered in Tom's ear. "He's a bit miffed. He wanted a full society wedding in London with all the trimmings, but Danny put his foot down, and Sally backed him up."

Sally's father sat down to polite applause, and the best man leapt to his feet. "We have been able to obtain – don't ask me from where – a whole hogshead of the best ale." The guests cheered. "And, courtesy of our great American allies," he nodded towards Tom, "two bottles of whiskey." The cheering was renewed.

"So charge your glasses, ladies and gentlemen. To the bride and groom!"

Everyone stood and raised their glasses.

Danny turned to Sally, took her in his arms and kissed her. The cheers rang out, accompanied with wild applause. Tom saw that Sally's father did not join in.

Tom awaited his moment. The reception had broken up into small groups, all talking about the wedding, the war, the future. He saw Sally's father on the fringe of the gathering, exuding his urbane charm where necessary.

"Excuse me, Gwen, I'll be back soon." Before Gwen could protest, he slipped away and cornered the man who had sent him to France. "Mr. Fortescue, may I speak to you for a moment?"

The Englishman's voice was cautious. "Certainly, but I think it would be better if…" He led Tom to the door and they went outside.

"By the way, I'd like to thank you for the work you did in France. You certainly got us out of a hole there. I spoke to Ike about it—"

"What about Priestley?" Tom could see Fortescue was embarrassed.

"Um, yes, bad show that. He'd been turned by the Germans back in the thirties and planted back in England as a long-term sleeper spy." He looked across at the church to avoid Tom's eyes. "He slipped through the net I'm afraid." He shook his head. "Bad show. Damned bad show." A brief smile cut across his gloomy face. "Still, you helped save the day there, too."

"Who was Philippe Josse?" Tom could see the question surprised the Englishman.

"I've no need to answer your question," he gave a thin smile, "but I think you deserve to know."

Tom bridled at the condescension, but said nothing. Fortescue pulled his gold cigarette case from his pocket and lit a cigarette.

"Philippe Josse was the finest double agent who ever worked for us. Priestley sensed he was important to the plan – that's why he tried to have him killed. Without Josse, our whole operation to fool the Germans about the invasion could have failed. He was a master. You know he's dead?"

Tom nodded.

"For Josse to fool Richter was a masterstroke. The Gestapo man unwittingly passed on the false information to Himmler, and Hitler believed that the Normandy invasion was a decoy. Even as late as July he thought Patton was going to invade the Pas de Calais. By then it was too late."

"But the plans for the Resistance, sent in by your courier, which were delivered into Richter's hands?"

"Completely false. Guaranteed to send Richter and his men on a wild goose chase all over Normandy."

But if Richter had captured Dalton and me he'd have tortured us. Wouldn't that have scuttled your plan?"

"I don't think so. You see, Dalton didn't know about Operation Fortitude. You did – I told you. The two of you would have given different stories – enough to keep the Germans doubting."

Tom realized he had been nothing more than a pawn in Fortescue's plan.

"But the man who took the plans? His parachute didn't open."

Fortescue drew on his cigarette and looked into the distance.

"Who was he?" Tom shouted, his voice full of vehemence.

"Look, Ford, in war we have to take all measures to win." The eye patch and the impassive face swung back to Tom. "I will tell you. But you must not divulge it. Even if you do, people will call you insane. An official denial will not be necessary."

"Who was he? What was his name?"

"His name is irrelevant. He was a German spy." Fortescue smiled at the incomprehension on Tom's face. "A German spy who had refused to cooperate like the others. He was due to be executed, anyway."

Despite the warmth of the May sun, Tom felt a chill grasp his body. "You mean you dressed him in Wainwright's uniform, then planted the plans on him and—"

"He was swapped for Wainwright at the last moment, after your friend had jumped." Fortescue ground out his cigarette. "There were other things, but they need not concern you." He turned to go back into the pub.

"Wait." Tom grabbed the Englishman's arm. "What about Gwen?" He was surprised to see embarrassment on Fortescue's face.

"I was not personally responsible for selecting the agent to go on that mission." He looked down disdainfully at Tom's hand holding his arm.

Tom released his grasp. Fortescue brushed his coat sleeve and let his fingers drop to toy with his gold cuff links.

"Ford, you should know that Gwen is a lucky woman. In all other matters, Josse was completely dependable, but he put our whole plan in jeopardy by rescuing her. I still cannot fathom why he did it." Tom saw Josse's face, the dark eyes set above the walrus mustache. Suddenly the coldness in his body became a fire of rage. He wanted to smash his fist into Fortescue's smug face.

"You're nothing but a calculating bastard, Fortescue."

"Say what you wish, Ford." The Englishman showed no contrition. "But we won the war. I'm sure you and your friends wouldn't want to be living under the Nazis, would you? And now, if you'll excuse me, I have to attend to my wedding duties."

He turned and was gone. Tom stood gasping, his mind numb as he realized the enormity of what the Englishman had said. The plan – Operation First Violin – had been paramount to Fortescue and his ilk. Everyone had been expendable as long as the plan succeeded. Gwen, Dalton, the hundreds of Americans who had died in the exercise had mattered nothing. Expendable. He looked across at the church. Major Fonseca and his men, Josse, Jacques the farmer and his wife, Bernadette, Augustine – all grist to Fortescue's mill.

Another face came into his mind. The big eyes, the little nose, the mouth smudged with chocolate. The child who, in all innocence, had saved Fortescue and Operation First Violin.

He forced his way through the reception, desperate to find Gwen. He found her talking to Sally. He pulled her away, cupped her face in his hands and kissed her.

"Gwen, let's go and find Céleste."

Author's Afterword

Many points of the story you have read are true. Over a million Americans were brought to England to prepare for D-Day in June 1944.

To help in their exercises, the British government did, as portrayed in *The Sobs of Autumn's Violins*, move everybody and everything – farmers, families and livestock – out of the area behind Slapton Sands, so that the Americans could have the use of a large part of South Devon to practice for the coming D-Day landings.

During one of these rehearsals – Operation Tiger – in the small hours of April 28th 1944, German torpedo boats attacked, sinking two American ships. Over seven hundred American servicemen were killed. Eisenhower ordered the disaster hushed up; servicemen were threatened with court martial if they talked of the disaster and the list of casualties was initially added to those suffered at Utah beach later.

In the early stages of the war, the British did, as described in *The Sobs of Autumn's Violins*, take control of the network of German enemy agents who had sneaked into Britain; they either executed them or "turned" them, i.e., persuaded them to switch their allegiance. By early 1944 there were twenty such German double agents in Britain, and their activities were vital in furnishing calculated leaks and spreading deception. Throughout the entire war, Germany remained unaware of this major breach in their intelligence system.

A major part of Operation Fortitude was the plan to deceive Germany into thinking that the main invasion would occur in the Pas de Calais rather than in Normandy. The non-existent First United States Army Group (FUSAG) was under the "leadership" of General George S. Patton, the Allied general Germany feared most. FUSAG was, as *The Sobs of Autumn's Violins* describes, an immense concentration in Kent, England of dummy landing ships, convoys, guns, ammunition dumps, field kitchens, and troop encampments made of plywood, rubber, wire, and cardboard and emanating a high volume of scripted radio chatter. The deception worked so well that, even after D-Day, Hitler remained convinced that the Normandy invasion was simply a decoy for a more major invasion and refused to move any of his units that were stationed north of the Seine.

Bad weather did force Eisenhower to postpone D-Day for twenty-four hours from its original date of June 5th. However, the Allies did make a successful landing, although heavy casualties were suffered by the Americans at Omaha beach. Hitler retained the whole German Fifteenth Army in the Pas de Calais area, where he believed Patton would arrive. But it took over two months of bitter, costly battle for the Americans to establish a firm bridgehead in western Normandy, before the eventual arrival of Patton. In late July 1944, his Third Army broke out at Avranches, leading to the armored pursuit that would drive the Germans from France.

These key events, around which the narrative of this book is woven, are all fact. Everything else in *The Sobs of Autumn's Violins* is a product of the author's imagination.

A. R. Homer is the author of the critically-acclaimed *The Mirror of Diana,* another novel of war and love.

Homer grew up in Birmingham, England. As a history major at Oxford University, he developed a serious interest in World War II. Later, he moved to Normandy, France, to study the battles in which ordinary men determined the course of history. The *Sobs of Autumn's Violins* is based upon his studies of D-Day and the events which led up to that turning point.

Homer and his wife live in New Jersey. Please visit him at:

www.arhomer.com
or
www.themirrorofdiana.com

Printed in the United States
90342LV00004B/81/A